PICTURE YOU DEAD

The Detective Superintendent Roy Grace books in order:

DEAD SIMPLE

In the first Roy Grace novel, a harmless
stag-do prank leads to deadly consequences.

LOOKING GOOD DEAD

It started with an act of kindness
and ended in murder.

NOT DEAD ENOUGH

Can a killer be in two places at once?
Roy Grace must solve a case of stolen identity.

DEAD MAN'S FOOTSTEPS

The discovery of skeletal remains in Brighton
sparks a global investigation.

DEAD TOMORROW

In an evil world, everything's for sale.

DEAD LIKE YOU

After thirteen years, has the notorious
'Shoe Man' killer returned?

DEAD MAN'S GRIP

A trail of death follows a devastating
traffic accident.

NOT DEAD YET

Terror on the silver screen;
an obsessive stalker on the loose.

DEAD MAN'S TIME

A priceless watch is stolen and the powerful
Daly family will do *anything* to get it back.

PICTURE YOU DEAD

PETER JAMES

MACMILLAN

First published 2022 by Macmillan
an imprint of Pan Macmillan
The Smithson, 6 Briset Street, London EC1M 5NR
EU representative: Macmillan Publishers Ireland Ltd, 1st Floor,
The Liffey Trust Centre, 117–126 Sheriff Street Upper,
Dublin 1, D01 YC43
Associated companies throughout the world
www.panmacmillan.com

ISBN 978-1-5290-0436-6

Map artwork by ML Design

Typeset by Palimpsest Book Production Ltd, Falkirk, Stirlingshire
Printed and bound by CPI Group (UK) Ltd, Croydon, CR0 4YY

To Anthony Forbes Watson – an inspirational leader and friend.

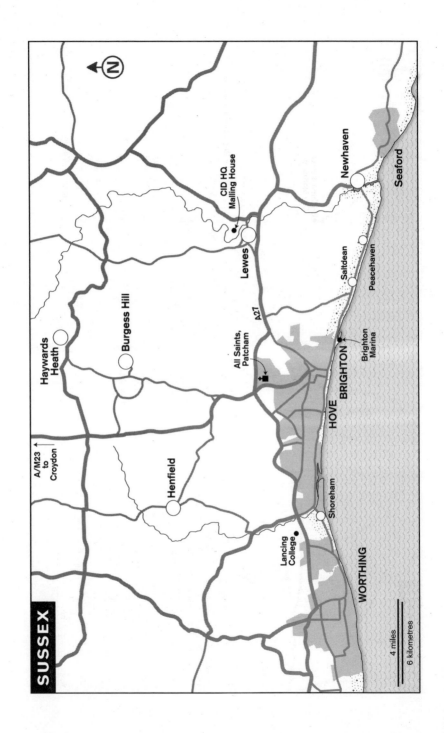

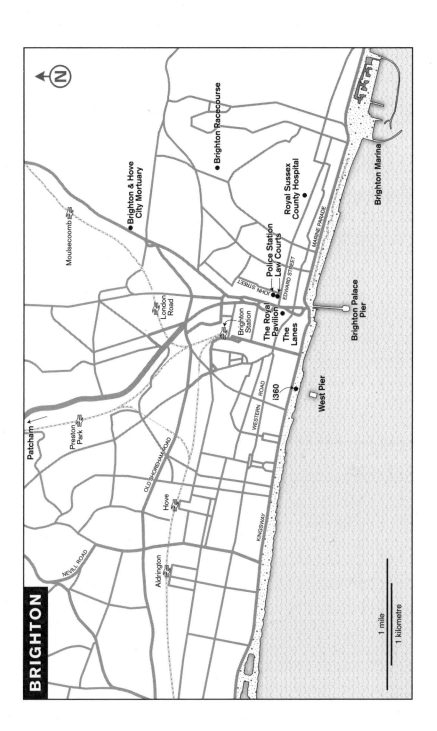

BRIGHTON

N

Patcham

Moulsecoomb

Preston Park

Brighton & Hove City Mortuary

Brighton Racecourse

NEVILL ROAD

OLD SHOREHAM ROAD

London Road

Hove

Aldrington

Brighton Station

WESTERN ROAD

The Royal Pavilion

JOHN STREET

Police Station

Law Courts

EDWARD STREET

The Lanes

MARINE PARADE

Royal Sussex County Hospital

KINGSWAY

i360

West Pier

Brighton Palace Pier

Brighton Marina

1 mile

1 kilometre

1

Charlie Porteous was fond of quoting Auden's poem, about the hare that was happy in the morning because it was unable to read the hunter's waking thoughts. But as he left home on this drizzling autumnal morning, he had no way of knowing that today, he was that hare. And that he wouldn't be making it back to his bed tonight. Or ever.

To all who knew him, and indeed to any casual stranger who happened to glance at him, the good-humoured sixty-two-year-old, who would always stop to drop a banknote on a busker's mat, appeared to be a man without a care in the world. With his confident gait, well-lunched face and stout frame, in his Savile Row three-piece chalk-striped suit, handmade shirt and salmon-pink-and-green-striped Garrick Club tie, he exuded the very image of *old money* and all the confidence that came with it.

But the much-liked – despite his mercurial temper – proprietor of the eponymously named Porteous Fine Arts Gallery was, right now, properly, badly and seriously in need of a big deal. Preferably cash. A lot of the stuff. The private bank which had once considered him an undoubted client, and for years had fawned over him, was now threatening foreclosure on a loan, on an amount which would bring his entire comfortable edifice crashing down.

But in his position he could not let his predicament show either to his staff or to any of his clientele in the rarefied circle in which he appeared the very model of respectability and trust-worthiness. Not to his recently retired wife, Susan, who revelled in her role as a major charitable benefactor in their home city, and not to his son, Oliver, who had spent the past decade working in the fine arts department of Sotheby's New York, to gain ex-perience before joining him, and eventually taking the reins, allowing Porteous, like his own father before him, to take life easier and enjoy a very comfortable dotage.

He felt particularly upset about Oliver, who knew nothing of his problems yet, that he had let him down badly. Let all his family and staff down. For months now he'd had constant sleep-less nights and had ended up taking antidepressants.

But finally it looked like Lady Luck had crapped on his head. Actually, in his right eye to be precise. It had happened as he'd looked up at the bird, a black crow, a few weeks ago. He remem-bered as a kid, when a magpie had dumped its load on his head, his deeply superstitious mother had told him it would bring him luck, and she had been right – that month he'd won £25 on his Premium Bonds. Result!

Grasping at straws, he wondered, was his luck about to turn now? Then, amazingly, it seemed it was.

2

Charlie Porteous did not tolerate fools gladly and his charming smile could turn into a withering glare at the flick of a switch. He had long been known as a man not to mess with but whose word was his bond, and his eye for a painting had long been the envy of many of his rival art dealers. That eye had served him well during the eight years he'd been on the team of experts, many years back now, on the *Antiques Roadshow*, for the peanuts the BBC then paid its experts – £100 per episode and a second-class rail ticket. But, being on the programme, he enjoyed the publicity and kudos it gave him – as well as the enhancement of his art gallery's reputation.

Eventually the relationship had soured, the BBC producer deciding his arrogance towards people who turned up with what Porteous considered to be rubbish was not in the spirit of the show. Two things had eventually led to his firing.

The first was when he'd reduced an elderly woman to tears when he'd harshly pointed out the supposed Turner seascape she'd brought him, which had been in her family for years, was nothing more than a painted-over print, cuttingly telling her that a child painting by numbers could have done a more convincing job. And the second when, in a rare error of judgement, he'd declared a sixteenth-century Abel Grimmer landscape as genuine and worth conservatively £200,000 – and it had subsequently turned out to be a fake. Concerned for his reputation, he'd stubbornly refused to back down and admit his error.

A fastidious man, with a love for beautiful things in both his private and work lives, Charlie Porteous was a creature of habit that you could set the proverbial watch by – in his case a £45,000 Rolex Submariner.

Every weekday he left his gated mansion, in Brighton and Hove's Tongdean Avenue, on the dot of 6.35 a.m., and drove his Bentley to Brighton station car park, catching the fast train to London's Victoria station. From there his trusty London driver, Meehat El Hadidy, would whisk him in his Mercedes S-Class to his gallery in Duke Street, arriving at 8.20 a.m., well before his five members of staff.

Four evenings a week Porteous would travel home on the train from London Victoria, and he would walk through his front door at 7.15 p.m. precisely. But on Thursdays, he would dine at his members' club, either with a client or with a chum from the art world, before taking a late train back. Tonight, however, he had spent a delightful evening socializing with his god-daughter at an Italian restaurant close to his gallery.

His father had given him a piece of advice he now bitterly wished he had heeded. It was to only invest in what he knew. But just over two years ago, a wealthy Australian property developer client, Kerry Dundas, who had bought paintings from him to the value of several millions over the past decade, had offered him a deal that, in the words of *The Godfather*, was an offer he could not refuse.

A rare chance to partner the man in buying an entire forty-two-storey block of flats in north London, Reynolds Heights, which was up for a bargain price for a quick sale, due to the current owner being overstretched. And named after a famous artist, it had to be a good omen, Porteous had thought.

For a £10 million investment each, they could turn a profit of, conservatively, £5 million within a year. His judgement had been clouded by the fact that the lease on the building adjoining his gallery was coming up for sale. If he could buy it, he would double the size of his gallery, leaving his son the legacy of being the largest dealer in their field in the country.

The bank had been happy to lend Porteous his share of the money, secured against his rock-solid assets, on a two-year term loan. Then, three months later, when they were in the process of making a sale every bit as profitable as Kerry Dundas had forecast, he was suddenly unable to contact the man.

The next thing he knew, after finally engaging his solicitors, was that Dundas was in prison in Dubai, under arrest for fraud, embezzlement and forgery.

Porteous had to face that he'd been duped and lost every penny of his investment. The bank, while initially sympathetic to his plight was, as he ruefully confided to a friend, just like the old joke: that bankers were people who lent you an umbrella when it was sunny and wanted it back when it was raining.

But tonight, for the first time in many sleepless months, he had an optimistic spring in his step as he alighted at Brighton station shortly after midnight, and he had good reason.

He had recently made, he was certain, one of the sweetest purchases of his life. Very possibly *the* sweetest by a country mile. One that potentially could get him out of the deep doodoo in which he was now mired.

His gallery, founded after the war by his late father, had built up a specialist reputation for paintings by leading French old masters such as Nicolas Poussin, Jean-Honoré Fragonard, Claude Lorrain and Élisabeth Vigée Le Brun. His old man, a former art student at Warsaw's Academy of Fine Arts, who had arrived in England as a penniless Jewish refugee from Poland in 1938, was a natural-born salesman with an eye for a painting and an even wider eye for a bargain.

He'd decided that his assumed name of Lewis Porteous would play better in the snooty British art world and anti-Semitic post-war climate than the one with which he'd landed in England – Jakub Lewandowski.

Charlie Porteous had inherited his father's appreciation of landscapes, portraits and mythological scenes of the French old masters, and like his old man he, too, had a talent for spotting a bargain. As well as that same instinct, possessed by all high-end art dealers, of being able to tell, pretty much instantly, whether a work was genuine or not. Mistakes were very rare. And through his network of well-paid scouts, with his knowledge and deep pockets, he was a feared hunter at auctions, especially those of provincial house sale contents.

The art business had been easier in his father's time, when it was much less regulated. Back then, in the 1950s, '60s and '70s, if you liked a painting, you bought it, paying by cheque or cash. Simple as that. But not any more. Today, it wasn't just about the provenance of the picture itself, it was about the provenance of the seller, too.

In this changed world, Porteous and his staff became, necessarily, bogged down in all kinds of due diligence, including money-laundering checks on the vendor. No picture for sale could be hung on the walls of the three floors of his Mayfair gallery until every aspect of its history and how it came to be here was bullet-proof.

In theory.

Like his father, Charlie was occasionally prepared to break the rules. Just so long as a painting he was offered was not on the Art Loss Register, which listed all known stolen works of art, he would occasionally take a punt on one that to his experienced eye looked authentic, and sell it straight on to one of a select few of his art collector clients who would take his word.

Like all dealers, he was well aware there were numerous major works that had vanished for many years and which once in a blue moon resurfaced. Paintings from way back, sometimes centuries ago, which had been hidden or lost during times of civil unrest such as the French Revolution or, more recently, looted by the Nazis in the Second World War. And some, while rumoured to have existed, had never been catalogued.

It was for this reason that, while he hadn't cared for the thin, nervous Frenchman – who gave his name as Jean-Claude Dubois – who'd come into his gallery two weeks ago with a rectangular parcel wrapped in brown paper, he'd been willing to take a look at what he had to show him. He hadn't cared either for the man's story about how he had come by this painting. A load of cock and bull, in Porteous's opinion, about cleaning out his late aunt's attic and coming across it in a trunk.

But he had cared very much about what he'd seen when he'd unwrapped the package in his office at the rear of the gallery's ground floor. A small, ornately framed landscape in oil, ten inches wide by twelve, of a spring scene. Two beautiful young lovers in elegant eighteenth-century dress, entwined in each other's arms in an idyllic woodland setting surrounded by daffodils, with a waterfall behind them. The depiction of the trees was simply exquisite, imposing, yet light at the same time, adding so much to the charm. It was a gem. Love's first bloom. Divine, powerful, awe-inspiring, classic.

He'd struggled to maintain an unimpressed poker face as he questioned Dubois on the provenance of this painting. Porteous knew all of the reputable fine arts dealers in London and indeed throughout Europe, and this sharply attired man, with the darting eyes of a feeding bird, twitching forehead and strobing smiles, wasn't on his radar.

If this painting was genuine and not an extremely good forgery – and from the surface craquelure, the spots of mould and seal on the back, the damages to the frame and its general condition, all his instincts told him it was – then he was looking at a highly important long-lost work by one of his very favourite

7

eighteenth-century painters, Jean-Honoré Fragonard. *Spring*. One of the four that Fragonard was known to have painted of the four seasons, but which had been lost for over two hundred years.

These Four Seasons were reputed to have been hanging in a privately owned French chateau but vanished, believed stolen or destroyed, during the French Revolution.

He was well aware, just as the man standing in front of him must have been – unless he was a total charlatan – that at the last major sale of a Fragonard, conducted by the auctioneers Bonhams, the artist's portrait of François-Henri, fifth duc d'Harcourt, realized a world record for his work of £17,106,500.

Calmly, Porteous had asked the man how much he was looking for. The reply had been £50,000.

'Why have you brought it to me?' he had asked, now convinced by the low asking price he was dealing with someone profoundly dishonest.

'I am told you are the leading expert in this period,' Dubois had replied in heavily accented English.

'Why don't you put it into an auction – at Bonhams or Christie's or Sotheby's perhaps, Mr Dubois?' he'd responded, testing the man.

The shifty look in the Frenchman's eyes told him all he needed to know. 'I thought I would come to you for a quick sale.'

Without even having to do any calculations, if genuine, Porteous knew its true value would be in the region of between £3 million and £5 million and maybe more in the right auction. If put together with the other three, to make the full set, that value could skyrocket by multiple times that amount.

This could be the ticket out of his financial mess.

3

Very reluctantly the Frenchman had agreed to leave the painting with Porteous overnight, for him to examine it further and to check with the Art Loss Register.

After the man left, Porteous knew that if he put the sale of this picture through his normal system, he would have to do all the due diligence on the Frenchman, and he doubted it would check out.

To mask his enquiry, he emailed a list and photographs of fifteen paintings, including this one, to the Art Loss Register. The following morning, he'd debated taking it to a trusted picture restorer, without revealing the artist's name, to ask his opinion on it, but had decided against, knowing the man would ask him awkward questions.

Among the fifteen enquiries that came back from the Art Loss Register, nothing was flagged up about the Fragonard.

Later the following day, after Charlie Porteous was satisfied enough to take a punt that the picture was not stolen, or a fake, and keeping it a secret from most of his staff, for one of the few times in his career he'd paid Jean-Claude Dubois for it from the cash fund he kept for such purposes in his safe.

During the past two weeks since then, he'd discreetly put word out to the more dubious dealers in his contacts list. None of them had been offered this painting, nor any of the three other Four Seasons of Fragonard. He'd also put word out to these same people that he was interested in finding anyone who had any of the three other missing paintings, *Summer*, *Autumn* and *Winter*, and that he would be willing to discuss a deal.

These were all dealers operating beyond the fringe of the coterie of respectable dealers, who'd helped him out on the occasions when he'd made an error of judgement either in acquiring a *hot* painting, or one that had turned out to be a fake, that he needed to dispose of in a hurry, with no questions asked.

Still concerned about the legitimacy of his purchase of this Fragonard, and wary of formally putting it up for sale, he had also discreetly notified a few of the wealthiest collectors among his clients, people who could comfortably afford to buy a painting of this value, and who would trust him.

One of these, George Astone, who had amassed one of the finest private collections of French masters in the country, had come straight back to him, very interested.

But Astone, a charming, ebullient character, who lived in grand style in a stately home ten miles north of Brighton, was immobile following a stroke. He couldn't easily travel to London – could Porteous bring the picture to his home? From the photographs Porteous had emailed him in strictest confidence, he was very eager to buy it. Porteous had agreed to bring it over to him in the morning.

By sheer serendipity Vivaldi's 'Spring', from his *Four Seasons*, was playing on Radio Three on the Bentley's sound system as Porteous turned into his street. A good omen. He smiled, everything was good tonight!

He drove along the dark, tree-lined avenue, turned in and pulled up outside the wrought-iron gates of his home, in the faint glare of the street light across the road. He was looking forward to the crazy greeting he would get from his lurcher, Poussin, and hoped his barking wouldn't wake his wife. It was 12.40 a.m. – Susan would be well asleep by now. He reached down into the cubby-hole below the dash, found the clicker and pressed it.

Nothing happened.

He pressed again, but still the gates did not move. He frowned. Was the battery dead? He pressed again and the little red light came on. But the gates didn't move.

It wasn't the first time this had ever happened. Cursing and making a mental note to call the gate people in the morning, he lowered his window and reached out to the panel to punch in the key code manually. But he was too far away.

Cursing again, he opened the car door and leaned across, oblivious to the shadow moving towards him from behind a tree as he tapped in the code: 7979 followed by the *plus* sign. Instantly the gates began, jerkily, to open and the bright security lights came on.

At the same instant, lights exploded inside his head as he felt a blow just behind his ear. It was followed immediately by a crashing whack from an iron bar. Shooting stars. Meteorites. The wildest fireworks display of his life going on in there while he stumbled forward and hit the ground, all his lights going out.

He never heard the words of his assailant, cursing him for being such a fat, heavy bastard as he heaved Porteous back into the driver's seat of the car.

He never heard the slam of the driver's door as blood oozed from the back of his smashed skull into the tan – with contrast cream stitching – Connolly leather headrest.

4

Harry Kipling made every customer feel like they were his new best friend. With his twinkly eyes, cheeky grin and messy hair, and invariably wearing shorts on all but the coldest of winter days, the stocky forty-five-year-old was constantly bursting with boyish enthusiasm and energy. He gave each customer the impression he could not do enough for them, and he sure tried.

Call me Harry and I'll hurry! was his catchphrase. Heck, when you inherited an identical surname to the brand of one of Britain's most famous cake makers, you either had to make a joke of it or change it.

And not so easy to change your name when your family business, Harold Kipling & Sons, Brighton's Premier Builders, had been established in 1892 and carried all that goodwill with it.

Besides, it was an icebreaker for a new customer, when discussing extensions to the rear of their house, invariably to tell Harry to make sure he brought some exceedingly good cakes with him, heh-heh.

Business was busy right now, the demand for extensions and for loft conversions better than ever, and a decent turnover was coming in. But he struggled to make a profit year on year. His business would be considerably more profitable, his wife Freya often chided him, if he wasn't quite so obliging to his customers.

Freya, also forty-five and his childhood sweetheart, was deputy head of a local school. Still the beautiful former head girl, with

12

her long blonde hair and trim figure, she was the organized one in the marriage, and in the rare free time she had after dealing with all the paperwork mountain from her school, and doing her workouts, she helped Harry out with the books of his business – something he was rubbish at. And sometimes what she saw worried her.

Because he always wanted to be helpful, and because he was a genuinely kind man, Harry constantly did his customers favours here and there at no extra charge – invariably eating into his all-too-thin profit margins.

It would be nice, Freya mentioned, and very pointedly, if just occasionally he would do them some favours, too. Such as fixing the floor tile in the downstairs loo of their house, which had been loose for months, or the damp patch in the ceiling of their fourteen-year-old son Tom's room. Not to mention the wonky wall light in their lounge. And the kitchen cabinet door which had had a broken hinge for as long as she could remember. And everything else that was wrong with their small, attractive but increasingly cluttered 1950s corner house in Mackie Crescent in the leafy Brighton suburb of Patcham.

'It's on my list, darling,' was his standard response. 'I'll do it at the weekend.'

But he never did, because most Saturdays, if he wasn't going with Tom to football at the Amex, to cheer on the Seagulls, or taking him to play rugby or tennis – the two sports Tom was obsessed with playing, which he and Freya encouraged – he would be putting in extra hours at a customer's house, trying to get a job finished.

And on the alternate Sundays when he didn't play golf, and while Tom slept in until midday, Harry enjoyed indulging with Freya in their favourite pastime together: scouring car boot sales. And then, when they returned home, after examining and cleaning or polishing their booty, he would take command of the kitchen – or the barbecue on summer days – to cook a roast.

Tom was a Type-1 diabetic. Increasingly, due to him badgering his parents that it was better both for the planet and his sugar levels, Harry had been experimenting with vegetarian and vegan roasts – and discovered to his and Freya's surprise that they enjoyed both of these, as well as his increasing repertoire of fish and seafood, as much as, if not even more than, meat.

Invariably, after lunch, any good intentions Harry might have had of putting in an hour or two of DIY on the house were nixed by the several large glasses of the red Rioja he and Freya favoured. It would be feet up in front of the television for pretty much the rest of the day and evening, while Tom, if there wasn't a major sports game on to watch, disappeared up to his room, into his world – alien to them – of computer gaming.

One of the passions Harry and Freya shared was a love of bric-a-brac, and on this Sunday morning they were among the first in line for the 8 a.m. opening of the Sayers Common car boot sale, five miles north of Brighton.

Both were well aware, from long experience, that if you wanted to snap up bargains, you had to be there at doors opening to have any chance against the professional dealers. And they had a well-rehearsed and practised plan of splitting up the moment they entered, Freya going left and Harry going right, scouring the stalls for bargains.

Freya collected Toby jugs, teapots, art deco figurines and Brighton prints. Harry loved police memorabilia – in particular badges – old photographs, Victorian watercolours and, more recently, silver teaspoons.

As usual, the scavenging dealers ran ahead of him, scouring the tables and the unpacked boxes below them, putting item after item into their old carrier bags. The grass was damp underfoot and the early morning air had a slight chill.

Harry was glad of his waterproof work boots, gilet and baseball cap keeping the mist at bay. There was an appetizing smell of coffee, doughnuts and frying bacon in the air. He looked forward to their Sunday guilty treat – which they didn't tell Tom about – of stopping at the stall serving all those, after they'd satisfied themselves they'd missed nothing, for their egg and bacon sarnie breakfast fix, with an Americano for him, latte for Freya.

He walked past a trestle table loaded with old clothes and soft toys. Another with horrible porcelain ornaments. But all the same, he stopped, checking them out carefully, and spotted a tarnished old Brighton Police badge. He negotiated it down from £7.50 to a fiver, slipped it into his pocket and moved on. The next stall was mostly Dinky and Corgi toys, with the occasional Matchbox car, but none of them looked particularly old. He scanned them for a police vehicle, but spotted none and moved on again.

On the next, he saw two hideous clowns and shuddered, wondering who on earth would want them – they looked like they would haunt you forever. But next to them were several Toby jugs, and he texted Freya to alert her. Then he noticed a large box containing pictures, on the grass beneath the stall. On the other side of the table sat a friendly-looking young couple, sharing a cigarette, the tantalizingly sweet smoke drifting his way.

Harry sniffed appreciatively. 'That smells so good!' he said.

'Have one!' the young man said, offering him an open pack.

'I just quit. I'd kill for one, but my wife would kill me if I did,' Harry replied. 'Thanks all the same. Mind if I take a look in that box?'

'Go ahead,' the woman said. 'We've just been clearing out my nan's house – the stuff that was up in her loft. Some frames are OK, but the pictures aren't that special.'

Harry pulled the box out and began to rummage through the contents, hoping for a Victorian watercolour or a Brighton print. She was right about the quality of the paintings, he thought; they were complete grot. A horrible vase full of flowers in an ugly cream frame; a Cornish harbour seascape with yachts looking like they were balanced on top of the water; a cheesy sunset over a flock of what he presumed were meant to be sheep.

Then he came to an ornate, gilded frame, which looked genuinely old. He lifted it out. The painting, in oil, was about ten by twelve inches. It was an ugly portrait, an elderly woman's face so thin it resembled a skull with skin stretched over it, with strands of wispy white hair. Some bad amateur's attempt at a portrait of their granny? he wondered.

But the gilded frame was beautiful. Real quality. He ran his hands around the edges, noticed some damage here and there, but he knew a chap in the nearby town of Lewes who specialized in repairing frames. He turned it over and looked at the rear. It was canvas, clearly old, with some markings too faded to read.

The frame alone, he figured, would be worth fifty quid, if not more, judging by the prices the restorer in Lewes charged for his. A few Sundays ago, he'd bought a watercolour of the old Brighton chain pier that was about this size. It would look stunning in this frame.

Standing up, holding the picture, he asked, 'How much do you want for this?'

'Twenty-five quid,' the young man said after a few moments.

'Would you take twenty?'

'Go on then.'

As he peeled off a banknote from his wad, Harry asked, 'Don't suppose you've got a bag for it?'

The young woman smiled. 'Actually, I do. It's your lucky day!' She dug an arm down to the ground and produced a white plastic bag.

Twenty minutes later, munching on their egg and bacon baps, Freya and Harry triumphantly showed each other their purchases. Freya produced a flat-sided teapot painted with flowers. 'This is similar to a Clarice Cliff, I really like it; it was nowhere near that kind of money but still worth something!'

He looked at it carefully, admiring it. 'You could be right, well done you!'

'What did you get, darling?'

'A police badge, and this!' He pulled the painting out of the bag.

'Oh my God, she is horrible!' Freya exclaimed. 'Like, really creepy! Yech.'

'Forget the picture, it's the frame! Don't you think it's lovely?'

She nodded reluctantly. 'Yes, fine, but the picture, yech, it freaks me out.'

'I agree, I don't like the picture either, but the frame is a total bargain.'

'As long as you get rid of that creepy head staring at me!' She wrinkled her face.

'I'll cut it out and burn it as soon as we get home.'

But, like so many jobs Harry promised to do, he didn't. When they got home, shortly after 11 a.m., Tom was still up in his room, no doubt asleep after spending half the night playing Fortnite or whatever the latest game he was now into. He leaned the picture against a glass wall in the conservatory annexe to the kitchen, which served as both family room and depository for their purchases, flopped on a sofa with another mug of coffee and watched golf on the television for half an hour, before jumping up to begin the lunch preparations.

As he did so, he saw their adored rescue cat, Jinx, was eyeing the painting suspiciously.

'See,' Freya said, walking in, 'Jinx doesn't like her either.'

'Reminds you both of your mother, does she?' he said, then ducked as, grinning, she threw a tangerine at him.

5

Monday, 16 September

Roy Grace sat in his small office, his swivel chair turned sideways, giving him a view of some of the particularly uninspiring concrete buildings of this part of the Sussex Police HQ campus, a patch of grass and a car park. The sky was overcast, matching his gloomy mood. It was just two weeks since his son, Bruno, had died, hit by a car crossing the main road outside his school, and he was finding work a welcome distraction.

As he had done so many times in the days since, he was fighting tears. A fight he regularly lost and was losing again now. He pulled his handkerchief out and dabbed his eyes. *Shit. Why, why, why?* A year and a half ago he hadn't even known that Bruno existed. Before she had disappeared, his former wife, Sandy, had kept it secret from him that she had been pregnant.

The first he had known about Bruno was a phone call from a friend in the Munich branch of the Landeskriminalamt – the LKA. Marcel Kullen informed him that a woman in a coma, after being hit by a taxi while crossing the road, might be his long-missing wife Sandy. And she did indeed turn out to be her. She had died then, and now the son they'd had was dead, in similar circumstances.

How Bruno came to be crossing that road, just an hour or so after he'd dropped him at school on that fateful morning, no one could explain. Nor could anyone explain, as yet anyhow, why Bruno had failed to see the car which had been travelling within the speed limit, according to the report from the Collision Investigation Unit. The only eyewitness to the accident itself, a woman walking her dog, had said he'd appeared to be absorbed in his phone.

Roy Grace was desperately sad, thinking about the upcoming funeral. And if it wasn't going to be harrowing enough, the presence of Sandy's parents, with whom he had never got on, and who at one point had suspected him of murdering Sandy, would for sure not make it any easier.

He dabbed his eyes again, took several deep breaths and turned his focus back to work, pretty much the only thing, along with Cleo's support, that had got him through these past days. They were expecting their second child together in December, which was at least something to focus on. And at work, fortunately, he had a cold case that deeply interested him.

The murder clear-up rate in the UK averaged around 90 per cent year-on-year – among the highest in the world. But that still left one in ten murders unsolved and he was acutely aware that for each of these there was a victim for whom justice had not been served, and bereft loved ones left without answers. Murders made sensational news headlines, but as the saying went, *today's news wraps tomorrow's fish and chips*. While the rest of the nation moved on to the next day's stories, for those loved ones of the victim the pain would never cease. But at least a successful conclusion, in the form of a conviction, would bring some closure and enable them to carry on with their lives.

And as the Detective Superintendent also well knew, most experienced homicide detectives had at least one unsolved case they'd handled that bugged them for years after. For some, that case continued to haunt them even beyond the end of their careers. The one that got away, leaving them forever thinking, *what have I missed – what vital clue?* Some retired detectives went to their graves with that question still unanswered.

Police files on unsolved murders in the UK never closed. And all the time, when there was the likelihood that the offender was still alive, or there were family members who would benefit from closure, these cases were kept under periodic review.

Relationships changed, and with them, sometimes, loyalties. A partner or spouse who had once provided an alibi might, after the relationship had ended – especially if badly and they were angry enough – come forward to the police. In addition, as technology advanced, improved techniques for recovering vital evidence such as fingerprints and DNA could put someone who had long thought they'd got away scot-free behind bars.

Every piece of evidence recovered from a crime scene was carefully tagged and filed in a locked storeroom. Ready to yield its secrets years, maybe even decades, after the crime had been committed.

As Head of Major Crime for Surrey and Sussex Police, Roy Grace had overall responsibility for both current homicide investigations and the regular review of cold cases. He'd recently had a drink with a newly retired colleague, Nick Sloan, a brilliant Detective Superintendent he'd greatly respected and had learned a lot from. Sloan had confessed, over a pint, that he had one regret in his career, a murder case that still haunted him, which he'd been unable to nail. He'd missed something, he was certain, but what?

A wealthy London art dealer, Charlie Porteous, had been bludgeoned to death in his Bentley in the entrance to the driveway of his house. The murder had happened late at night in a public street, in an exclusive residential area in the city of Brighton and Hove.

Sloan's team had established that Porteous had some cash-flow problems and, shortly before his murder, had been touting a painting he'd acquired from a dubious source. He'd paid cash – something apparently completely out of character, as ordinarily he would have paid by cheque or bank transfer, to leave a trail, as was the customary procedure for art dealers in case of any come-back.

On the night of Porteous's death, Sloan's team had established that the dealer had been out to dinner with his god-daughter, Carrie Hepworth. She worked part-time at the gallery and they had a close relationship. The investigation was satisfied that this was purely platonic, a totally avuncular relationship rather than anything untoward. They'd also established his wife, Susan, a pillar of Brighton and Hove society, was very fond of Carrie too, and she had stayed at the couple's house on many occasions. They'd taken her under their wing after some troubled teenage years.

But the massive and extensive investigation, given the name Operation Canvas, had drawn a blank. The long list of potential suspects had included Porteous's employees, a dealer they'd identified to whom he had touted this painting – seemingly a long-lost work by the eighteenth-century French artist Fragonard – and the wealthy collector in Sussex who had expressed interest in seeing the painting.

At the time of his investigation, Nick Sloan had been under pressure, due to a spate of murders in Sussex higher than the normal average for the county of twelve a year, and the then impatient Head of Crime had wanted him to move on as he'd exhausted all his lines of enquiry. Sloan asked Grace, when he next reviewed the county's cold cases, to take a close look at the Porteous murder.

Grace assured him he would. He now had the principal case files in his office.

He briefly turned his attention away from work to his best man duties at his friend and colleague Glenn Branson's wedding to *Argus* reporter Siobhan Sheldrake sometime later this year. It had been set for October but because of Bruno's death they had decided to postpone it and had yet to fix a date. So there were quite a few things to rearrange.

The current fashion seemed to be a three-day stag-do bender in some European capital, or even somewhere far away like Las Vegas, but Glenn just wanted something local and low-key – to Grace's relief. Even so, Glenn was a popular man both in and out of the force, so it was going to be more a question of who they didn't invite. At least that was a high-class problem, he thought, but he had a reputational responsibility. A bunch of drunk men, including a number of detectives, cavorting through the city of Brighton and Hove was never going to be a good plan. And he had made one solemn promise to Glenn, that, unlike one of their much earlier cases, burial in a coffin in remote woodlands was not going to be on the list of options at his disposal.

Fortunately, after successfully wrapping up his last case of an apparently missing wife, these past weeks had been a rare quiet time at work. And he'd been grateful of that quiet after the death of Bruno. His team's previous case – in which he'd had a relatively minor role – involved a bent legal aid solicitor running a county lines drug-dealing network. It had ended in a result, of sorts, but one which had tied him up in a major internal as well as an IOPC enquiry, which would be ongoing for some while. But he and his team had done everything by the book, and he wasn't worried about the eventual outcome.

Right now, his main focus during this period of downtime was on his cold cases so he could get his brain thinking about other things. And while looking through the list of some thirty unsolved murders in the counties of Surrey and Sussex that merited assessment for possible review, he found himself drawn to the one his old friend and mentor Nick Sloan had talked about a couple of months ago.

The thick master file, labelled *Operation Canvas*, sat on his desk in front of him, and fourteen boxes containing evidence, including witness statements, crime scene photographs, forensic reports, CCTV footage printouts, ANPR analysis, phone records and association charts, were stacked on the floor around his desk. There were another twelve boxes still to go through in the locked evidence store. Additionally, he'd requested the HOLMES team to load their entire file on his system.

His purpose in carrying out this assessment was to see if anything had been missed, as Nick Sloan felt there had been. Was it worth putting more money and resources into it or not?

He resumed the laborious task of reading through Sloan's policy book on Operation Canvas, in which the former Detective Superintendent had diligently noted all the decisions he'd made during the investigation, and his reasons, at the end of which were his conclusions before the unsolved murder had been filed.

This detailed report set out a summary of the murder of Charlie Porteous, followed by the lines of enquiry, strategies and forensic assessments that had been made. Sloan's purpose in writing this, as was normal for any SIO, was to allow any new Senior Investigating Officer, at a later date reinvestigating the case, to have an overview of what had taken place.

It had taken Roy Grace three days of reading through the paperwork, and the HOLMES report on his screen, to conclude that Nick Sloan's hunch was right. This was a case that very definitely merited review, to decide whether or not there was sufficient evidence to warrant the time and resources required to reopen it. In order to do that he would have to establish there was a more than reasonable chance of securing an arrest and conviction. And the more he read, the more confident he felt that there was.

6

Norman Potting was the last to arrive, as he usually was at any briefing, lumbering in through the door and shutting it behind him with the sound of a safe dropping from a great height onto concrete. Muttering an apology for being late, although he wasn't, he was actually on time for once – just – the DS grabbed a chair, joining his colleagues around one end of the oval table in the conference room of the Major Crime suite. 'Learned something interesting today,' he announced, his gruff voice more croaky than usual. 'Herrings communicate by farting.'

'That's very helpful to know,' Grace said, a little tersely.

'You obviously read a classy newspaper, Norman,' Velvet Wilde jibed.

After he had recently gone through a period of actually looking quite sharp, shedding some weight, and with his former comb-over long gone in favour of a modern, shaven look, Roy Grace noticed the DS was slipping a bit these days. Some of his shirts, like the purple-striped one today, had frayed collars. He guessed, sadly, that was the real Norman all over, a man becoming increasingly ragged around the edges through the trials of life, some of his own making, some totally undeserved and beyond his control. He felt a deep affection for this old war horse and his abilities as a detective that many others in the force failed to see.

Grace checked his watch, before looking up at his small, hand-picked group. 'The time is 4 p.m., Thursday, 19 September,' he

24

announced. 'This is the first meeting to review Operation Canvas, the unsolved murder of art dealer Charles Stuart Porteous in the early hours of Friday, 16 October 2015.'

In front of him lay a fresh investigator's notebook and a policy book, both labelled *Operation Canvas – Review*, as well as his printed notes. He glanced around at his team. DI Glenn Branson, his deputy SIO, wearing an unusually sombre tie and even more unusually sombre expression, was responsible for intelligence. Seated next to him was thirty-four-year-old Luke Stanstead, acting as intel researcher. Then Potting and DC Velvet Wilde, together responsible for reviewing all the witness statements and actions of Detective Superintendent Nick Sloan's former team and making recommendations. Next along sat twenty-seven-year-old DS Jack Alexander, tall with ramrod posture, smartly suited with shiny black shoes, responsible for heading up the forensic review assisted by CSI Chris Gee from the forensics team.

The final member was Pauline Sweeney – known as Polly. The energetic recent addition to his team had not long ago retired as a DC, then returned to join the force as a civilian investigator. With her fair hair pinned up, dressed in a black top, tight-fitting checked trousers and laced high-heeled sandals, Polly brought a touch of glamour to the team. Grace had known her for many years and liked her, as much for her sunny personality as for her brilliant skills at her job. And she was both a fighter and survivor, having taken two years out in the middle of her career to battle and defeat illness.

'We'll continue for now with the name originally given to this enquiry, Operation Canvas,' Grace announced.

'And who says computers don't have a sense of humour, eh chief?' Potting quipped.

Grace smiled; he was right. The names given to each enquiry were thrown up at random by a computer, but often they were uncannily close to the subject, as was the case here. 'Won't be long before we detectives aren't needed at all, will it, Norman?'

Potting tutted. 'Hope I'm long retired before that day, chief.'

Already well past his years of service to qualify for his pension, Grace secretly hoped that day would still be a long time off for his colleague. Focusing on his notes he announced, 'Right, I'd like to stress that this is only an initial assessment to decide whether a full reopening of this case should take place. And it must not interfere with any new and current Major Crime enquiry that comes in. Clear?'

Everyone except for Branson, who was preoccupied with his phone, nodded. Grace shot a glance at his friend, wondering what was wrong. Glenn's whole body language was odd; he normally radiated confidence but today he seemed decidedly downbeat.

Behind Grace were three whiteboards on easels. On one was a carefully curated selection of the original crime scene photographs, showing Charlie Porteous slumped dead in the driver's seat of his Bentley, in close-up and wide angle. On another were photographs from the postmortem, several close-ups of which showed his smashed-in skull. On the third was Porteous's family and association chart.

'Key evidence I've extrapolated so far from Nick Sloan's report is that at the time of his death, Porteous might have been in possession of a high-value painting. He had possibly brought it with him down to Brighton, from his London gallery, to show it to a potentially interested collector in Sussex. This person was identified as George Astone – who was subsequently eliminated from Sloan's enquiries. But at this moment it is only hearsay he had this painting with him, and we don't have full details of its provenance.'

Glancing down at his notes, Grace said, 'Paraphrasing from Nick Sloan's notebook entries, he was the duty SIO on the night the murder happened. He has recorded being called out at 8.10 a.m. on the morning of Friday, 16 October, by the duty inspector at Brighton police station. Earlier that morning a newspaper delivery person called the police, stating she had seen what looked like a body in the driver's seat of a Bentley at the front gates of Tongdean House, 173 Tongdean Avenue, Hove. The dead man was subsequently identified as Charlie Porteous.'

Grace sipped his mug of tea. 'Around 3 a.m. of that same morning, Porteous's wife, Susan, who hadn't left the house all day, had alerted the police as her husband had failed to arrive home from London and wasn't answering his phone. That call had been logged, with no action taken at the time. The then duty inspector at Brighton nick understandably took the view it was too soon to involve the police.'

Everyone on the team nodded, their eyes drawn towards the whiteboard with the gruesome blow-up photographs of the dead man, apart from Glenn Branson, who was still focused on his phone, texting.

The majority of murders that happened, year on year, in the counties of Sussex and Surrey were, sadly, Grace thought, domestic-related. Mostly, the law-abiding people of these prosperous so-called home counties were able to sleep easy in their beds, untouched by the violence happening in other less privileged strata of society – and in other more violent parts of the country.

Which was why the image of the portly, balding man, upright and lifeless in the driver's seat of his silver Bentley Flying Spur, the back of his skull smashed in, and a deep gouge behind his ear, the leather headrest stained by his brains and blood, drew everyone's attention. It stood out clearly among the very many murder scenes Grace had attended during his career to date. As it evidently did with his team.

The Detective Superintendent was equally well aware that it

wasn't his job to discriminate or decide which murder victims were more important. The life of a rich person was of no more or no less value than that of a street person. At every murder scene he'd ever attended, Roy Grace had looked down at the victim and felt profound sadness. That deceased human being had once been someone's child, someone's wife or husband or sibling. There was no unspoken hierarchy in homicide investigation. Whether it was a pillar of society or a particularly nasty criminal, you did your best to find out who had committed the crime, arrest them and bring them to justice.

But, in spite of that, Grace told his team that this particular unsolved murder merited a review. He went on to give his reasons, extrapolated from Sloan's very detailed notes, explaining that Charlie Porteous was by all accounts a well-liked and respected family man as well as a generous philanthropist, and a highly respected art dealer, with no known enemies. After her retirement his wife had started as a volunteer helper at the city's treasured Martlets Hospice, and the couple had been for years significant benefactors to many local charities.

Porteous had been struck on the back of his head, three times for good measure, by a heavy, blunt weapon that had never been identified, and he had a deep laceration behind his ear. The car was left tight to the gates of the property and upon examination there had been no obvious interference with the gate mechanism although his wife had mentioned they did occasionally have issues with their function. Nick Sloan's team had never been able to establish a clear motive for his death.

Charlie Porteous's rare vintage Rolex, which was insured for £45,000, was missing from his wrist, along with his wallet, in which according to his wife he only kept around £50 in cash, as well as his gold wedding band and his mobile phone. A possible random street robbery was one line of enquiry, and some credence was given to this when his wallet, minus any cash and his credit cards, but still with his driving licence inside, had been found dumped in a bin close to Brighton railway station.

Sloan's team had checked all the man's known credit and debit cards and no one had attempted to use any subsequently. With his reputation for being thorough, Sloan had his outside enquiry team check with every second-hand jeweller in the city and in a much wider area beyond, as well as eBay and other online sites, but neither the watch nor the wedding ring had appeared for sale.

Another major line of enquiry, Grace informed them, concerned the artwork. There was no painting found in the Bentley, but the team had come up with considerable evidence that Porteous may have had it with him at the time of his murder.

Earlier that night, the victim had been with his god-daughter, Carrie Hepworth, at a restaurant in London, although there was no evidence, certainly at the time, to implicate her in his murder. And from the information she had given in several interviews, Porteous, very excited about his bargain purchase, had showed her the painting at dinner, telling her he had broken his rule about paying cash. When he left the restaurant he carried the painting concealed beneath his raincoat over his arm.

Grace informed his team that CCTV at Brighton station had picked up Charlie Porteous alighting from the train from London's Victoria station at 12.17 a.m. The last sighting on the station's cameras had been of him entering the car park two minutes later, again with his raincoat over his arm.

Working in conjunction with the London Metropolitan Police Arts and Antiquities Unit, corroborating that story, Sloan's team learned that prior to his death, Charlie Porteous had made an acquisition that he was very excited about. A painting he'd bought from an unidentified Frenchman, for the sum of £50,000, which Porteous believed – backed up by an expert he had apparently mentioned or shown it to, who had subsequently been identified and interviewed – was the work of the eighteenth-century French master Jean-Honoré Fragonard.

The price Porteous had apparently paid, just a fraction of the true worth of the painting – if it was genuine – had been a major factor in the original enquiry, raising many questions. Why had a respected dealer, who must have known the true worth of the painting, bought it from someone unknown to the art world for such little money? And without a receipt or any financial record?

Neither the French police nor Interpol had been able to trace the seller, and Sloan's team concluded whoever this person was had given a false name. The team had been told it was possible the picture had been stolen to order by a collector in a country beyond Interpol's reach, but there were no reports of the theft of this painting. Equally, they had learned, from the outside enquiry team's conversations with dealers in the art world, assisted by Met detectives, that there were wealthy individuals who got a kick out of having a private gallery of paintings that no one else in the world could see. To date, the provenance of the painting remained unresolved.

ANPR cameras in and around Brighton had provided no leads, nor had any CCTV cameras in Porteous's residential neighbourhood.

Grace took a breath and then continued. 'The offender – or offenders – left no forensic evidence at the crime scene. However, a partial fingerprint was recovered from a restaurant bill inside the victim's wallet that was discovered in the bin. All members of staff at the restaurant in London where the receipt was from were printed, but no match was found. It is possible, therefore, that the print is from one of the offenders, at the time he or she rummaged through the wallet for cash.'

Norman Potting raised a hand. 'What about tapings, chief?'

'I was just coming to that, Norman. Good thinking, though. The forensics officers took tapings off Porteous's outside garments, and with the advances in forensics that have occurred during these past four years these should be sent for analysis to see if any potential fibres from the attacker's clothing might be identified. We should also see if anything new, such as blood from the attacker, might be present, which we could obtain DNA from.' He turned to Alexander. 'Jack, I'm giving you this action as part of your forensic review.' Then he looked up. 'Any comments at this stage?'

Alexander raised his hand. 'Sir, what is puzzling me is why Porteous was bludgeoned to death. If it was just a straightforward street robbery, the offender would have surely threatened him with a knife or maybe a gun and he would have handed over his valuables. It indicates something else going on, to me.'

'Such as, Jack?' Grace asked.

'If this was a targeted robbery and the offenders were primarily after the painting, maybe they didn't want Porteous reporting its theft. I've read that famous paintings are hard to sell in some territories, because they are instantly recognizable. Perhaps whoever the offender was knew this and reckoned it would be easier to sell if it wasn't reported.'

Grace thought about this for some moments. 'That makes sense, Jack, good point.' He made a note then looked up at Branson.

'Any thoughts, Glenn?' Grace asked him, deliberately to get his attention focused.

The DI looked up with a bewildered expression. 'I'm sorry, boss, I was elsewhere. Thoughts, boss?'

Not wanting to disrespect his deputy SIO, Grace said to his team, 'We'll take a five-minute break.' Then to Branson with a sideways nod of his head, 'Quick chat in private, something I need to ask you.'

'Sure, boss.'

7

Thursday, 19 September

Out in the corridor, closing the door behind him, Roy Grace said to Glenn Branson, 'Mate, what's the matter – you're not right, are you? What's up?'

The tall, powerfully built DI looked on the verge of tears. The last time Grace had seen him look like this was three years back when he had split up, badly, with his wife, Ari.

'I don't want to lump you with this shit right now.' He sighed and shook his head balefully. 'Siobhan and me had a big row last night – I don't know – I've a feeling we might be busting up. She thinks we should delay the wedding until—'

'Until when?'

He shrugged.

'What? Tell me? What's happened? You seem so good together.'

Branson stood in silence for some moments. 'Yeah, well, you know when we first started going out, I said she was keen to have kids, right?'

Grace nodded, vaguely remembering.

'Well out of the blue she's now told me that there's no way she wants any for years because she's too focused on her career. I'm gutted, mate, and it all kicked off yesterday.'

'Are you in such a rush? You've already got two lovely kids.'

'Yeah, and I don't want there to be a huge age gap between Sam and Remi and any kids I have with Siobhan.'

'Kids aren't everything, mate. I think she's a great person.'

'For a journalist?' Branson's expression briefly thawed.

Grace smiled. 'A great person, full stop.'

Again Branson nodded. 'I think that too, but I saw another side of her, she's so driven and ambitious, I've no hope of changing her mind at the moment. And I'd love more kids together while mine are still young. She's so good with my two, I thought we were on the same page and we'd have kids straight away. You know I love that movie *Brighton Rock*, right? The original with Dickie Attenborough, not the remake.'

Grace nodded again.

'I didn't realize it was actually a book first.'

'There's a surprise! Quite a lot of the best films are.'

'Yeah, well I was watching it again the other night – a kind of extended version – and they were talking about the author.'

'Graham Greene,' Grace added.

'So they were quoting Greene talking about his books and he said that every writer has to have a chip of ice in their heart.'

Grace glanced at his watch, unsure where this was going and mindful of getting back into the briefing. He had a meeting on diversity in the police force to attend in an hour's time. 'OK,' he said, 'so are you saying Siobhan has that chip? Of ice?'

'Right, so Siobhan told me she's been asked to write a big piece for the *Argus* on all the officers who've lost their jobs through misconduct in recent years. She asked me what names I could think of, and I just lost it, after the blow about kids. I asked her why the hell couldn't she write a piece about all the good work the police do, all the dangers they face, all the service they give to the community, rather than trashing them, trying to turn the *Argus* into some scandal rag like the old *News of the World*?'

'I agree with that!'

Branson looked forlornly back at him. 'Yeah, thanks. But it didn't play well. She said she wasn't going to compromise her journalistic integrity simply because she was engaged to a copper. And if that was going to be a problem for the future, as well as not having kids just yet, then maybe we didn't have a future.' The DI leaned against the wall, tears welling in his eyes. 'Shit, man, I love that woman. She's my future. I-I just – you know, ever since Ari – I've struggled.'

Grace said calmly, 'Glenn, this isn't a discussion we're going to be able to resolve in a couple of minutes now. Want a drink later, after work?'

'I'd like that, please.'

'You are going to have to look at it from Siobhan's perspective, too. She's ambitious, it's understandable she might not want kids yet and she will want to write stories that give her headlines, then you need to accept that it's the negative ones that get those headlines. How much happy news do you ever read in a paper? You and I both hate corrupt police officers as well as those that let down the force.'

'Guess you're right. I know you're right. But I care passionately about the police, Roy. I hate seeing us attacked in the press and media.'

'Then try using your influence, on a very influential journalist, to change all that?'

Looking only slightly convinced, Glenn Branson nodded.

8

As Grace and Branson sat back down in the room, Jack Alexander raised his hand again. 'It seems to me, sir, that the painting is key. If we could establish that Charlie Porteous had it with him when he was murdered, and it was taken, that would possibly rule out a street robbery, wouldn't it?'

'Possibly, but not necessarily, Jack,' Grace said. 'These people tend to grab anything they think they can flog – often drug users desperate to earn enough for their next fix. But I agree that if we could conclusively establish he had the picture with him it would give us another major line of enquiry. Nick Sloan did have his team contact all art galleries and auction houses in Sussex and the bordering counties, as well as wider afield and online, to see if anyone had been offered a painting by this artist – and drew a blank. But as you rightly suggest, it remained a major line of enquiry at the time he had to wind down Operation Canvas.'

Once more, Grace looked at his notes. 'The people remaining on the list of significant witnesses include his god-daughter, Carrie Hepworth, along with his other gallery staff, all of whom need to be interviewed again. As should his London driver, Meehat El Hadidy. But we need to bear in mind that the financial investigator, John Camping, had at that time been unable to provide evidence that any of them had benefited financially from Porteous's murder. The team had also eliminated the collector, George Astone, for whom Charlie Porteous had supposedly brought the painting down to Sussex for him to view, but he also needs to be interviewed again.'

Stanstead, next to Potting, raised a hand.

'Yes, Luke?' Grace said.

'Sir, over the last few days, as requested, I've been looking through the list of Charlie Porteous's neighbours who were interviewed by Nick Sloan's outside enquiry team. There's one missing.'

Grace frowned. 'There is?'

'I've done a search on Google Earth, against all the residences listed in the enquiry. There's one that's been omitted – a house some distance up the road, on the opposite side to the Porteouses' home, called Tongdean Ridge. It's a few hundred yards away. The report says that the owners were abroad at the time, at their second home in Marbella.'

'Which would explain it,' Grace replied.

Stanstead shook his head. 'No, they have two dogs – Rhodesian Ridgebacks – as well as a cat and seven hens. I've contacted the owners, Mr and Mrs Malby. They told me they have house-sitters whenever they are away, a couple called Joe and Liz Lee, who were in residence at the time of Porteous's murder. I've since spoken to Mr Lee. He says he was never contacted by the police, probably because they had left the country on a six-month house-sit abroad.'

Frowning, Grace looked at him. 'Did he see anything that might be helpful?'

'Actually, yes, he did. Mr Lee is a former army officer and told me he suffers from insomnia. He would often go for a walk in the early hours, and he remembers on that particular Friday morning seeing a car accelerating hard along Tongdean Avenue. He thought it was a little strange, as it's normally quiet – as you know, it's a very exclusive residential street – but he said that lately there had been more car drivers using these roads as a rat run.'

'Did he get a description of the car?'

Stanstead smiled. 'Better than that, boss. He managed to write down part of its registration – he often wrote down and reported cars driving too fast along there.'

'Nice work, Luke,' Grace said. 'Has the owner been identified?'

'Not yet, but we are narrowing the possible matching vehicles down.'

Grace then sat thoughtfully for some moments. 'Arrange to find and interview this Mr Lee as a matter of priority. We need the partial fingerprint found on the bill in Porteous's wallet to be run again against the database, to see if anything new comes up. Let's revisit the tapings from his clothes. As I said, we need to interview again this collector in Sussex that Porteous was going to show the painting to. And we want to find out and eliminate any dealer that he might have showed this picture to, prior to his murder.'

He was silent again for a short while, as he made more notes, before looking up with a specific list of actions for each member of his team. When he had finished, he said, 'I suggest we meet again here, at 9 a.m. on Wednesday, 25 September, to review everyone's findings. Any questions?'

There were none.

9

Thursday, 19 September

Roy Grace arrived home shortly after 10 p.m. and sniffed a very faint aroma of something appetizing, but also something burnt. As he entered the cottage, he was greeted by Humphrey, their dog, and a quiet hello from Cleo, although she didn't look up. She was on the sofa in the living area, surrounded by her Open University papers, which their recently fostered cat, Reggie, was clawing and playing with. Reggie's owner was in prison, and sadly the cat wouldn't be able to stay with them long term, but they were enjoying his antics so far. Cleo's dissertation was due to be handed in next month, hopefully well before the baby arrived. All going well, she would achieve the MA in Philosophy that she had worked so hard for and could graduate next summer.

'I'm sorry, darling,' he said, raising his arms as he went over, bent down and kissed her on the forehead.

'You said you'd be home at seven.'

He nodded ruefully, loosening his tie and pulling off his suit jacket. 'I'm really sorry. Glenn's in a terrible state, I had to try to help him.'

'I thought you had a phone, Roy? You could have called, texted, messaged me. My turn to cook supper tonight and I asked you what you wanted and you said fish. I got a lovely piece of turbot from the market, now it's overcooked and so are the vegetables. I'm afraid I ate over an hour ago. I've left yours in the warming oven of the Aga.'

'Thanks.' He perched on an arm of the sofa. 'Honestly, I'm so sorry, but he's genuinely worried.'

'Glenn?' She still looked cross.

'He wanted to have a quick drink after work to talk about it. I had to, I've not seen him like this since he broke up with Ari.'

'I have no problem with you having a drink,' she said. 'But next time just call and tell me?'

He raised his arms again helplessly. 'I know. I honestly thought it would be just a quick drink. But he was in bits, I couldn't leave him. I-I just lost track of the time, and—'

'And?'

He shrugged. 'I don't have an excuse, but I understand why it's annoyed you and I apologise. How's everything here? What's Noah been up to?'

'Fine,' she said. 'We've been cooking, painting, and he's helped me with the chickens. He's been asking me about Bruno still, and I got him distracted by making that dinosaur puzzle four times. Still no terrible twos just yet.' She frowned as if thinking. 'Oh, yes. We need to watch Humphrey with the hens, he's showing too much of an interest in them. Keeps licking his lips and obsessing over one of them, watching everything it does.'

'You think he might go for them? Maybe he's just interested.'

'I think if it flaps too much he'll grab it. It's just instinct, but we'll have to watch him,' she said. 'So, Glenn?'

After some moments he said, 'As I said, I have a feeling the wedding might be off.'

'Lucky I haven't bought a hat,' she said.

He gave her a half-hearted smile. 'I'm just not sure how they are going to work it out.'

'And? How did you leave it?'

'I told him to send a huge bunch of flowers to her at the office, in the morning.'

Cleo shook her head. 'Really?'

'You don't think that's the right thing?'

Shaking her head again, she said, 'You think any problem can be solved with a bunch of flowers?'

'A peace offering – no?'

She stared back at him. 'So what's happened, exactly?'

He told her the full story. When he'd finished she said, 'Do you remember what you told me when they first started dating?'

'No, what?'

'That it was going to end in tears. That at some time down the line, a cop in love with an ambitious newspaper reporter was always going to end in an ugly compromised situation. Take a bow, Detective Superintendent Grace, your powers of prophecy have proved correct.'

He smiled but she didn't smile back.

'So, what do I advise him?' he asked.

'To respect her, that's what women want, not sodding flowers or an expensive trinket. Tell him that if he really loves her and wants a life with her, he can't interfere with her career. He has to let her do what she needs to do for her work. And if that means delaying having children, he has to wait, and anyhow, she's still young. I really like her: she's smart, she's ambitious and she's a warm person – he told me those are some of the many things he loves about her. And I do genuinely think she's a *keeper*. So he is the one who needs to take a look at himself.'

Grace nodded. 'That's kind of what I said.'

'Glenn started his working life as a nightclub bouncer, if I'm remembering right?'

'He did.'

'Then after his son was born, he looked down at him and thought to himself, one day you are going to go to school, and when you do, someone's going to ask you what your dad does for a living, and I want you to be able to say something you are proud of. That's why he applied to join the police, right?'

'Right,' Grace said.

'And Glenn's ambitious too, isn't he?'

'Very.'

'You've always told me he has what it takes to get to the top, that he's bright, has real emotional intelligence, empathy, and people like him.'

'All of that.'

'If he has all those qualities, it shouldn't matter what his wife does, should it?' Cleo suggested.

'No, it shouldn't, but it does. God, you know how it is. The relationship between the police and the press has never been an easy one, and never less so than today. The Chief Constable is very wary of the *Argus*'s loyalties. If Siobhan is going to be seen as anti-police, which this piece would be, that's not going to help anything.'

'So what did you advise him? Other than sending flowers? The editor, Arron Hendy, his job is to sell newspapers, and he needs good stories. Think he's going to be happy to spike that one because his top crime reporter received a bunch of flowers?'

'I guess not.'

'Hello, Roy!' she said. 'Welcome to the real world. It's one in which, today, the *little woman* doesn't sacrifice her career for her *big breadwinner hubby's* advancement. In today's world *she-who-must-be-obeyed* doesn't sit at home all night waiting for her man to come home before cooking his dinner and popping out children on demand. The *real world*, as you are about to discover, is overcooked fish, burnt potatoes and soggy green beans in the bottom oven of the Aga. Enjoy. I'm going to bed.'

10

Win some, lose some, Harry Kipling rued. It seemed that no matter how hard he busted his balls working, the company's bottom line at the end of each year was always less than he'd hoped. His accountant would point out the need to increase his prices to keep up with his rising overheads and costs of materials, and yet Harry was always reluctant to act on her advice, fearing that would make him no longer competitive.

Between his and Freya's earnings, they just about kept in the black, but there was never enough left over to pay off some of the mortgage, as they started out every year intending to do, and their dream of upgrading to the pretty Sussex village of Steyning, a few miles to the west of Brighton and Hove, remained just that, a dream. Something always seemed to happen to scupper his profits and it had just happened again this week. Ironically, it was an extension in Steyning.

Vine Cottage was a job he should never have taken on, he knew. He'd already been overstretched with work, and the profit margin was a lot smaller than usual, but it had seemed a straight-forward and simple extension. He'd thought he could take on a couple of builders who worked for him occasionally, and who'd just had a job cancelled, and make a small but tidy profit on the job.

On Monday they'd cut very carefully through the bottom of a wattle-and-daub-rendered end wall, to make a doorway through

42

to the proposed extension. But the wall had started to crumble; the ceiling above had immediately begun to sag, urgently needed to be shored up with steel beams. And now, because it was a listed building, they were going to have to reconstruct the wall exactly as it had been. The time involved was going to dent his profit margin and he had already drawn up a revised estimate.

He'd finally put the nightmare of this past week with Vine Cottage behind him, with a blinder of a round at the Dyke golf course this morning, beneath a glorious, cloudless sky. Overjoyed at having played well below his handicap of 15, scoring three birdies, the couple of pints with his mates at the bar afterwards had further helped his mood.

And another pint of Harvey's now, as he sat in the conservatory of his home, with the patio doors wide open, the Sports section of *The Sunday Times* and a mail order catalogue on his lap, was helping his mood even further still. He'd sort out Vine Cottage, maybe the cost would be less than he feared – he'd figure something. He took another sip of beer and turned his attention away from the catalogue back to the television. South Africa were giving India a trouncing at cricket. That, combined with the smell of burning charcoal on the barbecue outside, and the sunlight streaking in, was improving his spirits even further.

He looked lovingly at their son, lounging at the other end of the sofa, orange headphones clamped over the fourteen-year-old's ears as always, head tilted down towards his phone, Jinx, their rescue cat, snuggled on his lap. Tom was dressed in a Seagulls T-shirt, Nike skinny tracksuit bottoms and immaculate white Air Force 1 trainers, which he scrubbed clean obsessively, almost every day – pretty much the only thing he did ever clean. The glass of cider they now allowed him as a Sunday treat sat on the coffee table in front of him, dangerously close to being knocked over by his clumsy, gangly legs alongside it. With his eyes half closed it was hard to tell, as it usually was these days, whether Tom was looking at his phone or was in a trance. And ever since the *big scare*, just over two years ago, both Harry and Freya always kept a close watch on him.

On his twelfth birthday they'd arranged for Tom and a dozen school friends to have an afternoon at the go-kart track at Albourne, for racing followed by pizzas and cake. But the following morning when Harry was at work, Freya had been unable to rouse Tom to drive him to school. For some dreadful moments of panic, she actually thought he was dead. Then she'd calmed enough to remember her first aid training and checked his pulse. Just a faint pulse she thought – hoped – prayed – and dialled 999, barely able to speak when the call handler answered. Then a long, agonizing wait for an ambulance.

Later the A&E consultant had told them, gravely, that Tom had been diagnosed as Type-1 diabetic. He had gone into a coma and if he'd been left for just a few more hours, he would almost certainly have died.

From that moment, Freya had become obsessed with Tom's sugar levels, to the point where Harry sometimes felt she was mollycoddling him. But he understood. Tom was their *miracle* baby, who had come along after over eleven years of their trying for one, including numerous very expensive and failed attempts at IVF. Finally, when they'd given up on all avenues and instead had decided to look at adopting, Freya fell pregnant.

The boy had always been particularly precious to both of them, as Harry guessed all kids were to their parents, but these past two years since his diagnosis, she worried constantly, especially as Tom resented that his diagnosis meant he wasn't supposed to eat the kind of treats all his friends enjoyed. While he was good much of the time, he regularly had major lapses, bingeing on chips, chocolate and soft drinks, sending his sugar levels into orbit.

Harry and Freya had had long debates over which school he

should attend. Freya had wanted Tom at her own school, where she could keep an eye on him, and Harry had resisted vigorously, feeling that being the son of the deputy head could have a stifling effect on him.

But now she had an even better way of keeping an eye on Tom, via an app on her phone. Tom wore a circular Libre patch on his arm which monitored his blood-sugar levels around the clock via a tiny needle permanently inserted in his skin beneath the patch, which was changed every two weeks. If the levels went too low or too high, an alarm pinged on both his phone and her own.

Freya was lying on the sofa opposite them, sipping a glass of rosé and reading through a thick pile of paperwork from her school. She wrinkled her nose a couple of times, sniffed, frowned, then focused on her reading again.

On the screen the Indian batsman blocked a fast ball and that was the end of the over. Harry jumped up, taking the opportunity to check on the barbecue. Hopefully the weather would stay fine, and they'd eat outside on the deck. The garden, with its hot tub, miniature plastic dinosaur, slide and swing – which Tom had long ago stopped using – immaculate lawn and lush flower beds and shrubs, was Freya's pride and joy.

Nearly ready. A row of bowls he'd prepared earlier sat on the table beside the Weber. King prawns, salmon steaks, No Bull vegan burgers, corn on the cob, and skewers of courgettes, red peppers and paneer. Sweet potatoes were baking in the oven.

He returned to the sofa and quickly glanced at a few more pages of the catalogue. Harry loved household gadgets and was forever buying them from the inserts that regularly arrived with the papers, much to Freya's amusement. His most recent purchase had been a tool to slice carrots into a floral spray, and it had done an effective job on his forefinger an hour ago, as the antiseptic cream and bandage she had patiently applied to his throbbing finger reminded him. Another gadget now caught his eye and he held it up to Freya.

'What's that? It looks like some medieval torture instrument,' she said.

'It's really clever – long-reach toenail scissors!'

She was about to reply when she was interrupted by two sharp pings, almost instantaneous, one from Tom's phone, the other from hers. She looked down immediately and saw a *high glucose* alert on her monitoring app. It was reading *28*.

She jumped up and went over to Tom who, with his headphones on, had been oblivious to the sound. She prised one away from his ear and he looked up at her, irritated. 'Mum!'

'Your sugar's high, darling,' she said. 'Have you been eating chocolate or ice cream or something?'

'Just Haribos,' he mumbled. 'Oh, yeah, and a caramel Magnum.'

'*Just* Haribos? You know how much sugar is in them?' she said. '*And* the ice cream?'

He shrugged. 'Whatever.' He looked back down at the game he was playing.

'You need to give yourself a jab,' she insisted.

'OK, I will.'

'Now!'

He glared at her, but then, trying not to disturb Jinx, reluctantly dug in his pocket for his insulin pen and clicked out a measure. She felt sorry for him. Tom was a kind person, and life had dealt him a crap hand by giving him this disease at such a young age. She used to binge on all the sweet treats he now craved and knew how she'd have felt if she'd been denied them.

As she settled back down on the sofa, she noticed again a smell that had bothered her earlier. She sniffed hard. 'Harry, can you smell something burning?'

'The barbecue, darling.'

She frowned. 'It's not a barbecue smell.'

Like a fish momentarily surfacing from the ocean depths, Tom raised his head and sniffed, then returned to the safety of the depths.

Without looking away from the television, as the Indian batsman hit a ball dangerously high in the air, Harry sniffed, too. The South African fielder dropped the easy catch, and the ball rolled towards the boundary. He sniffed again. Freya was right. There was a different, acrid smell, one he recognized instantly as the smell of burning paint.

He looked around, puzzled. Was it a light fitting or some other electrical problem? It was getting stronger. Coming from inside the conservatory.

Then, yelling, 'Shit, shit, shit!' he ran to the painting, the one he'd bought at the car boot sale and had left face out towards the glass side of the room. The south-west-facing side.

A thin, grey stream of smoke was curling up from that side.

He grabbed the frame, lifted it up, blowing frantically at the centre of the old crone's face, where the smoke was rising from a bulging blister.

Freya, who had followed him, watched him in horror as he ran through into the kitchen with the painting and over to the sink where he grabbed the spray mixer tap off its cradle, squeezed the lever and directed the fierce jet at the woman's face. After a few seconds the smoke subsided and stopped, as water ran down the picture.

Leaving it perched on the draining board, he went back into the hallway, momentarily baffled. After some moments Freya, looking at the window with the direct sunlight streaming in, and then at the shelf above the low sill where they lined up pots of cacti and a few other ornaments, realized what had happened.

She lifted up the offending article, a clear glass globe paperweight. 'This is what caused it.'

'Oh God, yes, it is!' he said, smiling with relief. 'Do any of your kids at school ever use a magnifying glass to refract the sun's rays and burn holes in pieces of paper? We used to do that all the time at school, in summer.'

She shook her head. 'No, we don't, things have tightened up since we were at school, sadly!'

'What, you don't teach them basic physics?'

'Yeah, but we leave out the bit about how to burn the school down.'

'When I was in the boy scouts, we used to do that to light camp fires. And we did it to piss off teachers! Don't you remember old Mr Leask?'

'The geography teacher?'

'Yep! No one liked him. We used to take magnifying glasses into his lessons and then, when he was sitting up at his desk, we'd try to set his things on fire by all focusing our magnifying glasses on his jacket!'

'I didn't realize I'd married a monster.'

He grinned. 'It would really annoy him and make him yell at us!'

Harry had been expecting her to smile at this, but she didn't. Instead, she was looking at him with a horrified expression. 'I can't believe you did that,' she said. 'You could have hurt him.'

Harry shrugged. 'Yep, well, we were just stupid kids, we didn't think about consequences.'

Freya nodded thoughtfully. 'Actually, remember my old friend Rachel?'

'Vaguely.'

'She spent a couple of years in Israel, living with a family. She told me they used to draw the curtains in the daytime to prevent the bright sun rays from refracting through glass objects and causing a fire.'

'That's exactly what's just happened.'

'Jesus, Harry, this is scary. Can you imagine if we'd been out today? The house could have burned down.'

He put the paperweight down on the island unit, shrugged again and went back to the kitchen. He checked the picture wasn't still burning before dabbing it dry with a tea towel. And stared at the blistered centre of the woman's face. He poked the blackened bulge tentatively with his forefinger, checking it wasn't still hot, and flakes of it fell away. He knocked away the rest of the fist-sized bulge, then stood still in amazement.

'Oh my God,' he said. 'Look at this. Look, look! There's something underneath. Another painting!'

11

Sunday, 22 September

'What do you mean?' Freya said, standing a short distance back. 'Something underneath? Like a palimpsest?'

Harry was beaming with excitement. 'A what?'

'A *palimpsest* – it's when you have a piece of paper – or parchment – with writing on, that's overwritten something else that was there before. But where if you look closely, you can see the original text beneath – or an impression of it.'

'Exactly – but in this case in paint. Look at the centre of the woman's face.'

She stared hard. At the jagged, roughly circular gap inside the blackened edges, at the space where most of the face had been. Replacing it was an exquisitely detailed painting of part of a tree, part of a woman's arm, and what looked like sunlit water beyond. After some moments she said, 'You're right, there is something underneath. Very definitely.'

'What if it's a long-lost old master?'

She gave him a reproachful look. 'Really? In a car boot sale?'

'It does happen, we've seen it on *Antiques Roadshow*, right?'

'We've also seen on *Fake or Fortune?* where people have bought what they thought was an old master, and which turned out to be a fake,' she said. 'Someone probably painted over it because it was a rubbish picture.'

He carried the painting out into the darkness of the hallway, laid it against the bottom of the staircase, safely away from light, then hurried upstairs to his den, grabbed his laptop and went back down into the conservatory. He sat on the sofa, flipped open the lid and began tapping the keys.

'What are you doing?' Freya asked.

'Googling,' he replied. 'I'm looking up solvents that could dissolve a surface painting.'

'To reveal whatever's underneath?'

'Exactly.'

She looked at him dubiously. 'My love, you're a house builder, not a picture expert. You don't want to risk damaging what's underneath – on the one in a million chance there is something of value. If you're not careful you'll dissolve what's underneath, too. You'd be better off looking up picture restorers. Talk to a professional. Maybe you should take it to an expert, to see what they think.'

He cocked his head quizzically. 'So, you actually believe there might be something of value, do you?'

She shook her head. '*One in a million* is what I said.'

'Yep, well, right now I'll take those odds.'

She gave him a strange look. 'Something I should know about?'

'No – I – you know – was just thinking wouldn't it be amazing if we found we had something of real value. It does happen.'

'Who was that guy you did the extension for a couple of years ago? The famous art forger – in Rottingdean?'

'Saltdean,' he replied.

'What was his name – Daniel something?'

Harry nodded. 'Hegarty. Daniel Hegarty.'

'That's it. He copied all kinds of artists, didn't he?'

'Yeah, he's really good.' Harry nodded. 'These days he makes good money by faking old paintings but signing them himself – his *DH* signature now has kudos – he has quite a celebrity clientele.'

'So, he'd probably know how to remove a surface painting, don't you think? Would he tell you?'

'Brilliant idea!' Cricket forgotten as well as the barbecue, he pulled up his contacts list on his phone. 'I'll bell him.'

Ten minutes later, ending the call to a very chatty Hegarty, Harry beamed at his wife. 'He's told me exactly what to do – acetone and cotton buds! He says it'll dissolve anything relatively recent, but if the painting beneath is genuinely old, it will be so hardened the acetone won't touch it. He said to do it slowly, bit by bit.'

He shot a glance at Tom who, oblivious to the excitement, continued to lie on the sofa, the world around him blotted out by his headphones. Whether he was watching the cricket or simply staring at the back of his own eyeballs, Harry had no idea.

'Where can you get acetone from?' he asked.

She smiled. 'Simples – my dressing table. Nail varnish remover.'

12

The crow was old, not long for this world. Like himself. Crows were lucky, Archie Goff reflected; their hair didn't turn grey the way his had long ago – it was now nearly white. Not that he was vain or had much to be vain about, with his ageing, beat-up face. Isabella told him affectionately he looked like a scarecrow that had been left out in too many storms.

But at least, unlike this bird, his time wasn't up, not just yet. Not, please God, for a while yet.

The words he'd read last time he was in prison came to mind. *The woods are lovely, dark and deep, but I have promises to keep, and miles to go before I sleep.*

And he had a big promise to keep. To his daughter, to pay for her studies through veterinary college. Ironic, Archie Goff reflected, looking down at the bird sitting, almost resigned, in a trap, that Kayleigh was studying to learn how to keep animals alive and he was paying for it by killing birds. But only crows. Nasty creatures that murdered chicks and ducklings. They were both bullies and thieves. But hey, who was he to moralize?

That was the thought he held, bending his gangly, increasingly creaky frame down, on the edge of the woods, dark and deep, as he removed the creature from the trap he'd baited the day before. It barely resisted as he placed it in the cardboard box, the top punched with air holes. There was food in the box, some strips of chicken, and a foil tray of water. Then he placed it in the bottom

53

of his large sack, alongside the brick. 'Enjoy your last supper, pal,' he said, feeling sorry for the creature. He couldn't help it. He didn't really like killing anything. But needs must.

There had never been a shortage of crows and never a shortage of country houses to burgle in these past forty-five years, to supply him with a living. Mostly a good one but sometimes less so. But all careers had their ups and downs, didn't they?

His times in prisons had been the downs, when he'd missed out on many of the important years when his kids were growing up, and when all three of his marriages had fallen apart. Prison itself was OK: the electricity was paid for, there was television in the cells and the grub was all right. And he had his mates, especially on those stretches when he was fortunate enough to be sent to his second home, as he jokingly called it, the local Sussex big house, Lewes Prison.

But now Archie was tired of the game. He wanted to settle down with his new love, beautiful Isabella from Cape Town, a lab technician whose hobby was belly dancing. She genuinely loved him, despite knowing his background, and he was crazy about her.

All he needed was a couple of good jobs. Maybe just one, if tonight panned out the way he hoped. And he was long enough in the tooth to know how not to get caught, these days.

Hope Manor.

Archie smiled. There was the sign right there in the name!

He checked his watch. Coming up to 4 p.m. It would be a long wait for darkness, but he didn't mind, he loved being in the woods, surrounded by nature and all the beautiful trees, many of which had been around long before he'd been born and would still be here decades, maybe even centuries, after he was gone. He was happy to wait, he had time.

As the Irishman he'd once shared a cell with told him, *When the Good Lord made time, he made plenty of the stuff.*

13

Hope Manor, a handsome Georgian pile five miles outside his home city of Brighton and Hove, was occupied by a couple, Martin and Juliet Fry. Their money had come from a chain of betting shops.

Archie had been tipped off by a bent antiques dealer during his last stay in prison, four years ago, that the couple spent their money on high-value antique silver objects. And that they also kept large quantities of cash in the house.

Archie had been watching the Frys' isolated residence, just beyond these woods, for the past three weeks and reckoned he knew the movements of the elderly occupants – both even older than himself – intimately.

Their guard dog, a German Shepherd, even more ancient in canine years than the Frys were in human ones, had been put down a few weeks ago and they hadn't yet replaced it. The gods were truly smiling on him, Archie thought. It was meant to be!

If all went to plan, tonight could net him all he needed – and more – from his fence, Ricky Sharp, who always paid him well, and from the cash – if he could find it. Enough tonight, perhaps, so he would never need to work again. He'd have a happy, successful daughter, his one kid who still talked to him, and a beautiful partner to share whatever years he still had ahead of him. And money for them to enjoy.

Finally, he'd be living the dream.

Just tonight to get through.

Sunset would be on his side. The moon was also waning – it was just a thin sliver, giving him near-perfect darkness – and he'd lucked out on the weather. No rain.

Dressed all in black, tool belt around his waist, he deposited the trap in the boot of his beat-up old Astra, concealed a couple of hundred yards away in a convenient picnic spot, then stood on the edge of those dark, deep woods, close to the wrought-iron gates of Hope Manor. They were flanked by pillars topped with stone pineapples, and he *hoped* – pun not intended – that Martin Fry and his wife, Juliet, would keep to their routine. And they didn't look like they were going to disappoint. Pretty much on the dot of 7 p.m. the taxi pulled up at the fancy entrance, the driver getting out and pressing the intercom button.

As the gates opened and the taxi drove through, Archie waited a few seconds, then slipped in, unseen, behind it, instantly secreting himself behind a dense bush in the rhododendron-lined driveway. The gates, needing oiling, creaked shut.

In!

Adrenaline surged as it always did, even though he now had a long wait. But he was used to that. Fishing was one of his hobbies and there was a lot of waiting in that.

A few minutes later, he watched the taxi returning. The silhouettes of the elderly Fry couple in the back. Off to their regular Tuesday night dinner at their usual table, no doubt, at English's restaurant in Brighton. Oh yes, Archie did his research on every job. A pro through and through, he had his sources. He even knew what they would be eating and drinking. Martin, six oysters followed by lobster thermidor. Juliet, prawn cocktail followed by Dover sole. A glass of champagne each, on the house, then a bottle of Chablis.

It would be three hours until they returned at 10 p.m. He

resisted the temptation to go for it during this gap, because that would be folly with the house's alarm system. Patience.

Removing the rucksack from his back, Archie made himself comfortable on a broad tree stump, took out the thermos flask and plastic picnic box he had packed, containing sandwiches and an apple, and munched on his supper, listening to the sound of the crow, more active now, flapping around inside its box. When he had finished, he popped in earbuds and resumed listening to his audiobook. It was a novel called *The Catcher in the Rye*. It was on a list he'd found called, 'One Hundred Books to Read Before You Die.'

Archie had left school at fifteen and, oftentimes since, regretted he'd had so little education. He was aware that his daughter, Kayleigh, thought he was a better person than he really was. So, albeit late in the day, he was trying to improve himself, as he wryly told his few friends, to try to cushion her eventual disappointment.

A handful of vehicles drove along the lane over the next three hours. Then, finally, he heard the sound of one stopping. Headlights on the gates, which creaked back open. He stiffened. Stopped the audio, pocketed the earbuds and stood up, heaving the rucksack, heavy with his safecracking kit, onto his back, and lifting up the sack containing the crow and brick.

The taxi passed by, heading up the drive towards the mansion a few hundred yards along, at the end of it.

Archie stepped out and strode up the drive, confident he was invisible to the driver's rear-view mirrors, then ducked back into the bushes as the couple climbed out, paid the man, then went in through the front door, leaving it open.

As the taxi headed away, crunching the gravel on the circular driveway, Archie heard the pip-pip-pip of the burglar alarm. Moments later it was silenced as, presumably, one of the Frys punched in the code.

The front door slammed shut.

A minute or so later, the downstairs lights went off and another came on in the upstairs bow window to the right. The master bedroom, he knew, from the plans of the house he'd viewed online and saved on his phone.

Another hour or so and he'd be good to go. Adrenaline coursed through him again. He was ready. He clicked his torch on and off quickly. Just to test it.

All good.

14

They called him Weasel as much for the way he moved as how he looked. Although, real weasels were diurnal, and he was mostly nocturnal. He was the kind of man, Daniel Hegarty had once joked, who would follow you in through a turnstile and come out in front of you without having paid.

The two of them went back a long way, to kids growing up on the Moulsecoomb estate in Brighton, where they had both begun their criminal careers. Hegarty had gone out burgling with his dad from the age of ten, when he was small enough to crawl through cat-flaps and unlock doors, and Weasel, back in his early teens, was adept at hot-wiring cars and taking Hegarty for joyrides.

Hegarty had ultimately carved out a successful career, initially as an art forger and latterly building up a celebrity clientele by honing his talents into copying the works of great artists, from the old masters to more contemporary artists such as Picasso, Modigliani and Lowry, and signing his own name on the paintings – at least most of the time. Weasel scraped a more modest living, in between spells in prison, turning his hand to any nefarious jobs he could get hold of, from couriering drugs to stealing vehicles to order, to fencing high-value stolen goods. He also occasionally acted as a runner for local art forgers, selling their work or obtaining new commissions for them.

At 10.15 p.m. on this Tuesday night, Daniel Hegarty and his

wife, Natalie, were relaxing on the sofa in their Saltdean home, to the east of Brighton, with their Jack Russell terriers, Rocky and Rambo, watching the news on television. Or at least, Hegarty was watching while his wife and both dogs dozed, snoring, when his phone pinged with a text from Weasel, saying he was outside their house and asking if they were still up. Daniel Hegarty had a feeling this wasn't exactly a social visit.

As he eased himself off the sofa, trying not to disturb Natalie and the dogs, she looked up at him with a start. 'What's up?'

'Weasel – he's outside, wants a quick chat.'

She rolled her eyes. 'God, not him. Be careful about anything he wants.'

Hegarty, a burly sixty-year-old, with greying hair gelled into short, tousled spikes, and a genial smile, said, 'Always careful of him, gorgeous.'

Their large semi-detached house was arranged with its open-plan living room down a short flight of stairs at the back, to take advantage of the fine views across the post-war urban development of Saltdean, with its wide expanse of greensward and the Lido, to the English Channel. As he entered his studio, off the living room, Rocky and Rambo got up and followed him, assuming their duty as guard dogs by bursting into frenzied yapping.

He walked past a copy of a huge Norman Rockwell painting which was leaning against a wall, one he'd recently completed for a client. He was particularly proud of this work, depicting a bunch of smoking jurors rounding on a female one who was clearly, as the story in the picture told, holding out on the verdict. Reaching the front door and doing his best to keep the agitated dogs behind him, he opened it cautiously.

It had been some months since he'd last seen Weasel and he

stood there, in the chiaroscuro of the security light and darkness beyond, clutching a small brown package. Slight, with badly dyed black hair that flopped over one side of his forehead in a style similar to Hitler, an oily smile, a cheap suit, huge shirt collar reminiscent of the 1960s and horrible green loafers, he looked like he always did – furtive.

Hegarty had been to his wedding, decades ago, and remembered Weasel, on the supposedly happiest day of his life, looking wary even on that occasion. He'd posed with his bride for the photographer, outside the church, and even in that moment seemed to be looking nervously beyond the camera, warily searching the assembled company for coppers.

'Dan!' He held out his bony free hand. 'Good to see you, Dan.' His voice whiny as ever.

Hegarty looked down at the package under his arm. 'You working for Amazon now, mate?'

'Very funny. I've got something a bit interesting here – a little job for you.'

'It's a bit late, mate.'

'Yeah, sorry about that.' Then Weasel's attention was drawn to the Heritage plaque beside the front door. It read, *Daniel Hegarty, Master Forger*.

'Blue plaque? That's new, yeah? Thought you only got one of these if you was dead?'

'Or if you reach one hundred years old.'

Weasel squinted at him. 'Pardon my ignorance, but you don't look like you qualify for either of those criteria. Know what I'm saying?'

Hegarty grinned. 'There is another criteria.'

'Yeah?'

He nodded. 'Forging it.'

Weasel broke into a grin. 'Brilliant, mate, well brilliant!'

Despite his annoyance at being disturbed this late, Hegarty realized he was pleased to see his old pal. 'Want a drink?'

'Better stick to something soft, I'm driving. Not like the old days when we drove around pissed all the time, is it?'

Hegarty opened the door wider, then realized Weasel was already inside the house.

15

'Finished!' Harry Kipling announced, carrying the painting down into the conservatory for Freya's inspection. 'Take a look at this beaut!'

He'd been working on it all last night and tonight, obediently following Daniel Hegarty's instructions of *bit by bit*, with cotton buds and nail polish remover.

And he could see from Freya's expression, as she yawned, putting down the bunch of essays she was reading through, that she was impressed.

As was he.

The painting was quite stunningly beautiful, and from the small cracks all over, it certainly appeared to be genuinely very old. The canvas depicted two elegantly dressed lovers picnicking in a forest, with the sun breaking through a swirl of tree branches above them, an idyllic lake behind them, the woman holding up a pink parasol. To their left was a Doric plinth on which sat a winged statue of Cupid.

'Wow!' she said.

'Couldn't have put it better myself,' he replied.

'Is there a signature?'

'I've looked and can't see one.'

She studied it carefully. 'I can't either. What about taking it to an auction house to see what they say? Gorringe's in Lewes are meant to be the best around here.'

'That's a good thought, but I've had another. I've just googled and there's an *Antiques Roadshow* coming to Sussex next weekend!'

It was one of their favourite TV shows.

'Really?'

He nodded. 'At Lancing College.'

'What do we have to do to get an entry?'

'Nothing! I looked on the website. It seems you just turn up and join the queue for the specialist in what you have!'

'That's all?'

'That's all. That's how they do it. What do you reckon? We could take it along and show it to the paintings expert.'

Freya shrugged. 'Let's go for it, why not? If it's a fake or a copy or just a piece of tat they'll tell us, right?'

'My thoughts exactly.'

16

As Daniel Hegarty led Weasel down into the living area, Natalie looked up. 'Ah, Jimmy,' she said with a raised eyebrow. She was one of the few people to call him by his real name, because even though she'd never cared for him, considering him a bad influence on her husband, she felt 'Weasel' was a bit harsh. 'Nice to see you.' Her tone of voice and her body language said anything but.

Standing up, she said wearily, 'I'll take the dogs out then I'm off to bed.' She shot a dubious frown at the package under Weasel's arm. 'Working for DHL are you now?'

'Haha! Dan reckoned it was Amazon!'

'Well,' she said with a frown, 'whatever it is, I hope it's not hot.'

Weasel shook his head. 'Nah, the owners don't know it's gone.'

She shot her grinning husband a cautioning glance, then called the dogs and took them out and down the steps to the garden below.

Weasel sat at the kitchen dining table and began unwrapping the package while Hegarty poured his visitor a Coke, and the last drops of the red wine in the bottle for himself. As he sat down opposite him, he noticed Weasel's nicotine-stained teeth, his nails bitten to the quick as usual, and the biro markings all over the back of both his hands. Names, phone numbers, symbols, some faded, some fresh. It was a habit Weasel had back in his school days and had never lost. The man smelled rank, and faintly of tobacco. 'So?' he asked.

Weasel raised a hand to his pocket. 'Mind if I smoke?'

'Only outside.'

'No worries, I'm trying to quit – take a look at this!' Weasel extricated a small, ornately framed painting from the packaging. It depicted a thin man with a big nose, almost as furtive-looking as Weasel himself. Dressed in a crimson robe, with a small velvet hat, his face caught a thin shaft of light in an otherwise dark space. '*Il Ladro!*'

'The Thief?' Hegarty hazarded a translation from the Italian.

'Yeah, very good, so you've not lost your touch, eh?'

'You sure it's not a self-portrait?'

'Haha, you might be one hundred years old to get that plaque outside, but I ain't five hundred years old – even though I may look it! This picture, *Il Ladro*, is documented as being painted by the Italian artist Caravaggio in 1605 – five years before his death. It was in private ownership for several hundred years, changed hands several times, then a rich Viennese merchant banker acquired it in 1927. He and his entire family were exterminated in the gas chambers during the Second World War, yeah?'

'OK.'

'The picture has been recorded as missing, possibly destroyed, on the Art Loss Register. Only it hasn't been, it's been stacked against a wall, along with a bunch of Canalettos and a whole lot of other insanely valuable paintings, in the stately home of a totally gaga aristo, just outside Burwash in East Sussex – Burwash Park.'

'Stacked against a wall – a picture like that?'

'Yeah, well, that's the aristocracy for you. Anyhow, they have a big damp problem, so they shifted all the paintings stacked against the wall into storage. My mate Larry, who's a damp-proofing expert, was called in to help out. He spotted the picture and thought we might be clever with it.'

'Clever in what way?'

'You do a copy of it that's undetectable from the original. We return the copy and we keep the original. The last Caravaggio sold was valued at a hundred and seventy million dollars!'

'Are you living in fucking dreamland, Weasel? The moment you try to list this for sale, you're going to get squashed like a cockroach.'

Weasel gave an oily grin. 'Nope. I've been doing some business with a Chinese billionaire who's obsessed with Caravaggio. He'll pay massive money, which I can split with you, yeah?'

Hegarty frowned.

'You told me once, you can do a copy of pretty much any painting that's undetectable from the original, yeah? You've done that loads of times, haven't you?'

Hegarty studied the painting carefully.

'You're a genius, mate. Reckon you could do this?' Weasel asked.

The master forger drained his glass, and debated whether to open a second bottle, but thought better of it. Instead he focused on the painting. 'I'd have to invest quite a bit of cash,' he said.

'How much?'

'The big cost will be buying a canvas from that period – something from around 1605. I've got an antiques dealer mate in France who can source me paintings from pretty much any period – there are old religious paintings that he can pick up for me from sale rooms. Something of this period's likely to cost between five to ten grand.'

'No probs,' Weasel said, then surprised him by pulling a thick wad of £50 notes, bound by elastic bands, from each of his inside breast pockets and placing them on the table. 'There's twenty grand, should cover your basics, yeah?'

Hegarty picked up one wad, counting through it hastily. 'These real?'

'What do you take me for? I'd never stiff me old mate. These are from my client as a token of good faith.'

Hegarty wasn't sure Weasel knew the meaning of those words, but said nothing.

'What you reckon?'

'I'll need time.'

'How much?'

'You want a pukka job? No possibility of any comeback?' Weasel nodded. 'Totally.'

'Then I'll need around two months.'

Weasel winced. 'That long? You can't do it any quicker?'

'Not if you want two Caravaggio originals for the price of one.' He raised his eyebrows.

'Why so long?'

'Well I've got loads of work on. Then I've got to source that canvas. Once I get it over here, I need to remove the painting on it. Then I paint lead white over the canvas which has a dual effect – first it's what Caravaggio would have used, and secondly it has the big advantage of blocking any X-rays that might be done. Then I've got to obtain some period clothing fibres from the kind of apron Caravaggio might have worn back in 1605 – I've a couple of contacts, one in the Brighton Museum who might be able to help. Then I'll need time to do the painting – and weave a few of the period fibres into it. When I'm done with that, making sure I've got Caravaggio's brushstroke technique correct, I'll need to leave it by a wood-burning stove for at least a couple of weeks to get the craquelure. Then I'll take it to my mate Billy the Brush's house – he's another forger and he smokes sixty fags a day – and leave it there for a while to get a good patina. After that I've got to work on the back, faking the markings that are on the original. Then we need a suitable frame – that's the easy bit.' He shrugged.

'Yeah, should be OK, those building works are going to take a while. Yeah.' Then Weasel hesitated, looking anxious. 'I need a gasper.' He stood up, went out through the patio doors and sparked up a cigarette.

Hegarty remained at the table for some moments. He stuffed the thick bundles of banknotes into his pocket, then continued studying the painting. It was a challenge, but hey, he'd copied Caravaggio before. He stood up and went through into his studio, where he had a stacked shelf of books on the pigments the old masters used.

One of the easiest ways a forgery could be detected was through spectroscopic analysis of materials. Modern oil paints would easily be picked up this way, which was why, when he was making a forgery he intended to be undetectable, he mixed his paints using the original pigments the artist would have used in that period.

He smiled. This Caravaggio would be no problem. And potentially a very nice earner.

Just as he went back into the living room, Weasel came in from the balcony, reeking of fresh smoke. 'What do you think, mate? Do we have a deal?'

Hegarty nodded, feeling the satisfying bulge of the banknotes in his pocket. 'We do.'

17

Basic physics. But not something they'd ever taught him at school. Two people sleeping in a closed room create warm air. As it hits the cold glass, condensation forms. Archie Goff had learned over the years that once there was heavy condensation on the glass, it was a pretty reliable indicator the occupants of the bedroom were soundly asleep.

And now, as he watched through his night-vision binoculars, sure enough, his buddy Mr Condensation was there. By midnight, the bay window was getting a little wet. He got the jitters, as he always did at this moment. Pulling on his tight-fitting, unlined leather gloves, then gripping his torch in his teeth, he reached into the sack and pulled out the cardboard box. Opening the lid carefully, he lifted out the now dozy bird and, with a quick movement, snapped its neck.

Then, dead crow in one hand, sack in the other, he walked in his sneakers, softly, softly, towards the lower bay window, the drawing room, where on a previous survey he'd seen the tell-tale flashing red light of an alarm sensor high up on the wall.

Held his breath.

Listened.

Sweet silence.

He swung the weighted sack back, then hard forward against the large pane of glass, shattering it. Immediately, he hurled the crow through the gap, straight up towards the blinking red light.

An instant later he heard the wailing siren of the alarm.

Yes!

He retreated across the lawn, took up his position behind a Japanese cloud tree, and raised his binoculars. Some moments later he blinked as a light downstairs flared in the green glow of the night-vision lenses. He watched old man Fry in pyjamas appear close to the window, holding a shotgun, then look down at the crow. Archie could see him mouth the words, lip-reading him.

Fucking stupid bird.

Fry leaned down, picked it up by its feet and lobbed it back out through the broken window, onto the lawn.

Archie knew the Frys had the kind of complex burglar alarm system, favoured by wealthy homeowners, which would require resetting by an engineer. He was betting Martin Fry wouldn't bother with that now and would wait until morning.

Sure enough, the old man turned and called out to – presumably – his wife. 'A ruddy bird! Flown through the bloody window! I'll let the alarm company know.'

The old man faffed around for some minutes, disappearing briefly then returning and taping what looked like a square of cardboard over the busted frame. Then the light went off.

Archie tossed the brick into a dense bush and waited. Half an hour. With the empty sack tucked down his front, he made his way over to the bay window. He pushed away the temporary cardboard and reached down his gloved hand for the latch, hoping there wasn't a window lock, but not a problem if there was. He had a glass cutter on his tool belt.

The latch lifted and the window opened silently. He hoisted himself up on the frame, ignoring the pain from his arthritic joints, found a purchase for his hands inside, and swung himself in, dropping silently to his feet on the carpet.

First rule, before he began work on any job, was to find a backup exit. He shot his torch beam around the large room, divided by two marble columns, and could see it was a treasure trove. Silver ornaments on every surface, on tables, on shelves, and in a number of fine antique display cabinets. Then out into the hall, with more silver on every surface, which he eyed greedily.

Along, past a grand staircase and through a doorway into a warm kitchen with patio doors on the far side. As he had expected from the plans on his phone.

Perfect.

Softly, he made his way across the conservatory, past the large, cushioned wicker chairs and sofa, to the doors. His escape route!

He kneeled and slid the bottom bolt then reached up and released the top one. He tested the handle and pushed one door a fraction. It opened easily. He left it ajar. Now he had two escape routes, should he need them.

Grabbing all the kitchen towels he could see, he returned to the hall, and began scooping up every silver object, wrapping each in a towel, then dropping them into his sack. On some jobs he would have checked for a hallmark, to make sure he wasn't wasting time with silver-plate, but here he knew it was all going to be pukka.

Next, he turned right through a door which, from his memory of the plans, should be the dining room. It was. And more ornate silver, some of it quite large. Two pairs of small candelabras sat on the table. He laid them in his sack, too.

He checked the drawers of a large cherrywood sideboard, after lifting all the silver from the top of it, starting bottom upwards, so there was no need to close a drawer before opening the next. But there were just plates and linen in these.

His sack was already heavy. And he was heady with excitement. He'd no idea how much value he'd taken already, but if his source was right, he must be well into thousands of pounds, if not more. Perhaps way, way more. The Frys had single pieces worth upwards of £20,000 each and some way higher than that. Most of what he was taking would end up in the melt, which was the safest way to dispose of it. No trace. He was in a treasure trove, and he was on a roll!

Just the drawing room to go, maybe chance a look around for the safe, and then he'd be out of here.

As he went back into the hall a light, shining from halfway up the stairs, blinded him.

'Stop right there, you bloody bastard, or I'll shoot!' a coarse male voice that sounded like it meant business yelled at him. 'I will shoot! I assure you!'

Archie froze. Dazzled with light and panic.

His brain swirled with confusion. *How? How the hell?*

He thought of Isabella. His promise. Doing night work as a security guard.

He was shaking, totally panic-stricken. Could he run with his loot?

'One move and I'll shoot, you scumbag! Stay right where you are!'

Archie knew just one thing, clung to that one thing. The man would not shoot him in the back from fear of being prosecuted. Still gripping the sack, he spun and fled towards the kitchen.

'Stop! Stop right there! Stop! I will shoot!'

In the jigging light of his torch beam, Archie sprinted around the island unit, across the kitchen and through into the conservatory. He reached the patio door, pushed it further open and ran through out into the night air.

Free!

He knew that the far end of the Frys' land ended at the woods. He began to sprint towards them.

Then the ground disappeared under his feet.

For a fleeting instant there was just nothing. He was falling.

Then he was underwater, choking on warm, chlorinated water.

Ridiculously warm, like being in a bath, his brain messaged him, for just a fraction of a second, before he got another message.

This time it was delivered by a pyjama-clad old man, standing at the edge of the swimming pool, as Archie broke the surface, gasping for air and coughing up water. Martin Fry was shining a flashlight and pointing a double-barrelled shotgun down at him.

'Don't even think about trying to get out,' the old man said. Then he kicked Archie hard in the face as he made a last, desperate try.

18

Chastened by Cleo's rebuke last week, but taking on board what she had said, Roy Grace had managed to catch Glenn for an early coffee the day after their drink and persuade him to ditch the idea of sending Siobhan flowers.

To his relief, Glenn had come to much the same conclusion, telling him that although they'd spent the night at their separate flats in the city, he'd spoken to Siobhan at length and apologized, and told her she should go ahead with her piece for the *Argus*, although he still had some private doubts. Nearly a week later, Roy was pleased to see his friend seemed a little less despondent today, but he still had a mountain to climb on the bigger family issue that was creating such a divide at the moment.

At 9 a.m., seated at the table in the conference room of the Major Crime suite, he made a note of the date and time in his investigator's notebook, then, addressing his assembled team, he said, 'OK, good morning, everyone, this is the second review meeting of Operation Canvas, and I'm pleased to say we have made some significant progress during this past week. Before we get onto that, I don't know if any of you saw on the serials that Archie Goff was nicked last night after breaking into a country mansion near Bolney?'

'That old dinosaur!' Potting exclaimed. 'He's still around? He's knocking on a bit, isn't he?'

'Like you, Norman?' Velvet Wilde said, making herself laugh out loud.

'Thanks, Velvet, very witty,' Potting said.

'Just saying.'

'Children!' Roy Grace addressed them. 'Let's not get personal, OK?'

'Sorry, boss,' the DC said.

'It's about time they binned Archie and threw away the key,' Polly Sweeney said, then added with mock sympathy, 'Bless his little cotton socks!'

Archie Goff had been on the police radar as a serial country house burglar for as long as Roy Grace had been in the police. He remembered, early on as a young PC on Response, being one of several officers who had attended after he'd triggered an alarm in a mansion in Dyke Road Avenue. 'I've checked the records and Archie was last released from prison on 2 October 2015, just two weeks before Charlie Porteous was robbed and murdered.'

Sweeney raised her hand and Grace nodded at her. 'Yes, Polly?'

'From memory, I don't think Archie Goff's ever been known to use violence in his burglaries, boss,' she said.

'Correct, Polly. I've checked his recent records and he usually goes after jewellery, silver and small high-value antiques. He's been known to steal art, small-sized pictures, but I've been reading through his case files and interviews earlier this morning and although he's never been a grass, he has admitted in the past to stealing items to order. While he's in police custody we should talk to him. I'd like you and Jack to interview him, scare him a little about being implicated in murder, and see if he says anything useful.'

'Yes, boss,' she said.

Alexander turned to Potting. 'Why *dinosaur*, Norman?'

'Because that's what crims like him are,' Potting replied. 'Career burglars are a dying breed. Today's younger generation have much easier pickings with drug dealing or internet scamming, but they're scum compared to the likes of him. Polly's right about him never using violence. I nicked him once and he was scrupulously polite. He actually said, "It's a fair cop, guv".' Potting looked around. 'When did anyone in this room last hear a villain say that outside of a re-run of *Dixon of Dock Green*?'

Smiling, Grace leaned over his shoulder and pointed at a large photograph that had been added to a whiteboard behind him. It was an elaborate, beautiful painting depicting two lovers in a forest, sun-dappled trees, a waterfall and hundreds of daffodils. It was in an ornate frame and looked as if it might be very old. 'We believe this is the picture Charlie Porteous had with him at the time of his murder.' He turned to Stanstead. 'Over to you, Luke.'

'I've been in contact with an organization, the Art Loss Register, which as its name indicates is a pretty definitive list of all known stolen or lost works of art. I'm informed it's the most respected database in the art world by all dealers who are offered a painting – or any other object of art – for sale – kind of like their first port of call. Its principal, Julian Radcliffe – incidentally, a very charming and helpful man – was contacted on Thursday, 1 October 2015, by Charlie Porteous, who he said was a regular client that he had a lot of respect for. Porteous asked him to check on a number of paintings he had been offered, which was a regular occurrence. Porteous emailed photographs of them, one of which he had identified as a possible work of the eighteenth-century French artist Jean-Honoré Fragonard.'

Stanstead turned to the photograph of the painting on the whiteboard. 'This picture.'

'The bloody paparazzi got me having a quiet picnic with my lover!' Potting said.

Everyone grinned, except Velvet Wilde. 'Which one are you, Norman?' she asked. 'The one having a pee behind the tree in the distance?'

That brought a laugh from the whole team, including Grace.

Then, serious once more, he said, 'Excellent work, Luke. What did Radcliffe report back to Porteous?'

'That painting wasn't on his radar, sir. I spoke to him yesterday and he told me that, while there is documented evidence that Fragonard created a series of four paintings of the four seasons in the 1770s, acquired by an aristocratic French patron a few years before the French Revolution, there has been no sighting of them ever since. He admits it is possible that they might have survived and still exist, but he couldn't possibly tell from this photograph whether this was a genuine painting by Fragonard or not.'

Grace nodded. 'So he concedes it's not out of the question this is a genuine Fragonard work and was in Charlie Porteous's possession at the time of his murder?'

'He does, sir, with the caveats I've just given.'

'Good work, Luke.' Turning to Potting, Grace said, 'OK, Norman, you have something to report – you seem to be going gangbusters!'

Holding his clumsy frame bolt upright and puffing out his chest, the DS looked rather pleased with himself. 'Well, chief,' he nodded at Stanstead, 'thanks to Luke's intel work, I met with the Mr and Mrs Lee who were house-sitting for a Mr and Mrs Malby, owners of a house a short distance from the Porteouses' at the time of his murder. Mr Lee is a professional dogwalker, and he and his wife, Elizabeth, also house-sit for a number of clients. And as Luke had correctly told us last week, Mr Lee is a bit of an insomniac. He told me he went out for a walk along Tongdean Avenue at 12.52 a.m. on the morning of Friday, 16 October 2015. He was able to be precise about the time due to his Garmin fitness watch which tracked all his movements.'

Potting coughed, clearing a frog in his throat, took a sip of water then went on. 'He saw a car accelerating fiercely away from the direction of the Porteous house – although he did not know exactly where it had come from. But he was surprised to see a vehicle at that hour being driven at speed. It's an expensive and exclusive neighbourhood, although Mr Lee told me it is favoured in the daytime by driving instructors as a good place for their customers to practise U-turns. He's a former soldier who worked for a time as a car salesman after his discharge from the army, so is very aware of car makes and models. He identified this vehicle as a recent model – at the time – an Audi A6, dark-coloured, and rather diligently made a note of as much of its registration plate as he could catch, just in case, he said. We've subsequently identified the vehicle through a process of elimination and run a PNC check and the plate turns out to be false – but cleverly false.'

'In what way *cleverly* false, Norman?' Grace asked.

Potting puffed his chest out even more proudly. 'A dark green A6 came up, registered to a Mr Brian Harris, with an address in Saltdean. I went to the address, a bungalow, and spoke to Mr Harris. He is an affable disabled widower of eighty-five. On the evening of Thursday, 15 October 2015, he was hosting a bridge evening at his home. He assured me he was not out burning rubber in Tongdean Avenue in the small hours of the Friday morning.' The DS gave a wry smile. 'I would have to say he doesn't seem the type, which makes me think whoever was driving that Audi was on cloned plates.'

'Norman,' Glenn Branson asked, 'did this Joe Lee see anything at the entrance to the Porteouses' house? Did he see Porteous's Bentley?'

Potting shook his head. 'He says he didn't – but you need to bear in mind that the home of the couple where he was house-sitting was a good quarter of a mile along the road, and Lee was walking in the opposite direction.'

'Did he hear anything, Norman?' Polly Sweeney asked.

'No, he said he was plugged in listening to a podcast. He just saw the car going past, in a hurry.'

'That timing fits with the CCTV from Brighton station,' Grace said. 'At that hour of night it would have taken Porteous about ten minutes to reach his home from the station. If it was just an opportunist street robbery, the assailant might have simply been prowling the neighbourhood and got lucky.' He paused. 'But if that car was the one the offender – or offenders – used then it smacks to me more of someone lying in wait for him. If I was wanting to park up and look inconspicuous in that smart street, I'd choose a car that blended in – smart enough to fit with the other cars that might be seen around that neighbourhood, but not too flash that it stood out. An Audi A6 is a perfect fit. How big a task would it be to identify all Audi A6s of that period in the Brighton and Hove area?'

Luke Stanstead raised his hand. 'Boss, I've checked and there are 339 registered to Brighton and Hove residents, and a further 1,700 across Sussex. In addition, it's a popular executive-level vehicle with car rental companies throughout the UK.'

Grace did some quick mental arithmetic. Over two thousand. It would take massive resources to check on that number of cars. On a live murder investigation he could justify it to his superiors, but not on a speculative cold case. 'Did you check any reports of stolen ones around that time, Luke?'

'I did, yes. And here's where it gets very interesting, boss.'

Grace's phone rang. Answering, he heard the voice of Lesley Manning, the Chief Constable. 'Ma'am,' he said and stood up. 'If you can just give me one moment, ma'am.'

He stepped out of the room and closed the door behind him. 'Sorry, I was in a meeting, ma'am.'

'I didn't mean to interrupt you, Roy.'

'It's fine, not a problem.'

'I just wanted to ask you a rather delicate question. As you know, I always regard all my officers as family. How would you and Cleo feel if I said I would like to attend your son's funeral?'

He was momentarily lost for words, and, suddenly choked up, had to take a couple of deep breaths before he could reply. 'My wife and I would be honoured, ma'am.'

'I'd like to be there, both in a personal capacity, but also on behalf of all officers and police staff of Sussex Police to pay our respects and to support you both – I'm sure it will be a difficult day for you, Roy.'

He felt tears welling and closed his eyelids against them. It took all his effort to get the words out. 'Thank you, ma'am.'

19

A subdued Roy Grace re-entered the room and took his place at the head of the oval table. He addressed Stanstead. 'Apologies, Luke, you were saying about the Audi?'

'Yes, boss, there was an A6 matching this vehicle reported stolen from near Haywards Heath, about twenty miles away, two days before the murder – and recovered the day after – and might be connected.'

Grace frowned. 'Did it have the false plates on?'

'No, it had the correct ones.'

'Was it damaged?'

'Quite severely, sir. They say it appeared to have failed to negotiate a sharp bend, mounted the pavement and hit the stone wall of a local recreation ground with the front near-side wing, deploying the airbags. Whoever was driving it seems to have reversed it back onto the road but been unable to drive it further.'

Grace made a note, then looked up. 'If these were professionals, which I'm inclined to think at this moment they were, they might have abandoned the car and removed the false plates. Do you have the name and address of the owner?'

'I do, sir. Her name is Monica Thaesler. I've made contact with her. She had the Audi repaired, then sold it two years ago – chopped in for a newer model with the dealer Caffyns. The current owner is a lady called Jo Dillan, in Haywards Heath.'

'Nice work, Norman and Luke,' Grace complimented them.

He was thinking of the age-old CSI boast that if anyone had ever been in a room or a vehicle, no matter how long ago, if you gave them enough time they would be able to find out who. All it would take would be just one single clothing fibre or hair follicle or blood spot or fingerprint, or maybe even a shoe print. From his own past experience, he'd seen an offender jailed from DNA obtained from a vehicle found twenty years after a rape and murder. And he knew from a recent discussion on another case with officer Andy Slark at the Sussex Police Collision Investigation Unit that a great amount of information could be obtained from interrogating the onboard computers of modern cars.

He turned to Norman Potting. 'This could be our vehicle, Norman. Modern cars have over a hundred computer and data recording systems – interrogation of these can reveal a range of information about their journeys and drivers – and passengers. Ask this lady, Jo Dillan, if she would let us have her car for a few days and we'll pay for a loan car. If she's not cooperative, you'll need to persuade her. It might help us eliminate Archie Goff – or not. We can get Forensics all over it, and at the same time see what the Collision Investigation team can come up with. I know they sometimes work with an outfit in the US, called Berla, which specializes in forensically examining onboard infotainment systems, and I understand there's a UK company doing something similar.'

'Will do, boss,' Potting replied.

'The UK company is called Harper Shaw,' Luke Stanstead said.

Grace thanked him and turned to Wilde. 'How've you been getting on, Velvet?'

'The Porteous Fine Arts gallery was sold after Charlie's death, boss, to pay his debt. After what happened, his son went down a different career path and didn't want to be in the art world any longer,' she replied. 'But the new owner, Harvey Myman, an American art dealer, kept on most of the original staff, and they are still there. They were helpful but didn't add much to what we already know. All I was able to confirm with Carrie Hepworth was that Mr Porteous had seemed very excited about a purchase he had just made, and that if he could prove its provenance, it would be the solution to his cash-flow problems. But he had kept tight-lipped about what the painting was. All his other staff members I spoke to confirmed the same thing. I'm still waiting to re-interview Carrie Hepworth.'

'So, we are no further forward on that,' Grace said.

Wilde raised a finger in the air. 'Well, we might be, boss. Yesterday, I drove out to Twineham, to talk to Mr George Astone. He is the wealthy collector who was interested to see this mysterious painting. As we know, the deceased had made an appointment to show it to Astone at 11 a.m. on the morning of Friday, 16 October. So it does seem very probable that Charlie Porteous had the painting with him at the time of his murder.'

Grace nodded. 'What did Astone have to say?'

'Wow, sir, you should have seen his house! It's more like a palace!' she said, sounding awed. 'It is vast, in huge grounds.'

'Was he ever burgled by Archie Goff?' Norman Potting interrupted.

'Not that I know, Norman,' she said dismissively. 'George Astone is pretty elderly and wheelchair-bound, very lucid and charming, and had very clear recall. He told me he'd bought a great number of paintings from Porteous over the years – and showed me some of his collection. I'm no expert, but as he took me around it felt like I was in an art gallery. He said that Charlie Porteous had the best nose for paintings of any expert he'd ever met.'

She had everyone's attention.

'A couple of days prior to his death, Mr Porteous had apparently phoned Astone, telling him he was certain what he had was a genuine Jean-Honoré Fragonard. That it appeared to be, in his opinion, one of four long-lost paintings Fragonard had made depicting the four seasons. He said these had apparently been documented a long time back in the eighteenth century, hanging in a French aristocrat's chateau, but had disappeared around the time of the French Revolution, when this particular aristocrat and his family had gone to the guillotine.'

She glanced at her notes. 'This fits with what we know. I've spoken to an art historian called Sir Toby Maguire, who specializes in this period, who said there is documented evidence these paintings had existed, but may well have been destroyed around that time, as they've never been seen since. But Mr Porteous believed this particular one, *Spring*, had survived. He was offering it for sale to Mr Astone for five million pounds, a bargain price considering, if it was genuine, that one recent auction of a Fragonard painting had sold for seventeen million and another, even more recent auction of a less important work went for over six million.'

'Can we eliminate Astone as a suspect?' Grace asked.

'I spoke to our Financial Investigations team. Emily Denyer checked and came back to me. George Astone has a net worth of over three hundred and fifty million pounds and no criminal record or known criminal associations. And he's been confined to a wheelchair following a stroke in 2012.'

Norman Potting cleared his throat. Everyone turned to look at him.

'You have something you want to say, Norman?' Grace asked.

'Ted Bundy, chief. Just saying.'

Grace frowned. 'Saying what, exactly?'

'That serial killer who raped and murdered scores of women used a false plaster cast on his arm. He'd get some of his victims to help him lift something into his van, then whack them over the head.'

'And your point is?' he asked curtly.

Potting shrugged. 'ABC, boss, it's what you've always drummed into us, isn't it? *Assume nothing, Believe no one, Check everything.*'

Velvet went on. 'If George Astone was faking being disabled, he deserves a sodding Oscar. One half of his face is lopsided and his speech is slurred. He has no movement at all in his left arm and can only move two fingers on his right hand, enough to press the buttons on his motorized wheelchair. Luke, as a wheelchair user, what do you think – does it sound like he's faking his condition?'

'From what I've heard, he needs the wheelchair,' Luke said.

'OK?' She glared at Potting.

'I surrender, Velvet,' the DS said. 'Humble apologies.'

She locked eyes with him for some moments, still glaring, then addressed Roy Grace. 'Mr Astone also said something that might be of significant interest, sir. He told me he'd heard rumours, through the grapevine, that there was another collector in Sussex who had two of the other three paintings – the other three missing Fragonard Four Seasons.'

'What was he able to tell you about this collector, Velvet?' Grace pressed.

She shook her head. 'He said it was only a rumour, and that was back then, four years ago.'

'Rumours always come from somewhere,' Grace said. 'Did he tell you the source?'

'No, sir. I did press him on that but he was very dismissive about it.'

'Do you think he was hiding something?' Glenn Branson asked.

'I don't think so, sir, no. He seemed genuinely upset about the murder – he'd regarded Charlie Porteous as a friend. He said he'd heard that rumour a couple of years earlier but couldn't remember from whom or where.'

'Couldn't remember or didn't want to say?' Grace pressed.

'In my opinion, he genuinely could not remember, sir. Possibly due to his stroke.'

Grace made a note then looked up thoughtfully, before continuing. 'Polly, I'm giving you the action of becoming an instant authority in French old masters. Find out all the dealers and collectors in Sussex, Surrey, Kent and Hampshire who might have an interest in these paintings – and among the collectors, all those with pockets deep enough to afford to buy a Fragonard.'

He turned to DS Alexander. 'Jack, although this smacks of being a specifically targeted robbery, the fact that at the same time Charlie Porteous's valuable Rolex, wallet and wedding band were taken indicates it could simply have been a random street robbery by a prowler in that exclusive neighbourhood. If so, that offender would either have offloaded what he'd stolen to a fence, or would have tried to sell the items himself. There are still many jewellers in the Brighton and Hove environs today who deal in second-hand watches and rings. I think it's worth talking to them again to see if you can jog any memories. The wedding ring had distinct markings on the reverse, the initials of Porteous and his wife and the date of their wedding.'

'Yes, sir.'

'As for the painting,' Grace continued. 'There are a number of local auction galleries in the area, such as Gorringe's in Lewes and Bellmans in Billingshurst. Talk to them to see if you can jog any memories of someone bringing a painting of this period into them around this time.'

He turned to Stanstead. 'Luke, work with Polly, it would be useful if you could compile a list of all London art dealers capable of handling a painting of this value.'

'Yes, sir.'

Next, Grace turned to Potting. 'Norman, check back with the ANPR camera records to see when and where the index of the Audi A6 was picked up between Wednesday, 14 October 2015, and Friday the 16th.'

'On it, chief.'

Grace checked his watch. He had a meeting with Cassian Pewe's temporary replacement, Acting ACC Hannah Robinson, in just under ten minutes and it would not make a good first impression to be late. 'Any questions, anyone?'

Branson raised his hand. 'Boss, if Charlie Porteous had one of the Fragonard Four Seasons paintings, and George Astone's rumour mill is correct and another local collector has another two, presumably that means the fourth might be around, somewhere, doesn't it?'

Grace nodded. 'It does, yes. It's a possibility. Any thoughts where to start?'

'I do, boss, yes,' Branson replied. 'I think you're on the money to get that Audi examined. What did they use to say in the old cop movies? *Follow that car!*'

Grace smiled, glad his friend had some of his humour back. 'Good,' he replied. 'Let's do it. Our next meeting will be Wednesday at 9 a.m. So, until then, follow that car!'

20

During Cassian Pewe's tenure as Assistant Chief Constable, standing outside his door had always sent Roy Grace time-travelling back to his school days where, for one misdemeanour or another – mostly being argumentative with those teachers who made their subjects crashingly dull – he was a frequent flier to the headmaster's office.

A somewhat fierce man, with a short temper and the arrogance of a hardened old lag, Reginald Bute showed very early on that he did not see eye to eye with young Roy Grace, and made that very clear in his school reports. *He has a lot to learn if he wishes to follow in his father's footsteps in the police force. At present he is on course for a career in manual labour or menial jobs,* he had written in one.

Reginald Bute's door had looked very similar to the door to the ACC's office, and with each ACC who had been his boss, he felt the same nervousness waiting for the call to enter. But not today. And this time there was no bellow from the room. The door was opened calmly by the new ACC, smiling warmly at him.

Hannah Robinson was a little shorter than Grace, neat and elegant in her uniform white shirt, epaulettes and black-and-white-chequered cravat. Her brown hair was clipped up into a small bun that looked both retro and modern at the same time. 'Roy,' she greeted him, 'how very good to see you, come in. Can I offer you tea or coffee?'

'I'm fine, thank you, ma'am.' He noticed just how very different this office felt to when Pewe was here, as if a dark cloud had dissolved and it was now flooded with light and even warmth. There were photos of her husband and two children on her desk, and her running shoes and kit were stacked on a chair in the corner.

Robinson ushered him to an L-shaped sofa and sat facing him. 'So, I thought it would be good to have a chat,' she said, 'and an update on Operation Canvas.'

'Indeed – first, ma'am, I'd like to congratulate you on your promotion. I'm very much looking forward to working with you. I remember when you were on my team, about four years ago, right, and without wanting to sound a creep, I always knew you were destined for the top.'

She grinned. 'That's very kind of you to say so.'

'I mean it.'

'Good, and you're not doing too badly yourself! Let's hope we can still work together well as teammates. I'm aware that you've had something of an unhappy history with the former ACC.'

'You could say that, ma'am.'

Again she smiled. 'I'm looking forward to a much healthier working relationship.'

'So am I – without saying too much about your predecessor, I don't think he always understood what was needed during a major operation.'

'Well, perhaps sometime you can elaborate on some of that history and we'll see what we can change going forward. Perhaps we can have that discussion before I meet with your Crime and Operations counterparts, as I really do want us as a team to work closely together. Joined-up, I think is the expression.'

Privately, Grace winced, hoping she wasn't going to start using any of the motivational gobbledegook that Pewe used to spout all the time. But he didn't let it show on his face. 'Yes,' he said.

'Absolutely.' Then he nodded towards her kit on the chair. 'I see you are still running, ma'am.'

'When it's just us, Roy, call me Hannah. How about we go out for a run one lunchtime and I'll see if you can keep up with me!'

'Ha!' he said. 'Fighting talk – is that a challenge?'

'Consider it a gauntlet thrown down!'

21

Buoyed by his meeting with the Acting ACC yesterday, Roy Grace sat in his office shortly after 8 a.m., buried in paperwork from the twenty-seven crates of files from Nick Sloan's original investigation on Operation Canvas, preparing for next week's briefing. It was a tedious but vital task. As he sipped his increasingly tepid coffee, he suddenly realized he'd not spoken to Norman Potting about his cancer scare for some time. He had been so consumed by his own grief he'd not thought about Norman. He picked up his phone and called the DS, inviting him in for a chat, and quite welcoming the distraction.

Potting responded eagerly, although his voice sounded a little strange, a bit croaky, and there was a knock on his door less than a couple of minutes later.

'Yes, chief?' he said as he entered, his voice definitely sounding a little hoarse, as if he'd been shouting. He stood massaging his neck between his finger and thumb, and Grace could see the worry in the detective's eyes.

Grace signalled for him to sit, and Potting perched on one of the two chairs in front of his desk. He was looking, as he had been for several days now, paler and less confident than normal. Grace knew the detective was living on his own and probably didn't have many people – if anyone – to share his worries with. But he saw something in the way the DS was looking at him that reminded him of the fear in his father's eyes, despite the brave face he'd tried to put on after his diagnosis of cancer.

'Sorry about my voice, chief.' He coughed as if trying to clear his throat. 'Woke up with it like this.' He grinned nervously. 'Just a bit of a frog in my throat. What can I do? Better than a toad in my hole some might say!'

'I just thought it would be good to have a quick catch-up on your health, Norman. Do you have any news?'

'Thanks for asking, chief. That's really kind. I don't want to trouble you with my problems at this really tough time for you. But I am worried – shit scared, to be honest with you.'

'I want to help. Where are you at with everything?'

'Well, as I think I told you, my GP sent me to an ENT consultant – she was a pretty cold fish. When I told her I smoked a pipe she said it was quite possibly laryngeal or oesophageal cancer, straight out, just like that. But she also said it might just be laryngitis.' He lowered his head, to avoid meeting Grace's eyes. 'I'm worried sick.'

Grace nodded sympathetically. 'But it could be one of a number of other things, couldn't it, Norman? Cancer is only one possible diagnosis. Have you tried Fisherman's Friends?'

Potting smiled bleakly, then shrugged. 'Yeah, I've tried them, they don't work. Used to, but not any more. It may seem strange to say this, but ever since Bella died, I've been feeling under a cloud, chief. As if it was my fault she died, and that if I'd been there, it wouldn't have happened.'

Grace looked at him face to face, with a sympathetic frown. 'Norman, Bella was on her way to work when she heroically went into a burning building to try to save lives. And in a couple of months we'll be recognizing that gallantry when we go to the Palace to receive her medal. How can you possibly blame yourself for not being there when she died?'

93

Potting shrugged and said lamely, 'I know, chief. It's daft, but I do.'

'So now you think you're being punished by being given a cancer diagnosis? Really? Do you have some kind of death wish to join Bella, where you'll both be happy together in an eternal afterlife?'

Potting shook his head. 'I'm not religious, chief. She's gone – the only woman I truly loved – and I know I have to move on. I don't buy all that crap that we'll be together in some kind of eternity.'

'So how can you believe you're being given terminal cancer as some kind of retribution, Norman?'

Potting shrugged. 'I know, it's stupid. But that's what I keep thinking.'

'Want to know what I think?'

'Please.'

'It's something my mother used to say: *Don't paint the Devil on the wall.*'

Potting grinned. 'I like that,' he said. 'I like that a lot. Maybe it is just laryngitis – I have had that before, although this somehow feels different. She sent me to the laryngologist, who asked me all sorts of things. How long has it been going on? Have I noticed blood in my phlegm? Does it feel like something is stuck? Do I smoke? Do I drink?'

'Well, she's got you there!' Grace said humorously.

'Fair enough, right. Then she massaged my neck to check my glands, which was all fine, but then she shoved a snake-like object down my nose and said she could see a polyp. They need to remove it.'

'So?'

'So, it could be anything,' Norman said solemnly.

'Well, whatever it is we'll tackle it; you are not alone.'

Potting coughed again, then squeezed his throat between his

finger and thumb. 'Bloody frog. They are down all our throats since Brexit, aren't they?' He gave him a wry smile.

Roy Grace looked him straight in the eye for some moments, then shook his head and said, trying not to sound too stern, 'Norman, we've known each other a number of years, right?'

Potting nodded. 'We have indeed, chief.'

'You're a highly valued detective and I'm very fond of you, and I do enjoy your humour, but we're in a very different world to when we first worked together, and sometimes you run your humour pretty close to the line. I'd hate to see your brilliant career ended because of something you said without thinking. I'm a good one to talk – I still occasionally say the wrong thing, but we've all got to be aware and think about other people's sensitivities. So here's my suggestion – before you open your mouth to say something witty, count to three, OK?'

'Good advice, chief. I'm suitably chastened.'

'I'm not criticizing you, Norman. I'm giving you a survival lesson.'

Potting nodded, looking downcast. 'I appreciate it, chief. I was always rubbish at maths, but I can just about manage to count to three.'

'I was pretty crap at maths, too.'

Potting shook his head. 'You and I – we'd never have made it into the force today, would we?'

Grace smiled.

22

Bail security had been set at £50,000, which Archie Goff did not have. So he was resigned to staying in prison until his trial. There were two big changes since he had last been inside, neither of which he was happy about. The first was the non-smoking rule; the other was that meals were no longer served in the canteen but had to be eaten in the cells. He'd been told it was to stop the violence that frequently erupted in the canteen. All very well, but he missed sitting at a table with his mates. His double-bunk cell hardly cut the mustard for a great dining experience.

After his arrest, he found himself back again in his second home, the remand wing of Lewes Prison. Although, with the amount of his life he'd spent in here, it was pretty much his primary home, with his time away from it more of a holiday.

To his amazement, Isabella had accepted his story that he'd been fitted up by the police, and came to visit him regularly. He still hadn't yet figured out how he was going to explain things to her when it came to his trial, but hey, that was some months away yet. Bless her, she'd done her best to raise the money for his bail, but all she had been able to come up with was just under ten thousand quid.

His brief had told him that although he'd been nicked red-handed in Hope Manor, he hadn't actually taken anything from the premises, since he'd only got as far as the swimming pool. Therefore he would only be charged with burglary with intent to steal. If he was lucky, he'd get away with a couple of years, unless he came up in front of a particularly mean judge. The potential downside was that, so far throughout his life, he'd not yet come up in front of a judge who wasn't mean – in his humble opinion.

At 5 p.m. on this Friday afternoon he left his cell and walked along the corridor to the meal trolley, collected his pre-ordered dinner of tuna bake and spotted dick with custard, and carried the cartons back to his cell. The telly was on, cricket, which had never interested him – he had no idea how the scoring worked – but his cellmate, three decades his junior, who reminded him uncannily of a former home secretary, Sajid Javid, was addicted to the game. Archie enjoyed ribbing him by calling him *Home Secretary*.

And right now, Mr Home Secretary was perched on the bottom bunk, forking vegetarian pasta into his mouth, watching a bowler hurl the ball at a helmeted batsman, who blocked it. Archie hadn't yet asked him what he was in for, knowing it could be a sensitive subject for many prisoners.

He sat down on the toilet, a few feet from Sajid – the only other place to sit in the tiny cell. Placing his dessert on the floor, he removed the foil from his warm tuna bake, on his lap. His body hunched over his food, he dug his plastic fork in, blew on it to make sure it didn't scald his tongue, then ate a mouthful. It was OK, it tasted like it might, once upon a time in its distant past, actually have been from a fish swimming free in the sea – albeit one filled with plastic waste – and the pasta might have come from something that had been grown in a field, rather than cultured in a lab.

Averting his eyes from the screen during an ad break, Sajid asked, 'How you doing, man?'

'Living the dream,' Archie replied.

Sajid smiled.

'Eating my meal on a toilet – what's not to like, eh, Home Secretary?'

Sajid smiled again. 'This is my first time – you told me last night you're not new to all this, right?'

'You could say that.'

'House burglaries? That's your thing?'

Archie nodded and ate some more. 'And yours is?'

'I was fitted up by the police. Isn't that what everyone here says?' He shrugged. 'You make good money burgling?'

'Yeah. Good enough, yeah.'

'How much is *good enough*?'

'Five to ten grand.'

'A day – or a week?'

'Yeah, a week, maybe, if I get lucky.'

'If I was to do what they think I did, know how much I could make in a day? Twenty grand, sometimes a lot more. Hypothetically, of course. Ever thought about doing something different? The world's moved on, mate. The internet and drugs, that's where the real money is today. Scams and dealing. Burgling's shit, isn't it? You're out in horrible weather, got to deal with dogs, lights, alarms and always the risk of getting caught. Seems to me that burglars are extinct.'

Archie bristled. 'You're calling me out of touch?' Sajid was a muscular hunk who worked out in the gym every day. It wouldn't be a smart idea to pick a fight with him, but his cocky arrogance was sure pissing him off.

'Just saying.'

'Saying I'm old?'

'Know what they say about new technology, Archie?'

Archie shook his head.

'Technology's like a steamroller. If you're not riding in the cab you're part of the road.' Sajid ate another mouthful of his food.

Archie stared at him. Maybe he was right, and he was just part of the road. Not even a motorway, just some sodding, crappy old B-road.

'How many times have you been inside, Archie?' he asked.

'A few,' he replied defensively.

'Like three times? Five? Ten?'

Archie realized he'd actually lost count. 'Maybe ten, maybe more,' he said, and ate some more of his own food in silence, as the cricket came back on, distracting his cellmate.

Sajid didn't speak again until the next commercial break, when Archie was scraping the last of the custard from the edges of the foil dish. 'You're how old?'

'Sixty-four,' Goff replied.

'You've been inside ten times, or even more, right?'

'Uh huh.' He licked the last sweet drops from his plastic spoon.

'You've got six kids with three different wives, you told me last night, right? You don't see any of your exes and you've only got one kid who speaks to you, your daughter who's studying to be a vet?'

'So?'

'Do you own a property?'

'Not yet.'

'Not yet? What does that mean?'

Archie shrugged. 'I'm waiting for the big one.'

'The *big one*? A burglary that's going to earn you enough to buy a property for cash, because you wouldn't get a mortgage in a million years.'

'What of it?'

'You don't strike me as being an idiot, mate. But you're gonna need two hundred K minimum to buy anything other than a shithole. What kind of burglary's going to net you that kind of dough?'

Archie stared into the empty aluminium carton. It was a good question, he knew.

With a kinder tone now, Sajid said, 'It's not too late. You're not an old man – yet. Why've you stayed with burglary, when you know you'll keep getting caught? Haven't you ever thought about nothing else? You're not a bad-looking bloke, you're in shape, there's plenty of wealthy widows out there who could be rich pickings for you.'

Archie shook his head. 'If you're so smart, how come you're in prison?'

He smiled. 'My first time and my last. Like I said, I was fitted up.'

'I thought the same, forty-five years ago, Home Secretary.'

'And you never once reconsidered what you were doing?'

Archie put his tray on the floor then sat bolt upright and a smile set his face alight. 'Nah,' he said. 'Not once. It's the adrenaline, you see, the rush, the buzz. When it goes right, there's no feeling like it.'

'And when it goes wrong, you're banged up in here with a bunch of mostly losers. How does that make you feel?'

Archie shrugged. 'You know what, Home Secretary, I actually like it here. I've got television, the electricity's paid for, the grub's decent, and I've got my mates. And I don't have to do my head in filling in tax forms. What's not to like?'

He wasn't about to share how much he missed Isabella.

23

Even this early, the cool September air was full of promise. A cloudless sky, the faintest hint of a sea breeze, a day to make anyone feel optimistic. And Harry Kipling was feeling very optimistic indeed, less so Freya.

At 8.30 a.m. they stood outside the grounds of the historic Lancing College, a little bleary-eyed from their early start, sipping their thermos flasks of scalding coffee, and munching on the egg and tomato sandwiches that they had made for their breakfast. Warned that it could be a long wait, they'd also brought along a packed lunch and plenty of water in a cooler bag.

Harry was glad they'd made the decision to come early, because there was already a sizeable queue gathered here, many sporting summery hats and caps of every shape, size and colour. There was a buzz of excitement, of anticipation, and many of the crowd of people were in a chatty mood. Harry and Freya learned that some had just come along in the hope of being caught on camera, so they could tell all their friends. Others had brought a vast assortment of stuff, some clearly junk, some family heirlooms, some items, like theirs, which they had picked up at a car boot sale and were hoping they would turn out to be worth a fortune.

All around them, amid a sea of the branded red umbrellas and small white marquees, people clutched unwieldy packages, some of them parcelled in newspaper, or bubble wrap, or in supermarket carrier bags, as well as many unwrapped objects. A woman stood near them holding a set of fire dogs; another a wooden side-table; another a small rocking horse, and another a cake stand. There were objects of every different size and shape. It felt like they were in a rather posh, modernist take on a jumble sale, Harry thought. Except no one was buying anything. They were all here to get an expert's appraisal on the objects they had. And all hoping for magic words from the expert. That the ugly vase they'd put flowers in, or the dreary bowl they fed their dog from, would turn out to be something from an ancient Chinese dynasty.

One excited couple they'd chatted with told them they had a Chinese marble-top table which had been collected from their home yesterday, by the show, because it had sounded of interest. They were hoping to be told it would be worth enough at auction to pay for the new kitchen they were planning.

Freya eyed the large Lidl carrier bag containing the bubble-wrapped painting on the ground beside them, propped against Harry's right leg as he ate. Tired, because she didn't do early mornings well, and especially not on weekends, she said, 'There's no wind, this would have been a great day to be on the beach with our paddleboards.'

'Well, if we're lucky and get seen early, we could get back in time to have an afternoon on the beach – and luxuriate in the knowledge that we're now millionaires!'

She put an arm around him, leaned up and kissed him on the cheek. 'My big dreamer! Let's try to manage our expectations, eh? I don't want you setting yourself up for a big disappointment.'

'I know. I'm not expecting it to be anything other than a copy and pretty much worthless.'

She stepped back and looked at him with the impish expression she had when she was teasing him and which he always loved. 'Fibber! I don't think you are expecting that at all.'

'Well, maybe I'm a little optimistic – but hey, I'm a realist.'

'Promise me one thing?' she asked.

'What?'

'That if this turns out to be a worthless copy or whatever, we just bin it, or give it to a charity shop – I don't want to keep it in the house.'

'It's very pretty.'

'So are a lot of poisonous plants.'

He grinned. 'OK, I promise. And if it turns out to be genuine?'

'Then I'll send you a list of all the things I'd like for my birthday. Got my eye on some Louboutin shoes I've always dreamed of, and a Chanel handbag would be nice, too.'

He looked down at the carrier bag and tapped it. 'You heard what the lady said.'

24

At 10 a.m., Harry and Freya Kipling had been marshalled, along with all the others – now numbering well over a thousand, he guessed – into various queues. Theirs was for the pictures expert. In spite of their early arrival, a good 150 people were in front of them and the queue was moving at a very slow pace.

The sun, already high in the sky, was beating down, and Harry, perspiring, wished he'd brought a hat, and had stuck with a T-shirt and his trademark shorts, rather than opting to dress a bit fancy in a cream linen suit. Freya had been more sensible, looking gorgeous in a broad straw hat, simple sundress and espadrilles with a blue bow on them.

On either side of them were more lines of people, clutching objects. The good, the bad, and the complete tat.

Harry said to Freya, 'You know, the one thing that I always find fascinating about this show is the expressions people have on their faces when they get told the value of what they've brought along.'

'Me too,' she said. 'Especially the ones who look so clearly disappointed when they're told it is worth fifty quid, when they were expecting to be told it's worth many thousands. Let's try not to look disappointed.'

'Or too excited?'

Harry and Freya suddenly heard a loud tut-tut behind them, and a horsey female voice exclaiming, 'Ridiculous! The way they organize this!'

Unsure who she was addressing, they turned to see a small, rotund woman in her late sixties, silver hair in a bun, tweed skirt and stout shoes. She was clutching a painting protectively to her chest.

'God knows what rubbish people here have brought along,' she said and tapped the back of her canvas. 'They really ought to separate us into those who have something clearly genuine and those who have an obvious waste of everyone's time.'

'Well I guess they have no way of knowing until the experts see it,' Freya replied pleasantly.

'What's the painting you have?' Harry asked.

'It's been in my family for three generations,' she said haughtily, then held it up, quite furtively, as if for them to sneak a peep.

It was a wooded landscape, with trees and water in the foreground and a Gothic cathedral with a very tall spire, beneath dark clouds, in the background.

'That's beautiful,' Freya said.

'Indeed, and so it should be, given its provenance.'

'What do you know about it?' Freya asked.

Lowering her voice, as if not wanting to be overheard by the people behind her, she mouthed, 'It's a Constable. John Constable. You've heard of *The Hay Wain*?'

'Of course,' Freya said.

She gave them a very smug smile. 'Well, this is one of the paintings he did of Salisbury Cathedral.'

'Wow!' Harry said. 'You've never thought of putting it into an auction – with one of the major houses?'

'Oh yes, but I've heard what a lot of rogues there are in the art world, so I thought I'd get its authenticity proven by Oliver Desouta – he's the paintings expert here today, a renowned authority on old masters – and then of course we'll take it straight to Sotheby's.'

'How wonderful,' Harry said, and waited for her to ask a

question about their painting, but she didn't. Instead she said, 'I don't suppose you'd let me go in front of you? I really would like Mr Desouta to see this before he gets jaded by too much rubbish.'

Harry had two pet hates, something he and Freya had always shared. The first was people you met who talked about themselves but never asked you a single question, and the second was pompous people who had a sense of entitlement. 'I'm afraid not, no,' he replied testily, the heat making him increasingly irritable. 'My wife and I got here very early and we're quite far enough back in the queue as it is.'

He turned his back on the woman and immediately heard her loud protest, 'Well, really!'

He shot a sly grin at Freya, who nodded back; she got it too.

A few minutes later he noticed a man in a sharp white suit, shirt and overtly conspicuous tie, and two-tone co-respondent shoes, in his late thirties, making his way along the queue ahead of them, stopping to examine each of the paintings the people in front of them had brought along. Over the next twenty minutes, he and Freya saw several despondent-looking people leave the queue and walk away with their pictures, and suddenly the line moved forward faster than before. Clearly this man was weeding out the obvious crap.

Was the same going to happen to them? he wondered, with a stab of panic. Were they going to be dismissed even before they got to the expert? Sent off, like a dozen in front of them, clutching their parcels on the walk of shame? And under the smug gaze of Lady Pompous behind them?

Eventually it was the turn of the young couple in front of them, who held a huge abstract painting of something that vaguely resembled, with a bit of imagination, a giant multicoloured grasshopper. White suit held it up, turned it around and studied the back, nodding approvingly. Straining to listen, Harry heard him murmur, 'Yes, very nice, very nice indeed.'

Harry removed his painting from the bag and then the bubble wrap just as the man handed the couple's picture back and approached them, preceded by a pleasant, if pungent, reek of cologne.

'Well, hello, good morning, so what do we have here?'

Prepared to be cut to shreds, Harry held the painting up. And saw the man's eyes widen. 'May I?' he asked, shooting his cuffs and putting his manicured hands out to the frame.

'Sure,' Harry said.

The man took it and studied the back a lot more carefully than he had studied the front, before turning it around and studying the front again. Then he frowned. 'This is very beautiful,' he said. 'Really, this is something quite exceptional. Has it been in your family a long time?'

'My husband – we – bought it in a car boot sale a few weeks ago,' Freya said.

'Well, actually there was another painting over it, we discovered what was underneath by accident,' Harry added.

The man produced a small tablet from his pocket. 'May I have your names?'

Harry gave them to him.

'Thank you,' he said. 'Thank you for bringing this along, it is very interesting indeed. Really quite special.' He handed the picture back to Harry. 'Please stay in this line, I think Oliver Desouta will be most interested to see this. Most interested indeed!'

Then he moved on to Lady Pompous behind them. Elated by what the man had said, Harry hardly heard the first exchange of words behind him. Then there was a very indignant protestation from her.

'Young man, this Constable has been in my family for three generations. You have no ruddy idea what you are talking about. I am going to see the expert.'

'Madam,' he replied, 'I am the senior old masters consultant to Bonhams. What you have here is a copy – I'm afraid to say a very mediocre copy – of one of John Constable's masterpieces, his *Salisbury Cathedral from the Meadows*. He was much copied because of his fame, and sometimes by very talented artists, and this was one of his most copied works. I'm sorry to disappoint you, the quality here is very poor indeed. I appreciate this may sound harsh, but you really would be wasting your own and everyone's time to stand in this queue. It's a decent frame, you might get a few pounds for it, but as for the painting itself, really I find it almost offensively bad.'

'And I find you quite offensive, young man. Are you saying that my family, which can be traced back to William the Conqueror, knows nothing about art?'

'No, madam, I'm not criticizing your family. I'm telling you it is not worth your while standing in this queue for the next two hours or so with this particular painting – it has very little value, fifty pounds perhaps if you were lucky. If your family does have such a wonderful history, perhaps you could find something else to bring along to a future *Antiques Roadshow*?'

Both Harry and Freya had been unable to stop themselves from turning round. The woman's face was puce with rage. As the man moved on to the next painting, Harry couldn't help himself. 'What a shame,' he said. 'How disappointing for you.'

'That man is an idiot,' she retorted. 'Mr Smarmy has no idea what he is talking about. I'm happy to wait, I'll show it to the proper expert.'

'Good luck with that,' Harry said.

25

In 1901, a French surgeon, René Le Fort, published his work on a series of experiments he had been carrying out on trauma to human skulls. Among these were dropping cannon balls onto cadaver skulls, crushing skulls in vices, whacking them with wooden clubs, kicking them or simply throwing them against tables and stone walls. From these experiments he determined that there were three predominant types of facial fractures.

This publication contained the definitive templates for surgeons carrying out facial reconstructions for much of the twentieth century. Excluded from Le Fort's comprehensive work was damage to the facial nerves inflicted by knife trauma, because no knowledge of that field had then existed and there was no mapping of these nerves.

In the early hours of a Saturday morning in 1979, outside a gay club in Brighton's Kemp Town district, a twenty-two-year-old man's face had been slashed repeatedly by a modified Stanley knife with a coin inserted between two blades, inflicting a series of parallel, tramline cuts – fortunately missing his eyes – as well as beaten and kicked to a pulp by a trio of youths, to the yells of *poof* and *poofter*, and he was left badly injured on the pavement.

The maxillofacial surgeon, Andrew Lyons, at the Royal Sussex County Hospital where Stuart Piper had first been taken, told him some days later, when he had eventually regained consciousness, that his skull had been so badly fractured it resembled a jigsaw puzzle. A week later, when he had been fully stabilized and the feared kidney damage from all the kicks had turned out to be no more than bad bruising, Lyons made the decision, in view of his extensive facial injuries, for Piper to be transferred to the Queen Victoria Hospital in East Grinstead, under the care of the specialist facial reconstruction plastic and maxillofacial surgeons there.

The Queen Victoria Hospital is credited as the place where the discipline of plastic surgery had begun. Back in the 1940s an extraordinarily talented New Zealander, Archibald McIndoe, later Sir Archie, ensured his fame, and that of the hospital, by treating severely burned Battle of Britain pilots. Such patients did not exist before the Second World War because pilots inevitably perished in their wooden-framed aircraft, which weren't equipped with parachutes and rapidly went up in flames.

The same was not applicable to the 1940s Spitfire and Hurricane fighter planes, whose brave pilots suffering horrific burns were soon arriving at the unit in East Grinstead. By transferring skin from other parts of their bodies, McIndoe was able to reconstruct their disfigured faces and hands. It was a painstakingly slow process. While they would never win any beauty contests, these airmen were given back functioning faces and hands that enabled them to lead normal, active lives again. Although many needed further skin grafts for many decades after.

During the months of reconstructive surgery on Stuart Piper's face, some former Battle of Britain pilots were still attending the hospital for review and further facial surgery.

Surgeons in the late 1970s did not have the benefit of computerized scanning and 3D reconstructions to tell them precisely where the bones should be and to give them exact details of facial height. Nor were they able to map and repair facial nerves. They simply had to do the best they could to patch up Stuart Piper's once-handsome features. During all this time, much of it with his face swathed in bandages, Piper had plenty of time to think. He was thinking about two things, with equal fervour. The first was how to build his future career. The second was how to exact his revenge on the people who had done this to him.

On a morning ward round a few days after the latest operation on Piper, the plastic surgeon he was under, Andrew Brown, noticed that Piper could not close his eyelids properly, leaving him with sore, dry eyes and problems sleeping. It was clear that the Stanley knife cuts had seriously and irrevocably damaged both the left and right nerves that controlled facial expression. He also noticed that Piper's face was flatter on the right than on the left. His eyes were wider apart than they should have been, because the canthal ligaments that should have kept the eyes close to the side of the nose had been crushed, causing a telecanthus.

Despite further surgery, the team of surgeons were unable to correct this, leaving Piper with his left eye further from the centre line than the right. This left him with an unnerving appearance; as it was such a small difference it wasn't obvious to anyone looking at him, but it made him seem menacing. No one meeting him could understand quite why he made them feel so unsettled. That sensation was worsened by his complete lack of facial expression, other than through his eyes and tiny movements of his mouth.

He was given a further operation to insert gold weights into his upper eyelids, to enable him to close his eyes properly, which left him with a squinting appearance to add to his lack of facial movement.

During the eight months Piper had spent in hospital, the three thugs had been subsequently identified by witnesses, arrested, brought to trial and sentenced, in Piper's opinion, to ludicrously short prison terms.

But he'd been ready after their release from prison, to ensure they would never do what they had done to him to anyone else, ever again.

A careful, calculating and financially independent young man, happy to bide his time to ensure he wasn't linked to the revenge attacks on these thugs, Piper picked each one of his attackers off at two-year intervals with the aid of hired muscle.

The first one, the ringleader, he had blinded and melted his face with sulphuric acid, while forcing him to listen, at maximum volume, to the Tom Robinson band playing 'Glad to be Gay'.

The second and third assailants he'd also badly beaten, satisfied in the knowledge that they would realize the reason for their assault.

Piper was too smart ever to be arrested, or ever connected to these attacks. Just as he'd succeeded in keeping his criminal activities largely under the police radar for decades.

Now approaching his sixty-third birthday, and a fitness fanatic, Piper was in lean shape. He had a narrow face, topped with slick, dyed black hair with carefully curated grey streaks, hard-man looks that reminded people of the actor Clive Owen, but the tramline scars down his cheek giving him a cruel aura. He was invariably dressed in a hand-stitched pinstripe suit, white shirt and sharp tie, even when he was relaxing.

No one could ever tell from Piper's face whether he was in a good or bad mood. A sarcastic man at best when he was in a good mood, when Piper was in a bad mood, none of the handful of people who worked for him dared say a word. Not even Robert Kilgore, even though he was well aware he was the one indispensable member of the boss's team, as well as the most highly paid, by a long margin. Piper had made him an extremely wealthy man.

And at this moment, Piper was in a proper bad mood. They were in the Long Gallery of his mansion, Bewlay Park, a Grade I-listed former stately home. It was a room with a stuccoed ceiling,

Wedgwood-blue pilastered walls, and hung with magnificent paintings.

Piper, suited, was pacing along, with Kilgore in tow and not knowing quite where his boss was going with today's bad mood. Kilgore worked out of converted stables at the rear of the house. The boss had called him at 1.45 p.m. this afternoon saying he wanted to see him, and when the boss called, Kilgore jumped – well, as much as a chain-smoking, albeit slim, seventy-two-year-old man, who'd not done a day's exercise since leaving the army, other than spirited sex, could jump.

26

Finally, shortly after 2 p.m., it was the turn of the couple in front of Harry and Freya in the queue, who were holding their watercolour of what looked like an abstract grasshopper. The paintings expert, Oliver Desouta, took their picture, placed it on the easel, securing it in place carefully. A tall man in his late fifties with gelled salt-and-pepper hair, pencil moustache, flamboyant pink suit and lime-green tie, oozing real charm and bonhomie, he examined the front and back carefully. A cameraman stood alongside with the camera trained on him and the young couple.

Then Desouta began to question them about the piece. He clearly liked it and named a watercolour artist neither Harry nor Freya had ever heard of. But both of them eagerly listened for his pronouncement of its value, as did its young owners.

'Well,' Desouta pronounced, finally, 'if I were to put this into auction, I would expect to see it realize between one thousand and fifteen hundred pounds.'

They looked both surprised and genuinely pleased.

He handed it back to them and they went off happily.

'Time to rock'n'roll,' murmured Harry to his wife as they stepped forward and a young female assistant asked their names.

As soon as Freya told her, the assistant's eyes lit up. 'Ah yes,' she said, and turned to a floppy-haired man behind her, in jeans and a T-shirt, holding a clipboard. 'Mr and Mrs Kipling,' she said and mouthed something that the couple were unable to hear.

Floppy hair nodded and made a note on his board, before turning to Desouta. 'This is the possible Fragonard, Oliver.'

Telling the cameramen to hold off, Oliver Desouta stepped forward and said, in his almost impossibly posh voice, 'Aha, Mr and Mrs Kipling – related to Rudyard by chance?'

Both of them, nervous as hell, smiled politely. 'Well no, but we do get asked that a lot, as you can imagine,' Harry said.

Desouta took the proffered painting from Harry's hands, glanced at it admiringly for some moments, then secured it on his easel. He studied the front carefully, then screwed a magnification eyepiece into his right eye socket and looked even more closely. Then he walked around the easel and spent what seemed to them both to be several minutes scrutinizing the back. Finally, he beamed at them and asked them how they came across it.

After they had told him, he responded pleasantly, 'This looks very interesting. Would you be willing to appear on camera, Mr and Mrs Kipling?'

Harry glanced at Freya, who hesitated for a moment before nodding. 'Yes,' she said.

Harry beamed at the expert. 'Absolutely!'

'Right, well, I'll repeat some of my questions when we're on air. In the meantime, Roger, our runner, will take you to the green room for a little powder on your faces, and some refreshments, if you are happy with that? It will give me a little time to do some research on this remarkable painting.' He nodded at the young man.

'Make-up?' Freya questioned.

'It's a hot day, they'll dab a little powder on to take off the shine, so you look your best on camera, nice and cool, eh?' the young man said.

The sun had been relentless and both Harry and Freya were wilting. Harry relished the chance of getting out of the heat for a while and Freya the chance to check her make-up before being filmed.

'Please come with me,' the young man said.

Extremely self-consciously, acutely aware of the gaze of dozens of onlookers, they followed him across the lawn and into a large striped tent, where the air was almost icy cool. Harry was ushered to a chair, with an array of soft drinks and snacks in front of him, while Freya was taken to the make-up artist. After a few minutes it was his turn.

The pretty female make-up artist chatted to him pleasantly, and it helped soothe his jangling nerves as she dabbed a soft brush over his face, then very carefully rearranged some of his hair.

Back with Freya, who had miraculously acquired a tan during her time in the chair, he said, 'You look like a movie star!'

'Really?' she retorted. 'I feel like a bag of jelly. What if he humiliates us and tells us it's a bad copy, like that other guy told the woman behind us?

Harry put his arm out and held her hand, entwining fingers. 'I don't think so – did you see Desouta's face as he was looking at it? He was impressed – proper impressed. And he said it was *remarkable.*'

'He also said he needed to do some *research* on it,' she retorted sceptically. 'Which to me means he's not sure about it.'

'I'm taking his reaction as a positive.'

She gave him a sideways look. 'That's my Harry, ever the optimist.'

27

Saturday, 28 September

Half an hour passed. Then another quarter of an hour. Followed by another. Harry became anxious, his mood swinging from optimist to pessimist. Maybe Freya was right. Maybe they were about to be humiliated, their hopes shattered on camera and broadcast sometime later this year to five million viewers. All their friends laughing at them. Perhaps, he thought, as time went on, and glancing continually at his watch, Desouta would have decided not to have them on camera at all. 'What time does it finish today?'

'I think they said six o'clock.'

He glanced at his watch yet again. It was now gone a quarter past four.

Then, suddenly, the floppy-haired runner, Roger, was standing over them. 'OK,' he said. 'Sorry to keep you, Mr Desouta asked for a bit more time, and he's ready to see you now.'

As they stood up, Harry asked, 'Do you know when this particular programme will be broadcast?'

'At the moment, no, it might be later in the autumn schedule, but it can change.'

They followed him back over the lawn, behind all the rows of experts and the queues until they were back in front of their painting. Harry's frayed nerves were very slightly mollified by the broad beam on Oliver Desouta's face.

Another camera had appeared from seemingly nowhere, and

there were now three – two on them and one on Desouta. In addition a bright light was shining on them. Harry was aware there was a crowd gathered around.

'So, tell me,' the expert asked, 'how did you come across this wonderful piece?'

'Well, actually,' Harry replied nervously, stumbling on his words, repeating what he had told Desouta earlier, off-camera, 'we found it in a car boot sale.'

Desouta's eyes widened.

'But not actually the painting you are looking at now,' Freya added, sounding a lot more assured than Harry felt. 'What my husband bought was what I thought was a hideous picture of a real old hag.'

'I really bought it for the frame,' Harry confessed. 'My wife hated it.' He glanced at her with a quivering smile. 'It was only some weeks later that we discovered there was another painting underneath.'

The expert nodded approvingly. 'Not uncommon at all for an original picture to be painted over,' he said. 'Canvases are expensive and many artists would use one with a painting on it that they perceived to be of no value. Or it could be that sometimes people wanted to mask the true painting – perhaps to conceal it during times of strife, or simply because through ignorance they didn't realize what the original was. Now, does the expression fête galante mean anything to you?'

Both of them shook their heads.

'Well,' he said expansively, 'fête galante is a category of painting first used for the French painter Jean-Antoine Watteau. His paintings show figures in ball dresses or theatrical costumes at garden parties, or fêtes, in bucolic settings, often with a romantic air about them. When Watteau applied to join the French Academy in 1717, there was no category to describe his works, so the Academy created one for him. Fête galante paintings reflected the growing shift at the time from the severe Baroque style to the more decorative, naturalistic Rococo period. What we have here, if it is original, is a wonderful example.' He beamed. 'And you really came across this in a car boot sale?'

'We did,' Harry said.

The couple waited expectantly.

Playing to his audience of not just the Kiplings but the considerable crowd, growing by the second, Desouta asked, 'Are you familiar at all with the works of Jean-Honoré Fragonard?'

Both shook their heads.

'He was born in the South of France, in Grasse, famous for its perfumes, and began painting in earnest around 1752. Artists loved the area, because of its beautiful light. So far as we know, Fragonard's lifetime canon of work was nearly six hundred paintings, many of which have been lost – as is the story of so many of the world's greatest artists. Looting during wars, especially by the Nazis in the Second World War. And, of course, the French Revolution, which deprived Fragonard of all of his private patrons, who were either guillotined or exiled. He left Paris in 1790 to return to his native Grasse, and did not come back to Paris until early in the nineteenth century, where he died in 1806, almost completely forgotten. Today he is ranked among the greatest painters of all time. Are you aware of what one of his paintings – a portrait – sold for at a Bonhams auction a few years ago?'

'No,' Harry said, his hopes, which had steadily been rising, now off the scale.

'Over seventeen million pounds!' Desouta said.

Harry felt a cold sensation in his stomach.

The art expert smiled for the cameras and paused, theatrically, for some seconds.

'Now, I don't want to raise your expectations falsely, but I will tell you that in my years of working for this programme, I've never been so excited by a painting. But what I don't know, of course, because I've not had sufficient time to examine it carefully enough, nor to carry out any tests on it such as pigment analysis, is whether this is genuine or a very clever fake. It has long been rumoured that Fragonard did a series of Four Seasons paintings, which were documented as existing prior to the French Revolution, but have never been seen since.'

Desouta stepped closer to the picture and pointed to the bottom right-hand corner. 'There is a very small but just visible signature, his trademark signature, just a simple *Fragonard*. So, tell me, how much did you pay for this painting at this car boot sale?'

Harry glanced at his wife before replying. 'Oh, we hadn't seen the signature. It was twenty pounds.'

'Twenty pounds,' Desouta echoed. He gave a tilt of his coiffed head, again addressing not just Harry and Freya but the crowd around them. 'Well, after what I've just told you, if it is indeed an original, have you now any idea what it might be worth?'

Both Harry and Freya shook their heads. 'No,' Harry tried to say, but no sound came out.

Desouta nodded and looked back at the painting on the easel. 'I would say you might have a bit of a bargain. You would need to have this picture examined a lot more carefully than we are able to on this programme. But if this were to turn out to be in the school of Fragonard, it will be a really valuable and desirable painting.'

There was a gasp from the crowd, and Desouta paused to let it sink in. The couple were staring at him, open-mouthed.

He went on. 'If it can be proven to have actually been painted by Fragonard himself, then it would be almost impossible to put a value on it. I would suggest that as a standalone, *Summer*, it could be worth, at auction, in the region of four to five million pounds.'

He paused again to allow the eruption of gasps, ooohs and wows from the crowd to be fully caught, as the camera lenses panned them, before continuing.

'But if this is part of the full set of Fragonard's long-lost Four Seasons, you could quadruple that, conservatively – and probably even more.'

There was an eruption of gasps from the crowd.

Harry felt faint. He gripped Freya's hand, which felt clammy. He forgot completely their plan to try to not show their emotions.

'Fuck me!' he said.

'I really could not put it better myself,' Desouta said. 'But as we are pre-watershed television, would you mind if we repeated your reaction without the profanity?'

'Sure,' Harry said, trembling. 'Yes, yes, of course.'

Desouta turned to the camera crews. 'We'd better do a retake.'

Moments later Roger jumped in front of them with a clapper board, arm raised. 'Mr and Mrs Kipling reaction, take two,' he said.

Bang.

'Blimey!' Harry said.

Someone a short distance away called out, 'Cut!'

'Perfect!' Desouta beamed. Then he turned towards the stunned couple and said, his voice quiet now so it couldn't be heard by the onlookers, 'Thank you so much for bringing this to us. If you would like, Mr and Mrs Kipling, we can arrange for Security to escort you back to your car.'

Harry nodded lamely, barely able to speak, glanced at his wife and said, 'Thank you, yes, I think we'd appreciate that.'

28

Saturday, 28 September

It was set to be a glorious Indian summer weekend, but Robert Kilgore was looking forward to proper autumn weather. Raised in the southern state of Georgia, he'd had plenty of sun, enough to last him all his life, and the truth was he actually liked this erratic British climate with all its distinctive seasons – well before global warming had come along and stuck its malevolent spanner in all of that.

His third wife had recently binned him in favour of a younger man and, hell, he was OK with that. His life was cigarettes and bourbon and doing the boss's bidding, in service of their great passion for – and lifelong expertise in – old master paintings, particularly the French Romantics. There were few collectors of these in his adopted country who were more astute – or ruthless – than the boss. And Kilgore had yet to be in a relationship that meant more to him than beautiful pictures. A failing, maybe, he rued, but hell, he was a happy and fulfilled man.

He was tall, with ramrod-straight posture, gained from his time in the military. He had served in Vietnam until he was hit by shell fragments, brought home, and invalided out – some of the shards were still stuck in his chest, too close to his spine to operate on and remove. Hugely annoying how they always set off airport sensors, pinging when he went through Security.

Bewlay Park was one of the largest stately homes in England still in private hands. It dated back to Tudor times, with its red-brick facade and elaborate chimneys allegedly copied by Henry VIII for Hampton Court, set in two thousand acres of grounds designed by Inigo Jones. There were two lakes connected by a waterfall, and anywhere you stood in the grounds, you could see one of the five Grecian-columned follies. The house, its owner and its contents were protected by a combination of high-tech security and plain, old-fashioned muscle. The two principal members of the latter, identical twins whom Piper had recruited from East London over a decade ago and paid way more than enough to ensure their unswerving loyalty, including giving each of them a cottage in the grounds, were seldom out of sight, visible at any hour of the day or night that Kilgore was here.

Just as they were now. Silent figures, dressed in black, whom no one in their right mind would want to mess with, standing a discreet distance behind them.

'Tell me something, Bobby,' Piper said, as they walked through the Long Gallery.

Bobby raised a flag. Piper only called him that when he was off on one – usually from all the white stuff he put up his nose. Normally and professionally the boss called him by his full name, Robert, as befitted the Southern gentleman that Kilgore gave every impression of being. As always, like the boss, he was immaculately attired. Even on this warm Saturday afternoon, he was dressed in a tailored suit and sporting one of his trademark bow ties. In his disarming Southern accent, he replied, 'Tell you what, Piper? What y'want to know, sir?'

Stuart Piper preferred to be addressed only by his last name. With his two Dalmatians in tow, followed by Kilgore, he strode past a Gainsborough, a Watts, a Stubbs painting of a horse and through into the Grand Salon, where he stopped and produced an ancient key from his pocket. He unhooked a Gainsborough miniature and inserted the key into what looked like a hole in the panelled wall behind, and turned it. A section of the oak-panelling, which was actually a secret door, swung open to reveal the stunning, windowless room that was Piper's private lair. Kilgore had only been admitted a couple of times in all the years he had worked for the boss.

It was a sumptuous cocoon. Also panelled in dark oak, it was furnished with deep, tasselled sofas and some fine antique pieces. It smelled of residual cigar smoke and furniture polish. A huge chandelier hung from an ornate ceiling rose, above a handsome coffee table. Silver, floor-standing candelabras, containing white, unlit candles, were positioned either side of a large fireplace, which looked freshly stacked with logs and kindling. Kilgore knew what the boss had once told him, that despite this room being windowless, there were ample ventilation ducts.

But the true wow-factor of this room was Piper's collection of fête galante paintings, the jewels in the crown of all his art. Twelve of them hung in their gilded frames, each with a lamp above it, along the walls. But there were three that meant the most of all to him. Jean-Honoré Fragonard's *Spring*, *Autumn* and *Winter*.

Despite being small, they had one entire wall to themselves, and were well spaced out, although there was an exceptionally large space between *Spring* and *Autumn*.

'See that gap, Bobby?' Piper looked at him coldly. Eyes the colour of high-tensile steel. Whatever genes Piper had inherited, he was missing the ones that carried humour. His charcoal-and-white-striped suit looked, as ever, like it had been freshly pressed this morning, and almost certainly would have been, by his butler, Wilson. Piper's father, who had been a racecourse bookmaker and died of an embolism when Piper was eighteen, had given him one piece of advice on his deathbed. *Always wear a suit and tie, son. People will always take you seriously in a suit and tie.*

His old man should have added that people would also take you seriously if you lived in a house with twenty-two bedrooms, Piper thought, because he did. And people did. They took the mutant – as he referred to himself – with the reconstructed face, very seriously indeed. The right people.

From as far back in childhood as he could remember, Piper had been obsessed by two things – history and the paintings of the old masters. Whether it was when his mother, who had a love of art, had first taken him to the Royal Pavilion or to the Brighton Museum, or to the National Gallery and later to the Louvre in Paris and the Uffizi in Florence, paintings had brought history alive to him. For good or bad, history had changed with the invention of photography and film. Before that, he so often thought, we only had paintings to give us an idea what the past actually looked like, and that had been a life-long fascination – and had become the source of his vast wealth.

The idea had occurred to him during those long, dark months of reconstructive surgery. He'd had plenty of thinking time. While the surgeons had been shaping his face, Piper was shaping his life. Making plans, big plans. The big realization.

Forget his father's hard work, long hours, out in all weather, reading betting odds from his tic-tac men, making lightning-fast calculations; it might have been a decent living but it never made the old guy rich. Nor for most people did robbery, drugs, all that shit, just pin money and long years inside for anyone getting it wrong. There was a different business, he realized, one that would combine his two loves, history and art.

A rogue's business with rich pickings. Extremely rich ones. As he went on to prove over the next forty years. Tracking down old masters that had vanished during times of upheaval. Ones that had been looted or hidden or painted over to conceal their true identity during turbulent times – such as during revolutions or countless wars. The library in his house was full of documentation detailing the existence of the original works and their provenance. And their likely whereabouts today. Documentation that Robert Kilgore accumulated for him and studied assiduously.

Kilgore was a renowned – and revered – expert in old masters. He'd worked for many years as a consultant for some of the world's foremost auction houses, including Sotheby's in New York and Christie's in London. He had become a go-to expert for art dealers and for insurance companies when they were trying to establish whether a painting was genuine or not. And they were utterly oblivious to the fact that he was a complete crook.

Robert Kilgore, with his impeccable appearance, his Southern gentlemanly charm and his encyclopaedic knowledge, was someone who everyone trusted. And he fully exploited that ever since he had first formed a working partnership with Piper.

Kilgore would take any painting he'd been entrusted with to a master forger in Brighton, Daniel Hegarty, rightly reputed to be the finest art forger in the world, retain the original and return the apparent *original*, an undetectable fake, to whichever client had entrusted it to him. He did this secure in the knowledge that the last thing any auction house or private collector or national gallery that subsequently bought the forgery would want to get out was that their picture wasn't the original.

During the past decade, Kilgore's reputation had become tarnished after a number of important works he'd once verified as originals had been exposed as fakes, through increasingly advanced forensic techniques. One by one, the prestigious houses had quietly dropped him. But Piper still saw his value. And knew that in the hands of Hegarty, a fake could be not only undetectable, but sometimes even more authentic to experts than the original.

Through the services of Robert Kilgore, as well as his own extensive network, over the past forty years Piper had found or had stolen for him – he didn't care how ruthlessly – lost paintings in Argentina, Brazil, Spain, Austria, Germany, Sweden, Holland among other countries, as well as here in the UK. Many originals he'd put into auctions, but some he'd retained, either because he loved them or to speculate on their values rising. On the ones he had retained, he'd also engaged the services of Daniel Hegarty to make exquisite copies, which he'd passed off as originals, relying on the increasing global feeding frenzy for the old masters.

See that gap, Bobby?

How many times, Kilgore wondered, had Piper talked about that *gap* on his wall? It was the boss's obsession. Like a child who had to have a particular toy or else it would throw a tantrum.

They remained in front of the three Fragonard paintings, with Piper still staring at the blank space, the *gap*. *Autumn* and *Winter* had both been acquired for a fraction of their real worth from a bent French lawyer handling an executor sale. He had asked Kilgore to identify them after they were found hanging in a modest house in Nantes in France. *Spring* he'd acquired through more ruthless means.

'Bobby, do you know the difference between five million and fifty million pounds?' Piper quizzed.

Puzzled, Kilgore shook his head. 'You got me on that one, boss. Forty-five million?' he ventured, taking a stab at humour, attempting to get the boss to lighten up, even though he knew that was doomed to fail.

The two dogs sat at heel. As he stroked their heads, Piper said to Kilgore, 'Bobby, your answer of forty-five million is about the right answer.'

Kilgore beamed, his face wrinkling. 'Well, goddamn it, I hit a home run!' Then he watched the boss closely for one sign that he was happy, which would be a faint glint in his eyes or a widening of his lips. There was neither. Piper stared back at him.

'You might be right on the maths, Bobby, but you're missing the point.' He walked up to the wall and tapped the empty space. 'That gap. That's the difference between five million and fifty million pounds. The missing painting. *Summer.*'

'Got you now, boss,' Kilgore said.

'It's out there somewhere, *if* it has survived. The one missing painting Fragonard did of the four seasons. I'm guessing it is still in France, but just maybe it's here in England like the third one we found. If we can get our hands on it, with the four together we are looking at a value of fifty million plus. I've asked you before, Bobby, and I'm running out of patience. We are going to find it, Bobby, aren't we?'

Kilgore nodded. 'Oh yes, boss. We found *Spring*, *Autumn* and *Winter*. We're going to find *Summer*. We sure are. It has to be somewhere. Lurking unidentified in some French house is my best guess. But, hey, you're right, boss. It might just be here – or anywhere in the world.'

Piper looked at him. 'I want it up on that wall. Find it. Whatever it takes. Fucking find it.'

29

When Harry and Freya reached the grimy old Volvo estate, they thanked the two security guards who'd escorted them to the car park. One of them, a cheeky chappie, had carried the painting for them. As he handed it to Harry, he jabbed a finger at the carrier bag and quipped, 'Didn't know you could buy old masters in Lidl.'

'Only on their special-offer days,' Harry retorted, smiling from ear to ear. He was walking on air, this was a dream! An absolute dream! In a minute he'd wake up, and yet, as he rested the painting down on the grass and rummaged in his pocket for the car keys, the two guards waiting patiently, saying they would keep watch just to make sure no one followed them out of the car park, Harry knew it wasn't a dream, it was real. And the possibility that he and Freya might now be rich was real.

'Shit.' He dropped the keys onto the ground, kneeled and retrieved them, then his hand was shaking so much he fumbled for some moments to hit the button on the key fob. Finally the locks thunked. He opened the front and rear passenger doors to let some of the heat out, then hesitated for a moment about where to put the painting. It had been in the boot, inside the tailgate, on the way here. But what if someone rear-ended them? he wondered. For safety he placed it between the front and rear seats, wedging it with the two pillows they always kept in the car for long journeys.

Easing himself behind the wheel, he thanked the security guards again, and as Freya belted herself up, he tried to push the ignition key in. And failed. His hand was still shaking too much. 'God, I don't know if I can even drive,' he said. 'I'm like – I'm just jangling!'

'Want me to?'

'No, I'll – I'll be – you know.' He shrugged, tried and missed again.

'A couple of deep breaths, darling,' Freya said.

He tried again, conscious of the guards still waiting, succeeded, twisted the key and the engine fired. He drove slowly over the bumpy grass until they reached the road, then pulled out onto it in the direction of Brighton.

After a few moments he glanced at Freya and said, 'Can you believe it? Incredible, eh? We might be rich – as in seriously rich! We might be *multimillionaires*!'

She gave him one of those smiles she always did when he got over-enthusiastic, and which annoyed him because they felt so damned patronizing. 'Harry, there's a very big if. You heard what the expert said – Mr Desouta: *If it can be proven to have actually been painted by Fragonard himself.*'

'Darling, he'd never have said that unless he was pretty certain.'

She gave him a sideways look. 'What the *Antiques Roadshow* team have to do is make good television. There's a reason why it's called *Antiques Roadshow* – because it's a *show*. They need the *wow* factor, they want the audience watching to get a thrill; you saw how he milked it for the cameras.'

'Did he?'

'You didn't?'

'Anyhow,' he said with a sly grin, 'I put a bottle of bubbly in the fridge last night, just in case. I think we should pop the cork when we get home.'

She shook her head. 'Let's save it. I don't want us to build up our hopes. He told us to take it to Christie's or Sotheby's to get it looked at properly, and that they might be able to tell us if it is genuine or not.'

'I'm planning to do that first thing next week,' he said.

'Can you afford the time? I thought you were on a deadline with that loft conversion. Aren't you on a penalty if you don't finish it by next weekend?'

'Afford the time? I can leave Darryl in charge for the day, it's all down to him and Phil at the moment for the next two days.' Darryl was his main carpenter, trustworthy and reliable, as was Darryl's assistant, Phil. 'Anyhow, whoever I take it to will probably need me to leave it with them. I've got to sort out Steyning on Monday, but I can whizz up to London first thing Tuesday and be back down by midday.'

'On the train?'

He shook his head. 'No way, I'm not risking doing something dumb like leaving it or getting it bashed in a packed carriage. I'll drive it up.' He reached across with his left arm, took her hand and squeezed it. 'I've got a good feeling about this, my love, a really good feeling. Don't you?'

Freya shrugged. 'I do but—'

'But what?'

'You know what they say: *if something seems too good to be true, then that's probably right.*'

'Yeah? You know what they also say? *Stay away from negative people, they have a problem for every solution.*'

She shook her hand free. 'Thanks, Harry, that's not a very nice thing to say.'

'I didn't mean it like that.'

Wet Wet Wet's 'Love is All Around' began playing on the radio. Harry turned the volume up. 'Our song!'

They'd had it playing in church when they'd got married.

She smiled fleetingly. 'OK, so how did you mean it?'

Harry drove on in silence, without answering, nodding his head to the music, the sun high in his rear-view mirrors. Freya was right to be cautious, of course she was. But this just felt – so – so good. 'Maybe just a glass of Prosecco tonight?' he suggested. 'We'll keep the champagne for when it is confirmed, yes?'

'OK.' Then she said, 'Just supposing the painting is genuine – just supposing.'

'Yes?'

'We should put it in the hands of a top auction house, right?'

'I've been thinking about that. And I'm wondering.'

'Wondering?' Freya said.

'Whether we should hang on to it. Just for a while, you know. You heard what Desouta said, that on its own, if genuine, it could be worth five million, but if part of the complete set of the Four Seasons paintings it could be worth multiples of that – like ten or twenty million or even more.'

She nodded. 'It's a nice dream, but how on earth would we start looking for the other three – even if they've survived?'

'I don't know. I don't know how the art world works. But if what we've found is original, who's to say the other three aren't out there somewhere? Maybe three other art collectors or museums that have one or more of them? Someone who has all three of the others who would jump at doing a deal?'

Freya shook her head. 'You are right, my love, we have no idea how the art world works. And we don't know anyone who does.'

'We do,' he replied. 'I built an extension on his house in Saltdean, and did his loft conversion, about three years ago. He paid us in cash, fastest payer we ever had!'

'Daniel Hegarty? The guy you called about the nail varnish?'

'Uh huh.'

'But he's a complete crook, isn't he?'

'No, he was once, but not any more. He's considered the best art forger in the country, if not the world. He can copy any painting and make it look even more authentic than the original. Collectors use him to make copies of paintings they own that are too expensive to insure, so they hang his copies in their homes and store the original in a bank vault.'

'So how could he help us?'

'I talked to him a lot when I was working on his house. He knows the art world inside out. I think he is the guy we need.'

'To find the other three Fragonards?'

Harry shook his head. 'Maybe even better than that,' he said. 'I have a plan. Trust me.'

'Really?'

'Really.'

'Don't tell me you're going to commission him to forge the other three?'

He shook his head. 'Just trust me.'

30

The cortège proceeded slowly up the narrow hill, then came to a halt outside the thirteenth-century exterior of All Saints Church, Patcham. Roy Grace and Cleo sat in the first black limousine behind the hearse. On the seats behind them were Anette and Ingo Lippert, who had acted in loco parentis for Bruno when his mother, Sandy, had died in Munich. Between Anette and Ingo sat their son Erik, Bruno's best friend. The three of them had flown over to attend the funeral and Grace was very touched that they had made the journey.

All of them were in sombre dark clothing. Roy Grace, wearing a dark suit and plain black tie, gripped Cleo's hand tightly. She was dressed all in black, with a hat and veil.

Grace's sister and her family were in the limousine behind, Sandy's parents in the one behind that, followed by another containing Cleo's parents, her sister, Charlie, and her boyfriend.

Throughout the journey from their cottage in Henfield, Roy had been mostly silent, staring fixated at the hearse in front of them, with the small coffin in the rear that was painted in the red and white colours of Bruno's favourite football team, Bayern Munich, the lid decked in red and white flowers. Inside the coffin, accompanying Bruno on his final journey, was a framed photograph of the Bayern Munich squad, signed *To Bruno*, by each footballer – which Ingo Lippert had somehow obtained. There was a second signed and framed photograph with him also, from

134

his local hero, Pascal Groß. The other item was a model Porsche 911 GT3, Bruno's favourite car.

Everything was feeling surreal to him. This son who he hadn't even known existed eighteen months ago was being buried today.

He'd originally wanted to be a pall-bearer, but Cleo had talked him out of it and now, numbly sitting here, occasionally looking down at the typed words of his brief eulogy on the two sheets of A4 paper, he was glad of his decision. With his emotions in utter turmoil, he really wasn't sure he'd have been able to hold it together. He wasn't even sure how he was going to get through the eulogy. Cleo had told him it didn't matter if he faltered, or cried, whatever, they would understand. All of those at the funeral who had ever had to give one themselves would know how hard it was.

And, shit, it was really hard. Far, far harder than the funerals of his father and later his mother – at least they'd had reasonably long lives, but poor Bruno had had just eleven years.

They'd decided on this church, because it was where he and Sandy had been married, where they'd had the memorial service for her after her death and where she was now buried, in the pretty graveyard at the rear. Later, after the service, Bruno would be interred in a plot close to her.

The current vicar of All Saints had kindly allowed their friend, and the man who had married them, the Reverend Ish Smale, to officiate today. Ish was a former rock singer, who'd taken Holy Orders relatively late in life, and Roy and Cleo felt he would bring a personal touch and warmth to this service.

Looking to his right, through the side window, Roy Grace was surprised by the number of people present. Far more than he had been expecting were gathered on the grassy knoll outside the church.

The funeral home director, Thomas Greenhaisen, in black top hat and tails, opened the rear door on Cleo's side and she slid out followed by Grace, squinting against the sudden, bright mid-morning sunlight, then politely waited for the Lipperts to climb out, too. The doors of the limousines behind were opened by identically dressed undertakers, and when all of them were out of their cars, Greenhaisen signalled for Roy and Cleo to follow him.

The crowd, which seemed even larger now, stood respectfully either side of the path. Grace could barely look at any of them as he walked side by side with Cleo towards the church's main entrance. Colleagues and friends, among whom he clocked Michael and Victoria Somers and their daughter, Jaye – his god-daughter – who was looking startlingly grown up.

Heading up the path he noticed, attached to a fence to his right, a green defibrillator sign. Bringing the dead back to life, he thought.

As they reached the porch, where a top-hatted figure stood on either side, he was handed an order-of-service sheet, which he clutched as he was ushered down the aisle of the empty Norman interior of the church and shown where to sit in the front pew. The dry, faintly musty smell brought back so many contrasting memories. He and Cleo stood aside to allow the Lipperts to go in first, Anette, then Erik, followed by tall, charming Ingo, who paused to squeeze his shoulder and gave him a solemn but reassuring smile.

Cleo went in next, then he followed.

The three Germans immediately kneeled in prayer, joined by Cleo. Roy sat, uncertain whether he had anything to say to a God who had allowed his son to die, and looked down at the service sheet.

A smiling Bruno stared at him from the cover, a photograph he remembered taking himself, outside the towering south wall of the Amex Stadium. It was one of the many games they'd attended together, where Bruno had been so passionate about the new football team he'd adopted.

Grace stared at the photograph. Bruno's fair hair was immaculate as ever, as he stood proudly in his blue and white Seagulls strip, arms behind him, beaming like he owned the place.

Below was his name, date of birth and date of death.

Death, Roy thought.

The past twenty years of his career had been all about death.

He unhooked the kneeler and went down on his knees, not because he had any religious views but because he could hear all the people shuffling in behind him, and he could not bear to face anyone.

Cupping his face in his hands, his eyes closed, blotting out everything, he kneeled and reflected. Life's slender thread. We took our existence so much for granted, but it could be snuffed out in an instant. He was remembering two traffic officers he was friends with telling him of two fatals they'd attended in the same week. In both, a person driving on their own, along a straight stretch of road on a dry day, had veered across into the path of an oncoming lorry and been killed instantly. The subsequent investigations had shown that both the victims had been texting in the moments before the collisions.

And Bruno, according to the eyewitnesses, moments after he had ducked out of school in the middle of the morning during a break and stepped out into the road, straight into the path of a BMW, had been looking down at his phone.

Grace had asked Aiden Gilbert, of the Digital Forensics team, if he could find out from Bruno's phone what had so absorbed his concentration that he'd failed to notice an oncoming vehicle. After three weeks, Gilbert had rung him last night, saying that in the moments before he'd been struck by the BMW i8, Bruno had been on the internet and he'd send through the details as soon as he could.

And Grace was now remembering the last conversation he'd had with Bruno, on the fatal morning he'd dropped him at the school gates. A bizarre one, as so many had been with him: *Education's a joke, don't you think? I can learn more from Google than any teacher can tell me.*

It had taken Grace a moment to process this. He'd not particularly enjoyed his own school days, and his performance in class had been disappointing to his parents, only just scraping through essential exams at pretty much the lowest pass grade.

Go for it, speak your mind. Tell them what you think they should be teaching you! he'd replied.

Bruno had hesitated. *Really? You think so?*

Sure. Be brave. Remember, fear kills more dreams than failure ever can.

Bruno looked puzzled. *Dreams? Is there any point in dreaming anything? Look at my mother. My mother had so many dreams, but they were all shattered and there was no way to put the pieces back together. Life sucks. School sucks.*

And that was it. He'd jumped out of the car and headed to school. Two hours later, he was on life support.

Grace sat back down on the pew. Behind him, the ever-increasing buzz of conversation convinced him that the large old building must now be pretty full, but he didn't have the courage to turn round and face everyone. Not yet.

Belinda Carlisle's 'Heaven is a Place on Earth' suddenly boomed through the speakers. He was aware from the sounds behind him that people were standing. He and Cleo had had long discussions about music for the service, consulting with Erik also on what music Bruno had liked, and Erik had told them this had been Bruno's favourite. A curious choice for someone of his age, but Bruno had long ceased to surprise him. He stood, along with Cleo and the Lipperts.

In slow, steady contrast to the music, they turned and saw Reverend Smale enter through the doorway of the church, leading the procession while reading out Bible verses of hope and comfort in a loud voice. The top-hatted pall-bearers followed with the far-too-small coffin, the red and white flowers.

They rested it on the catafalque and, as the music faded, solemnly walked back down the aisle, Glenn fleetingly locking eyes with him and giving him a chin-up grimace.

Then Reverend Smale, robed in a black cassock and white surplice, moved to the pulpit and addressed the congregation. 'On this sad day may I welcome you all to All Saints Church, and seeing so many of you gathered here is truly a great tribute of your love and respect for Bruno. Roy and Cleo have asked me to make our time together today more of a thanksgiving celebration of Bruno's short life rather than a solemn funeral service of his sudden and tragic departure and I'll do my best to do this but I'm going to need your help.' He smiled broadly. 'We all need to try and relax because that will help those contributing, who I am sure at this very moment are feeling extremely tense and emotional. I believe that Belinda Carlisle's lively entrance song we've just heard was a good choice. It's true that in heaven love comes first. But for now, our thoughts must turn from the insecure world that we live in to our perfect everlasting home that awaits us in heaven. Although this is an extremely sad occasion, I repeat that this is first and foremost a time of thanksgiving as we thank God for Bruno and for the happiness that he brought to many. We pray that Bruno may rest in peace and rise in glory in that place where he will never again know pain, sorrow or suffering.'

He paused. 'Our thoughts and prayers must also be with the bereaved close family that remain on earth. May the peace of God which passes all understanding be with Bruno's family and friends as they try and deal with their sad loss. Let us read together King David's much loved psalm of comfort, Psalm Twenty-Three. You will find it on page three.'

Barely listening to the words of the psalm, *The Lord is my shepherd, I shall not want,* Grace used the time to go over his eulogy once more in his head. There was a poem by his god-daughter, and a hymn, 'Abide With Me', before he had to walk to the pulpit, but he was already feeling sick to his stomach with fear. How the hell was he going to get through it?

31

As the organ struck up the final verse of the hymn, Roy's cue, he felt a tight squeeze from Cleo's hand, then stood and walked the few yards over to the pulpit and up its steps.

Years ago, he'd been advised by a mentor that when giving a speech you should look for a couple of friendly faces in the audience and focus on them.

But as he laid his notes on the lectern, he was so close to tears he wasn't sure he dared look up at the congregation. Finally, as the music faded, he risked it and looked up. The church was rammed and there were people standing at the back. And there was total silence. As his eyes roved quickly, trying and failing to spot Glenn again, he picked out the Chief Constable, Lesley Manning, as well as his new acting ACC Hannah Robinson; Bruno's headmaster; a retired solicitor, Martin Allen, who'd given Grace and Cleo some sound advice on the legalities around bringing Bruno to England. Then, suddenly, he was thrown.

There, sitting close to the rear of the church, was the unmistakable figure of Cassian Pewe.

Grace did a double take. Was he imagining it?

Pewe gave him a knowing smile. Grace immediately and angrily looked away.

What the hell was that bastard doing here?

Completely off his stride, glancing around the packed aisles,

140

he finally found Glenn, sitting with Siobhan and Norman, immediately behind Cleo's family.

The utter silence held. He felt a twitching of the muscle beneath his right eye. An air of expectancy along with the expressions of sympathy on so many faces. Everyone waiting for him, and he had all the time in the world. All the time to totally screw this up. He took a deep breath, then another and looked down at his notes. *Focus*, he thought. *Just focus. Take your time.* He looked back up at where Glenn was but for a moment couldn't locate him. Then he saw him, saw his concerned gaze. Saw his kind eyes and his *you can do it* smile. And he began, aware his voice sounded nervous and faltering.

'The American poet Maya Angelou said: "I've learned that people will forget what you said, people will forget what you did, but people will never forget how you made them feel".' He paused. 'Bruno was a truly extraordinary young man, who constantly challenged our preconceptions about so many aspects of our lives and of the human condition. A small boy who was wiser, in some ways, than many people very much older. Had he lived, I've no idea how much he might have achieved, but I have a feeling he might have been a truly great human being. Or at the very least, as he once told his headmaster, a benign dictator!'

He smiled and it prompted laughter.

When the congregation was quiet again, Roy Grace said, 'One of the last conversations I had with Bruno, before that morning when I dropped him off at school, was about music. He told me he was into the local artist Rag'n'Bone Man and that his favourite of his songs was "As You Are".'

Grace's voice choked and his eyes flooded with tears. He dabbed his eyes with his handkerchief, mumbled an apology, then took several deep breaths before continuing in faltering words. 'Bruno wasn't a misfit, in any conventional sense of that word. But throughout the short time that Cleo and I were lucky enough to have him with us, we always had the impression that he felt he belonged somewhere else, on some higher plane. We both hope that he has found it now, found that higher plane, found that mojo he was seeking. I suspect he has.'

Grace nodded at Smale, and moments later 'As You Are' began playing loudly from the speakers.

Clutching his eulogy, he climbed down from the pulpit and walked, avoiding all eyes, back to his pew and a warm, *well done* smile from Cleo.

32

Monday, 30 September

The service ended with Bob Dylan's 'Blowin' in the Wind', which Erik had said was another favourite of Bruno's. Thomas Greenhaisen and another of his funeral directors marched down the aisle, solemnly side by side, followed by Roy and Cleo.

Grace stared straight ahead, occasionally giving a slight nod of acknowledgement to a friend or colleague. He was looking for Cassian Pewe, although he wasn't sure what he would say when he reached the smug bastard. *Why the hell was he here?*

But when they reached the final row of wooden benches, there was a gap where he thought he'd seen the former ACC sitting. He was gone. Or had he walked past him and not noticed?

Outside, as they'd planned in advance, he and Cleo took up their positions a short distance from the porch, ready to greet and thank everyone for attending. But as the mourners filed out into the bright sunlight he was distracted and angry that Pewe had dared to show up, dared to intrude on this deeply personal service. It was as if this was some act of defiance from Pewe – *You might have got me suspended, Roy, but you don't get me out of your life that easily.*

Then the Chief Constable, in full dress uniform, was standing in front of him. A fair-haired woman, with a warm, kindly face that belied the steel behind it when needed. He and Cleo each shook her hand.

'That was a beautiful eulogy, Roy. I'm so very sorry for your loss,' she said.

'It's very good of you to come, ma'am.'

'We're family, Roy, you know that. Perhaps more than ever these days, and we all support each other, not out of any sense of duty but because we want to.' Looking at them both, she added, 'If there's anything I can do for either of you, just pick up the phone, and if you need any time out, please take it, as long as you want.'

Feeling her sincerity, he thanked her. 'You're probably busy, ma'am, but we are having drinks and bites back at ours after the interment – the address and directions are on the back of the service sheet.'

She smiled. 'Thank you. I've got the National Police Chiefs' Council conference call in an hour. If it doesn't go on too long I will try to make it.'

Next was one of Roy's team, Emma-Jane Boutwood, then Glenn Branson, who flung his arms around him and, pressing his cheek against Roy's, said, in a voice barely above a whisper, 'You did really well, mate.'

Roy Grace closed his eyes, crushing away tears, loving this man even more than ever. 'Thanks,' he managed to croak.

'Seriously, if I fall off the perch before you do – unlikely, I know, because of your great age – promise me you'll do my eulogy?'

'You seriously want me to tell the world what you're like?'

'Maybe not, on second thoughts.'

As Branson moved on, followed by Siobhan Sheldrake and Norman Potting, Grace saw his old police colleague Dick Pope and his wife Leslie. They'd first alerted him to the possibility that Sandy was living in Munich after they reckoned they'd seen her there while on holiday.

Next was Ray Packham, a former guru of the High Tech Crime Unit, now renamed Digital Forensics, and his wife, Jen, who worked as an ambulance despatcher. 'We're so sorry for your loss, Roy,' he said.

Aware the couple had recently lost their beagle, Hudson, Grace replied, 'And I'm so sorry for yours. Hudson was a character.'

'Yeah,' Ray Packham said. 'A fat thief. But we loved him.'

Jen nodded. 'He had a good heart, but he was so damned greedy!'

Behind them was Forensic Gait Analyst Haydn Kelly and his partner, whose name Grace was forever getting wrong. And he couldn't remember now – was it Emma or Gemma?

He extended the invitation to drinks and bites back at their cottage, where they had a heated marquee erected.

Finally, the queue of people ended. Thomas Greenhaisen approached them respectfully. 'Are you ready for the interment?'

Roy turned to Cleo, who nodded.

'Yes,' he said.

And a short while later, as the same four pall-bearers who had carried the little coffin into the church came back out with it, Roy Grace felt like the loneliest man in the world.

33

Tuesday, 1 October

Harry Kipling drove his grimy Volvo onto the forecourt of their house, parking in the gap between his equally grimy Toyota Hilux pick-up and Freya's sparkling Fiat 500. She loved her little car, which she'd nicknamed Daffy because of its daffodil yellow colour, and she kept it spotless, unlike his two workhorses, neither of which he'd taken through a car wash in as long as he could remember.

As he fumbled with his front door key, the door opened and Freya stood there, in jeans and roll-neck top, looking concerned. 'Darling, it's half past eight, I was expecting you back hours ago. Is everything OK?'

Harry, beaming like a Cheshire cat, kissed her then asked, 'Is that champagne still in the fridge?'

'What's going on – and where's the painting?'

He stepped inside and closed the door behind him. The house smelled of grilled fish.

'Where's the painting?' she asked. 'Why didn't you call me? I've been worried sick you were in an accident.'

'I wanted to surprise you with my news, my love.'

She gave him a dubious look. 'I called you four times and you didn't answer.'

'I'm sorry, but trust me!'

'Where's the painting?' she asked again.

'It's safe, don't worry!' He kissed her again and strode through into the kitchen. Opening a cupboard door, he removed two tall glass flutes, set them down on the work surface and walked over to their massive fridge. He took out the bottle of Taittinger that had been chilling.

'Harry,' she said, both irritated and grinning at the same time. 'Just bloody tell me?'

In reply he sat the bottle down beside the glasses, removing the foil and wire. Grabbing a clean dishcloth, he wrapped it around the top of the bottle and, after some silent exertion, popped the cork and poured. 'How's Tom?'

'Up in his room. He had his dinner earlier. His sugars were getting low.'

He carried their glasses over to the kitchen table. Then he pulled up a chair and beckoned Freya to join him. 'You need to sit down for this!'

Still looking hesitant, she sat.

He raised his glass. 'Well, it looks like we might well be multi-millionaires!'

'*Might be?*' she quizzed, almost reluctantly clinking his glass before sipping the wine.

'I took the painting to the valuations department of Sotheby's in Bond Street this morning, and the expert there got very excited. She studied the back of the painting almost as much as the front. I was with her for three hours, during which she showed it to several colleagues and made a number of phone calls and internet searches. She asked if I could leave it with her for a few days, to show to a gentleman she said was the number-one expert in Fragonards in the UK, but I didn't want to do that.'

'Why not?'

'I'll come to that. What she did say was that if, as she *suspects*, it's an original Jean-Honoré Fragonard painting of *Summer*, then it would be worth upwards of five million pounds, and she cited two recent sales of Fragonards, one of which had fetched well in excess of that figure!'

'We don't need that kind of money, Harry.'

He frowned. 'What do you mean, we don't need it?'

'We're good as we are, aren't we? We have everything we need. We have each other and we have Tom. We have a good life.'

Harry frowned again. 'Would it be such a problem if we had a whole lot more money? It would be like winning the lottery, right?'

Freya shrugged. 'I read a piece in a magazine about lottery winners – about how few were actually made happy by winning. Mostly, the vast sums destroyed their lives.'

'Fine, we could give it away to charity – or some of it, anyway. We could keep enough so we never needed to worry about money – wouldn't that be good? You find teaching stressful, more than ever these days you keep telling me, with all the regulations about how you can and cannot treat your kids. And I'm constantly stressed out by my customers, especially this bloody Steyning job. We could buy a place in Spain and give two fingers to the world.'

'And just abandon Tom? And end up among a bunch of drunk ex-pats who spend their time going from one bar to the next?'

He reached out and touched her arm. 'Hey, what is it, what's bothering you?'

Freya took a long gulp of her champagne, almost draining her glass. Harry refilled it.

'I've had a particularly stressful day. I've had to deal with an angry parent whose twelve-year-old boy has been playing up in school and bullying. Then, on top of that – and this may just all be in my mind – I think someone might be following me.'

'What?'

'Like I said, I may be imagining it but I don't think so. When I drove Tom to Varndean this morning, I noticed a Range Rover in my mirrors. Then a dark Range Rover, I don't know if it was the same one or not, seemed to follow me to Tom's school this afternoon, and then back home – and drove straight on past when I turned into the driveway and up Mackie Crescent.'

Instantly concerned, Harry asked, 'Did you get the registration?'

'No, I was so shaken I didn't think straight. Maybe it's nothing, just my imagination. I'm not even sure the two cars were the same colour.' She gave a thin smile. 'I'm probably just being paranoid.'

Harry nodded, thinking. The episode of *Antiques Roadshow* hadn't been broadcast. Only a handful of the public at the event would have seen the art expert's assessment of the painting, and he could give no guarantee it was authentic. It was too soon for someone in London today who might have seen it to pass it to a contact, surely. And anyhow, for a while, the painting would not be in their house. 'I think we're both jittery at the moment. But if you see the car again try to get its number plate.'

'I'll try. So – so where's the painting now?'

'You know I was mentioning Daniel Hegarty, right?'

'The forger.'

Harry beamed. 'He is my plan!'

Freya frowned. 'OK – do you want to explain exactly how?'

'I think you're going to like it,' he said, reaching for the bottle and topping up both of their glasses. 'A lot.'

34

Roy Grace had been intending to spend more time, especially weekends, at home with Cleo and Noah. Family had never been more important than right now, especially with the imminent arrival of their new baby. He needed to try to rebalance his priorities and leave behind at work the effects of the everyday violence he dealt with, separating it from his life at home.

But Sussex, with its crime hotspots of Brighton and Hove, Crawley, Hastings and once sedate and genteel Worthing, was going through something of a violence epidemic. The growing scourge of knife crime, which he'd seen first-hand during his secondment to London's Met Police, had started to permeate Sussex in particular, and there had recently been a spate of stabbings in the county, three of them fatal – and a new stabbing in the centre of Brighton and Hove last night, with the male teenage victim in hospital, in a critical condition.

In addition to the usual crimes which sometimes involved his team, the relatively new and iniquitous crime of illegal puppy farming was fast becoming a major problem. The same OCGs – Organized Crime Gangs – which had control over much of the drugs supply into Sussex, and its surrounding counties of Kent, Surrey and Hampshire, were now behind this new, lucrative, vile – and easy – trade.

Easy, because unlike the massive efforts that went into tackling drugs, at all levels, until very recently puppy farming was little known about, there were few resources thrown at it, and ludicrously light sentences, under the Animal Welfare Act, for anyone prosecuted. But fortunately this was starting to change, thanks to actions by the RSPCA inspectors bringing two successful prosecutions for illegal puppy-farming elsewhere in England on charges of conspiracy to commit fraud, which carried a much more punitive ten-year sentence.

Cruelty to animals of any kind was one of the few things that made Roy Grace really angry. The Surrey and Sussex Major Crime Team was now working closely with the RSPCA on monitoring the situation and steadily building files on suspects, but no arrests of any real significance had been made in Sussex – yet. But, with the blessing of the Chief Constable, herself a dog lover, he had delegated two detectives to liaise with the current Rural Crimes case officer, Sergeant Tom Carter, based in Midhurst, and work with him on monitoring the situation.

He'd also had the traumas in Glenn's relationship with his fiancée Siobhan on his mind. For a couple of days Glenn had seemed brighter, telling him that they'd patched things up and the wedding was back on. Then on Friday, Siobhan's article in the *Argus* had come out and it was, Grace had to admit, a hard read for Sussex Police.

Glenn confessed he'd lost it with her and they'd argued again about the article and family priorities. She'd said that if he cared to read down the comments he might be surprised. Many were in support of the police, agreeing that in an organization of some five thousand people you were bound to have the odd rotten apples, but that did not make Sussex Police institutionally morally bankrupt. Glenn told Roy he realized he'd been harsh and that he should just leave her to get on with her job. It had been a bumpy weekend, but they were making progress.

Sitting at the table in the conference room, Roy was aware of his team filing in. Glenn gave him a wan smile and an *I'm OK* nod as he sat down. To Grace's surprise, Norman Potting had been the first in, clutching a file and a mug of steaming tea or coffee, and looking very self-important.

'Good morning, everyone,' Grace said. 'This is the third meeting on Operation Canvas which started as a review but is now becoming a re-investigation.' Reading from his notes he said, 'Jack and Polly, I gave you the action of interviewing Archie Goff – how did that go?'

'We met him in Lewes Prison yesterday afternoon, sir,' DS Alexander said. 'It took a few days to arrange because he insisted on having his brief present. But he was all happy chatty despite having him there.' He turned to Sweeney, who nodded in confirmation, then went on. 'He said, quite openly, that his thing is antique silver – Georgian and Victorian – jewellery, and cash of course. Never touched paintings, except a couple of times a long while back when he was paid to target specific ones. Says he couldn't tell a Rembrandt from a child's painting-by-numbers. But that about sums him up: he's not the brightest, if you know what I'm saying, boss.'

'I remember going on a warrant to nick him about fifteen years ago,' Norman Potting said. 'He's definitely not the sharpest tack in the box. I heard at his trial he gave two different alibis that contradicted each other.'

Several of the team smiled.

'He's got no previous for violence in any of his burglaries, sir,' Alexander added. 'Murdering Porteous would not be his MO.'

'So we can eliminate him?' Grace said, looking at them both in turn.

'He also had an alibi,' Polly said, 'which he showed us in a five-year diary he'd brought along, that he'd been out for a birthday meal with his daughter at Pinocchio's restaurant in Brighton and had remained at home with her later that night.'

'Pinocchio?' Norman Potting interjected. 'Did Archie's nose grow as he told you this?'

Stroking her own nose, and smiling, Polly went on. 'We

subsequently spoke to his daughter who attends the veterinary college at Surrey University and she confirmed this.'

Glenn Branson looked up. 'They wouldn't have been at Pinocchio's all night. Could she verify that her father hadn't gone out after they'd arrived back home, Polly?'

'Well, she said she remembered the evening clearly because she'd never seen her father so drunk before. She told us she'd had a fair bit to drink, but he'd really been hitting it, and the taxi driver almost refused to take them because he was worried her father would throw up in the back. As it was, he passed out on the way home. She had to help him to bed.'

'Could have been faking it,' Potting suggested.

'She's a pretty sensible young lady,' Polly Sweeney said. 'Quite surprising, considering her old man. I think she'd have been able to tell if he was faking it.'

Grace nodded. 'I think we can rule him out for now, but not completely eliminate him.' He turned to Stanstead. 'How did you get on with art dealers in the area, Luke?'

Stanstead shook his head. 'I gave the details to Polly and we've been in touch with a large number of them, some who helpfully gave me the names of other dealers. I've a few more to go, but so far no one's been offered that painting – all of them said they would remember a Fragonard because it would be an extremely rare occurrence. Polly also covered all the house clearance companies who put some of their stuff into uncatalogued auctions, and none of them say they've seen it.'

Grace thanked them, then addressed Alexander. 'Jack, any luck with the jewellers?'

'I'm doing the rounds of jewellers as well as all the Cash Converters branches in Sussex, Hampshire, Surrey and Kent, and all the pawnbrokers, too, for both the Rolex Submariner watch and the wedding ring. Nothing so far, but I've still got some to go on my list.'

'Norman, your action to *follow that car!* How did that go?'

Potting grinned back, then puffed out his chest. 'Well, chief, I do have some progress here. The current owner of the suspect Audi, a Mrs Jo Dillan of Haywards Heath, who works freelance as a bookkeeper and financial manager, very kindly allowed us to take the car. I managed to persuade Caffyns garage to lend her a courtesy vehicle in the interim as she needs transport to get to her clients.'

'Well done,' Grace commented.

'Now, chief, this is where it gets interesting,' Potting said, beaming, and looked around to ensure he was the centre of everyone's attention. 'The Audi A6 that was used on the night of Thursday, 15 October 2015, was the then latest model, with state-of-the-art technology. Among its onboard monitoring systems are smart airbag sensors. These are able to detect from the position of each front seat at the time of impact, and the pressure on them, the approximate height and weight of the driver and passenger. We don't yet have all the information, but so far we know that both airbags were deployed, which indicates there were two people in the vehicle at the time of the impact.'

He paused to let this sink in. He glanced down at his open folder. 'The driver is estimated to be between six foot and six foot two. The passenger is estimated to be a bit shorter. I'm waiting for updated information.'

'How tall is Archie Goff?' Grace asked. 'I seem to recall quite tall.'

'Well over six foot, about six four,' Polly Sweeney responded.

'So this could further help eliminate him,' Grace said.

'I think so, chief,' Potting said. 'I also have a plot, from the Audi's onboard navigation system, of all the movements it made from the time it was nicked to the moment it crashed and was abandoned. And this is where it gets even more interesting.'

35

Wednesday, 2 October

Norman Potting now had everyone's keen attention. 'The dark green Audi A6 reported stolen sometime during the night of Tuesday, 13 October 2015, or early morning, Wednesday the 14th, by its owner, Monica Thaesler, was driven straight to an address off Blatchington Road, Hove, where it remained stationary until 11 p.m. on the night of Thursday, 15 October. At 11 p.m. it then moved to Tongdean Avenue, pulling up in the vicinity of the Porteous home. We don't have its precise location, but it was less than one hundred yards from this house.'

He glanced around, looking very pleased with himself.

'Possibly waiting for Charlie Porteous to arrive home,' Grace said.

'Indeed,' Potting replied.

'Which is further indication this was a targeted attack rather than a random street robbery,' Grace added.

'Very much so, chief.' Potting studied his notes for a moment, before reading out, 'According to the Audi's onboard navigation system, it left the vicinity of the Porteous home at 12.51 a.m. The car's system has additionally revealed data about its acceleration and speed. The car accelerated hard from where it was stationary near the Porteous house, covering four hundred metres in 13.1 seconds, the point at which the dog walker and house-sitter, Joe Lee, noticed it.'

'12.52 a.m.,' Glenn Branson said, looking down at his notes.

'What do we know about the location off Blatchington Road where it spent the previous twenty-four hours, Norman?' Grace asked.

Potting beamed. 'Well, chief, this is where it gets better still. The navigation system puts the Audi in Raglan Street, just off Blatchington Road. This street is a residents' parking zone, which means if the car had been parked there all the following day it would have been ticketed. I've checked and no ticket was issued either to this car or to the false registration it carried, but . . .' He raised a finger in the air. 'There is a row of five lock-up garages on this street, so it seemed likely to me that the Audi was parked in one of these – it made sense to keep it off the street and out of sight. I did some checking, with Luke's help, on the registered owners of these lock-ups.'

He paused to take a swig of his brew. 'Surprise, surprise, they're owned by someone well known to us – Ricky Sharp.'

Grace frowned. 'Ricky Sharp? That rogue? He must be older than God – is he still alive?'

'He was at 12.30 p.m. yesterday, chief,' Potting said. 'Drinking a pint of Harvey's in the Royal Albion on Church Road. He's all there, cagey as hell. And still got his curly hair, albeit gone very grey now.'

'Well, he would be cagey, considering all the time he's spent inside,' Velvet Wilde quipped.

Ricky Sharp was a fourth-generation member of one of Brighton's most notorious crime families. At one time the Sharps were major players in protection racketeering and controlled the drugs in a large number of Brighton's clubs. But in recent years they'd lost out in turf wars to the Chinese and Albanian gangs, and Ricky, an ageing, recidivist drunk, had scarcely troubled the police radar in recent years. He owned a few grotty properties, some occasionally busted for housing low-rent brothels, some for housing illegal immigrants, and always feigning ignorance

– and usually, through a cunning brief, getting away with it. The police also knew that Sharp made additional money as a relatively small-time fence.

'So what did he have to say, Norman?' Grace asked. 'Anything helpful?'

'Well, at first he told me to fuck off, that he wasn't a grass. Then when I told him there might be some cash from police funds to pay for information, he got interested. Could we find something to bung him, chief?'

'How much do you think would do it?'

'I reckon five hundred.'

'I'd have to run it by the ACC,' Grace replied, relieved he no longer had to kowtow to Cassian Pewe, who would have taken some persuading to make any speculative payment on a cold case. Hopefully he'd have better luck with Pewe's replacement, Hannah Robinson. 'Anything else?'

'Oh yes!' Potting beamed, giving the impression this was the moment he had been waiting for. 'The company that the Collision Investigation Unit took the Audi to, Harper Shaw, have come up with something that could be very helpful. It seems the numbnuts in that Audi were clearly unaware of the technology in the vehicle. One of these cretins had Bluetooth active on his phone.'

'Or *their* phone, Norman,' Wilde jumped in pointedly.

'Indeed,' Potting said, with a flash of irritation.

'Which would confirm one of my long-held views, Norman,' Grace said. 'That the majority of villains are crafty but, fortunately for us, not particularly intelligent.'

'I would agree with that, chief. The Audi's onboard sucked all the numbers out of this *person's* phone,' he went on, looking pointedly at Wilde as he said it. 'The phone itself wasn't registered to any user, clearly a burner, and there were only thirteen numbers. I gave them to Aiden Gilbert at Digital Forensics, and he's come back with three names he's matched to the numbers.'

Potting glanced down at his notes. 'The first, no surprise, is Ricky Sharp. The second is Jorma Mahlanen.'

'The Slippery Finn?' Branson said.

'The very one,' Potting confirmed.

'Funny how his name pops up from time to time. He's well rich,' Branson added, 'he could afford to collect art.'

'Do we know how he's made his money?' Jack Alexander asked.

'Not legitimately, from all I've heard about him,' Polly Sweeney said. '*Slippery* is the right moniker.'

'We've been looking at him for a long time,' Luke Stanstead said. 'Polly's correct, he's slippery all right. Every time we follow the money we hit a brick wall at the end of a blind alley. He'll make a mistake one day.'

'The third name is Stuart Piper,' the DS said.

'Stuart Piper?' Grace said, frowning. 'Doesn't ring a bell. Is he a person known to us?'

Potting shook his head. 'Not to Sussex Police, chief, no. But I've discovered he's on an Interpol watchlist. He lives in Sussex, near Horsham, and is apparently a major art collector – and dealer. He specializes in old masters – into which category the missing Fragonard falls. I understand he's a very rich man, who has made his fortune by tracking down and trading in lost works of art of historical significance.'

Luke Stanstead raised a hand. 'I've been doing a search on Piper at Norman's request, sir. The only thing I've found on him in police files was back in 1979; he was the victim of a homophobic attack, in which he was badly beaten, leaving him permanently disfigured. Three people were subsequently arrested and convicted of causing grievous bodily harm and served time.'

Grace nodded thoughtfully. 'Good research, Luke. Have you found anything else?'

Stanstead shook his head.

'Great.' Grace grimaced and thanked him. Turning to Potting, he asked, 'Any ideas why he is of interest to Interpol?'

'I've done my best to find out, chief, but haven't yet got very far. I talked to a Ludwig Waldinger, who is still a friendly contact in Vienna. He's getting back to me.'

'Maybe you should go and have a chat with this Stuart Piper, Norman.'

'I've already made contact, chief. It seems Piper has a second home in the Caribbean, on the island of Barbados, and he's just gone out there. I could fly out to talk to him, chief, if you like?'

Grace dashed the hope in Potting's voice. 'I think maybe we can wait until he returns to England, Norman.'

'It might not be for a couple of weeks, chief.'

Grace smiled. 'Much though I'd love to send you off for a holiday in Barbados, courtesy of the British taxpayer, as Porteous has been dead for four years, I think we can afford to wait.'

Potting nodded and mumbled, 'Just saying. Only a suggestion.'

'I appreciate your altruism, Norman,' Grace replied.

36

'Here we go!' said Harry Kipling, as he sat down beside Freya on the sofa in front of the television. Their best friends, Jim and Katie Morgan, were on the other sofa, turned round so they could watch, too. Even Tom had pulled up a chair and removed his headphones to watch. All of them held their topped-up glasses of Prosecco. They'd been alerted, only on Friday, by an assistant at the BBC that their episode of *Antiques Roadshow* was being broadcast much sooner than planned, due to a scheduling issue.

Jim, balding and two stones overweight, most of which he carried in his beer gut, on which he rested the base of his glass, had a substantial glazing business. His slightly built wife, Katie, was a care-home worker for children with learning difficulties. 'Get that art expert's whistle, Harry!' he shouted out excitedly. 'Was that your old man's demob suit from the army?'

Katie put a finger to her lips and shushed him, her eyes going from the painting on the screen in front of her, to the one hanging on the lounge room wall to her right.

As Oliver Desouta pointed at the painting on the easel and began talking, Jim said, nodding at the picture on the living room wall, 'Hope you've got it well insured, Harry?'

Harry shook his head. 'Not yet, not until we know for sure if it's an original.'

'Then it would cost a fortune to insure,' Freya said.

'But millions of people are going to see this tonight, Harry,' Jim continued. 'Aren't you worried about burglars?'

Harry shook his head. 'I've arranged to fit security lights, window locks and perhaps a CCTV camera.'

'They won't keep out a determined thief, mate,' Jim said.

Katie shushed him again. 'Let's watch!'

'I wouldn't keep it in the house, not after tonight.'

'Jim, shut it! Let's watch, OK?'

They all fell silent and watched.

37

There are decades where nothing happens, and there are weeks where decades happen.

That quote from Lenin, which Roy Grace had come across a couple of weeks back in *The Week*, had lodged in his mind. It was like one of those tunes that suddenly sticks and you can't get rid of. Earworms. And it had sure been true of these past few weeks.

As ever, the eternal yin and yang of life. Roy Grace wasn't a religious man, and never had been, but there were times when it felt like an unseen hand had reached down from out of the sky, instantly turning your life to shit, then with the other hand offered you a biscuit.

He was still grief-stricken over Bruno's death. The biscuit he'd been offered was in the shape of the arrest of the man, ACC Cassian Pewe, his direct boss, who had been making his life hell for the past two years.

He'd seen Cassian Pewe carted away in the back of an unmarked car accompanied by two burly detectives from the Metropolitan Police Directorate of Professional Standards. The ACC would be facing an internal disciplinary hearing, and very likely also a criminal trial for insider trading.

All the same, Roy Grace felt far from complacent at the thought of Pewe's impending fate of being sacked from the police force, as well as facing a jail sentence. The latter was a potential

162

nightmare for any copper – as police officers tended to be ranked alongside nonces and grasses by other prison inmates, and faced their own vigilante justice. His disgraced former colleague Guy Batchelor had drawn a lucky straw when he was sent to Ford open prison, a Category D. Cassian Pewe might not be so fortunate.

Grace wasn't complacent about it, firstly because he knew just how manipulative Pewe could be, and that if he did somehow manage to wriggle out of any charges brought against him, he would be back with a vengeance, on a mission to hang him out to dry. And secondly, because however much he loathed Pewe for all the hell he had made his working life for so long now, he felt a twinge of guilt – however irrational, and however much he hated the man – at potentially destroying his career and his future.

But for now the die was cast and he had to put all these thoughts behind him and focus on what lay immediately ahead. This included somehow coming to terms with Bruno's death, his cold case workload and, hopefully happier times, Glenn Branson's forthcoming wedding and his role as his best man – if the wedding went ahead.

He knew the best way to deal with his grief over Bruno was to do what he always did with every shitty curve ball life threw at him, by immersing himself in work. But he also needed to keep the balance with his family life, and a new baby on the way would help that. As a homicide detective, he could never bring the dead back to life, but the one thing he could do was to help those bereaved by a murder to find some kind of closure, to find some way of moving forward again in their lives. And his team on Operation Canvas was making some good progress on their review of the murder of art dealer Charlie Porteous. He was close to being in a position to inform the ACC that he was formally reopening the investigation. Porteous's killers were still out there, and he would love nothing more than to bring them to justice and to give closure to Porteous's widow, Susan, and his children.

Consumed during the summer by two large major enquiries, he and his officers had had to postpone the start of the cold case review. But now he had a gap – and not only that, but an itch that had been scratching him constantly that this was a case he could solve. And wanted so badly to. But it was a sensitive case at the same time, trying to deal with the fact that the dead man had been involved in an unorthodox, not to say shady, dealing over a painting.

He just needed that one break. The one that would cut the muscle of the oyster shell and let him prise it open. But this evening he needed to put all of that out of his mind and relax. He'd been sleeping badly for months and had recently read a book on sleep that told him, among other things, to switch off from work well before bedtime. And now on this Sunday night, on a week in which he wasn't the on-call SIO, he was doing just that. Seated with Cleo on the big sofa in front of the television, with a platter of cheeses, grapes, sliced apple and nuts in front of them, holding a glass of red wine in his hand – which Cleo, heavily pregnant, glanced at enviously – they were both enjoying one of their favourite television programmes, *Antiques Roadshow*. It had started a few minutes ago.

A tubby, middle-aged man was proudly displaying a staggering collection of Dinky and Corgi toy police and emergency service vehicles, all with their original boxes. The show's expert in these, attired in a purple jacket, pointed at a Mini Panda car, pale blue and white.

'I was out in one of those when I first joined!' Grace exclaimed. 'God, I remember them so well!'

'Wouldn't have been much use in a chase, would it?' Cleo asked.

He shook his head. 'Nope. The idea was for neighbourhood patrols – instead of bobbies on the beat, we cruised around in those. They were the start of the rot.'

'Rot?'

He nodded. 'The day they ended foot patrols was the day neighbourhood crime began to soar. When I was a probationer, we'd walk a specific beat, get to know the people in the areas, particularly the troublemakers, and be able to engage with them. And occasionally we'd be able to spot if something odd was going on, like a house containing a local terrorist cell. Once we were all put into cars, all that changed. Sure, we could cover more ground more quickly, so fewer neighbourhood police were needed – nice economics, but very short-sighted.'

'Weren't you out in one of those pandas when you had your first big job in the force?' she said, grinning. It was a dig. 'Your first Grade One shout? What was it – something involving a swimming pool, I seem to remember? And my brave soldier handled it in a manly fashion!'

'Yeah, yeah!' He grinned back, remembering all too well. It was his first week out of his probationary period, fresh in uniform, when he'd had to go and assist in pulling a donkey out of a swimming pool.

A cut on the screen from the toy cars to a painting on an easel on the television caught his eye and, instantly, his attention.

A couple in their mid-forties were standing in front of a rather fine and clearly very old painting of two young lovers in period dress, in an ornate frame. The couple were being addressed by the fine arts expert Oliver Desouta, whom Grace recognized as a veteran of this show.

The woman was in a floral sundress with a wide-brimmed straw hat; the man, evidently her husband, with unruly brown hair and wearing a rumpled cream linen suit, looked like a newspaper reporter out of a 1950s movie. Both wore the eager, puppy-like expressions of so many people featured on this show, waiting for the magical pronouncement of the value of what they had brought along, that might – just – be life-changing for them.

Then the flamboyantly dressed Desouta said, 'Are you familiar at all with the works of Jean-Honoré Fragonard?'

And Roy Grace jerked upright, almost spilling his glass of wine. 'Shit!' he said. 'Bloody hell!'

'What?' Cleo asked.

But he leaned forward, riveted, without answering.

38

Perspiring heavily, on the sixth mile of his treadmill run, Piper was irritated by the sound of his phone cutting out the soundtrack of the fourth episode of series three of *Game of Thrones* playing on the television screen in front of him. He glanced down at the display and saw it was Robert Kilgore calling. He ignored it and carried on, finishing mile seven, then mile eight, ignoring three further calls from Kilgore, then dutifully doing his three minutes of cool-down.

When he was done, he stepped off the treadmill, went through his routine of stretches, then drank some cold water from the dispenser, debating whether to call Kilgore back or wait until the morning.

The phone rang again. Sweaty from his exertions, Piper answered curtly, 'What do you want, Bobby? This had better be good to call me on a Sunday night.'

The soft Southern voice said, 'This is good, boss. This is very good. You anywhere near a television?'

Kilgore knew full well his boss had a television in just about every room in the house, including all the toilets.

'Why?'

'*Antiques Roadshow.*'

'Why would I want to watch that stupid show? A load of dumb fucking morons thinking they've found something of value in their attics or their dead granny's handbag?'

Calm as ever, Robert Kilgore said, 'I think you ought to take a look at tonight's episode. Take a look right away, check it out on catch-up. Then call me back.'

'What is this? Don't play fucking games with me, Bobby. What is it?'

'A solution to your mathematical puzzle. Remember the one you set me, sir? A few weeks back? Some kind of riddle, sir.'

'I don't do riddles.'

'Beg pardon, but back in September you set me a riddle. Y'asked me if I knew the difference between five million and fifty million pounds? Remember?'

'I did?'

'The three Fragonards on your wall. *Spring, Autumn, Winter.* Anything coming back now?'

'Uh huh. Kind of.'

'Watch tonight's *Antiques Roadshow* on catch-up or iPlayer or whatever. Then call me back, doesn't matter what time. I don't reckon I'll be sleeping much and nor will you.'

'I always sleep well.'

'Watch that show and you won't. Trust me. I'm guessing you're gonna be awake all night.'

39

Monday, 21 October

Roy Grace had been woken around 2 a.m. by the pitiful squealing outside, somewhere close, of a creature being taken by a fox, and furious barking from Humphrey. Worried that a fox might somehow have got into their now well-protected chicken coop, he'd pulled on his dressing gown and slippers and gone outside, with Humphrey in tow, to check. But all was quiet in the coop. Probably an unfortunate rabbit.

Just as he'd drifted back into sleep, Noah had begun wailing from a nightmare. Cleo had gone to comfort him and carried him back into bed with them. From then on, Roy had lain awake pretty much all night, or so it now felt as he looked at the smart metal tracker ring Cleo had bought him for his last birthday to monitor his steps, sleep and all kinds of other metrics.

Just gone 5.45 a.m. and he was wide, wide awake. Too bloody awake. Cleo was sound asleep, as was Noah. Right now, with her advanced pregnancy, her obstetrician had advised her to get as much sleep as possible.

He closed his eyes and tried to go back to sleep. Then, after what seemed like a good half hour, but was only seven minutes according to his watch, he gave up, slipped as quietly as possible out of bed, to not disturb Cleo and their son, and walked through into the bathroom, closing the door quietly behind him. Then he checked his sleep on the app on his phone.

Total sleep: *4.10*

Efficiency: *50%*
Restfulness: *Pay attention*
REM sleep: *24 minutes*
Deep sleep: *32 mins*

Shit. Thanks for that, *Antiques Roadshow*! A big day of meetings ahead to get through and on a fraction of the sleep he needed. He decided to deal with it the way he always handled stress, which was to go out for a run with Humphrey.

Half an hour later, on top of the Downs in the breaking dawn, maintaining a steady pace, with a happy dog bounding along near him, Grace was feeling a lot better, and thinking through what he had seen last night. The couple on the *Antiques Roadshow*, with the painting that the expert, Oliver Desouta, had become really animated about. He hadn't gone as far as declaring it to be an original, but his message to the couple was very clear. That it *might* be.

They'd come over as pretty ordinary folk, telling Desouta how they'd bought a painting in a car boot sale, and then discovered there was another painting beneath. Grace didn't think they were lying – why would they have been? If they were crooks, they'd never have gone public on that show, would they?

Oliver Desouta had told the couple that the painting could well be one of the four long-lost paintings Jean-Honoré Fragonard had created of the four seasons, a decade before the French Revolution and the Terror that followed under the regime of the maniac Robespierre.

Charlie Porteous had been murdered after openly touting around a painting he believed might be another in the same series by Fragonard, *Spring*.

The *Antiques Roadshow* was one of the most popular programmes on television, watched by many millions. Might whoever had murdered Charlie Porteous have seen it? And if not, might someone close to the killer have?

He needed to find that couple and interview them. Both to establish how they had come by this painting – if they'd told the truth on the show – and even more importantly, if the painting was genuine, how to safeguard them? He would get on it first thing tomorrow.

As he arrived back home, letting himself and Humphrey in through the garden gate, their newly acquired arrogant cockerel, whom Cleo had nicknamed Billy Big Balls, crowed loudly.

'Go for it, Billy!' Grace said. 'But don't take me on, because I'm a far meaner son-of-a-bitch than you'll ever be!'

40

Monday, 21 October

After dropping Tom off at his friend's to walk to school, at 8.15 a.m., Freya groaned in frustration at the roadworks that were causing a long back-up of traffic to the route she would have taken to her own school, to avoid the worst of the rush hour traffic by cutting through the backroads of Patcham.

Instead she diverted, heading down Surrenden Crescent to the London Road, where she had to wait, increasingly impatiently, as the heavy commuter traffic into Brighton streamed past in stop-start fashion, with no one having the courtesy to give her a gap.

'Come on!' she shouted through the windscreen. 'Let me out, it's not going to delay your journey one bit!'

As she edged her little Fiat cautiously forward, staring challengingly at each oncoming driver, a vehicle appeared in her mirrors. A black Range Rover.

She froze.

Then she saw a bus had stopped, politely, for her. Waving a thank-you, she pulled out across the road, checked there was a good gap to her left, and turned right, accelerating away, hard. As did she, she saw the Range Rover had made the dash too and was right on her tail.

Who the hell are you?

Her nerves tightened. For some moments she debated whether to pull over, forcing it to pass her, and get its number as Harry had suggested. But they were now approaching the mini-roundabout at the bottom of Carden Avenue. A white van had already started across it, and she cheekily accelerated across its path, getting an angry blast of the horn from the vehicle, then headed on towards Patcham, white van man giving her several angry flashes and another blast of his horn before he turned off left.

The Range Rover immediately closed the gap between them, looming larger in her mirrors again. She tried to see who was driving it, but the interior was too dark. Someone in a cap was all she could make out. And she was now approaching a long, almost stationary queue of traffic to the big roundabout at the bottom of Mill Road. As she braked to a crawl, the Range Rover appeared to brake harder, as if deliberately creating a larger gap between them. She tried to read the number plate in her mirror, then, realizing everyone in front of her had stopped, stamped on the brake pedal, locking the wheels with a scream of tyres as she almost rear-ended a taxi ahead.

Jesus. Calm down.

She was shaking. Trying to think clearly. To get to her school she needed to turn right at the roundabout. If the car behind turned right also it would be a further indication it was following. She was almost tempted to climb out, walk up to it and ask whoever was in it what the hell they were doing. But of course they might not have been following her, and then she'd have looked stupid. And besides, the cars in front were moving again.

Finally, she reached the roundabout. As she exited, the Range Rover followed.

Another option was looming in a few hundred yards. Worthing, Lewes or to the direction of her school.

But she didn't want the driver of the Range Rover seeing where she worked. Instead, she drove onto the A27, heading uphill in the direction of the Sussex University campus and Lewes beyond, but she had a plan if the Range Rover still followed her.

Shit.

It did.

A mile ahead, she knew, there was a slip road left, leading to yet another roundabout. She took it.

So did the Range Rover.

Fuck you!

What was its game? she wondered. Trying to intimidate her? Was someone going to get out and confront her when she finally stopped? She glanced at her phone on the passenger seat beside her. Should she dial 999 and ask for the police?

And say what?

Um, there's a Range Rover that's been behind me for a while, I think it might be following me. I think it might have followed me before. But I'm not sure.

The call handler would ask her for its registration, which she didn't have.

She looked at the car clock. 8.42. She was due to take a Geography class at 9 a.m. She couldn't go on playing this game, she needed to lose this bastard and get to the school. As she reached the roundabout, thinking wildly, it occurred to her what to do. The safe place.

She swung around to the right, reached another roundabout and took the second left, down the hill, past the old Sussex Police CID HQ.

The Range Rover was still following.

And now she was certain. And glad of her plan. Reaching the bottom of the hill, she braked sharply without indicating, and swung, almost too fast, into the entrance of the ASDA car park.

The Range Rover followed.

The superstore opened early morning, and as she had hoped, the car park was already fairly busy at this hour. She made a loop around, passing the filling station and heading towards the store itself. The Range Rover continued to follow as if attached to her rear bumper by a leash. Then Freya saw a space close to the main entrance. *OK, Big Boy, showtime. Confront me here if you dare.*

She drove straight in, turned the engine off and climbed out of the car defiantly.

And stopped in her tracks.

The Range Rover had pulled into a bay a short distance along, in the row behind, rear door and tailgate both open. A pert yummy-mummy, in skinny jeans and bomber jacket, blonde hair scooped through the back of a jockey cap, was busy unfolding a stroller. Through the rear door, Freya could see a toddler, swathed in pink, in a baby seat.

41

Roy Grace, sipping a strong coffee, checked his watch, then, as if for back-up confirmation, checked the clock on the wall of the conference room. 9.01 a.m. He addressed Velvet Wilde and Norman Potting. 'The action I gave you yesterday to find and interview the couple with the Fragonard painting on *Antiques Roadshow*. Any luck?'

'Yes, sir,' Wilde said. 'We contacted the producer, Robert Murphy, who was understandably reluctant to give us the name of the couple. But when we explained the situation to him, and scanned and sent copies of our warrant cards, he was helpful and gave us their names, a Mr and Mrs Kipling. He's a builder and she's deputy head of Patcham High School. It wasn't then hard to find their address in Mackie Crescent, Patcham – very coincidentally the previous residence of a former Sussex officer, Steve Curry and his wife Tracey.'

Grace smiled.

'DS Potting and I visited Mrs Kipling late yesterday afternoon, sir,' Wilde said. 'She told us her husband was in London meeting with an auction house. At the time we spoke to her she'd not heard from her husband. She tried to call him while we were there but was unable to reach him. She left a message.'

'What time was that?' Grace asked.

She looked down at her notes. '5.35 p.m., sir.'

'Have either of you heard from her since?'

'No, sir.'

'What did she tell you about the painting?'

'She said her husband, Harry, had bought it in a car boot sale some weeks earlier, for twenty quid. At that time it was just a mediocre portrait of an old lady – which she hated. He told her he'd bought it because he liked the frame and thought they could put something else into it. When they took it home, they left it, unintentionally, exposed to the sunlight, because they'd pretty much forgotten about it – they buy a lot of bric-a-brac, it's one of their hobbies. Then they saw that some of the surface painting had melted away and there was something else beneath. Her husband rang an art expert he'd done some building work for, Daniel Hegarty, to ask for advice on how to clean off the surface painting—'

Potting interrupted, 'Daniel Hegarty is an old rogue! I nicked him years ago for forging vehicle logbooks.'

'He's come a long way since then, Norman,' Luke Stanstead said. 'He's now considered to be an accomplished artist.'

Grace frowned and made a note in his notebook. 'He's been on my radar, too, but I can't recall exactly when. Thanks, Luke.' He nodded to Wilde to continue.

'Freya – Mrs Kipling – told us that they'd heard *Antiques Roadshow* was coming to a venue in Sussex and they decided to take it there, to see if the painting beneath, which looked old to them, might be of any value.'

'Did you believe her?' Grace looked at both detectives in turn.

'Yes,' Wilde said.

Potting nodded. 'I did, chief. She's a nice lady, I didn't get any sense of criminal activity. She is what it says on the tin.'

'Best before?' Wilde quipped.

42

Shortly after 5 p.m., Archie Goff was as usual eating his evening meal perched on the toilet. Chicken tagliatelle – well, some chewy lumps of protein that might once have had some brief and horrible existence in a battery farm, interred beneath slimy tendrils of pasta – with steamed jam sponge and fast-congealing custard for dessert. The television was on in the background, and his cellmate, the Home Secretary, was in a gloomy mood, prodding his plastic fork around the vegetarian moussaka in his foil tray.

'You all right, mate?' Archie asked. 'You don't look too happy.'

'Not had the best of days. My wife's filing for divorce, and I met my brief earlier who didn't have good news. Reckons I'll be lucky if I get only ten years.'

'Shit. Bummer about the missus – you love her?'

He shrugged, raised a hand and wiggled it in the air. 'It's the kids. Hate the idea of being one of those dads that gets to see them once every four weeks or whatever shit it is.'

'Can't the Home Secretary pull any strings?'

He gave a wan smile. 'Very funny.'

At that moment, one of the duty officers on their wing, a broad-shouldered woman with short, spiky hair, appeared in their doorway. She wore the same deadpan expression as always, and whenever she spoke to any of the prisoners, her voice was neither pleasant nor unpleasant, but faintly, nobody-home, robotic. 'Mr Goff,' she said. 'You're being released on bail. You will be free to leave after 7 a.m. tomorrow. The possessions you had with you at the time of your arrest will be handed to you then.'

Archie Goff looked at her in shocked surprise. 'Beg pardon?'

'You didn't hear what I said?'

'Well, yeah, but like – I dunno anyone who has fifty K. That was my bail.'

'Must be a secret admirer then,' she said, her expression easing into a faint smile before she turned and walked off.

'You lucky bastard,' his cellmate said.

Archie frowned.

'Maybe your missus found the dough?'

Archie said nothing, thinking. He finished his food, then hurried out in search of a free phone to use. They were all occupied, but after a few minutes' wait, one of his fellow prisoners hung up and walked away. Using up a credit, he dialled Isabella.

No, she said, she hadn't come up with the money, but she was beyond delighted he would be home tomorrow.

He walked away from the booth, then leaned against a wall, thinking. Happy but worried. Most times in the past when he'd been arrested, he'd been released on police bail by the Magistrates' Court. But this time the beaks had referred him to the Crown Court. He understood why: it was because the last time he'd been inside, at Ford open prison, he'd absconded.

Fifty grand. That was big money. Big money for someone to put up to have him released. And other than Isabella, who the hell cared enough about him to put up that kind of money?

He tried to think, going back in his mind through his list of contacts. Who was wealthy enough to stump up that kind of money to get an old lag freed? But equally, and more importantly, why?

43

It was sunny at 9.30 a.m, as Archie Goff walked, less jauntily than he might ordinarily, out through the ancient dark red prison gates between the portcullis-like twin flint towers, and into freedom. Well, a kind of freedom anyway. He'd been informed that the conditions of his bail were that he signed on at Brighton police station three times a week between the hours of 10 a.m. and 1 p.m., and he was not to seek any form of international travel document. Yeah, like he was about to jump on a jet and large it in Jamaica, he thought.

Well clear of the prison's grim Victorian walls, he stopped and stood still, in his baggy jeans, Seagulls sweatshirt, lightweight bomber jacket and trainers. He rummaged in the carrier bag containing the meagre possessions he'd had with him when he'd been fished out of the swimming pool of the Frys' country mansion one long month ago. He strapped on his Seiko watch, the St Christopher's necklace Isabella had given him, which he slipped over his neck, and the copper bracelet for his arthritis. Next he retrieved his wallet containing his driving licence, Co-op credit card and £35 in cash, all of which had survived his immersion thanks to them being in a zipped plastic pouch.

Looking around warily at the line of parked cars and the handful of people who looked like they were waiting for other prisoners being released today, and with his well-honed skill, he single-handedly rolled himself a cigarette and lit it, inhaling gratefully. It tasted sweet and good. He'd been able to get a few inside but not many. At least he could now enjoy a smoke without fear of being caught and having privileges taken, having started the habit again while on remand.

There didn't appear to be anyone waiting for him. Isabella had told him last night that much though she would have loved to have met him, she had a meeting in Cambridge today, but was preparing a special welcome-home meal of his favourite food. Something to look forward to, but he looked forward even more to holding her in his arms. He shrugged. Fine, it was a sunny morning, he'd enjoy the walk through Lewes, catch a train the short distance to Brighton, and then bus home.

But just as he set off down the long, sloping driveway, past the line of parked cars, an elderly, large maroon Jaguar saloon, badly in need of a respray, drove in and flashed its twin headlights at him, then pulled up a short distance ahead.

As he walked up to the car, frowning, wondering if this was the guardian angel who'd stumped up the bail security, he immediately recognized the man behind the wheel. The mop of grey, curly hair, the bulbous, drinker's nose, the ruddy, veined face, wearing an open-neck checked shirt and a paisley cravat. Leaning across the passenger seat, Ricky Sharp pushed open the door.

Archie lowered himself in and down onto the worn leather seat, placing his carrier bag between his knees, pulled the door shut and fumbled with his seat belt, finally clicking it home. The interior of the car smelled musty, as if it had been parked in a dank garage or barn for years. Part of the dashboard wood veneer was peeling away, and the panel of the passenger door had come unstuck, as had some of the roof lining.

'This is a surprise to see you, Ricky,' he said. 'I was expecting a limo.'

'Yeah? Well this is a long-wheelbase – prefer to sit in the back?'

'Nah, I'm fine.'

Ricky Sharp looked even older and more flaccid and booze-sodden close up than he remembered. 'Good to see you too, matey boy. They upgrade you to a nice room in there? A suite, with a sea view and Jacuzzi? Stamp your loyalty card? They oughta look after their regular guests properly, right – know what I'm saying?'

'Yeah, well they could start by putting a seat on the toilets. Make it a nicer dining experience. How you doing?'

'All right, I've gone legit – used cars now.'

Archie eyed the tatty interior of the Jaguar. 'Good luck with that one.'

Sharp began turning the car round, spinning the thin steering wheel with meaty, liver-spotted hands, his fingers bedecked with large rings. 'Like her? Could do you a good price – you know, mates' rates?'

'Fuck off. This shitbox?'

'It's a classic.'

'Right. So what's going on, Ricky? Was it you put up the money for my release?'

Sharp shook his head. 'No disrespect, Archie, but if I had that type of money I'd never bet it on you. I'm just the messenger, right?'

'Messenger for who?'

They were heading downhill, towards the large roundabout that would take them onto the A27. Archie could feel the vibrations of wheel-wobble, and hear the creak of a worn bearing and an ominous rumble from the transmission as they made the turn.

'Not enough sawdust in the diff, Ricky?'

'Funny.' They passed the Amex Stadium on their left and the campus of Sussex University on their right. Every few moments the gear shift popped out of drive into neutral and Sharp shoved it back brutally. 'I'll let him do the introductions and explaining, Archie – as I said, I'm just the messenger.'

'Let who?' Archie could smell burning oil. 'This shitbox actually going to get us anywhere?'

'Hey, pal, ever heard of gratitude?' Ricky Sharp said, looking hurt. 'Know what the old ads for big Jaguars used to say? *Grace, Space and Pace.*'

'And your point is?'

'You're in a piece of motoring history – you philistine! Enjoy the ride and maybe say thanks.'

'I'll say thanks when I know what's going on and decide if I like it.'

'You'll like it. That I have no doubt about.'

Archie gave him a sideways look. 'And I'll tell you what I have no doubt about. Want to hear it?'

'Go for it.'

'That whoever put up my bail has given you a big bung. And you're going to walk away with a wallet full of cash and I'm going to be left negotiating with the Devil.'

'Maybe, Archie, but just remember, dunno who said it, but *sometimes, the Devil is a gentleman.*'

44

Thursday, 24 October

Twenty minutes later, they were heading along Brighton seafront. The tide was out, with a vast expanse of sand flats before the slack, calm blue sea. It would be a good morning for digging up lugworm bait, Archie thought, before taking his little boat out, the one he kept beached at the Hove Deep Sea Anglers, to catch some plaice, and if he was lucky, a Dover sole. Maybe he'd do just that later on.

Ricky Sharp swung the Jaguar into the curved driveway of the Grand and pulled up outside the main entrance. A liveried doorman stepped forward and opened Archie's door. 'Welcome to the Grand Hotel, gentlemen. Do you need help with your bags?'

'Just dropping off,' Sharp said, getting out. 'This gentleman's meeting someone inside for a coffee. I'll just make the introduction, then I'll hang around out here.'

As Archie climbed out with his bag, the doorman did a sterling job of masking his frown at his shabby clothes and the carrier bag. Ricky greased his palm with a banknote clearly sufficiently large for the doorman to tell him to leave the car where it was and he would keep an eye on it.

They stepped out of the mid-morning sun and through the revolving doors into the air-conditioned cool of the lobby, Sharp leading the way past the front desk, through the lounge to the left and into a sunny, narrow conservatory with a fine view across the road to the sea. There were tables all along but only two were occupied. One by a young couple drinking what looked like Buck's Fizz, even though it was only just gone 10.15 a.m., and another by someone who looked, even though he might be the Devil, every inch a gentleman.

In his seventies, with elegantly coiffed white hair, he was immaculately attired in a lightweight navy suit, cream shirt and blue-and-white-spotted bow tie, with a matching handkerchief protruding with a neat flourish from his breast pocket. He sat with perfect-upright posture, at a corner table, a pot of coffee and a half-drunk cup in front of him, together with a large brown envelope and a small leather bag, reading a copy of *The Times*. As he saw the two men approaching, he stood up, head very slightly bowed in deference.

'Robert Kilgore,' Ricky Sharp said. 'This is Archie Goff.'

Kilgore extended a manicured hand, bearing a Wedgwood signet ring, to Archie. He smelled like he'd recently been outside for a smoke. 'I'm mighty pleased and, if I may say, honoured, to make your acquaintance, Mr Goff. It's good of you to make the time to come along.' His voice was a slow, Deep South drawl, warm and courteous and, Archie thought, almost genuine in the sentiments.

He shook the man's firm hand. 'Nice to meet you, too, Mr Kilgore.'

'Please take a seat. Let me order you coffee. Have you had breakfast? I can get you a menu – they do a mean Eggs Benedict which I can recommend.'

Archie had no idea what that was, but he was hungry. 'Sounds good.'

Ricky Sharp smiled. 'I'll leave you two to chat – I'll be outside, Archie, when you're ready for a ride home in the *limo*.' He walked away before Archie could acknowledge it.

Kilgore signalled for a server, ordered for Archie, asking him to add a fresh orange juice and coffee, then smiled at Archie. 'Mr Goff, I'm guessing you are wondering right now just what is going on, would I be correct?' He had a protruding Adam's apple that bobbed up and down his scrawny turkey neck as he spoke.

Archie, acutely aware he was feeling very out of place, attired as he was, in this smart room, replied, 'You wouldn't be too wide of the mark, no.'

Kilgore took a delicate sip of his coffee, folded his arms and leaned forward a little. 'Well, allow me to give you a little background as to where the bail money came from. I'm an authority in French old master paintings. You know the term, *old masters*?'

Archie shook his head.

'I know you are just out of a certain – ah – establishment, and I'm guessing you are eager to get on home so I won't bore you with a lecture on art history. The gentleman I work for – and let me tell you, this is one hell of a gentleman – is a connoisseur of fine paintings and he has one of the finest private collections in the nation of French old masters. Have you ever heard of a French artist called Fragonard?'

Again, Archie shook his head.

Kilgore picked up the envelope and removed from it a photograph of a painting that appeared to have been taken from an image on a television screen. It was indistinct, poor quality. As he studied it, Archie could see it was two young lovers picnicking in the sunshine against a backdrop of a lake and winged statue to their left.

'Jean-Honoré Fragonard, like many artists before and after him, made a series of paintings of the four seasons. Spring, summer, autumn, winter. If I tell you that at the last auction of a single Fragonard painting it went for over two million pounds, and the world record is over seventeen million pounds, it might start to explain my employer's interest in this particular painting. It was on a television programme last Sunday, the *Antiques*

Roadshow. This painting is in the possession of a couple in Brighton. What my boss needs is a better photograph of this.'

Archie frowned. 'A better photograph?'

'Let me explain. My employer has dedicated his life to discovering, and returning to their rightful owners, great works of art that have been stolen – looted – over the centuries during times of turbulence – most recently during the Nazi era, both from Jewish families in Austria, Germany and Poland as well as during the German occupation of France. But of course it is a delicate task, and the key to any great piece of art is establishing its provenance.' Kilgore flashed a smile, revealing nicotine-stained teeth, and Archie noticed the ochre staining around some of the man's fingers.

'And your employer has put up my bail of fifty thousand quid because he would like me to take a better photograph of this painting?'

Kilgore scratched the back of his head evasively. 'That's pretty much it, yes. My employer knows the location of three of these paintings, *Spring, Autumn* and *Winter.* The one missing to make the series complete is *Summer* and he believes this might just be that painting.'

'Where is it now?'

Kilgore smiled again. 'Well, this is where you are going to earn your money. Our understanding is that you have a reputation as someone who knows how to enter a house, regardless of the alarm systems it may have, that is correct, sir?'

Archie looked back at him, thinking hard for some moments before he responded. 'I have my methods.'

'You worked as an apprentice then a master locksmith for some years, I believe?'

'Correct,' Archie said reluctantly.

'Then more recently, after one of your – shall we say politely – regular residences in the establishment you have just left, you enrolled as a mature student in a City and Guilds electrician course, focusing on burglar alarm systems.'

Archie waited while his coffee and orange juice were served, then lowered his head and said, irritably, 'You've done your research. Want me to give you a prize? Go ahead, choose from the middle shelf – a fluffy duck or a pink sheep or a goldfish in a bowl?'

Kilgore smiled, but this time it was a less friendly one, his teeth looking more piranha than gentleman. More *Devil*. And his tone matched. 'Mr Goff, my employer did not put up this generous sum of money for your release in order to play games. He will expect value for his money, so can we stop right now the idea this is in any way – excuse my language – a pissing contest?'

Archie bristled. 'Perhaps you could tell me your employer's name?'

'That is not something, for now, you need to know. If you are not happy with our terms, your chauffeur outside will return you to prison, my employer will withdraw his security and that will be the end of it. The choice is entirely yours. Are you in or out?'

'Not much of a choice, is it?' Archie said resentfully.

'I would say, given your past form, it's a better choice than you deserve, sir,' Kilgore said, his tone becoming increasingly cold and hard.

Archie weighed the options in his mind. He could just walk out of this room and head home. But the menace in Kilgore's tone suggested that would not lead to a good outcome. And he wanted, very badly, to spend some time free with Isabella, before his inevitable prison sentence when he was convicted. He shrugged. 'OK,' he said. 'What exactly do I have to do?'

Kilgore leaned forward, picked up the brown envelope and removed from it some more photographs, which he laid out on the table, glancing a wary eye to ensure the server wasn't returning. 'Please take a look at these, Mr Goff.'

Archie picked up the first one. It was a photograph of a street he recognized immediately, lined on one side with similar-looking houses and bungalows. None of the properties were exactly grand, but Archie knew the street and knew they were all middle class and desirable.

'Recognize where this is, Mr Goff?'

He nodded. He'd burgled several of these houses earlier in his career before he'd made a speciality in the rich pickings of grander country houses. 'Yeah, Patcham.'

Kilgore looked pleased. 'I understand from the research my employer has carried out that one of your first prison sentences was for breaking and entering in one of these houses, some thirty years ago?'

Archie stiffened. 'How do you know that?'

'I can assure you, Mr Goff, my employer did not get where he is today through poor research. He chose you because he believes you are the best person for this task. Please take a look at the next photograph.'

Archie lifted it up and it was a close-up of one of the houses. A Volvo estate and a Fiat 500 were parked in the driveway alongside a van. The corner property looked less well kept than most in this street.

'How difficult would it be for you to gain access to this house, Mr Goff?' Kilgore asked.

'If your employer has done the kind of research you say he does, then I'm guessing he knows what security systems are installed, right?'

'Oh yes. In the past three days extra security locks have been fitted to all doors and windows. A fake burglar alarm box has been installed. Additionally, a CCTV camera has been fitted.'

'Urban properties aren't my thing these days, Mr Kilgore. But I'm sure this one is possible.'

'Well, I'm glad to hear that.' Kilgore picked up the small leather bag on the table and handed it to Archie. 'This contains a high-definition camera. I'm now going to instruct you on exactly the photographs my employer requires you to take of the Fragonard painting in this house. And anything else you can find that might tell us stuff of interest about the Kipling family, like financial documents – bank statements, things like that.'

'And that's all?' Archie asked, almost incredulous. 'You really just want me to take photographs? Not steal anything?'

The piranha teeth appeared again between Kilgore's thin lips. 'For stage one, yes.' Then he patted the pockets of his jacket, momentarily looking more anxious than confident Devil. 'What do you say about stepping outside for a quick smoke before your breakfast arrives?'

45

A note in Norman Potting's diary told him that Stuart Piper had been scheduled to return from his second home in Barbados a few days ago.

The DS had originally planned to pounce on him on his first day back, hitting him hopefully at a disadvantage when he would be jet-lagged and not thinking as sharply as he might otherwise. But a series of medical tests on Potting's suspected throat cancer had intervened and this was now his first opportunity. He was driving the unmarked Ford Focus along a narrow country lane accompanied by Velvet Wilde.

'How's it going?' he asked her.

'Going? With what?' she asked spikily, in her Belfast accent. Although they'd been buddied-up several times recently, she'd still not warmed to the ageing, totally non-politically correct detective.

'Your partner's pregnancy. The IVF?'

'Just had another failure,' she responded gloomily. 'How did your medical tests go?' She looked at the moving arrow on the satnav. 'We're close now,' she added.

'It's looking good. As I said to the boss, it may be just a polyp which the quack says could be removed easily, but I need some more scans and stuff.'

'That's good,' she said. 'That it might just be a polyp.'

'Hopefully.' He paused then said, 'Look, don't take this the wrong way, but if you need a donor, I'd always be up for it. You know, just to help out a colleague.'

For a moment she was floored, but not by his generosity. 'Well, yep, thanks, Norman, but that won't be necessary.' She restrained herself from adding, *not if you were the last man on earth.*

Then she said, 'Coming up on our left!'

They drove alongside a tall, imposing and clearly very old stone wall, topped with spiked defences, for several hundred yards, before they reached what looked like it must be the main entrance. A pair of closed wrought-iron gates set between pillars topped with stone balls, with a lodge just inside. A discreet sign, gold lettering on a black background, read BEWLAY PARK. Two CCTV cameras, perched like birds alongside the balls, looked down at them, and there was a phone panel inset on the right-hand pillar, with another camera.

Potting lowered his window, reached out his arm and pressed the button with a bell symbol. Almost instantly, a stern voice with a heavy London accent said a curt, 'Identify yourself.'

'Police,' Potting replied. 'We would like to speak to Mr Piper.'

'You have no appointment,' came the blunt reply.

'Correct but we would like a few minutes of Mr Piper's time.'

'For what purpose? Mr Piper doesn't see visitors without an appointment.'

'It is in connection with a murder enquiry we are conducting. If this isn't a convenient moment for Mr Piper, then we can make an appointment for him to come in and talk to us at Sussex Police Headquarters in Lewes,' Potting said. 'If that doesn't suit him we can return with a search warrant.'

A moment's silence, then, 'Wait please.'

Velvet Wilde looked at Potting and, her voice lowered, asked, 'A search warrant? Would we get one for this?'

'Probably not.' He grinned, lowering his voice too. 'But whoever that wanker is doesn't know that.'

'You're terrible!' she said.

He shook his head. 'After you've been doing this job as long as I have, you'll learn.'

She thumped him playfully. 'Always keen to share your wisdom, aren't you?'

'I'm taking that as a compliment.'

After a few minutes, during which the two detectives became increasingly convinced they'd been cut off, the gates suddenly began opening, and the same voice came back through the speaker. 'Hold up your warrant cards.'

Potting held his up to the panel's camera. 'Detective Sergeant Potting,' he said. Then he took Wilde's and showed that, too. 'And Detective Constable Wilde, both from the Surrey and Sussex Major Crime Team.'

There was an abrupt, 'Mr Piper will see you now for fifteen minutes.'

'Very gracious of him,' Potting responded, and without waiting for a reply, drove on through.

They headed, for a good quarter of a mile, along a straight avenue lined on both sides with tall trees, until a huge, elegant, Tudor mansion appeared ahead. Beyond were acres of immaculately mown lawn, and a lake with what looked like Grecian statues on an island in the middle.

Velvet Wilde murmured, 'Where did it all go wrong for poor Mr Piper?'

Potting nodded. 'Yeah, my heart's bleeding for him having to live in this shithole.'

'Mine too.'

'I mean, why would anyone want to live here, with all the bills, when they could be in a nice council flat in Brighton, with everything paid for and drug dealers on the floor above and below?'

193

'Beats me.'

A moment later Potting's tone changed abruptly as he nodded at the rear-view mirror. 'Hello, we've got an escort.'

Wilde glanced in her wing mirror and saw, just a short distance behind them, the menacing grille of a black Mercedes G Wagon. 'Thoughtful of them to provide security for us,' she said.

Potting carried on, pulling up outside the portico, and switched off the engine. The Mercedes had stopped, effectively blocking the exit to the driveway, as if signalling they could forget thinking about making a run for it if they weren't who they said they were.

Turning to Wilde, he said, 'If you lived with your partner in a pad like this, would you want to have all this security stuff?'

'I think I would,' she replied. 'Because if I'd made the kind of money that could buy this place, I'm unlikely to have made it honestly. So I'd always be looking over my shoulder.'

Potting smiled. 'My thoughts exactly.'

46

The two detectives walked up the steps to the grand, white front door, noticing the pair of CCTV cameras on either side of it. Before they'd even reached the door it swung open and a surly man, the height and width of a double fridge, filled most of the space inside the frame.

He was dressed all in black, with a mandarin-collared suit jacket, wet-look black hair and a coiled earpiece. It sometimes seemed to Norman Potting that there was a secret organization that cloned door heavies. All these types looked the same and dressed the same. And all had attended the same charm school.

'Your ID?' he asked in a way that particularly annoyed Potting.

The detectives displayed their warrant cards and received just the faintest reluctant nod in response. Both of them noticed, standing a few yards behind him, another security guard who must be his identical twin, both of them wearing gold bracelets and rings.

'Mr Piper will see you for fifteen minutes. Exactly and no more,' he said.

Potting moved confrontationally up to the guard until they were just inches apart and retorted, jabbing a finger at him, 'Mr Piper will see us for however long *we* decide, not you or him. Understood?'

The man spun on his booted heels without replying and led them along a corridor hung on both sides with, even to Norman

Potting's untrained eye, clearly old and fine paintings. Velvet Wilde trailed behind, looking enraptured at them, aware of the footsteps of the man's twin close behind her. 'This is incredible!' she said when she caught up with Potting. Then for his ears only she added, 'When I went to that art expert's house, George Astone, last month, I thought I'd seen something amazing, but it's got nothing on this. I'm not an expert but I do know a little bit about art, and there is serious stuff here.'

Their escort stopped in front of a pair of oak-panelled double doors, rapped then swung round to face the detectives, giving Potting a particularly hostile look. 'Enter please.' He opened the doors.

There were offices and there were offices, Potting thought. And the room he now entered eclipsed pretty much any he had ever seen. It was a simply vast gallery beneath a domed stuccoed ceiling. The walls were lined with large, magnificent ancestral-style portraits of men in military uniforms, and there was a railed minstrels' gallery running all the way around the room, with further paintings above that.

In the centre of the room was an enormous antique desk on a circular Persian rug. Potting recognized the man seated at it from having googled him earlier, and his uncanny resemblance to Clive Owen was even stronger in the flesh. A Dalmatian sat each side of the desk, both dogs so motionless Potting thought at first they must be statues, until getting closer he saw they were moving, their eyes watching him. The room smelled of old, polished wood and a faintly musky aroma that he guessed came from the two diffusers on the desk.

Piper's mouth extended into the hint of a smile, but the rest of his face did not move. 'Officers,' he said. 'How may I be of assistance?' His voice was sharp, bordering on acidic, and he made no attempt to stand up. His grey eyes held a toxic gaze.

Both Potting and Wilde were disconcerted by the complete

lack of movement of his facial muscles. And there was something else about his face, which neither of them could immediately put a finger on, that was equally disturbing. As Piper's lips formed the words, it felt to Potting almost like he was looking at a hologram rather than an actual human being.

'We appreciate you are a busy man,' the DS said. 'We would just like to ask you a few questions. I'm Detective Sergeant Potting and my colleague is Detective Constable Wilde from Surrey and Sussex Major Crime Team.'

Piper raised an arm and indicated to the two tall-backed chairs in front of the desk. 'Have a seat. Can I offer you tea or coffee? Or would that involve you in hours of paperwork afterwards, since you people are not permitted to accept gifts?' It was impossible to tell whether he was being humorous or not.

They shook their heads. 'We are fine, thank you,' Potting said as they sat down, noting the vast surface of the desk was almost completely bare, apart from the computer monitor and the diffusers. 'Actually we don't have to declare gifts of a value less than twenty-five pounds. Or is your coffee very special?'

There was no reaction from Piper. Potting glanced at his tablet. 'Does the name Charlie – Charles – Porteous mean anything to you, Mr Piper?'

'May I ask why it should?' he replied, again the only facial movement being his lips.

'Mr Porteous was a highly respected art dealer,' Potting said. 'As you may perhaps remember from the news, he was murdered in October 2015.'

'I don't recall. I am usually abroad in October, through to the spring.' He touched his face. 'The damp English winter isn't kind to my skin, but I've had to return on business.'

'Did you ever have dealings with Mr Porteous?' Wilde asked.

Piper replied, impassively, 'The art world is a large place, with a great many dealers. I personally only do business with a very small number of them, those who I trust implicitly.'

'Would that mean that Charlie Porteous was a dealer you did not trust?' Potting pressed.

Piper stared back at him levelly. 'Why should it?'

Potting shrugged, a little thrown by the reply. 'Did you ever have any social interaction with Mr Porteous?'

'No.'

Potting waited for Piper to say something more but he didn't. 'Do you remember anything about his murder? Did any associates of yours in the art world talk about it, or perhaps speculate who might have killed him and why?'

'No.'

Piper stared at both of them hard, with his weird, cold eyes. For some moments he drummed a rat-a-tat-tat beat on the top of his desk with his manicured nails, then he opened his arms expansively and pointed at some of the pictures around the walls, before zeroing in on one. 'Recognize this person?'

It was a head and shoulders portrait of an arrogant-looking man, with hair that looked too young for his aged face, and dressed in a red tunic with gold braid. The background was dark and sombre.

Potting and Wilde shook their heads.

'It is one of three portraits of General Arthur Wellesley, first Duke of Wellington, painted by the Spanish artist Francisco Goya in 1812. It was stolen from our National Gallery in 1961 by a bus driver called Kempton Bunton and not returned for four years. He claimed to have taken it as a protest against the introduction by the BBC of licence fees. But there has been speculation ever since whether this was his real motive – and whether during that time one or more perfect copies were made of this painting.'

'What are you saying?' Velvet Wilde asked. 'That is a copy?'

'No, I'm not. It might be, or it might be the original. Sometimes with clever forgers it is impossible to tell. But this is not my point – I appreciate this painting for the beautiful work it is regardless of provenance. I love the history it represents.' He fell silent for a moment then continued. 'I see you both looking at my disfigured face. Maybe you are wondering what happened, but as you are detectives, I will credit you that you already know. Yes?'

He waited. They both nodded.

'What happen to me changed my life and my thinking. The Danish philosopher Søren Kierkegaard said that life must be lived forwards, but it can only be understood backwards. From that moment when I began to recover from my assault, I turned to the past to try to understand. I have little interest in current news, the past is where I live my life.' He raised his arms and pointed around the room. 'These great people and the past great artists who preserved them for us so we can still see them today. This is the world I consider my manor, not the twentieth or twenty-first century.'

'Well, I'm sorry to have to bring intrusive twenty-first-century technology into your world, Mr Piper,' Potting said. 'But the reason we are here is that one of the persons we believe murdered Charlie Porteous had your number on his phone and we need to know why. Can you explain that?'

Piper stared coldly back at both of them for a few moments, then simply said, 'No, I cannot.'

'And you definitely never had any business dealings or social interaction with the late Charles Porteous?'

'What part of the word *no* don't you understand?' Piper's body language was impatient. 'Who is this person who has or had my number in his phone contacts list?'

'We don't know that,' Wilde said. 'We were hoping you might be able to help us identify him.'

He looked at her sharply. 'Your accent – you're from Belfast?' he questioned, abruptly changing the subject.

'I am. Have you been there?' she smiled, attempting to soften him a little.

'My brother was there, in the army, during the Troubles. He was blown up by a parcel bomb, lost both his eyes and both his arms.'

There was an awkward moment of silence. 'I'm very sorry to hear that,' she said. 'It was a bad time.'

Piper did not respond and sat drumming on the desk surface again. 'Is there anything else I can help you officers with?' he asked, finally.

'Does the eighteenth-century French artist Jean-Honoré Fragonard mean anything to you, Mr Piper?' Potting asked.

Piper gave him a withering look. 'Is the Pope Catholic? Is Luxembourg small?' He stared at them in silence.

'You'll have to forgive me, I'm not an expert on art.'

'Clearly.'

'Do you have any of Fragonard's works in your collection?' Potting continued.

Both detectives noticed the minutest hesitation before Piper replied. 'That would be a dream for any art collector, Detective Sergeant Potter.'

Potting stood, not bothering to correct him, and Wilde followed his cue. 'We won't take up any more of your time, Mr Piper. Thank you.'

Piper said nothing, he just gave a faint nod of his head in acknowledgement.

The doors opened behind them.

47

Sunday, 27 October

The taxi dropped Harry and Freya Kipling at their house. Harry was always extra generous when he'd had a few drinks, and tonight he'd had more than a few at the dinner party at their friends, Jim and Katie Morgan. He pressed a £20 note into the palm of the driver, on top of the fare.

'Are you sure?' he said.

'We've had a good week!' Harry said, slurring his words, ignoring his wife's disapproving stare.

'Very generous of you, gov.'

As they walked up to the front door in the mild night air, Freya, who'd drunk only marginally less, held on to his arm in case he stumbled. 'Shit,' Harry slurred. 'That the time?' He glanced at his watch. It was a quarter to two.

She smiled. 'I did suggest we left a good hour and a half ago.'

'Yeah, but that Armagnac – that was so good.'

'Hope it still feels that good at eight o'clock in the morning – when you go off to play golf.'

'Hmm,' he murmured, fishing in his pocket for the front door key. He got it in the slot and pushed the door open. As he did so, Jinx shot out past them.

'Hey, boy!' Freya called out to him, concerned. He never normally went out the front.

Harry tripped on the doorstep and would have fallen flat on his face if she hadn't been holding on to him.

'Darling, was that a twenty-quid tip you gave the driver?'

'Was it? I meant to give him a fiver.'

She looked at him, grinning. 'You are totally sloshed.'

'What the hell, we're rich! Pay it forward! Brighton cabbies have been struggling ever since they let Uber into the city. We can afford to be generous to them.'

'Not yet,' she said. 'We still don't know if what we have is real.'

'Trust me,' he replied. 'It is. Think I'll just have a quick nightcap.'

'Darling, don't you think you've had enough? And keep your voice down, you'll wake Tom.'

'Wake him? He *sleeps* with bloody headphones on! I dunno how, but he does!' He staggered through into the living room, went over to the drinks cabinet, picked up a brandy snifter and poured himself a generous slug of cognac.

'I'm going to get Jinx back in,' she called out.

'Yesh, sure.' He sat down on a sofa, more sharply than he had intended, spilling some of the brandy into his lap. Then he heard Freya calling out, 'Jinx! Jinx!' Then after a few moments the tone of her voice changed. 'Good boy! Very good boy!' He heard the sound of the front door closing and she said, 'Biscuits? Like some biscuits?'

He looked up at the painting on the wall and smiled. Raised his glass towards the courting couple. 'Your health!' he said. 'Your very good health indeed, eh?' He winked at them and took a large sip of his drink.

Then Freya screamed. 'Harry! Jesus, Harry!'

He put his glass down on the coffee table and jumped up, wobbling for some moments, then made his way through to the kitchen, fending off the walls and door frames on the way. Freya was standing in the conservatory, her face sheet white, pointing at the back door and looking in total shock.

For a moment he couldn't see the reason for her concern. But then, moving closer, holding onto the worktops to keep his balance, he entered the conservatory and saw it, too.

The glass door, leading from the conservatory into the garden. One of the panels was broken, with shards of glass lying on the floor. Despite his inebriation, he felt a cold flush in the pit of his stomach.

'The door's unlocked,' she said. 'Has Tom left it open or has someone been in here?' Then, lowering her voice, she said, 'They might still be in here.' Her eyes darted in panic. 'Tom?' She raced to the stairs.

Harry looked around for a weapon. His golf clubs? But they were in the garage. He grabbed a carving knife from the block and brandished it, stumbling up the stairs after her, then lurching along the landing. Freya opened Tom's door and switched on the light. To her relief he was there, headphones on as Harry had said. He blinked at them in confusion.

'Are you OK, darling?' she asked.

Tom lifted away the headphones and replied sleepily, 'What's – what?'

'A window's been broken. Did you hear anything, darling? Anyone downstairs?' Stupid question she knew. He never heard anything.

Tom frowned. 'I dunno. Like what? I didn't break the window.'

'Go back to sleep, darling,' she said, backing out of the room, switching off the light and closing the door.

Harry was opening the spare room door.

'Be careful!' she urged. Speaking quietly, she said, 'We need to call the police.'

'Jinx might have broken it,' he said.

'And unlocked the door?'

'Are you sure it was locked?'

She looked at him. 'We double checked all the windows and doors.' She lifted the landline phone from its cradle and dialled.

48

Sunday, 27 October

Twenty anxious minutes later, during which Harry had downed a double espresso while standing near the foot of the stairs still brandishing the carving knife, they heard a car pull up outside, and saw blue flashing lights through the glass panels at the top of the front door.

Two officers came into the house, a tall, burly man who introduced himself as PC Alldridge and a shorter police officer whose warrant card showed PC Dave Simmons. Freya explained they'd recently been in a broadcast of the *Antiques Roadshow*, at which they'd shown a painting that might possibly be of very high value.

'Has that been taken?' Simmons asked.

'No.'

'Is anything missing?'

'We've not had a good look around, but if someone was going to break in that's what they would most likely have been after.' She led them through into the lounge and pointed the painting out to them.

Over the next fifteen minutes the two police officers made a thorough search of the house, opening all wardrobe and cupboard doors, as well as checking the loft, then the garden, the shed and the greenhouse.

Back inside the house, PC Alldridge said, 'You have a CCTV camera at the property. Is it active?'

'It is,' Freya said. 'But it's pretty basic – we'd have to take the card out and look through it on a computer.'

Alldridge nodded. 'That will take you a little time. I think we've established there isn't any intruder present in your house now – are you both comfortable with that?'

'We are, thank you, officers,' Harry said, glancing at his wife for confirmation.

'And you've not been able to establish that anything is missing?'

'Not that we are able to tell so far,' Freya said.

PC Simmons was looking puzzled. 'It's possible you might have surprised the intruder by arriving home unexpectedly.'

'At a quarter to two in the morning?' Freya replied sharply.

Simmons looked nonplussed. 'Perhaps you should do a careful check on all your possessions to make sure nothing is missing – any watches, jewellery, anything like that.'

He gave them his card. 'When you've checked, if you find any valuables have been taken, get in touch immediately.'

They thanked the officers and saw them out into the night.

49

Monday, 28 October

Daniel Hegarty's dad, Len, had been a small-time career criminal, who had missed his true vocation. That had been a real talent for drawing wildlife in his spare time, and, spending over half of his adult life in and out of prison, he'd found himself with plenty of spare time on his hands. The art forger's fondest childhood memories had been the times he'd gone fishing with his dad, sitting on the banks of the river Arun, keeping an eye on the bobbing float while his dad worked away on his easel.

His dad had committed burglaries when Daniel was growing up. From when Daniel was ten, Len Hegarty had taken him out with him, sending him climbing in through tiny windows to open up bigger ones or doors. But, Daniel rued, the old sod never gave him a cut of anything he had stolen. By the time he reached seventeen, his dad had graduated to bank and post-office robbery, and, two months after getting nicked for the last time, he'd dropped dead of an aneurism in prison, leaving Daniel to care for his mother and three younger siblings.

All he had inherited from the old bugger was an eye for the main chance, and a talent for drawing. His last school report had damned his consistent lack of attendance with the faint praise that if he could ever bother to apply himself, he could have a future as a graphic designer.

And that chance presented itself two years later, when Daniel had been on a fishing holiday in Ireland with a couple of mates and was returning on the car ferry from Dublin to England. Going through customs, he'd overheard two Border Control officers talking to each other, saying how hard it was to identify faked Irish vehicle logbooks.

Hegarty set up a studio in his little bedroom in their council house and created a lucrative business forging logbooks, making enough money over the next year to buy his mum a small house on the outskirts of the city, which he paid for in cash.

His bigger chance came in the form of the looming handover of Hong Kong, when the British Government were due to cede it to China on 1 July 1997, after 156 years of British rule. Many of its citizens were desperate to leave and flee to the United Kingdom and there was a rush for British passports. Hegarty realized there was a potential goldmine for him and set about exploiting it.

He began producing, initially in small batches, seemingly very accomplished passport forgeries – and soon had a queue of Chinese customers lined up. Within three months, charging £1,000 a pop, he'd made enough to buy a period terraced property in the centre of Brighton, close to the Clock Tower, where he set up a full-scale mini-factory, employing a printer, a binder and a salesman. He began literally minting money.

But unfortunately for Hegarty, his printer was lousy at spelling. On the inside front cover of every British passport is the wording, *Her Britannic Majesty's Secretary of State requests and requires in the Name of Her Majesty all those whom it may concern to allow the bearer to pass freely without let or hindrance, and to afford the bearer such assistance and protection as may be necessary.*

The printer managed to make two spelling errors in his otherwise impeccable forgeries, by having just one 'N' in Britannic and replacing the 'J' in Majesty with a 'G'. Despite the crass mistakes, it took over a year for it to come to the attention of the police, during which time Daniel Hegarty had made so much money he'd put down a £300,000 deposit on a small castle in

Scotland, intending it as his bolthole should the balloon go up. But he never got the chance to flee. One morning, while the team in his handsome period house were flat-out printing, binding and dispatching passports, the front door was kicked open and five police officers burst into the premises, bringing his dream to an abrupt halt.

During the ensuing five years he served at Her Majesty's Pleasure – or Magesty, as spelled on his passports – he learned to paint, and discovered he had a real talent for copying the works of almost any artist.

Immediately on his release from prison, Hegarty began another lucrative career, forging the works of big-name artists and selling them for big money on eBay, until, following complaints, eBay took him down. Undeterred, he continued making copies of the work of these artists but now signed them with his own distinctive interlinked DH. Rather than his business falling off, it grew even larger, his clientele, as befitted his celebrity status, including rock stars, DJs, actors, authors and even politicians. Galleries in both Brighton and London eagerly offered him permanent space to show his work.

In addition he was in demand by serious art collectors unable or unwilling to pay the escalating insurance premiums on their works, to make copies which could still be displayed in their homes, while the originals remained secure in bank vaults.

Which was why Daniel Hegarty was totally unfazed by the photographs of the front and rear of the painting he was now looking at, early on this glorious October Monday morning. Two lovers in a forest of sun-dappled trees, with a lake behind them, and a plinth close to them on which sat a winged figure. He was already familiar with this painting and had some difficulty concealing a smile.

The man who had brought them to his Saltdean home was Robert Kilgore, for whom he had done a number of previous commissions copying old masters.

'Yeah, Robert,' Hegarty said. 'No problem. How long can you give me?'

'How long do you need, Mr Hegarty?' Kilgore asked him politely.

They were seated in the large open-plan living room, the walls lined with Hegarty's paintings ranging from Norman Rockwell to Caravaggio, and there was a smell of oil paint in the air.

The artist wore his years well; with an elegant head of gelled, spiky silver hair, he exuded the aura of a fit man comfortable in his skin, and had an easy demeanour to go with it, as well as his charming and confident wife, Natalie, who sat in the room with them.

'Well, Robert,' he said, staring at the highly detailed photographs, 'that would depend as usual on how far you went and how much you want to pay. If you want a pukka job that would stand up to every forensic test, that will cost you more. I'd use an old French religious canvas – I've a mate in France who's an antiques dealer and sources them for me – that would be several grand extra. Up to you. But I'll tell you, what you have here, if it is real, is one of the most stunning pieces anyone has ever brought me.'

'Do you think it is real, Mr Hegarty?'

He shrugged. 'Hard to tell from photographs. But from what I can see, if it is a Sexton Blake, whoever did it is a better man than me, Gunga Din.' He shrugged again. 'What about you? Do you think it's real, Robert? Do you believe it's real?'

'My employer and I have reason to believe it might be.'

Hegarty whistled. 'So, two questions. Firstly, where the hell is it, and why couldn't you bring it here – assuming it's not hot? And secondly, why do you want a copy?'

'Too many questions, Mr Hegarty.'

He gave Kilgore a sideways look. 'Meaning?'

'Just tell me how long you'd need.'

'Four weeks, maybe six weeks to be safe.'

'What? Six weeks? You're busy?'

He nodded. 'Yeah, but that's not the issue. I can do the copy in a couple of days, no problem, but I need to get rid of the smell of the oil and the varnish – that's the giveaway with a copy of an old master. I can buy canvas from around this same period that Fragonard was painting, in the late seventeen hundreds, but not the paints themselves. I'd have to grind them up from the same plants and insects Fragonard used to make his pigments. Cochineal, all of that, if you want to avoid modern tests rumbling it. Then I'd need to get the craquelure on it. After that, my mate Billy, a chain smoker, has it in his house for a few days – that way the paintings get properly aged.'

'For my purposes and my employer's none of that will be necessary,' Kilgore said. 'All we need is a perfect facsimile. We're not talking about sophistication here. The people who currently have this picture already think it might be a fake – a Sexton Blake, as you call it – but they aren't certain. Let's just say all we want to do is convince them it is a fake, for sure.'

Hegarty looked at him levelly, then grinned broadly. 'I think I'm beginning to understand your game.'

Kilgore nodded, unsmiling. 'A perfect copy, two days?'

'Give me three.'

'And your price?'

'Ten thousand.'

'That's a lot more than the last commission we gave you.'

'This is a lot harder.'

The American pursed his lips, then nodded. 'I'll grant you that. It had better be good.'

'Robert, it will look good. Just don't smell it or subject it to forensic analysis. Do we have a deal?'

Kilgore reached into his inside pocket and pulled out a wad of £50 notes held together by an elastic band.

50

Monday, 28 October

It was an old habit, dating back to when, early in his career, Roy Grace had first transferred from uniform to CID. As a junior Detective Constable at Brighton police station, he tried to learn as much as he could about the city's crime and its criminals, and found the best resource was the constantly updated computer log of all reported crime and incidents, and the follow-ups. These were known traditionally as serials, as each incident was given a serial number.

From his very first day in CID, he would come in early, before his shift began, and read through the serials of the past twenty-four hours. Over the years, with his highly retentive – near photographic – memory, he had built up an encyclopaedic knowledge of all the regular offenders, as well as being on top of any changes in crime patterns, from house burglaries to moped theft, to street crimes, to internet fraud.

Even though he had long since moved into Major Crime, dealing mostly with homicide, reading the serials was still the way he liked to start his working day, seeing what was going on in his city, which he still considered his *manor*, as well as throughout the counties of Sussex and Surrey, which came under his remit. And scanning them at 7.45 a.m. on this Monday morning, he saw all the usual weekend detritus of fights in pubs, bars and streets in many of the town centres of Sussex, as well as burglaries, vehicle thefts, street robberies, a flasher, an assault, and someone missing after a midnight swim. But then he came to one serial that stopped him in his tracks.

He read it through carefully, noting the names of the victims and the attending officers then, fifteen minutes later, carried it in his head through into the briefing of Operation Canvas.

Seated with his team in the conference room, he opened the meeting by saying, 'Last week at our meeting I raised the issue of the couple who had brought along a painting to the *Antiques Roadshow*. The pictures expert was very excited. He thought it might be one of the long-lost paintings the French artist Jean-Honoré Fragonard had done of the four seasons.'

He continued. 'In light of the possible connection to Charlie Porteous, we made some enquiries and found out the name and address of the couple who took it to the show, a Mr and Mrs Kipling – Harry and Freya. He's a builder and she's a teacher, living in Patcham. Norman and Velvet subsequently visited them and talked to Mrs Kipling.' He glanced at both detectives by way of acknowledgment. 'They reported back that they believed Mrs Kipling's story that they bought the painting in a car boot sale because they liked the frame. At that point there was another painting over the possible high-value one beneath.'

Potting and Wilde both nodded in confirmation.

'I've just this morning checked the weekend serials and guess what? It appears the Kiplings had a burglary at their home on Saturday night.'

'Was the painting taken, boss?' Jack Alexander asked.

'Nothing was taken, apparently.'

Grace looked around at the sea of frowns. 'The couple called it in at a quarter to two on Sunday morning. A response crew, PCs John Alldridge and Dave Simmons, attended. They reported there was very clear evidence of a break-in – a windowpane was smashed – but nothing appeared to have been taken. In a follow-up post on the serials, Alldridge concluded that the couple may have disturbed the intruder who fled empty-handed.' He paused. 'My sense is that it is too much of a coincidence to dismiss that an attempted burglary was made on the Kiplings less than a week after *Antiques Roadshow* broadcast their possible Fragonard painting.' He looked at the team and saw nods of agreement.

'Norman and Velvet, how did you get on with Stuart Piper and with the Slippery Finn?'

Jack Alexander raised a hand. 'Boss, Polly Sweeney and I went to see Jorma Mahlanen, at Norman's request, because Norman had a series of medical appointments he needed to attend. Mahlanen was, as expected, evasive. He did finally admit, under questioning, that he knew Charlie Porteous, and had over the years bought a number of works of art from him. He also said that Porteous had contacted him, a few days before his death, saying he had what he believed to be an original Fragonard painting of spring, part of his Four Seasons. But he said the price Porteous wanted was too rich for him.'

'And that was how much?' Grace asked.

'Five million pounds,' Alexander replied.

'That fits with the value Desouta put on the painting on the *Antiques Roadshow*,' Grace said. 'Could Mahlanen offer any explanation why his number was on the burner phone of one of the offenders we suspect murdered Porteous?'

Alexander shook his head and Sweeney nodded in confirmation. 'He couldn't, no.'

'Did you believe him?'

'He showed us some of his paintings and said that a quarter of a million pounds is pretty much the top price he ever pays.' He shrugged.

Grace turned to Financial Investigator Emily Denyer. 'Emily, what intel do we have on how Mahlanen accumulated his wealth?'

Denyer shook her head. 'None, sir. He has a large number of legitimate business interests, and from the research I carried out, while the maths don't add up, so far we have nothing to prove any criminal activity.'

'But you believe Mahlanen is involved in some?'

'Oh yes. But whether it's drugs or cybercrime, I can't yet say.'

'OK,' Grace replied. 'You'll keep on him?'

'For sure, sir.'

'So what about Stuart Piper?'

'Norman and Velvet interviewed him later in the week,' Alexander said.

'Yes, chief,' Potting said, taking over. 'And a real charmer he is.' He looked at Wilde for confirmation. She nodded. 'A real charmer – not.'

'He lives in a proper fuck-off historic house, guarded like Fort Knox,' Potting said, 'with hunks of hired muscle.'

'He has unbelievable artwork on the walls,' Wilde added. 'Like, the National Gallery eat your heart out!'

'He gave us an alibi for the night of Porteous's murder, on 16 October 2015, chief,' Potting continued. 'That he was in his home in Barbados, where he normally spends the winter months. He has a very disfigured face, from a homophobic attack on him back in 1979, and claims that damp weather hurts his skin.'

Grace looked down at his notes. 'Norman, in a previous briefing you told me that while Piper is not on the British police radar, he is on Interpol's watchlist. What's that about?'

'Well,' Potting said, looking pleased with himself. 'I've been doing some digging over the weekend and spoken to a few of our Interpol contacts. It would appear that Piper has amassed a fortune from recovering works of art that have disappeared over the centuries – looted during times of trouble dating back from the French Revolution to the Nazi occupations. On the surface, all legit, and Piper has never had charges brought against him in any jurisdiction, but it would appear that many of these works of art that he has *miraculously* found might be very good forgeries. But here's a big problem for us, chief.' He fell silent.

'And that is?' Grace quizzed.

'Well, from what I've discovered, the last thing the galleries or private collectors of these works, for which they've paid huge sums, want to know is that they might be forgeries, which makes identification extremely difficult. Added to which there are a few forgers, working with old canvases and old materials, whose work is apparently near impossible to detect.'

Grace frowned. 'Does Piper have Fragonards amongst his collection?'

'He said it would be a dream to have one, sir,' Velvet Wilde said.

'Do you believe him?' Grace asked.

'He's very hard to read, sir. He has very little movement of his facial muscles.'

'There is something I'd like to add from my research of the weekend, chief,' Potting said, and shot a glance towards Stanstead. 'I asked Luke to look back into Stuart Piper's history. Back in 1979, when he was attacked, he very nearly died from his injuries and spent the best part of the following year having his face reconstructed. The records show that the three offenders who carried out this attack were subsequently identified and convicted. During the six years after their release from prison, at two-year intervals, all three were attacked and left with serious injuries. None of these link back to Stuart Piper, but it does seem perhaps a little coincidental.'

'You're suggesting these were reprisal attacks either carried out by Piper or orchestrated by him, Norman?' Grace asked.

'They might have been, chief. Just a thought. But just supposing Piper was capable of carrying out – or ordering – retribution back then, is it a big stretch to imagine he might resort to murder to get his hands on a painting as valuable as the Fragonard *Spring* that Charlie Porteous had in his possession?'

Grace considered this for some moments before responding. 'It's an interesting hypothesis, Norman, but as you just said, a bit of a stretch. It sounds from what you've said that Piper's MO is finding long-lost works of art around the world, ostensibly returning them to their rightful owners, and either collecting reward money or being duplicitous, having them expertly copied by forgers, retaining originals and passing off forgeries. There's nothing to suggest he is a brazen art thief, is there? Does he have any past form for burglary or suspected burglary?'

'Well – no, chief,' Potting replied reluctantly.

'It doesn't make any sense that someone of his wealth would need to resort to murder.' He looked at Wilde. 'What do you think, Velvet?'

'The only reason I can think of, sir, is if he knew the whereabouts of some or all of the other three Fragonard paintings in the series. Or indeed had them himself.'

'He told you he didn't, right?' Grace pressed.

'He alluded to that, yes.'

'But he might not have been telling the truth,' Potting added.

Grace nodded. 'The only way we'd find that out is by searching his house, and from what you're telling me, we don't have anything like enough to obtain a warrant. I think we should add him to our list of POIs, but with no further action for the moment.' He looked again at Potting and Wilde. They nodded agreement.

51

Thursday, 31 October

The upper level of the car park of the Miller and Carter, formerly the Black Lion pub, in Patcham village at the northern extremity of the city of Brighton and Hove, had been the scene of one of Brighton's most notorious murders.

It was where, on 12 January 1976, former glamour model Barbara Gaul, wife of millionaire businessman John Gaul, was blasted in the back with a double-barrelled twelve-bore shotgun by two men he had hired to do the hit. She died two months later from her injuries, but while the hitmen were subsequently arrested and given life prison sentences, John Gaul fled to Malta and evaded justice for over a decade before eventually dying, still a free man, from a heart attack.

This secluded car park, accessed by a steep ramp and shielded by bushes, was the location where Robert Kilgore had chosen to meet Archie Goff. The American, always scrupulously punctual, had arrived twenty minutes before his 8 p.m. appointment, reversing his Tesla into a space against the rear of the car park, giving him a clear view of every vehicle arriving. Quickly, he removed a traffic cone from the rear of the car, placing it at the front of the empty space immediately to his right.

Thursdays, traditionally pay day, was a big night out for many, and the car park was filling up rapidly, as a steady stream of vehicles flowed in. Kilgore figured he was unlikely to be noticed by any of the customers arriving, dressed up for their evening out, looking forward to meeting friends and having drinks and a good meal. No one was going to give a toss about a solitary old guy in a car in the dark smoking a cigarette.

He clocked each of the headlights flaring up the ramp: a Porsche; a Jag; a Mini; a plumber's van. Then, finally, a tired old Astra, its front number plate cracked and at a wonky angle, the exhaust shot. Instantly identifying the car from its registration and from the description Goff had given him over the phone, Kilgore flashed his headlights, once, then opened his door, jumped out, removed the cone and climbed back in, putting the cone in the passenger footwell. Goff drove straight in and wound his window down.

Kilgore lowered his, checking there was no one in earshot. 'Are we good, Mr Goff?' he asked.

'We're good.'

'You're all clear what you need to do?'

'Yep, I'm on it.'

Kilgore lifted the bubble-wrapped copy of the Fragonard off the passenger seat and passed it through the window to Goff, followed by a burner phone. 'It's got one number programmed in. Text it when you're done and you'll get back my instructions for the handover.'

'Leave it to me. That's when you'll pay me the balance, yeah?'

Kilgore said nothing for a moment, he just sat staring at the old burglar's face. There was something about the man he hadn't cared for when he'd first met him for breakfast at the Grand Hotel, something shifty and evasive in his eyes, and he saw that same look again now. In addition to paying the bail, Mr Piper had agreed a £2,000 fee. 'That's when we'll pay you the balance, Mr Goff.'

52

Archie Goff drove slowly up the steep residential street of Mackie Crescent in Patcham. It was, coincidentally, just half a mile or so from where he'd been handed the painting last night. As he passed a row of tennis courts to his right, the Kiplings' house appeared on his left, on a street corner, and he clocked that the driveway was empty, apart from Harry Kipling's pick-up. Neither Harry's Volvo estate nor Freya's Fiat 500 were there. Good.

From the daily surveillance he had carried out this week, he had established that Harry Kipling left for work at 7.30 a.m., pretty much on the nose, every morning, and Freya Kipling around twenty minutes later. She always returned around 4.30 p.m., with their droopy-looking son with his headphones. Yesterday she had gone out again, twenty minutes later, dressed like she was going to some kind of fitness class. And yesterday, instead of 5 p.m., her husband returned closer to 5.30 p.m. and unloaded a bunch of groceries from his car.

The only time Harry had come back in the morning had been on Monday, when he shot home around midday to pick up some building supplies.

Turning left in front of the house and heading up the hill, with small houses and bungalows on either side of the road, Archie found a parking space between two cars. They were outside the yellow-line zone here, so he didn't need to worry about the car getting ticketed and logged.

He climbed out, wearing a hi-vis jacket, black trousers, trainers and a baseball cap. Then he lifted the bubble-wrapped painting, now in a layer of brown paper, from the rear seat, along with a clipboard, locked the car, then walked casually away, parcel and clipboard under his arm, and back down towards the Kiplings' house.

It was a tip an old lag in prison had given him many years ago, that if you didn't want to arouse curiosity in a neighbourhood, then wear a yellow hi-vis jacket and carry a clipboard, it would make you pretty much invisible.

Mackie Crescent was deserted, apart from a tubby elderly woman on a mobility scooter, heading away from him, down the hill on the pavement on the far side of the road, along by the tennis courts. Heading to the shops in the village, he guessed, patting his jacket pocket for the copy of the back door key he'd had cut from the wax impression he'd taken when he'd broken into the house last Saturday night, although he guessed it might not be of any use now. He was still annoyed at himself for breaking that rear windowpane. He'd intended to simply cut it out, reach in and unlock the security chain in place on the back door, then re-putty the glass back. But he'd not been expecting the pane to be rotten – certainly not in a builder's home – and it had fallen out, taking him by surprise.

He was pretty sure that the locks would now have been changed on all the doors, but no problem. In another pocket he carried a few pieces of kit, one a tool for picking just about any commercially available door or window lock, the other items for removing security chains.

As he walked down he slowed his pace, taking in all his surroundings, while pretending to make the occasional note on his clipboard. As he did so, he glanced surreptitiously for any signs of anyone watching him, especially any twitching curtains, but saw none. Urban burglaries had never been his thing, at least not since the first time he'd been nicked. But hey, this was the deal, and it was a sweet one. And it enabled him to be out of prison and home with his beloved Isabella.

Just this morning to get through.

Adjusting his cap so the peak was low over his face, and pulling on dark glasses, he clutched the parcel and the clipboard, trying to look every inch that he was here on business, strode up to the front door, keeping his face low, out of sight of the cameras, rang the bell and then rapped the brass leprechaun door knocker, with his cover story – that he was in the wrong street – at the ready in case anyone surprised him by appearing.

Silence.

He rang and knocked again.

Still silence.

Nice.

Still acting all casual in case a nosy neighbour was observing, he walked around to the side of the house, negotiated the bins and round to the rear, clocking the garden with its small pond, and a shed framed with tall leylandii trees. The last time he had been here it was in darkness, and now he was pleased to see the garden shrubbery and the trees at the far end gave it total privacy from the neighbours.

He tried his new key in the back door, but as he had suspected, the lock had been changed. Not a problem. It took him less than a minute of working his slender metal picks for the lock to click open. Pushing the door, it only moved a few inches before resisting. A security chain.

In less than a further minute, using a flat, plastic schoolboy ruler and a strong elastic band, he popped that open, too.

Inside the house, which he'd only previously seen by torch-light, he hurried through to the lounge, which was at the front. He checked the street, through the windows. All clear. Then out of habit he glanced around the room to see if there was anything small of value he could nick that might not be missed. The coffee table between a sofa and two armchairs had a glass top, making it into a display cabinet. It contained dozens of tiny silver spoons – mustard spoons, salt spoons, some shiny, some tarnished and in need of polishing. Worth a few bob. Maybe he'd come back for them one day, he thought. But it would only be small pickings.

There wasn't much else of any real value in the room, from what he could see. A few family photos in nice frames, some vases filled with flowers, a large television, a pair of tall Sonos speakers. Then he focused on the painting hanging on the wall, which he'd photographed in detail, front and back, on Saturday night. Not his kind of thing, a bit chocolate-boxy in his opinion – he liked old Brighton prints, and some pictures that local modern artists painted of the broken West Pier and the beach huts along in Hove – a few of which he'd bought on the rare occasions when he'd had spare cash. Isabella really liked them, too, and that pleased him.

He worked quickly, lifting the painting off the wall and setting it down on the floor. Unwrapping the copy, he had to admit he was impressed by just how good a job the artist had done, even down to the detail on the back, and the identical thin string looped between two hooks. He'd have struggled to tell the difference, he reckoned.

Then he heard a car approaching outside and slowing down.

He held his breath, his brain momentarily paralysed.

Shit, no no no.

He saw the blue and yellow Battenberg markings of the front of the police car crawling down the hill and fell to his knees and out of sight, his heart knocking seven bells out of his chest.

Don't stop. Don't stop. Don't stop.

He cursed his stupidity in breaking his own golden rule of never entering a building without having a planned exit route. At the rear of the house was a garden, with a high fence around, which he wouldn't be able to climb. His only way out would be through the front door or around the side of the house. Straight into the arms of the Plod.

He crawled close to the window on his hands and knees and risked a peep. There were two uniformed officers in the car, a bulky male in the passenger seat, the female driving, both peering at the house. The male was saying something, whether to his colleague or into the radio Archie couldn't tell.

Shit.

He ducked down. Had they seen him? Had someone reported him? Had he triggered a concealed alarm?

You idiot. You idiot.

God, if they nicked him it would be goodbye to his dream, to everything. He'd be straight back in the big house, without passing GO. It would be goodbye to Isabella. And it would be goodbye to the £50,000 bail that his benefactor had put up – and would doubtless want back.

Shit, shit, shit.

He heard the rattle of the car's engine. Listened for the sound of a door opening, his entire body throbbing. So much to lose, he was thinking. Isabella had taken next week off work and he'd booked a room for two nights in a lovely-looking hotel in the New Forest. He figured he could just make it work between his appearances at Brighton police station that were part of his bail conditions. Tomorrow he had planned to nip into the town centre and buy a ring and surprise her by proposing to her over dinner on their first night in the hotel. He'd had a lot of false starts in his life, he knew, he hadn't been so clever in his previous choices of partners, but Isabella was the one. He wanted to spend the rest of his life with her, no question in his mind at all.

And no question in his mind at all that if he got done for burglary while he was out on bail, she wouldn't be giving him any more second chances. He'd already used his last one up.

Then, to his immense relief, he heard the car drive on. Risking another peep over the windowsill, he saw the rear of the patrol car disappear down the street.

He hung the replacement up, all the time checking through the window. Then clumsily, in his hurry to get out of there, he pulled the bubble wrap around the original, securing it with the roll of gaffer tape he had brought along, followed by the brown paper, into a right mess of a parcel.

Checking he had hung the copy straight, he slipped out the back door, using the ruler and elastic band to replace the safety chain and then his tools to re-lock the door.

As he strode back up the hill, with his seemingly undelivered parcel, he was smiling. The Kiplings would never know. Job done!

All he had to do now was the handover in the pub car park at 8 p.m. tonight and he'd get the balance of the payment. Plenty enough to buy Isabella a nice ring, and to pay for a glorious week ahead in their New Forest love nest, loads of drinks, nice meals and wild sex.

And just maybe, his brief reckoned, because he hadn't actually nicked anything at Hope Manor, and because prisons were over-crowded, he might get away with a suspended sentence when his trial came up in three months' time.

Whatever. He planned to get that ring onto Isabella's finger as quickly as possible. And a registry office wedding as soon after that as they could.

The future sorted. Well almost. He still needed one big job, the one that Hope Manor would have been, to pay for his daughter through veterinary college. Just that one final big one, and he had a list of houses to choose from. But for the next ten days, he didn't need to worry about a thing.

He climbed back into the car with a big smile on his face. Happy days!

53

'Happy days, boss!' Robert Kilgore said, standing in Piper's office and presenting him with the clumsily wrapped package. 'As you Brits say!'

Piper, his face revealing nothing, as usual, took a pair of scissors from a drawer. He carefully removed the brown paper, cut through the gaffer tape securing the bubble wrap, and finally lifted the picture clear.

Kilgore beamed as his boss studied the front carefully, then turned it around and examined the back. Then the front again. Even though it was virtually impossible to read anything in his expression, Kilgore saw what he interpreted as the shadow of a flicker of doubt.

Then Piper brought it close to his face and sniffed.

An instant later he slammed it down on his desk. 'This is a forgery,' he said. 'This is a fucking forgery!'

Robert Kilgore had seen his boss angry plenty of times over the past fifteen years he'd worked for him, but he'd never seen him as angry as this. He was like one of those fireworks that kept firing exploding bombshells into the air, each one bigger and louder than the previous.

Piper stood, apoplectic, behind his desk, the debris of bubble wrap and brown paper strewn around him, as he held up the painting again. 'It's a fucking forgery!'

'This is what Archie Goff removed from the Kiplings' living

room wall, *sir.*' It was partly due to his Southern breeding and partly due to the sheer coldness Piper exuded that he rarely, in all these years, used his boss's first name. And Piper only used his last name when he was angry. He was seriously angry now.

Piper shook his head. 'No, Kilgore, it's what that toe-rag, Goff, *told* you he'd removed from the Kiplings' wall. I know that *Antiques Roadshow* expert, Oliver Desouta, I've bought pictures from his gallery, and I called him on Monday morning, to ask him his opinion – what he really thought. He told me that while he would need more time to fully establish its provenance, that he was as certain as he could be, with his forty years' experience of the art world, specializing in French old masters, that it was the genuine article. Didn't you fucking smell it?'

'I did not, sir, no. It was all wrapped up, as I brought it to you just now.'

Piper shook his head, all the explosions fired from his shell now, and sat back down, a dangerously simmering husk. 'We bailed him out because he was recommended, you told me, as the finest house burglar in the county.'

'That is correct, sir.'

'So does he think we're a bunch of monkeys? Does he seriously think he can walk off with the original and pass off Hegarty's forgery to us without us noticing? Do I look stupid, Kilgore? Do I look like someone who just rode into town on the back of a truck?'

'I wouldn't say so, no, sir.'

Piper thrust the painting at him. 'Smell it!'

Kilgore took it, held it close to his face and sniffed. And immediately noticed the faint reek of varnish. He nodded. 'Yep.'

'Yep?' Piper retorted. 'That's all you have to say?'

'No, sir, I reckon you are right.'

'You *reckon*? Bobby, we've been royally stiffed by a low-life scumbag dickhead. I don't know what's going on in his head

– clearly not much if he thinks he can get away with this. You have his contact details? His address? Phone?'

'Both,' Kilgore said.

Piper stabbed a button on his desk intercom. Moments later the twin guards came into the room. He gave them their instructions.

54

Even though he'd got up early in order to beat the Saturday crowds
and had arrived at the Cannon Place car park just before 10 a.m.,
Archie Goff still had to drive up to Level Five before he found a
free parking space. It was a tight one at that, between a Porsche
Cayenne and a squat sports car he didn't recognize.

After reversing the Astra in carefully, there was barely enough
room for him to squeeze out, and he had to tap the side of the
Cayenne with his door. He paid no attention to the white van
that followed him in, and had now driven on past.

There was a jeweller in the Brighton Lanes, Anthony Horowitz,
a ten-minute walk away, with whom he had done business many
times. He knew that Horowitz only stocked quality. And, Anthony
owed him a favour. On the last big job he'd done, before Hope
Manor, he'd held back a bunch of watches and jewellery, instead
of handing them along with the rest of his haul to his fence, Ricky
Sharp. He knew fine well he'd get a better price from Horowitz,
even with a big knock-down. Horowitz had handed him ten grand
in cash knowing the goods were worth a good fifty grand, if not
more, at current retail prices. 'I owe you one,' Anthony had said
as his parting words.

Archie intended to call in that favour now and bag himself a
nice antique engagement ring for just a few hundred quid.

Less than half an hour later he was climbing, with some
difficulty, wheezing, back up the car park staircase. Elated,

he repeatedly patted the lump in the inside breast pocket of his bomber jacket. Checking his purchase was still there. Inside the small blue cotton-wool-lined box Anthony Horowitz had found for the ring.

He could not wait to see Isabella's face when she popped the lid off that box to see the white-gold ring with the tiny ruby set in the head. She'd let slip some while ago that rubies were her favourite stones, and this one was just plain gorgeous.

Horowitz had tried to stiff him for £750 for it, and he'd managed to haggle him down to £500, still more than he'd budgeted to pay, but what the hell. She was worth it.

He stopped to get his breath back when he reached the fifth floor, feeling a little giddy from the exertion, his chest hammering. He felt a sharp pain in his left arm and then another down his chest, and for a moment panicked that he might be having a heart attack.

Oh God, not now, please not now.

He was hyperventilating.

Took some deep breaths. Slowly, steadily, he calmed down. Felt fine again after some moments. Although he was aware he was drenched in perspiration. Maybe he would join a gym after they got back from the New Forest. Hell, he was only sixty-four – no age today. Get his fitness up. He owed that to his future bride. Hell, he owed it to himself and to his daughter.

He walked along the deserted floor of the car park, trying to remember exactly which row he'd left the Astra in.

He never heard the soft footsteps behind him.

Never registered the single blow to the base of his neck that knocked him, instantly, unconscious.

55

When he opened his eyes, Archie Goff was confused and disoriented. The back of his head was throbbing. He had been in the Cannon Place car park behind Churchill Square. Who were these people? Big, unsmiling identical faces, in matching black mandarin collars and with identical shiny black hair slicked back.

Was he seeing double? For a moment, in his befuddled state, he thought he might have been mugged. That this face or these faces belonged to his rescuers.

But he wasn't seeing double, he realized, after some moments. And there was something in their eyes that he really did not like.

Slowly he became aware of his surroundings. He was in a huge, cold, empty warehouse, as vast as an aircraft hangar. Some wooden pallets were stacked over in a far corner; a couple of grey-sided containers. Over to the right, as far as he could crane his neck to see, was a white van. There was nothing else in here except for the two massive, muscular men who looked like identical twins. He was stark naked, he realized with shock, and seated in a chair, but as he tried to move, neither he nor the chair budged. It felt like the chair was cemented to the floor and his bum and back were cemented to the chair. He was bound by a rope across his midriff and by something sharp around his wrists and ankles.

Suddenly his right palm was seized in a vice-like grip; his fingers were straightened out by a hand as strong as steel, then something pressed against the tips. Tighter. Tighter.

Crushing them.

He cried out in pain.

Crushing them further.

'Stop! No, please, please stop!'

Tears of pain streamed down his face, blinding him. The pressure eased but his fingers throbbed in agony. Then the same thing began happening to the fingers of his left hand. The tips were being crushed in a vice. As he screamed and sobbed and pleaded, the man on the right spoke. His accent was London.

'Did you ever see that film *Reservoir Dogs*, Mr Goff?'

Through his blur of tears he vaguely registered the almost ridiculously large gold watch on one wrist, and a gold ring on his middle finger, with an equally over-sized ruby in the clasp. The stone was too big to be genuine, he thought. It was ten times the size of the ruby he'd bought Isabella. Total bling. Archie tried to think, to disassociate, to take his mind to anywhere but here.

The crushing stopped but the throbbing agony just worsened, hurting more and more by the second.

'*Reservoir Dogs*, Mr Goff. Directed by Quentin Tarantino? Great movie, wasn't it?'

In pain and terror, close to hyperventilating, Archie nodded and blurted, 'Yes.'

'So you would remember the nicknames, right? Mr White, Mr Brown?'

Unsure where this was going, but liking it less by the second, Archie tried to think through the excruciating agony in his fingers. 'Yes.'

'Very good. You may call me Mr White, and my brother Mr Brown. Are you OK with that?'

'Fine, fine with that.'

Who were these people? What did they want? Who had sent them?

Suddenly, the man on the left leaned over and grabbed a military-looking fuel can. The kind that could hold several gallons. He held it up right in front of Archie's face. 'Have you ever seen someone badly burned, Mr Goff?'

And now Archie began to tremble. He struggled with every ounce of strength in his body but was unable to move anything. 'What do you want? What – what do you want? Please tell me what you want. Money? What do you want?'

'Oh, I am sorry, but it is not what *we* want, Mr Goff,' the man with the red ring said. He sounded almost genuinely apologetic. 'It is what our boss wants that you have stolen from him.'

Archie stared back in terror. 'There must be a mistake. Your boss? What does he think I've stolen?'

'A painting.'

'A painting? You mean your boss is Mr Kilgore?'

'Mr Kilgore is not our boss. Mr Kilgore works for our boss.'

There was a brief, tense silence.

'I-I don't understand.'

The one on the left flipped back the lid of the can and held the spout under Archie's nose. He smelled the strong, unmistakable stench of petrol.

'N-n-n-no, please, n-n-n-no,' Archie stammered.

The one on the right, with the red ring, pulled a pack of cigarettes from his pocket, shook one out and offered the thin white stick with the filter tip to Archie. 'Smoke? Like a snout?'

Goff shook his head wildly.

'Not good for your health, are they, Mr Goff.' Replacing the pack in his pocket, he then pulled out a plastic lighter and clicked. A large flame burned. He clamped the cigarette between his own lips, lit it and drew in a deep lungful, smoke spurting from his mouth as he spoke. 'But I don't think it is the snouts that are going to kill you right now.' He smiled and took another drag. 'We don't have the luxury of time to wait for that to kill you; it could be years, couldn't it?' Then the smile fell off a cliff and he looked deadly serious.

'Our boss don't like being made a fool of, Mr Goff. He would like the painting you removed from the wall of the Kiplings' house, not the copy that the artist Mr Hegarty had made. If you'd like to see your lady, Isabella Reyzebal, again, it is very simple. All you have to do is direct us to where the original painting is.'

Archie stared back at him, totally confused through his terror. 'I-I'm sorry – I – the painting I handed Mr Kilgore last night is the one I took off the Kiplings' wall.'

The man slammed his fist into the side of Archie's head, momentarily dazing him. Archie felt agonizing stinging pain as the ring gouged out a chunk of flesh. Then blood running down his cheek.

'My boss does not think so. Maybe we should jog your memory, Mr Goff.'

His twin circled Archie, pouring petrol in a steady stream all around him. Then, holding the can, he stepped back a few paces. 'Is this helping you to think any more clearly?'

'I swear!' Archie screamed. 'I swear the painting I gave Mr Kilgore is the one I took off the wall. I don't know anything about art. Why the hell would I try to screw the man who'd bailed me out of prison? You have to believe me. You HAVE to. Please!'

'Are you familiar with the television show *Who Wants To Be A Millionaire*, Mr Goff?' the one with the ring asked.

'I-I've seen it, yes,' he croaked, the reek of petrol all around him, and watching the glow of the cigarette in utter terror.

'So is that your final answer?'

'NO!' he screamed, realizing where this was going. 'NO, this is NOT my final answer.'

'So, just tell us where the original painting is.'

'I just did what I was told,' Archie yammered. 'I photographed the painting, front and back, as instructed and gave the photos to Mr Kilgore. Then, as instructed, I switched the painting he gave me with the one on the wall.'

'So why do we think you are lying, Mr Goff? And why does our boss think you are lying?'

'I'm not lying. Please, you have to believe me.'

Both of his tormentors shook their heads. 'We are paid to believe our boss,' the one on the left said. 'Not a piece of used toilet paper like you.'

'We'll give you one more chance to think clearly,' his twin with the ring said. Then he began to empty the contents of the petrol can over Goff, dousing him from head to foot. 'Where is the original?'

Archie was sobbing, the petrol fumes stinging his eyes, almost overpowering him. 'Please,' he choked. 'Please believe me, I gave you what I took from the wall of the Kiplings' house. Please believe me.'

'Final answer?' the twin on the right said.

'Please believe me!'

The twin took a hard drag on the cigarette, now burned down almost to the tip. It glowed bright red. He tossed it onto Archie Goff's petrol-soaked lap.

56

Shaking uncontrollably, heart pumping, Archie closed his eyes, waiting for the explosion, the *whuuuuumpppp*, the flames, the searing pain.

Nothing happened. Time stood still. Time was frozen.

Finally, he looked down through blurred eyes and saw to his astonishment the cigarette was extinguished.

'You like movies, Mr Goff?'

Barely able to speak through his fear, the stench of petrol fumes making him dizzy, Archie looked up at the two men and croaked, 'Some.'

Both twins nodded approvingly. 'We like movies, too. But we like the ones best that have their research correct,' the one with the ring said. 'There are so many movies where petrol is ignited by a cigarette, but you see, as you may perhaps know yourself, Mr Goff, as an intelligent man, the ignition temperature for gasoline is way higher than the heat a cigarette can generate. Which means that the movie makers have simply not done their research. Pretty crap, eh?'

Archie nodded dubiously. He was thinking about his daughter. About that ring in the box inside his jacket. About Isabella and the trip ahead with her. What did he need to do to convince these psychopaths to believe him?

Please don't let it end here.

Please.

235

There had to be a way out of this.

Fear coiled and unspooled and coiled again in every cell of his body.

Money? he thought. The universal motivation. 'Look, please, how much do you want? I-I can give you back the money. I've – I've got most of it. I've—'

He screamed as a cigarette burned into his skin, then he screamed again as he felt something clamp to his scrotum, then another cigarette burn. He felt clamps on his nipples. Drenched in perspiration, he cried out again just as his body convulsed with electric shocks.

'Please,' he yelled. 'Please—' He was stopped in mid-sentence by an agonizing pain in his left arm, as if someone had stuck a sharp knife all the way up inside the skin and muscles. He cried out again, but the sound jammed somewhere inside his constricted gullet.

Neither of the men had done this. They were both still standing in front of him, looking at him. Frowning now.

The pain shot up his left arm again, even more excruciating, but this time only a tiny gasp jetting from his mouth. The men blurred as a volcanic pain erupted inside him. It felt like his entire chest was being clamped in a vice that was tightening, crushing his insides.

Images of Isabella's face floated in front of him.

Heard one of the twins say, 'He's ill.'

'Isabella!' he whispered.

The last sound he ever heard was the voice of the twin with the big red ring saying, loudly, 'Shit.'

57

Daniel Hegarty's house, which had a commanding view to the south – facing out onto the English Channel – and to the north of the open fields of the South Downs, was sunk down below the street level.

Hegarty and his wife had bought the house largely because of the inspirational views for his painting. He always woke early, loving the pre-dawn light. His routine, seven days a week, was to dress, down a quick espresso, then take Rocky and Rambo – tough names but wusses of dogs – for a long walk across the open countryside before returning home for breakfast, a scan of the papers and then settling into his studio to paint – sometimes commissions, and sometimes more works for his next exhibition at the Brighton gallery which had endless demands for his pictures.

It was a dry, fine, if chilly, autumn morning, and still half an hour to sunrise. Wrapped up well in a fleece and beanie, the artist climbed the steps to the street in the half-light, the dogs tugging on their leads, almost pulling him up, and opened the gate latch, letting the over-excited animals run out onto the pavement, yanking his arm.

'Hey!' he said. 'Hey, calm down, boys!'

But Rocky and Rambo seemed even more excited than usual this morning. And instead of turning right, as usual, to drag their master as fast as they could towards the Downs and where they would be let off their leashes, they ran straight ahead, stopped and began barking loudly.

'Sssssshhhhh, Rocky, Rambo!' Hegarty hissed. 'You'll wake the neighbours!'

Then, to his surprise, the leads slackened as they stopped pulling and just stood barking.

Barking at the dark shape lying on the pavement.

A human body, he realized. A tall thin man, with congealed blood down the right side of his face.

Hegarty's first thought was that it was a drunk. Shouting at the dogs to calm down, he kneeled down and touched the man's face. It was stone cold. The flesh stiff and unyielding.

He recoiled in shock. Then stood up, shaking, and dialled 999.

'Emergency, which service please?' the calm female voice answered after several rings.

'There's a body – a man – lying on the pavement outside my house, I think he might be dead,' Hegarty said.

'I'll put you through to the Ambulance Service, sir.'

Moments later, Hegarty repeated the same thing to the Ambulance Service controller who answered. He was asked for his name and address, which he gave, and the controller asked if he could stay at the scene and an ambulance would attend as quickly as possible.

Hegarty said he would, then walked the dogs a short way up the street, stopping to let first Rocky and then Rambo relieve themselves, scooping up their poop with plastic bags. Less than ten minutes later, he heard the faint doppler wail of a siren.

Then his phone pinged with an incoming text.

He looked at the display. And froze at the words he saw.

**I hope you haven't double-crossed my boss, Mr
Hegarty, by keeping the original – you know what**

I'm talking about. If you have, the next body on the pavement outside your house will be yours.

Hegarty replied, with shaking fingers, struggling to get the words right and having to correct his text several times before it was ready to send. All the time, the siren getting louder and nearer. As he finally sent it, the siren had stopped and he saw light approaching, streaking across the pavement on both sides.

Why would I double-cross your boss or anyone? I make a good living doing what I do best. Assuring you and your boss of my best services at all times, DH.

58

There had been plenty of weeks in his life that Roy Grace would like to forget. Among them had been the week between his beloved father's death and his funeral, and another when his mother, whom he adored, had died. The weeks following his former wife Sandy's disappearance had until now been perhaps the worst of all. Not to mention the months and then years of torment, during which he'd begun to give up all hope of ever living anything approaching a *normal* life again.

But now, finally, in these past few years, Cleo had changed all that. This gorgeous, smart, amazing woman lying in bed beside him, with her swollen, heavily pregnant belly, had given him a whole new life, a new home, a new passion for living. He loved her with all his heart and he would do anything for her. He would take a bullet for her without a moment's hesitation. She had given him the gift of something he thought would elude him for the rest of his life.

The gift of happiness.

That had been torn away in the weeks that followed Bruno's death and his funeral, which Cleo had helped him so much to get through.

The sadness would never leave him but he knew he had to try to live his life and be there for his family. And at work there were still some unresolved issues with his former boss, Cassian Pewe, that he was yet to get to the bottom of. But for now it was

Sunday, his favourite day of the week. In a few moments he would prise himself away from his luxuriously soft pillows, slip out of bed quietly, then change into his running kit and take Humphrey for a good long run along the Downs. 10k at least, maybe more. Then when he came back he was eager to try out a new recipe he'd read, an omelette, but with the eggs mixed with rolled oats and a little English mustard, wrapped around grilled mushrooms, with tomatoes and steamed spinach on the side.

He loved experimenting, and the picture of the finished dish he'd seen in a magazine looked amazing.

Later they were going to meet Cleo's sister and her boyfriend at one of his favourite pubs, the child-friendly Griffin at Fletching, for Sunday lunch. Grace had mixed views about this. He liked Cleo's sister, Charlie, a lot, although he was less keen on her boyfriend, Lance, a pompous know-all who enjoyed belittling Roy by telling him how much money he made in financial services and wondering why Roy persisted at his relatively low-paid job with the police.

The last time they'd spent a day together, at Christmas last year, when, after their boozy lunch Lance had again told Roy he was wasting his talents in the police, and that he would never become rich as a copper, Roy had retorted, 'Maybe not, but I have something you will never have.'

'And what's that?' Lance had asked, through a blue cloud of cigar smoke.

'The knowledge that I have enough,' Grace had said.

They hadn't spoken again for the rest of that day. And Roy wasn't much looking forward to seeing him now. But, big bonus, despite Cleo in her advanced state of pregnancy not drinking, he'd be able to have a couple of glasses of red wine. It might help him cope with the boyfriend.

Then his job phone rang.

He grabbed it quickly, slipped out of bed and answered, whispering, 'One moment!'

He hurried through into the en-suite bathroom. As he did so, he remembered he had completely forgotten that he was doing a favour to the previous week's duty Senior Investigating Officer, Mike Ashcroft – who had helped him out by covering his shift last week – taking over from him today instead of the customary 6 a.m. Monday morning.

A slightly nervous female voice he didn't recognize said, 'Detective Superintendent Grace?'

'Uh huh,' he said, closing the door behind him.

'It's DI Sapna Patel at Brighton.'

'You're new?'

'I am, my first shift, sir.'

'Tell me?'

'We've a possible suspicious death, sir. The victim has been identified as someone well known to Sussex Police – Archie Goff.'

'Very well known,' Grace confirmed. 'A proper recidivist.'

'He was found two hours ago on a pavement in Saltdean, by a gentleman walking his dogs. DS Walker attended and there are a number of things that make her concerned that this is not a natural death. The first is that the dead man reeks of what apparently smells like an accelerant, possibly petrol, as if he has been doused with it. He also has a wound behind an ear, and the fingers of both hands look to have been crushed.'

'Sounds like he might have upset someone,' Grace said. 'Anything else?'

'No, sir, but I felt you should be informed.'

'Where is the body now?'

'Still in situ, sir.'

'Has a coroner been notified?'

'No, sir, not yet. DS Walker felt that should be a decision by Major Crime.'

'Let me have the address.' She gave it to him and Grace did a quick calculation. 'OK, I'll be there in half an hour. Is the body taped off?'

'It is, sir, and we've a scene guard present.'

'Good work, Sapna. What I'd like you to do is arrange a CSI team to attend the scene as quickly as possible, and I'll meet them there.'

'I will do, sir.'

Grace had a quick shower, dressed hastily, knotting his tie, then explained the situation, apologetically, to a drowsy Cleo.

'So you won't be making lunch,' she murmured.

'I'll do my best to be back in time.'

'It wasn't a question,' she said, sounding more awake now. 'It was a statement.'

'I'll do my best.'

'I'll get those words engraved on your tombstone,' she said.

He looked down at her. 'Baby.'

Then she pursed her lips. 'I'm sorry, that wasn't very sensitive. I understand what you have to do.' She raised a hand from under the duvet and waved it. 'Let me know how it's going, and when you know you'll be back.'

He lingered for some moments, temporarily lost for words, leaned over and kissed her, then headed downstairs.

A heart laden with guilt. And worry. And grief.

There was a dead body lying on a pavement in a suburb of Brighton. And quite likely a loving partner wondering why he hadn't come home last night.

Could a police officer responsible for finding the answers as to why he hadn't come home and to who had killed him, sit comfortably in his skin on a chair in a Sussex pub, enjoying a prawn cocktail, perfectly roast beef and a few glasses of a decent red wine? If so, that person was in the wrong job.

You had to make choices in life and live with the

243

consequences, not only those of your actions, but of your inactions.

Roy Grace went downstairs, ate a piece of toast spread with Marmite, peanut butter and slices of cucumber, downed it with a Nespresso, then hurried out to his car.

Before he drove off, he texted Cleo:

Love you so much, babes. XXXX

59

Thirty minutes later, following the satnav on his phone, in its cradle on the Alfa's dash, Roy Grace passed the Lido then turned off the coast road, winding up through the network of Saltdean's pleasant residential streets.

There had been no reply yet from Cleo.

Cresting the brow of a steep hill, a glorious, sunny view of the English Channel came into sight. Then a short distance ahead he saw a cluster of vehicles – two marked police cars, a white CSI van as well as an unmarked saloon. There was a small knot of members of the public standing well back down the road behind crime scene tape and he kicked, almost on autopilot, into full work mode.

A uniformed officer stood steadfast behind another line of blue and white crime scene tape. A motionless male human shape sprawled on the pavement behind her, between the grass verge and a low brick wall that protected the car port of the long, low house beyond that was sunk down below street level. A large off-roader was parked on the far side of the wall, obscuring the view of the front door area.

On the outside of the tape a bewildered-looking man, with gelled silver hair, was in conversation with a police officer. Three officers stood nearby. One he recognized as Detective Sergeant Sally Walker, the other two, a male and a female officer, he didn't know.

No press, so far, but that wouldn't last long. He wouldn't be surprised to see Glenn's fiancée, Siobhan, arrive any minute – as the *Argus*'s senior crime reporter, she was normally the first of the press pack at any scene. He parked and approached the group.

'Good morning, sir,' DS Walker said. She was tall, fair-haired and all smiles despite the seriousness of the situation.

'What do we have?' Grace asked.

She indicated the silver-haired man, who looked, in Grace's view, very traumatized – and he wasn't surprised. Finding a dead body on your doorstep was rarely going to be the best start to anyone's day.

'This is Mr Hegarty, who lives at the house, number 20, who called it in. He was about to walk his dogs when he came across the body.'

Hegarty, Grace thought. Interesting. Then out of the corner of his eye, he saw the youthful-looking figure of Crime Scene Manager Chris Gee, in full protective clothing, climb out of the CSI van.

Grace hurried back to his car, opened his go-bag in the boot and wormed into a hooded protective suit and then pulled on overshoes and gloves. He greeted Gee, then both of them signed the crime scene log, ducked under the tape and walked towards the body.

Grace could smell the reek of petrol while he was still yards away. He pulled on his mask, glad for the protection against the stench it gave him, and kneeled down a few inches away.

The dead man lay on his back with congealed blood behind his right ear. He was in his sixties, Grace estimated, lean and tall with thinning strands of grey hair. He was dressed in jeans, trainers and a jacket, with a white T-shirt beneath. His pasty face was craggy, tiny shrivel-creases in the skin indicating he had probably been a heavy smoker, this backed up by the ochre shade of his visible front teeth. The fingertips of both his hands looked crushed, the nails dark with congealed blood. Torture? he wondered.

He studied the injury behind the man's right ear carefully, wondering if it could have been made from impact with the pavement, but it looked too deep, as if something had gouged it. And there were no blood spots on the pavement. It had been a dry night, so no rain could have washed it away.

From what he could see, other than the wound, there was no other injury. He touched the man's arm with a gloved hand. The flesh was stiff.

It was currently just gone 9.30 a.m. From his observations, he probably died a good few hours earlier at the very least, and possibly longer. Which meant, if he had died here, he'd been lying in this residential street some time and no one had noticed. Pretty unlikely.

Not wanting to disturb the body's position more than he needed, he asked Gee to help lift him up a little to check for any obvious injuries to his back. But they could see none – no visible wounds to the back of the head, or slash marks from a knife or visible gunshot holes in his clothes.

'Clearly been dead a while,' Gee said.

Nodding, Grace replied, 'I know him. I once nicked him, around twenty years ago, when I was in uniform. He looked a bit prettier then. Archie Goff is – was –' he corrected himself, 'a career house burglar.' He stood up, wanting to get away from the smell, but continued staring down at the body, trying to study it dispassionately, but at the same time unable to detach himself from it emotionally.

There was always something intrusive about being in the presence of a dead human being. All the time you were alive you had options about who you invited into your personal space. The moment you were dead, those ceased. You didn't even own your body any more, it had become the property of the coroner.

It was coming back clearly now, when he had arrested this man, all those years ago. Archie Goff had broken into a mansion on the outskirts of the city, where the unfortunate man had subsequently been cornered in the garden, backed up against a tree after fleeing, by a particularly aggressive Rhodesian Ridgeback. The owners were out, and it had required two Sussex Police dog handlers to restrain the Ridgeback and cuff the man.

So what was Goff doing here? His normal MO, from memory, was large country houses. And he'd been nicked again back in September for just such a burglary. But he'd made bail. Goff had recently been of interest to Roy and his team as part of the Porteous investigation but was just one of many lines of enquiry. This was a comfortable middle-class area, but not somewhere that would generally house the kind of valuables Goff specialized in nicking. And why doused in petrol?

From the way Goff lay, it looked to Grace highly unlikely that he'd doused himself in petrol and then collapsed on this spot. He had died somewhere else and his body been deposited here. But how had he died, who had dumped him here and why had he been doused in petrol – and why this location? What was that about?

And how inflammable was he now?

'We need a fire extinguisher,' he said to Gee. 'As a precaution.'

'I'll get one from the van.' Gee hurried off.

Grace glanced around at the neighbouring houses, looking for any outward-facing CCTV camera that might provide a clue. There were none he could immediately see but they could be hidden anywhere. To get to this house, whoever had brought Goff here would have to have driven along a zigzag of residential streets. Hopefully one or more of the houses in this neighbourhood might have cameras that would have picked up the vehicle. Or at least someone might have seen an unfamiliar vehicle.

As the Crime Scene Manager returned with a small fire

extinguisher, Grace said, 'Chris, I'm treating this as a suspicious death.'

'I agree, sir.'

Grace turned to DS Walker. 'Sally, we need to liaise with the Coroner's Officer and be authorized to contact the on-call Home Office pathologist. Once we know who it is, get their sanction to move the body.'

Home Office pathologists these days were paid by the job, not the hour, so it was rare for them to spend time at the crime scene itself, although occasionally they insisted on doing that.

'I'll get right on it, sir.'

Grace turned back to Gee. 'We don't yet know what we're looking for, but we need a Police Search Adviser and a POLSA team doing a fingertip search in the area.'

Gee nodded. 'I'll organize it.'

Grace then thought hard and calmly about what Hegarty's link might be to the body. A major league art forger. Charlie Porteous and the Fragonard. The Kiplings, who had taken a Fragonard to the *Antiques Roadshow* and had subsequently reported a break-in after the programme had aired. Was there a link with Archie Goff?

It could of course be a complete coincidence that the old lag's body had been dumped here in this particular location, but, just as the petrol on his clothes didn't smell right, the deposition site stank.

But what the hell could the connection be? Goff had been assaulted, doused in petrol. Now he was dead. It looked like he'd been murdered.

Hopefully the postmortem might provide the evidence.

Whatever had ended Archie Goff's life, Grace was as certain as could be that *natural causes* was only a bit-part player in his demise. He pulled out his phone and called Glenn Branson.

When his sleepy friend, colleague and protégé answered, Grace asked, 'How's your Sunday, so far?'

'It was pretty good until now,' Branson retorted, with a yawn. 'I've got plans – me and Siobhan are going to have a nice day and talk through all our issues. Don't tell me you're going to mess all that up?'

So the reporter wasn't about to turn up here, Grace thought. And he was pleased to hear his friend sounding positive. Which made what he had to say next even harder. With his voice tinged with genuine apology, he replied, 'Sorry, I am going to mess all that up.'

60

'You're not really sorry at all, are you, boss?' Glenn Branson said, a few hours later in the mortuary.

It was just gone 2 p.m. The one positive about today, Grace thought, was that Dr Frazer Theobald was unavailable. Instead they'd been assigned Nadiuska De Sancha, who was far quicker, just as thorough and much more fun to work with.

'Depends, how do you define sorry?' Grace raised his eyebrows. They were gowning up in the cramped changing room of the Brighton and Hove Borough Mortuary.

The DI shook his head, seated on a bench and pulling on white gum boots. 'There you go again, pissing me off by answering a question with a question. You've screwed up my Sunday, and you've probably screwed up my life,' he joked.

'Welcome to the Major Crime Team,' Roy Grace retorted. 'Anytime you want out and decide you'd like to return to your former life working nightclub doors, be my guest. I won't stop you.'

'But seriously, Roy. My wedding – it's like hanging on a knife edge.'

'Because you've been called out to be Deputy SIO on a murder enquiry?' Grace was being serious now. 'Siobhan's a top crime reporter. Get real, she didn't achieve that by sticking to office hours. Reporters and coppers are part of the same breed. We have to drop everything for a murder, reporters have to drop everything for a story. If she doesn't get why you're here at this moment, instead of having a cosy Sunday brunch with her in some trendy cafe, then the optics aren't good.'

Branson gave him a sideways look. '*Optics?* So Cassian Pewe's lingo's rubbed off on you?'

Grace pulled on his cloth head-cover, then selected a fresh gauze mask. 'It may not seem like it at this moment, but I'm doing what I always try to do, which is to advance your career.'

'Really?'

Grace shrugged. 'You've gone from a PC to DC to DS to Detective Inspector in how few years?'

'And lost my wife, nearly lost my kids and now I'm about to lose my fiancée in the process. Should I be grateful?'

'Depends; how do you define gratitude?'

'There you go again, you bastard! Answering with a question.'

'So tell me?'

Grace saw Glenn wringing his hands in frustration. 'Glenn,' he said, trying to calm him, then secured his mask. 'Let's go do it.'

They walked out into the narrow corridor and turned right, passing the closed door of the isolation room and into the wide, open-plan twin postmortem rooms separated only by an arch.

The mortuary operated normal working-week hours, on the basis that in general, their occupants weren't in any particular hurry to be postmortemed and nor were their loved ones, most of the time. So the regular team of three pathologists who carried out postmortems on deaths that weren't suspicious had the luxury of weekends off.

For Home Office pathologists, who specialized in suspected murder victims, where time was almost always critical, there was no such luxury. They were far more highly paid, but they earned their money by being on-call 24/7, ready to travel anywhere, instantly, and spend however many hours it took, both at the crime or deposition scene, and then in the mortuary, examining every aspect of the body, and often of the surroundings where it was found, in scrupulous detail. Few took less than six hours, and some far longer.

To Grace's left were four empty stainless-steel postmortem tables. To his right were another four that were empty, on this Sunday afternoon, and one on which lay the body of Archie Goff, still at this moment fully clothed, beneath bright lights, and the centre of attention of a number of people, all in identical blue gowns, white boots and blue and white gauze hats and face masks. Coroner's Officer Michelle Websdale, Crime Scene Photographer James Gartrell, alternating between taking stills and video, Darren Wallace, the Assistant Anatomical Pathology Technician, and Cleo, who was taking notes alongside centre-stage, flame-haired Nadiuska De Sancha who was at this moment taping every inch of Goff's clothing, while Gartrell moved his plastic ruler up the body each time she nodded.

This was the part of the murder investigation Roy Grace always found unpleasant. If he'd had any other Deputy SIO, he would have happily left them to it and gone home to enjoy his Sunday. But he felt obligated to Glenn. The moment they'd first met, when Glenn had joined his Major Enquiry Team as a very junior Detective Constable, Grace had taken a liking to him, recognizing in him, perhaps, something of his own young, ambitious self and ability. Ever since then he'd been on a mission to nurture Glenn, becoming close friends in the process.

'Daniel Hegarty,' Grace said.

'What about him?'

'He lives in the house right where the body was dumped outside.'

'He does? You found that out already?' Branson questioned.

'Elementary, my dear Branson. Isn't Rule One to check the ground under your feet?'

61

Freya Kipling lay back on the recliner sofa, a glass of red wine in one hand and a novel, *Where The Crawdads Sing*, in the other. Harry sat beside her with a can of lager, watching a replay of *Match of the Day*, his team, Brighton and Hove Albion, beating Norwich 2–0. Tom was up in his room, gaming with friends online, and Freya glanced at the Libre app to check his glucose level. 8.9. At the high end of the range, but OK.

She and Harry had spent the morning covering three different car boot sales and returned with a small amount of booty. Harry's purchases had been an ancient, empty tin of Players Medium Navy Cut cigarettes, a tiny bronze statuette of a golfer swinging his club, and a Brighton print, in remarkably good condition, of the old, ill-fated Daddy Long Legs railway, which ran on stilts above the English Channel, along part of Brighton seafront between Kemp Town and Rottingdean, from 1896 to 1900 before being closed down. Freya had bought a pair of matching, purple-tinted glass vases which the vendor had said were Victorian, and a silver salt and pepper cruet set.

Yet again, there had been no sign of the matching paintings that Harry hoped against hope they might find. To Freya's relief, he was finally coming around to the view they ought to put the Fragonard – well, *possible* Fragonard – into a major auction house sale and see what happened. Sotheby's, Christie's and Phillips were all interested and had kept in regular contact, updating them on their future fine arts sales.

As the game ended, Harry put his can down on the coffee table, then slipped an arm around her shoulder, and nuzzled her ear. She grinned, knowing exactly what he wanted. And why not? Despite being engrossed in her book, even after all these years she still did really fancy him.

She felt an erotic tingling deep inside her, put down her glass and book and turned to kiss him, knowing Tom was in his room and absorbed in the computer game with his mates.

At that moment, their landline phone rang.

As she reached for it, Harry restrained her. 'Later, baby.' He nuzzled her ear again, whispering, 'Now's not the time for phone calls. It's probably some insurance company telling us we've been in an accident.'

'It might be Dad, he gets lonely on Sundays sometimes.'

Freya's mother had died two years ago and her father, whom Harry liked, had been a lost soul since, but determinedly and fiercely independent, refusing to leave his home in Scarborough and come down to live with them.

Harry leaned forward and picked the cordless up off the table and saw it said *Number Withheld*. He hesitated then answered, 'Kipling residence, Harry Kipling speaking.'

It wasn't his father-in-law, but another elderly-sounding man who spoke with a soft, measured American drawl.

'Good afternoon, sir,' the man said, consummately polite. 'I apologize for intruding on your Sunday, but I understand you own a painting that is a good copy of one by the French artist Jean-Honoré Fragonard. Would I be correct?'

'Who am I speaking to?' Harry asked.

'I'm calling on behalf of my employer, who is a major collector of works of art from this period. He would be interested in making you an offer for a private sale – such a sale would save you the very costly fees of an auction house.'

'And what makes you think I might be interested in selling, even supposing I have such a painting?'

'Mr Kipling, my employer saw you with this picture on *Antiques Roadshow*. He is willing to make you a very generous offer, given that the painting is almost certainly a fake.'

'Really?' Harry sounded more belligerent than he had intended. 'Exactly how generous?' He put the phone onto loud-speaker so Freya could hear.

'I'm instructed to offer you the sum of fifty thousand pounds.'

Harry caught Freya's frown. 'You are joking?' he replied.

'Mr Kipling, I am deadly serious. If the picture is a fake, it would be worth, at very best, a few hundred pounds – and that much only if you were lucky. I appreciate that if it did turn out to be original, then it would be worth many multiples of that sum. But really, do you seriously believe something you bought from a car boot sale could be genuine?'

Freya was signalling to him to consider the offer, waving a hand in the air to get him to negotiate upwards.

Ignoring her, Harry said, 'Actually I do. Three of the major London auction houses want to include it in their next sales. I've been given estimates of around four to five million. Your offer is a joke.'

Sounding offended, the American said, 'Mr Kipling, my employer is a gentleman who doesn't joke about art.'

Freya signalled. *Negotiate*, she was indicating.

'So what would be your employer's best offer?'

'I just gave you my employer's best offer.'

The phone went dead.

Harry, shaken, stared at the phone for some moments, then put it down. Had they been cut off? He looked at Freya.

'Maybe we should have taken it,' she suggested.

'No way! You've seen the auction estimates from those houses.'

'Yes,' she said. 'The estimates *if* the painting is original.'

'None of them would be offering to list it if they thought it was a fake. That American was just a dickhead – a chancer.'

'Fifty thousand pounds would be very useful money, darling,' she said.

'Five million would be a lot more useful. He'll ring back, don't you worry.'

The American did not ring back.

62

In this room that always felt to Roy Grace like it was perpetual winter, a grey and bleak winter with its grey walls, grey steel tables, sinks and worktops, and the grey faces of the cadavers unlucky enough to fetch up here, the Home Office pathologist worked in steady, quick, concentration.

Thinking hard about the dubious coincidence of Archie Goff's body being dumped outside Daniel Hegarty's house, Grace shivered from the refrigerated air. Even on the brightest summer day, the dense frosted glass of the exterior wall leached all the colour from the sunlight, and the bright overhead lights added only starkness, no warmth. He tried to breathe through his mouth, as he always did in here, to shut out the cloying smells of death and disinfectant.

Nadiuska De Sancha had been looking at her watch regularly, and then at the clock on the wall, as if to double check it, and he wondered if she was on some kind of a deadline. She had certainly been proceeding refreshingly quickly, assisted by Cleo, who had cancelled the lunch with her sister. They were positively galloping through the postmortem compared to Dr Frazer Theobald, who carried out his so slowly that one of the team had once joked it was hard to tell which was the corpse and which the pathologist.

Including the brief time she'd spent with the body in situ on the pavement, less than five hours had elapsed in total, and De

258

Sancha was almost done. It was coming up to 5 p.m. If they'd had Theobald, Grace doubted they would even be halfway through by now.

Archie Goff lay naked on the steel table, with his hair shaven directly above the gash behind his right ear, giving that side a bizarrely fashionable look. There was also a contusion at the base of his neck. His clothes had been removed when he'd first been brought here, each item carefully bagged and labelled for later forensic examination for fibres, hairs and blood spots that might yield clues about who had killed him.

Nadiuska dictated into her machine at intervals throughout the process, providing Roy Grace and everyone else present with a steady commentary. Despite her decades of living in England, she still retained some of her origins in her accent, and it was a voice, Grace thought, that even in a situation as grim as this, was laced with charm as well as frequent flashes of humour.

'The deceased was found on a pavement in a Saltdean residential street, so one of my tasks is to try to establish if that is where he actually died. Was it on this street or in another location and his body later deposited there? I don't have sufficient information to give a clear time of death but,' her eyes twinkled, 'our good friend Dr Rigor Mortis is very happy to share some of his little clues with us. When I first began my examination, the deceased had fairly well-developed rigor mortis over his whole body – the fingers, jaw joints, arms and legs all stiff, the joints all difficult to move, and he was completely cold to touch.' She turned to Grace.

'Roy, it would be helpful if we could establish how long he had been lying on the pavement, because the length of time he was exposed to the elements would help us to be more precise about the rigor mortis development.'

'I have a team doing a house-to-house in the area, Nadiuska,' he replied. 'They're asking if anyone saw anything, and also whether anything was picked up on any private CCTV cameras.'

'Excellent.'

Grace saw her look at her watch again, then shoot a glance at the wall clock once more. 'What's your gut feeling about where he died, Nadiuska? The pavement or somewhere else?'

'It's more than a gut feeling, Roy. I'm fairly confident from what I've seen so far that he died in another location and was subsequently deposited on the pavement – possibly thrown out of a car. One thing that leads me to that is he was lying in the street in a different position to the one in which he lay at the location where he died.'

Grace glanced at Branson and saw him frown; he was pretty sure why she had deduced this but asked her all the same, for confirmation. 'OK, interesting, what makes you think that?'

'A major clue is the presence of what I would term *inappropriate* hypostasis.' She pointed at the purple mottling colour around part of Goff's stomach. 'Hypostasis develops gravitationally after death, in the parts of the body lowest to the ground. When the heart stops pumping, the blood pools instead of circulating, and it collects wherever gravity draws it. This purple blotching around the stomach indicates the deceased lay on his front for some hours after death, allowing the blood to pool in the stomach area. But, on the street, he was lying on his back. If he had died in that position, we could have expected to have seen hypostasis on his back, but there isn't any present.'

Grace nodded in agreement. He looked at the gash and the congealed blood behind Goff's right ear. 'Have you been able to determine the likely cause of death?'

She pointed at the injury. 'That didn't happen from a fall – it looks to me that he was struck deliberately – if I had to hazard a guess, I'd say that wound could have been made by an object with a sharp edge.'

She turned to the CSI, James Gartrell. 'James, please take a series of close-ups with right-angle scale of this injury.'

The photographer complied meticulously. Grace knew this would allow for any images to be subsequently produced on a 1:1 scale and compared by the forensic scientists. This could be invaluable evidence if the object that had caused this wound was subsequently found.

Next, she pointed at the dead man's right nipple. 'See that tiny mark? This looks to me like a burn – possibly from an electrode clamp.' She walked down the body and pointed to a burn mark on his scrotal sack. 'This too indicates he may well have been tortured.'

Out of the corner of his eye, Grace saw Branson wince. 'Shit,' he said. 'Poor bastard.'

'I can only imagine the pain,' she said.

'Not sure I even want to imagine it!' Glenn Branson added.

Next, she pointed to a blackened circle in the middle of his chest. 'That looks to me like a cigarette burn.' Then, with a gloved hand, she raised the dead man's left arm. 'You noticed his fingers, Roy, when you first saw him on the street. All four fingers of both hands crushed, the nails blackened, as you can see. Did you ever hit one of your fingernails with a hammer, or slam one in a door?'

'Yeah, I did,' Branson said. 'I was sitting in the back of my dad's car when I was about twelve. Had my arm out of the rear window and curled round, holding the driver's door frame. Then my dad got in and without realizing, slammed the door on it. It was probably the worst pain of my life – and I lost two nails.'

Nadiuska nodded. 'Yes, it is the worst pain. Something like that happened to me once, too. But you don't get the fingers of both hands slammed in a car door, or any door. I'm only speculating, but I would say this was done to him as part of his torture.'

'That's a classic gang method of torture,' Branson said. 'I've seen that before.'

Grace added, 'From my experience it's a form of punishment widely used in turf wars by Eastern European drugs and human trafficking gangs, including the Serbs and Romanians.'

The pathologist next pointed at red marks on the dead man's wrists and ankles, and in a line across his chest. 'I'd say these were made by restraints of some kind, cord or wire ligaments.'

All of Goff's internal organs had been removed, sliced into segments, scrupulously examined visually, weighed and then – apart from his dissected heart, which was still in a steel basin, bagged in white plastic – inserted inside his hollow midriff before it was stitched up, to ensure that all of him, barring the fluid samples she had taken for lab analysis, would be present when he was finally released to the undertaker for burial or cremation. All of the segments of his heart would eventually be placed in there, too.

She walked over to the weigh scales, on which lay the stainless-steel bowl containing the pieces of Goff's heart, and carried it back over, placing it on a table, nodding for everyone to look, then shooting another glance at the clock. 'This level of torture, the pain combined with the fear it would have caused the victim, would have been sufficient to bring on a heart attack in a man of his age and health.' She picked up a scalpel and sliced slowly through one of his heart valves. There was a distinct crunching sound as she did so. Looking at both detectives, sharply, she said, 'Did you hear that?'

'That sound?' Branson asked.

She nodded. 'Calcification. Badly furred arteries constricting the blood flow. This gentleman was a heart attack waiting to happen.'

Roy Grace considered this for some moments, then asked, 'Would you be able to say this was definitely causal, Nadiuska? I'm asking because if and when we bring his killer – or killers – to trial, we need to make sure we can prevent a defence brief from saying he died because he had a heart problem, and that his clients never had any intention of killing him.'

'It's good you've raised this, Roy.' She pointed a finger down at a segment of Goff's heart, a reddish brown colour, with white blotches. 'I found a fresh thrombus – blood clot – blocking one of his main coronary arteries, actually the left anterior descending artery. This reveals the immediate cause of death as a myocardial infarct.'

'Can you translate that into layman's language?' Grace asked.

'I can, Roy, but I'm not sure it's going to be helpful in the way you need. This gentleman died of a classic heart attack. The left anterior descending artery is pretty much the worst coronary artery to have a blockage in – that's the reason the more cynical members of the medical profession refer to it as the widow maker.'

'Great,' he replied flatly. 'So a smart brief could argue that he had a heart condition that the torturers could not have known about, and that's what killed him, right?'

'I'm afraid so, Roy. He could have died at any moment – during any exertion like climbing a staircase, or,' she smiled, 'at the moment of orgasm.'

'Yeah, well, when I peg it, I'd like to go that way,' Glenn Branson said.

'Wouldn't we all?' Nadiuska retorted. 'The reality is that most of us with heart conditions will die in a hospital corridor, with a hungover medical student jumping up and down on our chest.'

Grace and Branson laughed.

She looked at her watch, then at the clock again and switched off her recorder. 'This is as far as I can go today. Perhaps the fluid samples I've taken will indicate something more helpful, when we get the toxicology report back from the lab. But for now, I have to tell you that the apparent cause of death is heart attack induced by torture.'

'Thanks, Nadiuska,' Grace said.

She raised her gloved hands in the air. 'I'm sorry, I know you need more than this, but let's see what we get from the lab. Would you forgive me if I have to run? It's my birthday actually, and my husband has arranged something for tonight.'

'Your birthday? Your thirtieth?'

'Ha! I wish – and thank you for the compliment.'

He grinned. 'Happy birthday!'

'Happy birthday, Nadiuska!' was echoed by everyone else present.

Cleo turned to her husband and said quietly, 'I'll see you at home – I may be a little while.' She pointed at the gash on Goff's head. 'I want to check something out.' She gave him a strange look, as if she was trying to indicate something.

He frowned, then smiled, taking the hint. 'Sure,' he said. 'I'm not going back to the office. I'll take Humphrey for a walk and get supper ready.'

'We've got those nice cheeses we bought at the market last weekend, in the fridge. All hard ones, no soft ones.' She patted her swollen belly by way of an explanation. 'And there are those oatmeal biscuits you wanted to try in the cupboard.'

'I'll make up a platter. Anything you want me to get on the way home?'

'No, we're good.'

He lowered his mask and blew her a kiss.

Glenn Branson followed him into the changing room where they began disrobing by kicking off their boots. 'Bummer,' the DI said.

'Archie Goff,' Grace said, reflectively, ignoring the comment. 'A proper crim, with a speciality in country houses. What's he done to get himself tortured to death?'

'Burgled the wrong person?' Branson suggested.

Grace nodded. 'Quite possibly. Something feels odd to me

about where his body was dumped, doesn't it to you? Outside Daniel Hegarty's house.'

'It seems to be stretching coincidence rather far.'

'It does. We're investigating the cold case of an art dealer who was hawking around a possibly rare Fragonard painting. We've now got a couple, the Kiplings, who brought what might be a rare Fragonard to the *Antiques Roadshow*. Someone burgled – or attempted a burglary – at their house soon after their appearance on the show. Now we have a dead burglar outside the house of a major art forger.'

Branson questioned, 'We need to be sure we're not making too big a leap here, despite the coincidence, don't you think?'

Grace shook his head. 'Put yourself in the crim's mind. You've just tortured someone for burgling you or, more likely, your boss, and he's died on you, which you weren't expecting to happen. So now you have a problem on your hands – a corpse to dispose of. Let's imagine it happened in Sussex, in the country – country houses are Archie Goff's MO. You've got woodlands, forests, and you've got the sea. But no, you decide to ignore all of these options and drive your deceased tortured victim into a nice, middle-class residential area and dump him on a pavement where he was absolutely bound to be found.'

Branson nodded. 'I get your point.'

Grace, fumbling with the bow at the back of his gown, said, 'Whoever did this wanted the body to be found. It's a message to someone. A very loud and clear message. *Mess with me and this will be you.*'

'A message to Daniel Hegarty, is that what you're saying?'

'We're on the same page.'

63

Sunday evenings were for flopping in front of the television, Daniel and Natalie Hegarty had long agreed, the way they agreed, comfortably, on most things. They lay back, large glasses of red wine in their hands, the bottle on the coffee table in front of them, Rocky and Rambo snuggled between them on the sofa, both watching, as attentively as their owners, the start of a new crime drama on catch-up.

It had been, by any stretch of the imagination – and the master forger's imagination stretched a very long way – a different Sunday. Certainly, an unusual start to the day, finding a dead body outside your front garden gate. And he could tell, from his long involvement with the police – not all of it great – that this wasn't just any Joe Schmo who'd pegged out on the pavement in front of their house.

Certainly not judging by the speed at which a CSI tent had been erected to shield the body from view, and the number of police vehicles that had rocked up during the following hours, the crime scene tape that had sealed off the pavement around the body, and then the fingertip search by officers that had gone on around where the body had lain, long after it had been bagged and removed.

But despite his questions, they'd remained tight-lipped, both to him and to the newspaper reporters who had turned up, about the dead man's identity – he'd seen them take out his wallet and then his driving licence, so they knew, for sure, who he was.

266

In the absence of any information forthcoming from the police officers, the media had turned to him. The reporters from the *Argus*, the *Brighton and Hove Independent*, the *Sussex Express*, Radio Sussex and camera crews from BBC South and ITV News Meridian had relentlessly interviewed, recorded and filmed him. Always the publicity hound, Hegarty had relished the exposure, making sure to get his message across that his new art exhibition of Lowry, Picasso and Modigliani paintings – each dutifully signed by him – was opening next week.

But despite his bonhomie towards the media, after they had all drifted away he was left feeling increasingly uneasy. With his artist's eye for detail, he'd observed the injury on the side of the dead man's head carefully, noting it had been caused by something sharp. And he'd noticed the crushed fingers on both hands. Neither of these things had happened to him out on this quiet and pleasant street. They'd been done somewhere else.

He'd not conveyed this to his wife, and she seemed relaxed by the story he'd fed her. But then, he hadn't given her the full low-down. All he had told her was that the police were doing their normal due diligence that they would do whenever a dead body was found, and it looked like the poor sod had dropped dead from a heart attack, or a stroke. Whatever.

Natalie and he loved each other. They were cool. Life was good. Actually sixty but feeling closer to thirty, his reputation in the art world was beyond his wildest dreams. Never ever had he imagined, way back in his earliest teens, that one day he'd achieve this kind of success and fame. He didn't reckon anyone who'd known him had. Certainly not his art master at Patcham High School, who told him, drily, he had a talent for drawing and maybe he should consider a career using that skill.

Yeah, right, Mr Tosser Turner. You might have shared the same name as one of England's greatest ever artists, but that was as far as your talent – and vision – stretched. One of his biggest regrets was that his teacher had died long before he'd become a household name in the art world.

As the opening credits of the crime drama rolled, along with sombre, moving, orchestral music, Hegarty sipped his wine distractedly, trying to figure out just what it was that was making him so uneasy. Was it that text?

He didn't have to wait long.

His phone, which he'd switched to silent, to not be disturbed during the programme, was vibrating.

A number he did not recognize.

He was tempted to leave it to ring out, but then he wondered – a little irrationally – if it was going to be some information about the dead man outside his house, and made the decision, nodding apologetically to Natalie, to answer it.

He was right, in the wrong way.

64

'I'm real sorry to be intruding on your cosy Sunday evening, Mr Hegarty,' said the polite Southern US accent. 'I know how sacrosanct Sunday evenings are to you English folk.'

Hegarty put down his wine glass, jumped up from the sofa and headed to the living room door.

'Want me to pause it, darling?' Natalie asked.

He shook his head and hurried out, closing the door behind him. 'How can I help you, Mr Kilgore?' he asked breezily.

'Well, Mr Hegarty, I'm guessing you noticed some activity outside your home today?'

'You guess right. It was a little hard not to notice. The whole of Saltdean noticed it, and all the local media.' He didn't like the tone of Kilgore's voice.

'They sure did, I saw it on the news. Very tragic.' Kilgore hesitated. 'If I'm still guessing right, you are wondering about the location. Did this gentleman drop dead on the street outside your house, did someone deposit his body there randomly, or was the location chosen specifically for a reason? Am I correct that's what you might be wondering right now, Mr Hegarty?'

'You seem to be talking in riddles, Mr Kilgore. I'm a little confused.'

'Well, Mr Hegarty, I apologize for that,' he said, his voice maintaining his courtly charm but with a steely undertow. 'Confused is the last thing I want you to feel – and my boss, too. We would just like you to understand loud and clear the message we sent to you this morning.'

'Like a message in a bottle?' Hegarty said facetiously. 'Like a dead man in a bottle?'

'Mr Hegarty,' Kilgore said, his tone now sounding more steely, 'a short while ago I gave you photographs of an original Fragonard to copy, and you were paid good money for this job. When we swapped the pictures over at the Kiplings' house, we discovered the painting on his wall was also a fake. You are the only forger good enough to have done that. So here's what I think: Goff brought the original to you – and I want it. Here's the deal. I will come by tomorrow morning, and you will hand me the original. Mess with us again, and the next time you head out to walk your dogs, it won't be a stranger lying dead on the sidewalk. It will be your wife. Goodnight, Mr Hegarty. Enjoy your evening.'

'Hey!' Hegarty said. 'I haven't—'

But Kilgore had hung up.

Hegarty quickly hurried upstairs to look out at the pavement to see what was happening. But all looked quiet. The floodlights the CSIs had erected, along with the tent, had gone, and so had the crime scene tape. It was all back to normal, as if nothing had happened.

Which, ironically, now made him feel more vulnerable.

65

Arriving home shortly after 8 p.m., deep in thought, Roy Grace thanked their nanny, Kaitlynn, for coming in on a Sunday and staying so late, but asked her if she could hang on a little longer while he walked the dog. She told him that Noah was sound asleep and had been good as gold all day.

He pulled on his Barbour and a baseball cap, against the falling drizzle, grabbed his torch and took Humphrey out for a short walk. As he walked through the darkness, wondering about Archie Goff's deposition site outside Hegarty's house, he called the Force Control Room to get an operation name assigned to the enquiry into the man's murder. He was given Operation Porcupine and the option to have another if it caused any issues.

He said it was fine.

Where Goff had been deposited could of course have been sheer coincidence. But his body could have been dumped in any number of woods or lay-bys, or outside any of the 430,000 houses and apartment buildings in and around the city of Brighton and Hove and its neighbouring towns and villages.

But it had been dumped on the doorstep of the city's most famous art forger.

Grace wasn't a gambling man, but he understood odds. One and a half million people lived in the county of Sussex – East and West. The odds of Goff ending up on Hegarty's doorstep by sheer chance were astronomical.

He spent the next twenty minutes of his walk, guided by his torch beam, up through the fields behind their house, using the time to call the key members of the new team he was assembling, asking them to attend an 8.30 a.m. briefing on Op Porcupine in the morning.

Before going back inside, he entered the hen run, checked on the birds, which were all in their shed, asleep on their perches, and retrieved four eggs – two dark brown, his favourites, one white and one blue. As an added precaution against foxes, he shut their door with a breezy, 'Goodnight, girls and Billy!'

Then he went into the kitchen, said goodbye to Kaitlynn and used the date stamp Bruno had bought to mark each egg, then laid them at the back of the tray on the work surface. His son was always in his thoughts. Feeling pensive, he turned his attention to preparing supper, Humphrey sitting on the floor at his feet, looking up expectantly.

'Still hungry, are you, boy? You've already been fed by Kaitlynn, you gannet! Are you ever not hungry?' Grace asked. Cleo had told him after her last visit to the vet that the vet had said he was five pounds overweight.

But as he removed the cheeses from the fridge, unwrapping them and putting them on a wooden board, Humphrey continued staring up at him, making him feel guilty. He cut a few slivers off and slipped them to the dog, who swallowed them like he was inhaling them, and then looked up at his master for more.

'Last slice, boy, OK? And don't tell your mistress.' He kneeled down and patted the dog, hard. 'Fatty boom-boom, are you? Or is it all muscle tone?'

Down on his haunches, Humphrey barked at him. One sharp bark. Grace cut him one more slice – a large one. As he did so he heard the front door opening. Quickly, he slipped it into the dog's jaws and immediately heard Cleo's rebuke.

'Hey, you, I saw that!'

Turning towards her, he grinned. 'I had to – he was fifteen seconds away from dialling the RSPCA to complain we were starving him to death.'

'Yeah yeah, you big softy!' She stood there, in mock disapproval, in a leather jacket over a turtleneck sweater and jeans. 'Overweight dogs are much more likely to get arthritis – no more cheese treats, OK?'

'Understood.' He went across and kissed her. 'Long day, eh, my darling.'

She nodded. 'How about a couple of Virgin Marys? I really crave one.'

'Great idea, I'll make them.'

She grinned and looked at the platter containing an array of cheeses, crackers, nuts, fruit and pickles. 'I'm impressed.'

He mock-bowed, filling two glasses of cold water from the fridge dispenser and placing them on the kitchen table.

'You have recently become quite the Domestic God, haven't you?' she said with an approving grin.

He grinned back. 'Every team needs a water carrier.'

'Is that in the *Murder Manual*?'

'Page one! So, what was it you needed to go and check?'

'Tell you over supper – I think you'll be impressed. Maybe I should be a detective too!'

'Oh?'

66

Cleo helped herself to slices from each of the cheeses, taking a particularly large chunk of the Manchego, then, after hungrily eating several mouthfuls of the cheese and biscuits, as well as a couple of grapes and a slice of cucumber, she said, 'That gash behind Archie Goff's ear, right?'

Grace frowned. 'OK?'

'Nadiuska said she thought it was made by an object with a sharp edge.'

'She did, yes,' he said, picking up a sourdough cracker and smearing some beetroot chutney on it.

'It reminded me of something I'd seen before – it had really been bugging me all afternoon and I needed to go and check to see if I was right.'

'Were you? Tell me.'

She popped another grape in her mouth, chewed and swallowed it, then looking decidedly pleased with herself, she said, 'I think I might be. You've been reviewing the case of that art dealer who was murdered in Brighton a few years ago, right?'

'Operation Canvas. It was one of Nick Sloan's. His name was Charlie Porteous. Yes, we are reopening it, some significant new evidence has come to light.'

She ate a walnut, then another sliver of cheese. 'So you've looked at the crime scene photographs?'

'Of course.'

'I remember it all very clearly: it was the first unsolved murder case I was involved with after joining the mortuary team. Charlie Porteous had a wound on the right side of his face, behind his ear, do you recall?'

Grace thought for a moment, it was coming back to him. 'Yes, he did.' He stopped eating, very curious now. Had he missed something?

'I just looked up the postmortem report on our records – it took a while as it had been misfiled, somehow, when we changed our system. The postmortem was done by Frazer Theobald, and he had put in his notes that the wound was caused by something sharp. Do you see where I might be going?'

Grace looked at her excitedly. 'Go on!'

She smiled. 'From my examination, I think the wounds of Porteous and Goff are similar and may have been caused by some sort of ring with a stone. I've seen similar injuries on other bodies where they have been badly beaten. Maybe I should be on your team?'

'Brilliant, Cleo! You are on the team!' he said.

Humphrey nudged his master's leg, hoping for another scrap but, deep in thought now, Grace ignored him. 'You're right, it could possibly be a link and, if so, a very significant one. Might be a long shot, but – hold on a sec.' He jumped up from the table. 'I'll be back in a mo.'

He hurried upstairs to his den, and it was several minutes before he returned. 'Sorry, darling, I had to look up the name of a specialist in identifying and matching wounds – I've got it. Dr Colin Duncton at Liverpool University Hospital – he's developed some very smart software that can analyse damage to every skin and muscle cell and run a database search for matches. He's been to the mortuary before to look at a wound on a case a while back. Talk me through this again, all you have found.'

Cleo showed him the paperwork and photographs and explained what she had identified, with the potential link between the two murders.

'Darling, this is brilliant. You could be on to something here. I'll have the team looking at it first thing tomorrow. If the doctor can positively link the injuries this could be a breakthrough!'

She smiled. 'Good. Now we've solved that, how about next weekend, regardless of work, we take Noah to the petting zoo at Middle Farm? He'd love that – and it would do us both some good to at least have an afternoon out together as a family.' She nestled her chin in her hands, her eyes looking up at him.

'Love your face!' he said.

'I love yours too. I don't get to see enough of it. So?'

'You're right, let's do that. It's a plan.'

She patted her tummy. 'Bump agrees.'

'He or *she*?'

Cleo shrugged. 'We don't know, do we?'

'Nope.' He thought for a moment. 'But we have that envelope the obstetrician gave us after the last scan. Would you like to know?'

'Would you?'

He hesitated.

'It would help us to know, to choose the right colours for the baby's bedroom, wouldn't it? Shall we?'

He grinned. 'It's in a drawer in my desk. Do you care whether it's a boy or a girl?'

'We'll love her or him just as much. I don't care at all. Do you care?'

Roy Grace smiled back at his wife. 'I'll go get it, but I'm the same as you, I don't care.'

67

Stuart Piper cared.

In truth, he cared far more for the past than the present. You had to live in the *now*, you were trapped in that, he knew. But the present was a conveyor belt that was forever tipping you off its edge, unprepared, into an uncharted future. You could only get perspective by looking at the past and – unlike the present and the future – if you had the luxury to choose, you could decide where in the past you wanted to be.

Piper had just that luxury of choice. And this Sunday night he spent surrounded by the past in his favourite room, the Hidden Salon. It was windowless and paintings hung on all four walls. Soft light glowed from the crystal chandeliers suspended from the ceiling, and subtle light from the lamps over each picture. The log fire blazing in the hearth made it as warm as the womb. Real candles burning in two candelabras on the table in front of him completed the ambience he loved so much.

In the sixteenth century, Europe was under the spiritual leadership of the Roman Catholic Church. Religious beliefs were a matter of life and death. When Henry VIII sought an annulment of his marriage to Catherine of Aragon, who had failed to give him a male heir, the Pope refused. Henry responded by splitting from the Catholic Church and founding the Church of England. After his death, his son, Edward VI, during his brief reign, helped turn England further into a Protestant nation.

Edward was succeeded by his sister, Mary, who did an immediate reversal, turning England back into a Catholic state. Anyone who refused to give up their Protestant beliefs was burned at the stake, earning the Queen the soubriquet Bloody Mary. Subsequently, her sister, Queen Elizabeth, who wanted a strong, independent England with its own religion and trade and foreign policy, re-established the Church of England. She made it high treason for a Catholic priest to even enter England, and anyone found aiding or abetting a Catholic priest faced torture and death.

Priest hunters were established to locate any such Catholic priests. Hiding places, known as priests' holes, became commonplace. Sometimes, in smaller houses, these were little more than cubby-holes behind fireplaces, in attics and in cellars. But in grander Tudor houses, such as the one Piper owned, there was often fine accommodation behind false walls. Like this salon, concealed behind a secret door in the library.

Some collectors bought art for investment. Others to display their wealth. Both kinds of people, Piper despised. The art on his walls was there because he loved it, much of it representing a world he wished he could have lived in. At least through these paintings he could achieve some of that, albeit vicariously.

This Hidden Salon was where he loved to spend his evenings. Oftentimes thinking about who might once have been concealed here. Catholic priests. Outcasts, like himself.

Cohiba cigar in one hand, 1967 Hine single cask cognac in the balloon in the other, he loved to lounge back, in his crimson smoking jacket, on one of the three ornately embroidered – and original – Louis Quatorze sofas arranged around the Queen Anne coffee table, surrounded by the paintings on the wall that brought him the most happiness of all the art in his vast collection.

All of these in this room were by French artists of the fête galante period.

He found such tranquillity in these works in particular. They took him back to a place long before he'd had his face irreparably smashed and where his bitterness and anger had been ignited. Long before the humiliation of his parents when he'd come out, at eighteen, and they'd pretty much disowned him from that point. They could never accept his sexuality.

These paintings were from a point in history where hedonism rocked and anything went. These elegant people, in their fine clothes, in such beautiful settings. Where lovers forever stared into each other's eyes; where musical instruments were played with abandon; where breasts were proudly and shamelessly bared; where life was eternally bacchanalian and sublime. A world where the trees were forever dappled by a sun that never set. Where time was suspended on a state of permanent elegance and joie de vivre.

Like the Keats poem of the two lovers frozen forever on a Grecian urn, all these characters on his walls lived eternal gilded lives inside their gilded frames. They gave the delicious lie, Piper thought, that the past was somehow a less dark and murderous place than the present.

And in this room, with everything old or vintage, including his cigar and Patek Philippe watch – although, at sixty years old, that pretty much counted as modern in this environment – the only real intrusion of the modern day was the presence of the three mobile phones laid out on the table in front of him.

Unless anger counted as an intrusion, too.

And Piper was feeling anger tonight. He didn't like being screwed over, and someone was doing just that, royally. Instead of indulging his normal Sunday evening pastime of looking at one of these paintings, studying the characters, trying to imagine their lives, and visualizing himself there, he was staring at a blank piece of wall. Onyx-coloured. A blank space where there should have been a painting hanging tonight.

Spring. Autumn. Winter. Those three pictures by Jean-Honoré

279

Fragonard were there, with the glaring gap of the missing *Summer* between them. A painting that right now he was being cheated out of by a clever-dick forger.

He took a deep sip of his drink and puffed hard on his cigar to bring it back to life, then blew a series of smoke rings at the ceiling. He always blew smoke rings when he was angry, to calm himself down. Watching their perfect grey-blue circles rise upwards and slowly dispersing. Then he allowed his mind to reflect on how he'd acquired these first three of the Four Seasons.

Starting with *Autumn* and *Winter*.

They'd been discovered ten years ago in the priest's hole of a derelict French chateau west of Paris. The owners, a prominent aristocratic Roman Catholic family, had been guillotined during the Terror of the French Revolution, following the de-Christianization acts of France, in 1793. France did not have the same reverence for historic buildings as England and this ruin was in the process of being demolished when the discovery had been made.

Fortunately for Piper, the foreman was a crook with no knowledge of art, and quietly flogged the two pictures to a local antiques dealer for a few euros. Piper's second stroke of luck was when the dealer, aware the paintings were old but having no idea of what they actually were, took them to a fine art specialist. The man was part of Piper's international network of contacts constantly on the lookout for just such missing grand master works of art. The specialist had bought them from the dealer for the equivalent of £20,000, which the dealer was deliriously happy with. And the specialist had then flogged them to Piper for £100,000 the pair.

It had been a punt for Piper, but Robert Kilgore had been reasonably confident, both from all the history of the paintings he'd been able to glean, and from his own personal eye and judgement, that these were genuine Fragonards. Knowing his boss's ruthlessness – and violent streak – it had been a gamble for Kilgore, too. Piper would not have been a happy bunny if the pictures had been by a pupil of, or other lesser artist than, Fragonard. But he would have been even less happy if they'd subsequently turned up in a saleroom at a major auction house and gone under the hammer for millions.

Fortunately for Kilgore, his subsequent attempts at establishing the provenance – while maintaining the total anonymity of his boss – looked increasingly promising. Two scholars, considered the world's experts on Fragonard, had created in 1982 what had become accepted as the authorized list of his works. It included an entry for the four lost Fragonard paintings of the four seasons. Their provenance, right back to the family who had owned the now-demolished chateau, was well documented along with prints of each of the paintings that had been made in Fragonard's studio.

His next step, to confirm his assessment, had been to hand the paintings over to the octogenarian fine arts consultant to several top auction houses, Sir George Shaw, the renowned world expert on French masters. Shaw had first taken microscopic paint samples from a certified original Fragonard to compare the pigments that had been used by the artist. They had passed this test. Shaw had one final stage – the one he had told Kilgore about many times before – and which had previously exposed as a forgery many seemingly perfect originals.

The brushstroke technique of an artist was as unique as his or her handwriting. It was sometimes, but not always, possible through microscopic examination to detect if these brushstrokes were the original flourish of the artist with gay abandon, or the slower and more painstaking attempt at mimicking them. In much the same way, Shaw had explained, that a handwriting forgery could be detected.

Shaw had declared these pictures, without doubt in his opinion, to be the work of Fragonard.

Just as he had, subsequently, made the same declaration on the painting Charlie Porteous had had in his possession.

When word had reached Piper that Charlie Porteous was surreptitiously showing around to an expert what might be another of the missing Four Seasons paintings, Piper's interest – and excitement – had been piqued. Quite apart from how it might enrich his life, he was well aware how having three of the four would potentially enrich his coffers, should he ever need to sell. But there was a big, pretty near unsurmountable, problem. He'd done business with Porteous once, and to his chagrin was well aware that the dealer would never in a million years do business with him again.

It was his own fault, he rued. He'd stiffed the famous London art dealer a few years earlier with a brilliant Tintoretto fake, commissioned from Daniel Hegarty, and executed to perfection by the forger, right down to the stencils on the back and the auction lot numbers of previous salerooms. Every detail was correct, especially the brushstroke technique that Tintoretto himself employed and which Hegarty had perfected.

Then, out of the blue, the long-lost original of the Tintoretto had turned up in Venezuela, in a haul of art looted by the Nazis – and with unassailable provenance. Charlie Porteous had come after him for the two million quid he'd paid, and Piper had told him to go fuck himself.

Porteous had been faced with a massive hit, both financially and reputationally. Even after the Venezuelan art dealer who had made the discovery had been found shot dead in an underground car park, and the original had conveniently disappeared, there was not a lot of love lost between Porteous and Piper.

Which was why, when Piper heard that Porteous might have a long-lost Fragonard Four Seasons painting, and that the expert was excited that it might be original, he knew that the respected dealer wouldn't have sold it to him, not in a million years. Not for any money.

But he had to have that painting.

Which left him with two options.

Pay big money through an intermediary.

Or.

He'd gone for the second option, and it had worked out fine. Since October 2015, the Fragonard *Spring* that Porteous had been in possession of was securely hung on the wall in front of him, to the left of the onyx gap. Because of the vagaries of proof in the art world, regardless of who had seen and opined on this painting, no one was ever going to be able to definitively link it to the death of Charlie Porteous.

Piper blew another smoke ring. A magnificent one, even if he said so himself. It circled, then spiralled towards the three Fragonards, getting broader and thinner as it rose. Just one more, to fill that gap.

Tomorrow morning, after that scumbag forger had been taught a lesson by Bobby Kilgore, that gap would be gone. Filled by the original that Hegarty would hand over.

Filling a long, aching and hard-won gap in Piper's life.

As well as adding several zeros to his net worth.

68

Monday, 4 November

When one door slammed shut in Daniel Hegarty's face – and on two occasions in his distant past it had been a cell door – another always opened. Born with a happy disposition, he sailed through life, riding the waves on a combination of charm and immense talent. And, normally, he slept well, the sleep of the innocent.

But not last night, after Robert Kilgore's deeply unpleasant phone call, which he hadn't shared with Natalie. In the past, whenever he'd had a problem he would talk it through with her, and his sanguine wife would always have a pragmatic solution. *A problem shared is a problem halved* was one of his mantras. He should have shared this particular one, but last night she'd seemed in such a happy and relaxed mood, he hadn't wanted to break that. So instead he'd kept it to himself, ending up drinking more red wine than he should, in the hope of it making Kilgore's menacing words go away.

But of course, it hadn't. And as always when he'd drunk too much, he lay awake in the middle of the night, his head aching and his thoughts in turmoil, sleeping fitfully and waking frequently at the slightest sound, with a feeling of dread.

Finally, his bedside clock showing 6 a.m., feeling exhausted but wired, he slipped out of bed, pulled on a tracksuit and fleece, went downstairs, tugged on his wellingtons, then opened the kitchen door to Rocky and Rambo, who jumped up at him, barking excitedly. He shushed them with their first treat of the

284

day, a cocktail sausage each, clipped on their leads and took them out on the dark pavement, where there was no dead body today. The forensics teams had not returned.

Wanting to clear his head, he took the dogs for a much longer walk across the Downs than his usual forty-minute morning constitutional before returning home. He showered and then had a breakfast of porridge and fresh fruit at the kitchen table, while watching the 8 a.m. local news.

The main item, ahead of Brexit for a change, was the dead body outside his house. Natalie joined him, eating some even more healthy, high-protein gunk the colour of dog faeces she'd whizzed up in the Nutribullet. 'So, my darling, you never told me about that call last night. Who was it?'

He shrugged. 'It was—'

He stopped as a familiar face appeared on television. It took a second to realize why it was familiar – it was himself, standing on the pavement with the blue and white crime scene tape and the white tent in the background. Talking directly to the camera, he was saying, 'It was just a complete shock! I took our dogs out for a walk, as I do every morning, and saw this man lying there. I rushed over to see if I could help him, but he wasn't moving. I did a first aid course years ago and tried to remember the protocols. But as soon as I touched him, I was pretty sure he was deceased. I-I did the only thing I could think of, which was to dial 999.'

'You have no idea who this man was?' the reporter asked.

'None at all – I've never seen him before – ever.'

'Do you have any idea why he was here outside your house?' she pressed.

Hegarty watched himself shrug and give a bemused smile. 'Absolutely none at all.'

The interview ended and Natalie looked at him. 'Is that true?'

He frowned. 'What do you mean?'

'You know what I mean. I married you because I love you, but I'm not naive. I know that you work for some dodgy people. A dead body outside our front gate? Was that pure chance or is someone you've upset sending you a message? I think you owe me that answer, at least.'

Suddenly both dogs began barking and ran upstairs towards the door. Moments later the bell rang. A long, sharp, insistent ring.

Hegarty saw the instant look of panic in his wife's face.

'It's OK,' he said.

'Is it?'

As he approached the front door, the dogs barking even more frantically, Natalie called out, her voice wracked with concern, 'Use the spyhole.'

'Don't worry, I will.'

He raised the flap and peered through the tiny hole in the door. Despite the distorted image, he instantly recognized the man standing a short distance back.

'It's OK,' he said. He unhooked the safety chain, and leaning down, with one hand holding both of the dogs' collars, opened the door with the other.

Robert Kilgore stood there, all smiles, dapper and faintly flamboyant as ever, in a dark suit with a small green-and-white-spotted bow tie. 'I'm real sorry to intrude so early, Mr Hegarty, and without an appointment,' he said, his voice so sincere he almost sounded as if he meant it. 'Would this be a convenient moment to have a chat?'

'Come in,' Hegarty replied tersely.

Kilgore stepped through the doorway, then kneeled and made a massive fuss of the dogs, letting them lick his face, tickling their bellies, then to Hegarty's surprise digging a couple of treats out of his pocket.

'All right with you if I give them these?'

'They'll love you forever.' Kilgore seemed very different today from his cold, threatening voice of last night, Hegarty thought.

Kilgore fed the treats from the palm of his hand, then stood up and addressed Natalie, who was standing warily behind her husband. 'Good morning, Mrs Hegarty, nice to make your acquaintance again.'

She responded with a polite but cool, 'Nice to see you again, too, Mr Kilgore. Can I offer you some tea or coffee?'

'Coffee would be good, black, no cream.' He smiled. 'My apologies, guess after thirty years in your country I should have gotten used to saying *milk* rather than *cream*, but some habits, you know . . .' He shrugged.

'Shall we go to my office?' Hegarty suggested, then turned to his wife. 'I'll do the coffees, darling.'

'I'll get them, no problem. One for you, too?'

'Please.'

As Natalie walked off towards the kitchen, the two men stood for a moment in uncomfortable silence. Then Kilgore said, his voice lowered to little more than a whisper, 'I'm here on serious business, Mr Hegarty, so I hope you're not going to mess with me. I've come here to save your life.'

69

Because, at the time, Roy and Cleo had wanted the sex of their new baby to be a surprise, after Cleo's first ultrasound scan, several months ago, the obstetrician had kept the secret. But she had given them a sealed envelope containing the answer written on a note, should they ever decide to change their mind. Last night they had finally opened it. The small sheet of paper inside had just one scrawled word on it, in the barely decipherable handwriting doctors seemed to favour: *Girl!*

They were having a sister for Noah! Roy Grace, normally reserved about all aspects of his private life, was so excited he wanted to shout it out to the world. But as he sat at the oval table in the conference room at 8.30 a.m. on Monday morning, the only person he'd shared the news with, so far, was a genuinely delighted Glenn Branson. And he'd had to stop Glenn from telling everyone else in the room. They weren't here to celebrate his joyous news. They were here to find who had killed Archie Goff.

And the more he'd thought about Goff during a restless night, the more he wondered about the connection with Hegarty. Someone had paid his hefty bail of £50,000 to get him released from prison. Within days, the Kiplings, who had appeared on *Antiques Roadshow* with a potentially genuine Fragonard worth millions, had their house broken into – but nothing taken. Possibly the burglar had been surprised and legged it. Then Goff was tortured and his body dumped outside the home of the well-known art forger. Just what the hell was that all about?

On his notepad in front of him Grace had written, *Fragonard – fake or original? Goff bailed in order to burgle Kiplings and steal Fragonard? Punished for failing? Dies. Had his torturers planned to kill him or was death a surprise? Deposition site of his body – random or Hegarty targeted? If so why? Message? For who? And about what?*

He addressed his team. 'This is the first briefing of Operation Porcupine, the investigation into the death of Archibald – Archie – Goff, who was found on the pavement outside a house at 20 Saltdean Close, Saltdean, at approximately 7.15 a.m. yesterday, Sunday, 3 November, and subsequently confirmed as deceased by paramedic Kirsty Nelson, who attended the scene.'

Grace had added to the Operation Canvas team Chris Gee as Crime Scene Manager, DS Exton and DC Boutwood.

'Operation *Porcupine*, did you say, chief?' Norman Potting asked, his voice still croaky.

'Yes, Norman. Come on, give us what you've got!'

'Well, seeing as you ask, I read a good line about porcupines once in a Len Deighton thriller.' He looked around. 'Don't suppose many of you are old enough to remember him. He wrote a brilliant novel about confidence tricksters, with this great line, something like: *"Don't the spines on your back hurt?" said the dog to the porcupine. "No," replied the porcupine, "only when I laugh."'*

'Do you find that happens to you a lot, Norman?' Velvet Wilde asked teasingly in her Belfast accent.

Grace looked at him. 'Is that your best, Norman?'

The DS shrugged. 'Just saying, chief.'

'Thank you, Norman,' he replied and moved on swiftly. 'Before I go into the full details of what we have so far, there is a likely link between this case and Operation Canvas: a very similar wound behind Charlie Porteous's right ear and Archie Goff's right ear that might have been made by the same object. I would stress at this stage it is not evidentially confirmed, but I've requested the services of Dr Colin Duncton at Liverpool University Hospital, who is a leading authority in the field of wound comparisons.'

'He was very helpful on the Jodie Bentley case,' Jack Alexander said. 'On snake bites.'

'Yes, he was, Jack,' Grace replied. 'A second, possibly more tenuous link – at this stage – is the deposition site itself. Goff was dumped on the pavement outside 20 Saltdean Close. The owner of that house – the person who discovered the body – is art forger Daniel Hegarty, who has a quality criminal pedigree.'

'Like his dad before him,' Potting interjected.

'And his granddad, Norman?' Velvet Wilde suggested. 'You must have nicked him, too, at some point, surely?'

Potting harrumphed.

'Can we focus, please.' Roy Grace looked at them both sternly. 'Archie Goff is – or rather *was* – a career burglar, as some of you know, specializing in large, isolated country houses. At the time of his death, he was out on bail awaiting trial on a new burglary charge. The Crown Court, to which magistrates on the bench had referred him, set bail at fifty thousand pounds. I'm frankly surprised, considering his past record and that the occupants of the house were in residence at the time of his burglary, that bail was granted at all. I'm guessing we have to thank the overcrowding of our prisons for that.'

'Do we know anything about who put up the bail – did Goff himself know?' Polly Sweeney asked.

Grace shook his head. 'No, he was in prison for a bit before bail was paid. It was arranged through his solicitor, Paul Donnelley.'

'I thought Donnelley had been struck off?' Potting said.

'Appears not, Norman.' He turned to Polly. 'Can you follow that up, see where it takes us?'

'Yes, sir.'

'What we do know,' Grace continued, 'is that Goff had an accelerant, believed to be petrol – which the lab will verify – poured over him, but it wasn't ignited, which indicates it was done to frighten him. He was badly beaten up and had electrical burns on his body, according to the pathologist, as well as a cigarette burn on his chest. At some point during the torture process, he suffered a fatal heart attack.' He took another sip of coffee.

Velvet Wilde raised a hand. 'Boss, wouldn't the cigarette have ignited the petrol?'

Grace shook his head. 'That burn might have been done before the petrol was poured on him. But even if the petrol was already on him, it only ignites at a certain temperature – unlike what we see in movies when someone drops a cigarette into the petrol tank of a car. All that would happen then is that it gets extinguished.'

'So who said smoking is bad for your health?' quipped Potting.

Several of the team laughed. Grace glanced at him sympathetically. That was some show of bravado, he thought, considering Potting was awaiting a possible diagnosis of cancer related to his pipe smoking. Then he continued.

'Some of you are experienced enough to know that as and when we track down Goff's assailants, a smart defence brief will have a field day with his pre-existing medical condition, but we don't need to concern ourselves with that now. We have four significant lines of enquiry. The first is to find out more about who put up Goff's substantial bail. Second is tracing Goff's exact movements from the morning of his release from Lewes Prison to his death. The third is why he was tortured and by who. Finally, who deposited his body outside 20 Saltdean Close – and why there? Is that location relevant? Is it too coincidental not to be relevant?'

EJ Boutwood raised a hand. 'Sir, does Goff have any history of stealing art? Could that be a link to the occupant of 20 Saltdean Close – Daniel Hegarty?'

'I think it's a possibility, EJ. We'll need to interview Hegarty and see if he has anything useful to tell us. Norman and Velvet, can you pick that up?'

He turned to Alexander. 'Jack, I asked you yesterday to organize an outside enquiry team to do a house-to-house in the vicinity of 20 Saltdean Close. Any luck with anyone who might have seen anything suspicious the evening before, or any CCTV footage?'

'We talked to one lady a few doors up, who's obsessed with people who let their dogs foul pavements, sir,' the DS said. 'She's a little eccentric in my opinion.' He glanced at Polly Sweeney who nodded in confirmation and Alexander continued. 'She has an outward-facing CCTV camera covering the pavement in front of her house and the road beyond, which is there mainly to spy on a neighbour, who she's convinced deliberately gets his German Shepherd to dump outside her house every evening around 7 p.m. We spoke to her at approximately 8 p.m. last night. She said she'd been reviewing the footage and a white van she didn't recognize drove past at approximately 6.45 p.m. She claims to know every car and van in her neighbourhood, and this one struck her as odd, especially at that time on a Saturday evening.'

Sweeney took over. 'She invited us in, to view the footage. The vehicle was a white Ford Transit with no markings. The number plate was recorded but in poor lighting, with a couple of options on one of its numbers and one of its letters. Jack and I ran both through the PNC and came up with two possible vehicles, one belonging to an electrician in Brighton, the other to a funeral director in Eastbourne. We've managed to speak to the owners of both, and we're pretty confident that neither were in Saltdean Saturday evening.'

'The van was on cloned plates?' Grace asked.

'Looks like it, sir,' Sweeney replied.

'Good work, Polly and Jack,' he said, then reflected on this development.

Nadiuska had estimated, very roughly, that Goff's body had been dumped sometime between 6 and 9 p.m. yesterday evening. And during that time a van, on possibly cloned plates, drove in the direction of the deposition site. 'Do you have anything more on this van?' he asked them.

'No, sir,' Alexander said. 'But we've been checking the serials for any similar vans that might have been stolen in the Sussex area during the past week, and we've been on to – and are still working through – all the local and regional car rental companies that might have rented out a vehicle of this description. We have one so far, from SIXT.'

Grace had long thought that Jack Alexander had a big future as a detective and this latest initiative reinforced that even more. He always acted on his initiatives. 'Have SIXT got any CCTV, Jack?'

'They have, sir. They record every customer. Polly and I are hoping to get the CCTV of the one who rented their Transit two days ago, later this morning.'

'Great stuff. I'm going to see the ACC and suggest it's about time we merged the investigations. I'm pretty confident she'll agree.'

70

Monday, 4 November

Hegarty led Kilgore into the open-plan living area, with its magnificent view through the picture-window across to Saltdean Lido and the English Channel beyond, and then into an adjoining room. The bare, stark concrete walls with no windows made it feel like being inside a cave, which was exactly how the artist felt every time he came in here. His man-cave, the place where he was most inspired, away from all distractions.

Copies of paintings, including a Banksy, were among many other works stacked higgledy-piggledy against the walls. Wooden bookshelves on three of the four walls heaved under the weight of reference books on great painters past and modern.

Next to them was a shelf laden with technique manuals. One was titled *Master Class in Seascape Painting*, another *Anatomy Perspective Composition*, and above those, *Dog Painting – the European Breeds*, *Techniques of the World's Greatest Painters* and *Seventeenth- and Eighteenth-Century Colour Palettes*. They were weighted down by a small, plump, white bag labelled *L. Cornelissen & Son, Genuine White Marble Dust. Medium. 1 Kilogram.*

Another shelf contained glass jars with brushes of every size in cleaning solution, as well as a rack of palette knives. And in the centre of the room stood a paint-spattered easel, on which was mounted an elaborate Lowry, evidently a work in progress, as some of the dozens of thin figures populating what looked like a factory forecourt had not yet been coloured in.

PICTURE YOU DEAD

The tart reek of stale cigarette smoke on Kilgore's clothes mingled with the smells of oil paint and turpentine. The American looked around in wonder, as he did every time he came here, into the master's inner sanctum. 'Banksy now?' he said.

'Uh huh.'

'Oh boy, Mr Hegarty, is there any artist, past or present, you can't copy?'

Hegarty smiled, waiting for Kilgore to get to the point of his visit, but the man seemed in no hurry. 'I can copy anyone. But if you want me to forge something that a world authority on the artist could trust, then yes, there is a limit. It's hard to buy canvases dating back much before the sixteenth century. So if you wanted me to fake a Giotto, who was painting back in the fourteenth century, I'd have to level with you and say I could do an exquisite copy, but not a fake that would stand up to analysis.'

Kilgore walked across the room and looked at the densely stacked rows of framed and unframed canvases leaning against the walls. Without being invited, he lifted a few blank canvases out of the way and began rummaging through a stack of paintings behind them.

'You said you've come here to save my life, Mr Kilgore.'

The American took his time before responding, picking his way through several paintings – all bearing the Daniel Hegarty signature. 'Mr Hegarty, I can assure you this is why I am here.' His focus immediately returned to the paintings. He looked at several Hegarty-signed Picassos. After some moments, he said, 'You know, I always thought Picasso was a bit of a jerk and so overrated. Hell, the guy signed napkins in restaurants instead of paying the bills. You ever tried doing that?'

'I've dined out courtesy of Señor Picasso plenty of times,' Hegarty replied with a cheeky grin. 'He's been good to me.' But despite his humour, he was feeling increasingly uncomfortable having this man in his house, in his cave. And the tone of his

295

voice wasn't helping. Despite Kilgore's exaggerated politeness, Hegarty felt a growing sense of menace.

'Is there a dead artist of stature who hasn't been *good* to you, Mr Hegarty?' Kilgore challenged.

'I've not tried the *Mona Lisa* yet – Leonardo set the bar pretty high, although I've heard rumours that the one in the Louvre might be a fake – a very fine copy. What do you think?'

Kilgore nodded thoughtfully. 'Nothing ever surprises me in the art world, Mr Hegarty. But then, nothing ever surprises me about conspiracy theory, either.'

'How about you and your boss commission me to paint the original?'

'Very witty,' he replied, with no trace of humour now in his voice. He flipped around a canvas that was face-in to the wall. 'Well, hey, what do we have here?'

At that moment, Natalie appeared with a tray, and set down mugs and a plate of biscuits on a small table.

Hegarty blew her a kiss of thanks.

She mouthed back, 'I'm off to the S.'

Natalie volunteered as a Samaritan. Their rule was that they always remained anonymous – just in case someone who knew them rang in.

Hegarty blew her another kiss, deeply proud of the tough and incredibly worthwhile work his wife did, then turned to Kilgore, who was studying the painting carefully. As she left the room, he asked, in a distinctly abrasive tone, 'You want to explain just what this is exactly, Hegarty?'

After his wife's footsteps had faded away, Hegarty replied, 'Mr Kilgore, I have a busy morning – do you want to get to the point?'

'Oh I do, yes. But I'd like you to explain just what in hell's name is this picture, Fragonard's *Summer*, doing here?'

Both men were briefly distracted by the ping of the doorbell. Natalie would get it, probably the postman, or a delivery of materials, Hegarty thought. He breathed on his coffee to cool it down, then took a sip. 'It's a copy. Whenever I'm commissioned to make a copy of a very special painting, I make an extra for myself. It's what they call in the rag trade *cabbage*. That's when they're making dresses, frocks, whatever, for a designer label, the factory pattern maker regularly over-estimates the amount of cloth they need and they make an extra one or two outfits for themselves, to sell on eBay or in markets. I do something similar with my art.'

'And how do you tell these *copies – cabbage –* apart from the original – without lab analysis?'

'That's simple. Turn it over and look at the wooden frame of the stretcher.'

Kilgore complied.

Hegarty pointed at an almost microscopic groove in the right-hand cross-member. 'That's done with my fingernail, that's how I tell.'

Kilgore nodded. 'It's an impressive copy. I've made a point of studying Fragonard's brushstroke technique and you've darn well captured it. The frame's not the right era, and it's clearly not an old canvas, but otherwise it's a great forgery.'

His words were praise delivered with glacial warmth.

'I'll take that as a big compliment, coming from you.' Hegarty stared at him, his unease increasing. 'So, you said you've come here to save my life. I'm all ears.'

The American's demeanour changed in a way Hegarty couldn't quite read. 'Do you have a picture in your home that you value above all others, Mr Hegarty? Or, let me put that question to you another way: do you have a picture here in your home that is worth proper money? Perhaps your favourite painting?'

Without hesitation, Hegarty pointed at one hanging on the wall. It depicted a medieval troubadour in a red tunic and knickerbockers, playing the flute to a beautiful woman in a flowing red dress. She was seated on the ground, in a rural setting, with a man in a tricorn leaning over two more seated ladies and two children behind them. In the immediate background was a surreal latticed archway. Classic fête galante.

'I thought you might choose this,' Kilgore said. 'Watteau. The original is in the Uffizi in Florence.'

Hegarty smiled wryly. 'Or so the Uffizi thinks.'

Kilgore frowned. 'I've much admired it. I make a point of going to see Botticelli's *Birth of Venus* and this particular Watteau on every visit I make to that beautiful city – or a city that would be beautiful if it wasn't for the constant noise of those infernal mopeds the Italians are obsessed with.'

Hegarty nodded, still smiling. 'I'm glad to hear it, Mr Kilgore. It makes me happy to know you are able to admire my art when you go to Florence.'

Kilgore walked over to the painting and studied it closely. 'Are you saying what I think you are, Mr Hegarty?'

He raised his arms defensively. 'If you admire a painting and it gives you pleasure, does it matter whether it's the original or a near-perfect copy?'

'Of course it does,' Kilgore snapped back with deepening iciness. 'The original connects you to history, to the world as it was then. If it's a fake, you are cheating everyone who admires it.'

'Exactly.' Hegarty nodded at the painting. 'In which case, I'd strongly advise you to admire this version.'

Kilgore looked back at the painting and then at the forger. 'You're telling me that the Watteau in the Uffizi is a fake and this is the original here?' he laughed.

Hegarty shrugged.

'How in God's name?'

'I'm asked to copy paintings all the time, Mr Kilgore, mostly to save their owners money on the insurance, and mostly I do a clearly identifiable copy. But just occasionally I make a copy that no one can tell from the original.' He smiled. 'And I keep the original for a bit of fun.'

Kilgore looked up at it. 'You realize what this painting is worth, if it is indeed the original, as you are suggesting?'

'Of course. Fifteen, maybe twenty, million pounds, but I can never sell it, as you well know. This is one of the most documented and authenticated paintings in the world today. And here it is on the wall of a humble residence in Saltdean.'

Kilgore gave him a look that Hegarty interpreted as almost respect. 'Well, I'm impressed, Mr Hegarty. If you are telling me the truth, I'm very impressed indeed.'

Hegarty shrugged again. 'It's what I do, Mr Kilgore. Can we now get to the point of your visit?'

An instant later there was a terrible scream. Natalie's voice.

'DAAAAN!'

71

After he had updated the Acting ACC and obtained her agreement, Roy Grace returned to the next briefing meeting, deep in thought. The words of that sage, the thirteenth-century monk, William of Occam, who posited that the most obvious explanation for anything would usually be the correct one, resonated so often for him. He was looking for that *obvious* explanation now.

Archie Goff had been badly beaten. Had his assailants planned to kill him after torturing him, or were they just teaching him a lesson? Had his dying on them spared them the job of finishing him off – or had it created a major problem for them?

Or an opportunity?

Thinking out loud, he said, 'Was Goff being given a punishment for crossing someone, or was he being tortured for information? If the latter, did his torturers get what they wanted before he died?'

'Isn't that level of brutality something we associate with Eastern European gangs, boss?' Jon Exton, who had recently joined the investigation team, replied. 'From what we know of Goff, he operated as a lone wolf burglar – he's very unlikely to have been doing business with any of the gangs, he doesn't have any past form for drugs, or people trafficking. That's not his thing.'

'What about if he'd burgled the wrong person?' Jack Alexander suggested. 'Perhaps the house of an Albanian mobster – someone like that?'

300

Grace nodded. 'It's a possibility.'

'Should we look at all the reported burglaries of substantial properties in the time since Goff's release from prison – and before he went in?' Alexander suggested.

Grace nodded. 'But if Goff upset someone enough to have all that done to him, the person he burgled isn't necessarily the type to think of calling the police as their first resort.'

'Good point, sir,' Alexander conceded. Then he appeared distracted by his computer screen.

Grace thought hard again for some moments. 'We need to try to establish what Goff's torturers wanted and how many of them there were. Nadiuska identified fresh marks from restraints on Goff's wrists, ankles and around his chest. I think it's likely there was more than one person involved in his torture,' he said to the team. 'A minimum of two, maybe more.'

'I agree, boss,' Branson said.

'I'm trying to put myself in the mindset of someone torturing their victim, either for retribution or to get information from them, and then their victim unexpectedly dying on them,' Grace said. 'They chose a street in a smart residential area. The only thing that makes any possible sense to me, as we discussed, is that this street was specifically chosen, for a reason. To make a statement? To Hegarty?'

'We do know that some of the Eastern European gangs put bodies of people who've crossed them outside the homes of their enemies as a warning,' Polly Sweeney said.

'Yes, I've had experience of that,' Grace said. Throughout his career investigating major crimes, he well knew that while every murder was a huge puzzle, hundreds and sometimes thousands of pieces that had to be painstakingly put together, often it was either a piece of sheer luck, or out-of-the-box, blue-sky thinking that ultimately nailed the offenders.

And a wild, blue-sky thought was going through his mind right now. Stuart Piper's name had showed up on the crashed Audi linked to Charlie Porteous's death. Potting and Wilde had interviewed Piper – a significant art collector – in his grand country house, filled with fine paintings. Archie Goff was a career country house burglar. His body had been deposited outside the house of a renowned art forger. Stuart Piper, despite having no criminal record, was of interest to Interpol, and a major player in the art world. Charlie Porteous had a seemingly high-value painting in his possession at the time of his murder. The Kiplings had had an attempted burglary shortly after appearing on the *Antiques Roadshow* television programme with a potentially high-value painting. The burglary had happened very shortly after Archie Goff had been released on bail from prison.

How to make the connection, if there was one . . .

Follow the money? That had in recent times become one of the tenets of major crime investigations. He turned to Denyer. 'Emily, make sure your financial profiling confirms who might have put up the bail money.'

Luke Stanstead raised his arm. 'Boss, intel on Goff is that he had a new love in his life, a lady called Isabella Reyzebal. What we know about her is that she is a lab technician with a hobby of belly dancing.'

'Woo-hooo!' exclaimed Potting. 'If I had a lady like that in my life, I'd do anything to find fifty K to get out and be with her!'

Smiling, and ignoring the reaction of his team, Grace replied, 'You're saying, Norman, if you were Goff, you'd sell your soul for that bail money?'

Potting frowned. 'Meaning what, chief?'

'Meaning just that, Norman,' Grace replied. 'Perhaps Goff, desperate to be with his girlfriend, agreed a deal with one of his network of dodgy pals in exchange for a favour. A pretty big favour.'

Potting nodded. 'I think I'm on your bus, chief.'

'Hope you bought a ticket, Norman,' Velvet Wilde said. 'Or did you use your free Senior Citizen bus pass?'

Everyone laughed, including Grace. 'What I'm positing is that someone wanted Archie Goff out of jail to do a job for them.' He noticed that Jack Alexander was no longer listening but absorbed in reading something on his screen.

'Sir.' Jon Exton raised a hand. 'Are you thinking Goff might have been tortured because he failed to deliver whatever the person who stood his bail wanted?'

'Exactly that, Jon, that is my primary hypothesis right now. We need to find out who really provided the fifty thousand pounds, and establish Goff's movements from his release from Lewes Prison to the time of his death. I'd like you and Polly to see what you can establish from the prison's exterior CCTV – did someone pick him up on his release, on the morning of 24 October, or did he take a bus or train back to Brighton that morning? If someone picked him up in a car, then you might be able to track its movements through the ANPR cameras and Brighton Police's own network of CCTV cameras – we know they cover all the main routes in and out and through the city.'

'Will do, boss,' Exton said and looked at Sweeney, who nodded.

Grace glanced at his notes. 'Our next briefing will be at 6 p.m. Does anyone want to add anything?'

Alexander raised his arm. 'Something of interest has literally just come in, sir.' He pointed at his laptop. 'It's from Andy Slark at the Collision Investigation Unit. It's quite long so I'll summarize. He's managed to retrieve the data from the airbag sensors of the crashed Audi A6 that was discovered in Burgess Hill, on the morning of 16 October 2015. This is the vehicle that was linked to the murder of Charlie Porteous.'

Grace felt a surge of excitement. 'Yes, Jack.'

Alexander continued. 'Slark reports that the airbag sensors fitted to this vehicle – and many other of the more modern upmarket models – measure and record the weight and height of the driver and front-seat passenger with a fair degree of precision, in order to gauge the force of deployment in the event of a collision.'

'Anything else?' Grace asked.

'Slark says that the height and weight of both the driver and passenger were similar.'

After a brief silence, Norman Potting quizzed, 'How similar, Jack? Do you know how accurately the sensors measured? After all, we knew they were about the same height already.'

'He said that within the sensor computer parameters, the driver was six foot one and the passenger six foot. Both weighing approximately one hundred and ten kilograms.'

Potting turned to Velvet Wilde. 'Stuart Piper's house? His hired muscle, they fit that description, right?'

'So do a lot of people, Norman,' she replied.

Potting raised a finger in the air. 'Ah, but the muscle guys are identical twins.'

'Piper's bodyguards?' Grace quizzed sharply.

'Yes, chief,' Potting said.

'It wouldn't necessarily rule them out, Norman. Identical twins aren't always exactly the same height, and we're talking just one inch difference here.'

Potting conceded with a reluctant nod.

Grace carried on. 'First Piper pops up on the crashed Audi's phone list. Which indicates that Porteous's killer knew him. He appears to be a major player in the art world, and significantly, although he has no criminal record, he is on an Interpol watch list. You don't make that list without good reason.'

Potting raised his hand. 'I have spoken over the weekend to a helpful American detective at Interpol, sir,' he said. 'To see if we can get any updates on what we already know, and there is something of possible significance. They believe Piper and a former US national who works for him, by the name of Robert Kilgore – now domiciled in the UK – have an inside track on a substantial number of high-value art works that were looted by the Nazis during the Second World War and ended up in Brazil, Chile and Argentina. They don't have enough for an arrest warrant for either man at this stage, but they have a financial investigation team looking into recent payments that may be linked to them.'

'Do we know the whereabouts of this Robert Kilgore?' Grace asked.

'I'm working on it – he owns a property, an apartment on the seafront in Kemp Town. He also has properties in Savannah, Georgia, and in Buenos Aires, Argentina.'

Grace frowned at the latter. 'A bolthole?'

'Could well be, chief. But it could simply be for business purposes – several countries on the South American continent have historically provided a safe haven for looted art.'

'As well as for looters themselves,' Grace added. 'Yes, it would make sense for someone like him to have some kind of a base there. Good work, Norman. If he's here in England at the moment, we need to talk to him.' Grace turned to Wilde and Potting. 'Remind us, what impression did you get from Stuart Piper when you went to his house recently?'

'Apart from the bum's rush from him and his heavies, chief?' Potting said, only partly in jest.

'I think we got that he's not the nicest or most helpful man,' Wilde added. 'He was very reticent about Porteous, claiming he'd never had dealings with him. Almost pretending he'd never heard of him. Norman and I discussed that afterwards and it seemed strange. Piper is clearly a very rich man, with vast amounts of period art in his house. Porteous was a major London art dealer. It struck us as unlikely that they wouldn't have known each other.'

'Perhaps we'd get more out of him by bringing him in for

questioning,' Grace said. 'A proper cognitive witness interview out of the comfort zone of his home.'

'I don't think he'll make that easy, chief,' Potting replied. 'Just to give you a heads-up on him, he's like a lion who reckons he's king of the jungle.'

'So we should be afraid of him, Norman?' the Detective Superintendent quizzed. 'Are you scared of him, is that what you are saying?'

Potting mumbled, awkwardly, 'Well, no, not exactly, no, chief.'

Grace replied, 'Norman, it's a very dangerous world if police are ever afraid of a criminal, and that will never happen on my watch, OK? A lion might be king of the jungle. But throw him into the shark tank and he's just another meal.' He paused. 'Do you understand?'

'I do, chief.'

'Good. After you and Velvet have spoken to Hegarty, I'd like you both to invite Stuart Piper to come in voluntarily for questioning. But in case he doesn't want to do that willingly, suggest you may return with a search warrant. I've a feeling he's the kind of guy who might not want his house searched.'

Potting looked at Wilde and saw her complicit smile. 'With pleasure, chief,' he said.

In her Belfast accent, DC Wilde said, 'When I was a child, Sundays were a day of rest. The Lord's day. Not yesterday, though.'

'The Lord works in mysterious ways, Velvet,' Grace retorted.

'You'd like to think, wouldn't you, sir, that even murderers turn up for Holy Communion?' she said.

With a wry smile, Grace said, 'That's the problem. Far too many of them do. It's something my old mentor said, many years ago. *Do you know what a murderer looks like? I'll tell you. He looks like you and me.*'

72

Daniel Hegarty, reacting to the terrified scream from his wife, made a desperate lunge for the doorway of his man-cave. Kilgore blocked it, startling Hegarty by pulling out a gun with a silencer attached as he did so. 'I'd be obliged if you'd stay right there,' he said icily, pointing the small black weapon straight at him.

Hegarty hesitated.

Moving the gun closer to the forger, Kilgore said, 'My employer doesn't like vermin, as you've already seen.'

The two men stared at each other with hatred in their eyes.

'My employer also doesn't like being cheated, Mr Hegarty. And I can assure you no one will hear a gunshot in here.'

Hegarty debated charging the old man but hesitated at the deadly serious expression on his face – he looked like he really would pull the trigger. An instant later, another man appeared behind Kilgore. A tall, muscular hunk, dressed in black, with a face that looked tough enough to break a sledgehammer.

'Would you mind turning around please, Mr Hegarty, and putting your hands behind your back.'

'Go fuck yourself.'

Unfazed and still consummately polite, Kilgore said, 'Mr Hegarty, we really do not want to have to hurt your wife, but if you don't do what I ask you, I'm afraid we will.'

As if on cue, Natalie screamed again in terror. 'Daniel – Daniel!'

Again, Hegarty stiffened, preparing to lunge. 'You do not touch my wife,' he yelled at him.

'We'll do whatever the hell we want, Mr Hegarty. If you do not cooperate we will hurt her real bad. Now turn around.'

Very reluctantly and slowly, Hegarty obeyed. He heard footsteps, then rough, powerful hands seized his arms, forcing his hands together, palm to palm, then sharp wires cut into his wrists. He tried to move his hands, but they were bound together as if he had been handcuffed.

A massive hand on his shoulder spun him around until he was face to face with the hulk in black, breathing in a reek of last night's garlic only faintly masked by mint gum. 'Follow me, yeah?'

'Where's my wife? What have you done to her, you bastards?'

Behind the hulk, he now saw Kilgore standing in the middle of their living area, still with the gun in his hand. 'Fuck you, Kilgore.'

'There's really no need for bad language, Mr Hegarty,' he said calmly.

'Not in your twisted fucking mind,' Hegarty retorted.

Before he could duck, Kilgore swung at him. The force of the gun striking his cheek sent him flying; dazed, he lost his footing and fell painfully on his back, on the floor.

The henchman hauled him to his feet. His face was stinging.

'Let's have some manners and some decorum, Mr Hegarty,' Kilgore said, his Southern drawl sounding totally out of place here. 'And let's all calm down before someone gets hurt bad.'

'My wife,' Hegarty said. 'If you touch—'

He stopped in mid-sentence as he saw Natalie, a gag tied across her mouth, her eyes a picture of terror, hands cable-tied in front of her, appear at the bottom of the stairs, with another big thug, also all in black. The two men could have been twins. They *were* twins, he realized. The right hand of the one with

Natalie sported a ring with a massive, vulgar-looking ruby-coloured stone. His twin wore a similar ring, with an emerald.

Elbowing the henchman beside him hard in the groin and hearing a satisfying grunt of pain, Hegarty hurled himself towards his wife. But before he'd got close, he received a massive punch in his stomach, which sent him staggering back, completely winded, and crashing into the pine dining table. He reeled off it, unsteadily, lost his balance and fell, painfully, back onto the floor.

'Just calm down, Mr Hegarty, and take a seat,' Kilgore said, pulling out one of the wooden chairs while still steadily holding the gun in his other hand.

Before he could react, a powerful hand hauled Hegarty back up to his feet, propelled him towards the chair and pushed him down onto it. An instant later, a tie-cord was pulled around his midriff and secured behind the chairback. Then the thug similarly secured his legs. All the time Hegarty looked impotently and helplessly at Natalie, who stared pleadingly back at him.

Kilgore stepped into centre stage. 'Are you sitting comfortably?' he asked.

'Very funny.'

'My friends and I are not here on any laughing matter, Mr Hegarty.' He nodded at the henchmen in turn. They were standing on either side of Natalie now. 'I'd like you to take a look at your wife, Mr Hegarty. She's a very attractive lady, wouldn't you say?'

Hegarty glared in silence, thinking hard, desperately, about what he could do.

'Oh,' Kilgore frowned. 'You don't agree.'

'Touch her and I'll kill you. I'll kill all three of you.'

Kilgore smiled. 'Nice sentiment, but I don't think any of us three are too worried right now about that. What I would say is that your wife has very elegant hands. Beautifully slender fingers. My mama would have called them *pianist's fingers*. Or maybe more appropriately right now, *surgeon's fingers*.' He walked over to her, dragging another wooden chair behind him, and raised her cuffed hands in the air, as the two henchmen forced her down onto the chair. Then he dropped her arms, dug into his inside jacket pocket, and produced a small pair of bolt-cutters.

Fear coiled in Hegarty's stomach as he saw them.

'Here's the thing, Mr Hegarty. My employer and I originally thought that threatening to cut off some of your fingers would be a good way to get what we want from you, and you know exactly what that is. Then we thought about it some more and figured that would prevent you from painting further copies for us. Not smart, right? Not smart, because you are one stubborn son-of-a-bitch.'

Increasingly terrified for Natalie about where this was going, Hegarty said, 'Do what you want to me, but please don't hurt my wife. She's got nothing to do with you people.'

Kilgore smiled. It was the kind of smile that reminded Hegarty of the jaws of a predatory fish frozen inside a block of ice. 'Is that right? Well, the choice is yours, Mr Hegarty.' He pocketed the gun and then the bolt-cutters, raised Natalie's arms and harshly prised two of her fingers apart. 'I'm a very fair man, Mr Hegarty. So I'm going to give you the choice of which two of your wife's fingers I cut off first.'

A terrible, plaintive sound came from his wife's gagged mouth. It tore Hegarty's heart to shreds. 'No, please, cut mine off, not hers.'

'Well, I'd sure like to, but as I explained, Mr Hegarty, that really would not be forward thinking.'

'You seriously think I'm ever going to work for you bastards again?'

Kilgore nodded then frowned, as if he was suddenly deep in thought. 'Oh, I think you will, Mr Hegarty. Because when word gets around the art world about what you've done, no one else is going to touch you with a goddamn ten-foot barge pole.'

'Please,' Hegarty said. 'Please tell me just what the hell I'm supposed to have done? You brought me photographs of a Fragonard painting of *Summer* and you asked me to make a copy of it, which I did. I just kept another copy for myself. What the hell is your problem?'

'It's not my problem, Mr Hegarty. It's your problem.' He pulled out the bolt-cutters again and held them in front of Natalie's terrified face. 'You thought you could cheat me, and more importantly my employer. I think at some time you've had the original painting in your possession. So, if you want your pretty little lady to retain all her fingers, it's very simple. Give me the original that you've stolen, I'll take it back to my employer, and we'll all be friends again.'

'You have this all wrong, and you've a very weird idea of friendship, Mr Kilgore.'

The American lowered his head and looked directly at Hegarty. 'Any more weird than your idea of honesty? Integrity? Do you know the definition of *integrity*, Mr Hegarty?'

The forger stared back at him without replying for some moments. 'And you think you know it, do you?' he retorted acidly.

'Integrity is doing the right thing, even when no one is watching.' Kilgore smiled. 'True?'

'And your point is?'

'You have that Watteau which you claim is the original, and that one of your undetectable fakes is the version hanging in the Uffizi in Florence. You were given that original painting in good faith. No one was watching you make a fine copy. No one could challenge you when you duped the gallery into thinking you had given them back the original, as you've proudly boasted to me.'

'I was just joking,' Hegarty said, nervousness raising the pitch of his voice.

A sharp noise startled them all. It came from behind them.

Kilgore turned and looked in horror at the huge picture-window. Hegarty turned his head, along with the two henchmen. They saw a squeegee on a wooden pole rubbing up and down the glass.

'The window cleaner,' Hegarty explained, unnecessarily.

'Get him the hell out of—'

A moment later a reedy-thin man in his fifties, in dungarees, gave them a happy smile and a wave.

'You have curtains? Blinds?' Kilgore demanded, with panic in his voice now.

'Afraid not.'

'Tell him to go get the hell out of here,' Kilgore said.

'You tell him yourself, I'm a bit tied up right now.'

The American instinctively slipped his hand inside his jacket pocket and gripped his gun.

'Shoot him, why don't you?' Hegarty suggested. Then, gathering confidence, he added, 'He's seen your face and your two gorillas. You're going to have to shoot him. POW! POW!'

'Shut it. Make one signal to him and you're all dead, you both and him. Understand?'

'Actually, Kilgore, I don't understand. You're not in the Wild West of the nineteenth century. You are in twenty-first-century England. Saltdean has one murder every ten years. Three in one day isn't going to look good on your CV.'

'I said shut it.' Kilgore ushered the twins to stand behind the table and, by joining them, the three of them blocked the window cleaner's view.

'He's a Jehovah's Witness,' Hegarty said. 'Very nice man. He could save your soul, and your mates'.'

'Don't push me.'

'I don't need to push you, you're already on the edge of the cliff. That nervous twitch in your eyes is a dead giveaway. Oh, and further bad news, he and his son, who is probably around the front at the moment, will be coming inside in a few minutes, using the key we leave in the shed.'

'You tell them both to go away and come back some other time.'

'I'm not doing that,' Hegarty said, emboldened now as he saw the menace in Kilgore's face turn to concern. 'They are very busy and I need clear windows. We get a lot of salt off the sea – hence the name of this place, *Saltdean*.'

'You are starting to really piss me off, Mr Hegarty.'

'Not half as much as you are pissing my wife and me off.'

An instant later the doorbell rang.

'You do not answer it,' Kilgore said.

Hegarty smiled. 'Not a problem, I don't need to.'

A young male voice called out from upstairs. 'Mr Hegarty, Mrs Hegarty, it's Charlie and Joey, just come in to do the windows!'

73

'I'd advise you untie us pretty quickly, Mr Kilgore,' Hegarty said quietly. 'It won't look too good. And I'd also advise you to put your piece away. Charlie up there is a black-belt mixed martial arts fighter, and if I ask him nicely, he'll shove that gun so far down your throat you'll need an enema to get it back.'

'You're not in any position to threaten me, Mr Hegarty.'

'Actually, I am, and you know that.'

'Shall I start upstairs, Mr and Mrs Hegarty?' the window cleaner called down.

Kilgore, momentarily panic-stricken, told his two heavies not to react.

'Great, thanks, Charlie,' Hegarty called out. 'Tea with three lumps?'

'Top man!' the reply came.

'Tell him to get lost,' Kilgore demanded, but his voice had lost its authority. He stepped back, blocking the view of the window cleaner outside.

'You tell him,' Hegarty retorted.

Kilgore frowned, looking thrown and uncertain what to do next, the gun jigging up and down. Then he said quietly to the twins, 'Untie them.' Levelling the gun first at Hegarty then Natalie, he retreated to the bottom of the staircase.

As the twins removed the bonds around the couple, and the gag from Natalie's mouth, Kilgore announced quietly, 'Here's

314

what we're gonna do, Mr and Mrs Hegarty. We're all going to sit calmly around your kitchen table, like we're having a real friendly meeting, until these two jokers have done their stuff and gone away.'

Still covered by the gun, both Hegartys shook some blood back into their arms, then complied. Natalie exchanged a nervous glance with her husband, sitting next to her. The hired muscle perched opposite and Kilgore took the head of the table, holding his gun low, out of sight. Addressing the couple, Kilgore said, 'If either of you attempt to call for help, I'll shoot you both and the window cleaners, I promise.'

'I don't think so,' Hegarty said.

'Darling,' Natalie cautioned her husband.

Hegarty grinned at Kilgore. 'Four dead bodies? Really? You and these apes don't want to spend the rest of your lives in prison, do you?'

'I mean what I said, Hegarty.'

'You do, so go ahead, shoot me.' He stared at the American hard in the eyes. 'Might be wiser to talk, don't you think?' He stood up.

'Sit down,' Kilgore said.

'I have to make our window cleaners their tea. For Charlie upstairs and Joey outside.'

'SIT!' he snapped.

Rambo growled at Kilgore, who glared down at the dogs then up at the forger. 'I never took you for being a comedian, Mr Hegarty.'

'And I never took you for being a man without a plan, Mr Kilgore,' he said, calmly walking over to the kettle and switching it on.

The twins stood, but Kilgore snapped a hand at them, indicating them to remain seated.

A Banksy copy was mounted on the wall above the cupboards

over the worktop. It depicted two helmeted male police officers embracing passionately and snogging.

Kilgore pointed at it. 'That does not do anything for me.'

'Really? Banksy is one of the greatest modern artists of our time,' Hegarty said, taking two mugs from the cupboard and setting them down on the worktop.

'There are no greatest artists of our time. Good art stopped in the nineteenth century,' Kilgore said.

Hegarty looked at him. 'And there I was thinking you were an art connoisseur.' He dropped a teabag into each mug.

'Excuse me,' Natalie butted in. 'Could we not discuss your issue in a calm and sensible manner, Mr Kilgore? I'm needed on duty, where we are already short-staffed.'

As the kettle started to come to the boil, Kilgore looked at her. 'It's very simple, Mrs Hegarty. On behalf of my employer, I commissioned your husband to paint a copy of a Fragonard for which he was paid well. I believe he has the original painting and I want it. All he has to do is give us the original, *Summer*, and we'll be out of here.' He nodded at Hegarty. 'I'd be prepared to say, *nice try* and let it rest at that. How fair does that sound?'

'My husband is not a liar,' Natalie said firmly.

Pouring water into the mugs, Hegarty shook his head. He counted out sugar lumps from a bowl, dropped some into each mug then turned. 'Mr Kilgore, do you really think if I cheated my customers I would have survived this long in business? You asked me to paint a copy of Fragonard's *Summer*. I obligingly made the quality of copy you requested – one that would stand up to visual inspection, but not a forensic one. And last week, having done the job, I gave it to you. Sure, I made an extra copy for myself, as I've already explained. You can tell from the back easily enough – there are none of the markings you'd expect to find on a painting of that age.' He shrugged.

'What exactly are you saying, Mr Hegarty?' Kilgore asked.

'Let me explain some background, which you are very clearly unaware of. Several weeks ago I was contacted by Mr Harold Kipling, who did some building work here for us a couple of years ago. He told me he'd bought a painting in a car boot sale, which he believed might possibly be an original Fragonard – *Summer* – part of the artist's long-lost Four Seasons paintings. He asked me if I could make a copy which he could hang on a wall in his home, saying he wanted to put the original into a secure storage unit for safe keeping until he could establish whether it was an original or not.' Noting the surprise on Kilgore's face, he went on. 'I duly made a copy for him and gave him the copy plus his original back and kept my *cabbage*. As I've just told you, Mr Kilgore, what would be the point in trying to hang on to the original, which would be unsellable? My business is copying famous paintings, and forging originals. I'm not in the business of stealing art.'

'You know fine well that is bullshit, Mr Hegarty. There are plenty of collectors around the world, in Russia and China among other countries, who pay big money for famous works of art regardless of their provenance.'

The kettle came to the boil and Hegarty filled each of the mugs, then put the kettle down, allowing the tea to steep. 'Not my scene, Mr Kilgore.'

Kilgore looked like he was about to explode. 'You must have known it was your own goddamn copy that we took from the Kiplings' house. Why the hell didn't you say something? You knew why we wanted the copy.'

Ignoring Natalie's anxious glance, Hegarty pulled the teabags out of the mugs, opened the fridge, removed a carton of milk, poured out two measures into each of the mugs, then popped a teaspoon from the drying rack into each.

'Mr Kilgore, I never question the motives of my clients. I make copies of paintings to order, that's a big part of how I earn my living.' He calmly opened a cupboard door, removed a pack of Jammy Dodger biscuits and emptied some onto a plate. Scooping up the two mugs with one hand, he picked up the plate with the other and headed towards the staircase. 'Excuse me,' he said.

Too discombobulated to respond, the American stepped aside.

As he walked out of the room, Hegarty called, 'If you want to threaten anyone, then go and threaten Mr and Mrs Kipling. We saw them on *Antiques Roadshow,* just like you or your employer did. That's where I would start, if you're after the original. You're barking up the wrong tree by coming here.' He hesitated on the third step and went, 'GRRR, WOOF WOOF!'

Rambo and Rocky immediately responded by barking back.

'I don't think they like you and your buddies, Mr Kilgore. Let me give you some advice: always trust the instincts of animals.'

'Why the hell didn't you tell me this about Kipling in the first place?' Kilgore demanded, his voice close to a snarl, as Hegarty came back into the room. 'Why didn't you tell me?'

He smiled. 'Because you never asked.'

74

Monday, 4 November

'Never asked?' Stuart Piper exploded. 'Because you never fucking asked? We're going to fix that bastard good and proper for this. I'll send the boys over. He'll have his arms and fingers broken so badly he'll never be able to pick up a brush again.'

Robert Kilgore had been brought up by parents with proper manners. His father, a lecturer in fine arts at the Savannah College of Art and Design in Atlanta, Georgia, and his mother, who had lectured on the history of art at the same college until she'd stopped to raise her large family, of which Kilgore was the fifth child, had instilled values of morality and decency into all their children.

Despite the fact that he had been employed for the past fifteen years by a criminal, Robert Kilgore had justified this, by his own moral compass, because he was engaged in the work of recovering fabulous works of art by the great masters of the fête galante period, which he particularly loved. Nothing thrilled him more than hunting down and securing their works. But as he grew older, he was increasingly concerned that his employer, who he had once thought shared his values of preserving these works for posterity, was far shallower than he'd assumed. He was beginning, increasingly, to feel conned. Used. That Stuart Piper did not really want all these fine paintings for any altruistic purpose, but purely to satisfy his own massive ego.

Nevertheless, seated in Piper's study, he kept his calm. Lighting

319

yet another cigarette, he said, 'It seems like we've been fooled by the sheer quality of Hegarty's work.'

'*We?*' Piper queried acidly, tapping the end of his cigar in a large grey ashtray, with the name Courvoisier emblazoned in gold lettering along the side. 'There's no *we* about this, Bobby. I pay you a big salary and you can't tell the difference between an original and a fake?'

'Not when it comes to an artist of Hegarty's skills, no, sir, I sometimes cannot. Not without a lot of forensic tests. But what we do know now is that the original is with Mr and Mrs Kipling, and that's a real positive.'

'Is it? They turned down our last offer for the picture. A very generous offer, considering we had no evidence that it is an original,' Piper reminded him. 'Now word on the street is that it is the original. Are you hearing that?'

Kilgore nodded. 'I am, yes.'

'So, any day, those fuckwit Kiplings are likely to hand it to an auction house. Sotheby's or Bonhams or Christie's or Phillips, right?'

'We don't know that for sure,' Kilgore said.

'They want money.' Piper, behind his desk, tapped a sheaf of papers, with a bunch of blown-up photographs clipped to them. 'What I have here are my notes from the report Archie Goff gave us when he first went into the Kiplings' house. We asked him to photograph any financial documents he could find, right?'

'We did,' Kilgore agreed.

'We figured from these statements that the amount we offered, fifty thousand pounds, would get the Kiplings interested – and they threw it back in our faces.'

'Maybe we should have gone higher?' Kilgore suggested.

'I've never paid over the odds in my life, Bobby.' There was a sneer in his voice that did not appear on his face. 'And I'm not going to now. Archie Goff did a better job for us than we realized.'

He slid out some of the close-ups of bank statements, and held them up, one at a time.

Kilgore dug his half-frame spectacles from his pocket and pulled them on, although he had already studied all of these statements some while back. 'He did do a good job, sir,' he agreed. 'It enabled us to figure out that the Kiplings' finances could be better.'

Kilgore picked up one and studied it. In a corner of the picture, near the bank statement, was the partial image of a small yellow box, marked FREESTYLE LIBRE 2. FLASH GLUCOSE MONI-TORING SYSTEM. SENSOR. He looked at his boss and frowned.

'Look at the other one, Bobby.'

It was a photograph of a paper bag bearing a chemist's logo. On the side was stuck a prescription label, marked TOM KIPLING. Kilgore frowned again. 'This is what, exactly?'

'A diabetes monitor,' Piper said. 'I know all about it because Frank's a Type-1 diabetic.' Frank was his head gardener. 'It's a smart bit of kit – he wears a Libre sensor on his arm and moni-tors his blood-sugar levels through it via an app on his phone. It tells him if his sugar levels are too low or too high. If they drop too much he can pass out and if he doesn't get sugar, die in a matter of hours. Similarly, if his sugar levels get too high and he doesn't inject enough insulin, he can go into a coma, and again die in a matter of hours. The Kiplings' kid is evidently, from this, a Type-1 diabetic.'

'And you are saying what, exactly, sir?' Kilgore asked.

'I think you know exactly what I'm saying, Bobby.' His lips widened a fraction into what, in Piper's almost frozen face, Kilgore had long ago learned to interpret as a smile. 'And what I'm also saying is that we need to move fast. This is our chance, and I'm coming up with a plan.'

75

Monday, 4 November

Daniel Hegarty, in his paint-spattered smock, stepped back from his easel, which he had set up in the bright living room. It was where he liked to work on fine days, the dogs curled up asleep close by. He was putting the finishing touches to the Lowry painting he'd been commissioned to do by a radio celebrity.

Nice work, five thousand quid for something that had taken him just three days. Half a dozen spindly bookies, each sporting a trilby at a jaunty angle, stood on their stools beside their boards displaying betting odds, bagmen to their right, while racegoers in their finery paraded in front of them.

It had been a very long morning, after the unwelcome intrusion earlier, but he smiled with some satisfaction looking out across the Saltdean vista, which he could now see through sparkling windows. And thanks to the window cleaners, Kilgore and his men had been shown a clean pair of heels.

But he was deeply upset about the trauma Natalie had been put through, and she would no doubt have a few choice words about his promise to her of going straight, when she returned from her shift with the Samaritans. But maybe she'd appreciate the situation when he told her what the truth really was. He grinned again at the knowledge. His little guilty secret. *Hegarty one, Kilgore nil!*

He was feeling hungry, and as he now needed to leave the painting for an hour, while the cocktail of chemicals he'd just

322

brushed on did their work in ageing the picture, it was a good time for lunch. He would make himself a ham and tomato sandwich on sourdough, using some of the delicious Serrano ham he'd bought from a local deli, and maybe a small beer to steady his nerves, and inspire him to dash off a few convincing saleroom marks on the rear of the canvas this afternoon.

The doorbell rang. Instantly the dogs raced up the stairs in a tornado of yapping. He frowned, not expecting anyone. Probably a new book he had ordered from Amazon to help him with a very lucrative fresh commission, copying a Dante Gabriel Rossetti painting for a rogue middleman he'd known for years, Ron Patchouli, as slippery as the oil but less fragrant.

The fixer, who had handed him the picture along with a down-payment of £10,000 in cash, had told him the copy was for a wealthy Saudi client who loved the English poet and artist's work. Hegarty knew the painting, it was famous, considered one of Rossetti's finest works, and formed part of a collection in a Midlands stately home. 'Is this hot?' he'd asked him dubiously.

'Nah,' Patchouli had replied brazenly. 'We've only borrowed it!'

Rocky and Rambo raced ahead of him up the stairs and began jumping up and down against the front door. Warily, he peered through the spyhole, in case it was Kilgore and his boys, and saw two people standing outside, a portly man in a suit and a smartly dressed woman beside him. Engaging the safety chain, he opened the door a crack, and above the yapping of his dogs asked, 'May I help you?'

'Mr Daniel Hegarty?' asked the female with a Belfast accent.

'Who are you?'

The man held up a warrant card. 'Detective Sergeant Potting and Detective Constable Wilde from the Surrey and Sussex Major Crime Team. Could we have a word with you, sir?'

'Is this about the body?'

'We won't take up too much of your time, sir,' the female officer said pleasantly. 'We appreciate you've probably had your fill of police around here in the past twenty-four hours.'

Unhooking the chain and grappling with the dogs at the same time, Hegarty let them in, closing the door quickly to keep the dogs safe. Immediately the female detective kneeled and began making a fuss over both of them, while her male colleague stood looking at them warily.

'Do they bite?' Potting asked.

'Yeah,' Hegarty replied. 'All dogs bite, that's how they eat. But it's all right, they've already had a whole postman today, so they're not hungry.'

As he led them through, Hegarty heard a voice and a crackle of static behind him, then indicated for the detectives to sit at the table at which he and Natalie had, just a few hours earlier, been held captive by Kilgore.

The female officer stopped to look at the Lowry on the easel. 'I like that – is this the kind of painting you do?'

Hegarty waved his arms expansively around the room, pointing at a Picasso, the Banksy and a Caravaggio. 'I like to think I can turn my hand to pretty much any artist,' he said. 'Like art, do you?'

'I do.' Then she gave him a pointed look, her voice turning sharper. 'When it's genuine.'

He laughed. 'You've come to the wrong place then.'

The one with the cheap suit and gruff voice looked up at the Banksy on the wall. 'Two coppers snogging – what's that about?'

'Two million quid, if it's the original,' Hegarty retorted facetiously.

Potting cleared his throat, then focusing on the purpose of their visit asked, 'Mr Hegarty, does the name Archie Goff mean anything to you?'

He thought for a moment. The name rang a very faint bell,

maybe somewhere way back in the city's criminal community. He shook his head. 'No, why?'

'He was the unfortunate person you found yesterday morning on the pavement outside your house. We are trying to establish whether his body was put there at random or whether you might have had some connection with the deceased.'

'You're a detective?' Hegarty said.

Potting gave him a wary look. 'I am, yes.'

'Well, Detective Sergeant Potting, I was the one who found the body yesterday morning. Don't you think if I knew him, if I recognized this *Archie Goff*, I'd have said so?'

'Unless you had something to hide,' Potting fired back sharply. He leaned across the table a little closer to Hegarty and, watching his face carefully, asked, 'Does the name Stuart Piper mean anything to you?'

The hesitation before Hegarty replied was enough. Further confirmation came as, shaking his head and smiling politely, he raised a hand and scratched his hair at the back of his head. Both signs, Potting knew, might indicate someone was lying.

'No, no, it doesn't,' he answered.

'Are you certain, Mr Hegarty?' Potting pressed.

'Stuart Piper, you said?'

'Correct. You've never done any work for him in the past?'

Hegarty felt a flash of discomfort. Something in the expression of the two detectives indicated they knew more than they were letting on at this moment. 'Stuart Piper?' he repeated, feigning deep thought. 'Actually, that name does ring a bell.' Then, as he lapsed into deep thought again, he was no longer feigning it. And he had to mask his smile as he came up with his response. 'I've not dealt with Piper directly, but there is a gentleman you might want to talk to. He's an American, based here, name of Robert Kilgore. Nasty piece of work; you might find it helpful to have a word with him.'

'Where might we find him?' DC Wilde asked.

'I believe he's employed by Mr Piper. But I'd be grateful if you didn't mention I told you that.' He shot both detectives a look which they acknowledged.

'You've been very helpful,' Norman Potting said.

'What kind of dealings with Mr Kilgore did you have?' DC Wilde pressed.

Hegarty shrugged. 'None that I was very happy about.'

'Can you expand?' she asked.

'Client confidentiality,' he replied with a wink.

'Do we gather you don't care for Mr Kilgore?' Potting asked.

'You could say so,' Hegarty replied with a grin. 'And I'm not faking it.'

76

Monday, 4 November

Harry Kipling never normally stopped off at a pub for a drink on his way home. Nor was he much of a person for drinking alone, but at this moment he felt badly in need of a pint. Needed to think. Needed some Dutch courage before telling Freya the bloody awful news.

Just one pint then he'd go home and face the music. Shit, what a day. And with the clocks having recently gone back it was dark as he drove towards Brighton, passing the bleak, vast hulk of the long-closed cement works on his left.

Vine Cottage in Steyning had turned in the past days from a minor disaster into a bigger one, and he cursed himself. If only he hadn't tried to cut corners and make a quick profit, all this could have been averted. But now the structural engineer had glumly informed him that as a result of knocking down the end wall, the house needed to be underpinned. The occupants had been advised to move out and stay in a hotel until it was made safe. He wasn't quite sure how he was going to explain to Freya that he was now likely to at best break even on this project and more likely make a loss.

At the large roundabout, instead of turning onto the A27 dual carriageway and the quick route home, he chose the coast road, making for a pleasant-looking pub he'd driven past dozens of times, but had never been inside. It was just past 5.30 p.m. and the forecourt was almost empty. He parked, went inside, ordered a pint of Harvey's in a jug, ignoring a couple of pub bores who were arguing with the landlord about a new striker Brighton and Hove Albion had paid big money for, and took his drink over to a table in a deserted corner.

As he sat down, his phone rang. It was a number he didn't recognize and he hesitated, debating whether to hit the decline button, but instead he answered it, warily, just in case it might be a new potential client. 'Hello?'

He heard a buoyant, forceful male voice he vaguely recognized. 'Mr Kipling?'

'Yes?'

'It's Barnaby Jackson!'

'Yes, hello,' he replied, trying to place the name as well as the voice.

'From Bonhams in London.'

Now it clicked. 'Ah, yes, hello.'

'How are you doing, Mr Kipling?'

'Yep, OK,' he responded.

'Have you had a good day?'

'Actually, I've had better.'

'I'm sorry to hear that. I was wondering if you still have that painting you brought along to us, the one that might be an original Fragonard?'

'Actually yes, I do.'

'Have you been able to establish anything more about its provenance, Mr Kipling?'

'I'm afraid not, nope, it's pretty much as you saw it.'

'Well, OK, good. Fine. My colleagues and I have been doing some research and we are pretty certain it could well be authentic. The reason I'm calling is we have a major sale of art from the fête galante period coming up and I thought it might be of interest to you to consider entering this work.'

'Really?' He spoke quietly, although the only other people in the saloon bar were still engaged in their discussion with the landlord.

'This will be the biggest sale of works of this period for some years and we'll have the top buyers from around the world bidding. There won't be an opportunity like this, to get top money for this picture, for some while. Obviously, we'd need to run further checks on its authenticity, but I thought I'd give you the chance to consider it for inclusion in this sale. That is of course if you haven't already made other plans for it?'

'No, my wife and I haven't,' Harry replied, perking up a little. Maybe this was the solution to his problems. So long as the experts Bonhams consulted gave the painting the thumbs-up.

And if they didn't?

Then no one else would and they'd be no worse off. He didn't need to speak to Freya, he knew what she would say. *Sell it!*

'When is this auction happening?' he asked.

'23 January. So we have plenty of time to get its authenticity and provenance checked.'

23 January, Harry thought. Nearly three months away. Hopefully the bank would support them until then. 'Could you send me an email with your thoughts on the value this could realize, if genuine?'

'Absolutely!' Barnaby Jackson replied.

77

Monday, 4 November

Roy Grace started the 6 p.m. briefing by handing a bunch of photocopies to Glenn Branson on his right and EJ Boutwood on his left to circulate. Crime Scene Manager Chris Gee looked like he was bursting to say something, but the Detective Superintendent signalled with a finger for him to hold fire.

After everyone around the table had a copy in front of them, Grace said, 'What you're looking at is a mock-up of a ring with a large stone. We sent the forensics expert at Liverpool University Hospital, Dr Colin Duncton, images of similar gash marks found behind both Charlie Porteous's and Archie Goff's right ears. The professor needs more time, but his initial assessment is that both contain sufficient identical features to link them, and he believes they were most likely caused by contact with a ring with a large stone cut as the one illustrated. He's made a computer mock-up of the kind of ring, which is what you have in front of you.'

'Christ!' EJ said. 'Who wears a ring like that?'

'Someone into bling,' Branson said. 'Someone who likes to show off.'

'Not you, then, Glenn?' she ribbed him.

'Haha.'

After studying the image intently, Potting glanced at Velvet Wilde. 'Both Piper's muscle men were wearing rings with big rocks, weren't they?'

'One red, one green,' she confirmed.

'Port and starboard.' Potting turned to Grace. 'Chief, I appreciate this is not conclusive, but in terms of matching height and weight, and now this information about the rings, Stuart Piper's bodyguards are ticking a few boxes.'

Grace grinned. 'Sounds like the Piper mansion could be a very happy little household, all cosied up together in the nick.' Then he shook his head. 'I agree with your thinking, Norman, but I don't think we have enough yet to bring them in for questioning. As I've said, the information from the Audi gives us two people of similar height and weight, but we can't extrapolate from that that they're twins. A lot of people wear big rings – male and female. And you're making the assumption it was a male wearing the ring, but we don't have strong evidence for that at the moment.'

Chris Gee interrupted as if he couldn't contain his news any longer. 'Actually, sir, I have something that may be very helpful.'

'Go ahead, Chris,' he replied.

Gee held up another sheet of paper on which was a blown-up section of a fingerprint. 'I've been doing some work around the partial dab recovered from a restaurant bill inside Porteous's wallet. It was too smudged for a match to be obtained, but that was then, and this is now. Technology has moved on and while the owner of the print is still unidentifiable, the lab have discovered DNA on the bill. They're working on it right now.'

Everyone stared at him in silent expectation.

Grace felt the beat of excitement he always got when the net was closing in on suspects. 'When do they expect a result, Chris?'

'I would hope within the next forty-eight hours, sir.'

He turned to Alexander. 'I think Jack has something to add to this mix,' he said, nodding at the DS.

'I do, sir,' he said, then addressed the team. 'I was tasked with tracking Archie Goff's movements from the time of his release from prison, which I've done with the assistance of Lewes Prison's external CCTV cameras, ANPR and the CCTV network around Brighton. On the morning Goff walked free from Lewes Prison he was picked up by a Jaguar XJ6, registered to none other than Ricky Sharp – a gentleman well known to us!'

Grace smiled. 'Good work, Jack.'

Alexander continued. 'Sharp, assuming he was driving his car, then drove Goff to the Grand Hotel, depositing him there at approximately 10.15 a.m. At 11.05 Goff emerged and was driven in the Jag, again presumably by Sharp, to the home he shared in Hollingdean with his girlfriend, Isabella Reyzebal. After that, Sharp's Jaguar headed back to the Southwick district of the city, where he resides.'

'What about Goff – any vehicle registered to him or his girl-friend that could be tracked?' Grace asked.

'There is, sir – a Vauxhall Astra, index Alfa Victor Five-Two Uniform Yankee Romeo, was spotted, seemingly abandoned, by an alert lady walking her dogs. It was in a clearing in woods half a mile from the main entrance to Hope Manor, two days after Goff was nicked for attempting to burgle that house. She phoned it in and, guess what, the vehicle was registered to one Archie Goff! It was checked over, and then recovered to the police pound at Hickstead, where forensics went over it before releasing it for collection by Goff's girlfriend, Isabella Reyzebal.'

'Thank God for dog walkers!' Exton said. 'Would we ever solve any crime without them?'

'God bless 'em!' Chris Gee said. 'I agree!'

'I've done an ANPR trace on the Astra,' Alexander continued. 'It didn't ping any cameras until the day after Goff's release from prison, so it may have been parked up. Then over the days following his release – I have the exact dates and times – it twice pinged cameras close to the Kiplings' house in Mackie Crescent. I'm guessing that the Kiplings' house was his destination, but on each occasion he didn't ping any further cameras. Other venues in that vicinity he might have visited are the Miller and Carter pub and the Elizabethan Cottage Tandoori.'

'For a takeaway, Jack?' Potting quizzed. 'That's kind of his style, isn't it? He likes to *take away*.' He chortled at his own thin joke.

Alexander, looking down at his notes, continued without reacting. 'The last journey the Astra made before Archie Goff was found dead was into central Brighton. The CCTV team in the Control Room have done a brilliant job of mapping his journey, down the London Road to one of the car parks behind Churchill Square at around 10.30 on Saturday morning. He was also picked up by two cameras on foot heading down into the Lanes, and returning to the car park just after 11.15, seemingly holding a carrier bag, but they can't identify any shop or brand label on the bag. That's the last sighting of him alive.'

'And the Astra, Jack?' Grace asked.

'It's still in the car park, sir. An attendant located it for us.'

Grace made a note. 'So that's possibly where he was seized,' he said.

Alexander nodded. 'Seems likely, sir.'

'Kidnapped and bundled into a vehicle?' Grace suggested. 'By offenders who either followed him in or were lying in wait for him. Most likely is they followed him in – unless it was a pre-arranged rendezvous.'

'I've requested Associated Car Parks let us have copies of all CCTV cameras in that car park from 9 a.m. that morning until midday, to see if we can spot any vehicles that arrived before or with him and left soon after,' Alexander said. 'But there's a delay thanks to their GDPR policy.'

'Really?' Grace sighed.

'Afraid so, sir,' Alexander replied. General Data Protection Regulations had recently become, in Roy Grace's view, yet another obstacle put in the way of police crime-fighting efforts.

'So they're not allowed to give us information that could help us arrest a murderer,' Norman Potting said. 'Because that might invade his privacy?'

'Right, let's focus, everyone,' Grace said, restoring order. 'Jack, how long before the ACP deign to hand over the footage? Tell them this is a major crime investigation and should be GDPR exempt.'

'It's with their lawyers now, sir, who know the urgency. I'm hoping for a call at any moment.'

'OK, let's wait to see what we get from the cameras.' He looked at Potting and then Wilde. 'You went to see Daniel Hegarty, how did that go?'

Potting glanced at Wilde who indicated for him to respond. 'He's quite the geezer, chief.'

'And joker,' Wilde added.

Potting concurred. 'He claims not to have any knowledge of Archie Goff, although personally I find that hard to believe, since they both come from crime families on the Moulsecoomb estate where they grew up at around the same time. Be that as it may, he came up with a name that could be very significant for us – Robert Kilgore.'

'The name that Interpol told you is associated with Stuart Piper in international art dealings?' Grace questioned.

'The very same,' Potting said. 'It was very clear to both DC Wilde and myself that Hegarty is not a member of the Robert Kilgore fan club.'

'What made you think that?' Grace quizzed.

'Just the way he spoke about him, sir,' Wilde said.

Potting looked in his notebook on the table surface in front of him. 'You might like to listen to this, sir, and everyone.' He read from his notes.

'*I've not dealt with Piper directly, but there is a gentleman you might want to talk to. He's an American, based here, name of Robert Kilgore. Nasty piece of work; you might find it helpful to have a word with him.* These were Hegarty's words. Then Velvet asked Hegarty where might we find him.'

Potting continued to read from his notes, '*I believe he's employed by Mr Piper. But I'd be grateful if you didn't mention I told you that.*'

'Very interesting,' Grace said. He tried, but failed, to hold a grin back. 'We'll call it useful information for now, Norman, but not admissible evidence.'

'Fair play, gov. I should have got him to sign the notes.'

Grace looked around his team. 'Anyone else have any information? If not, we'll reconvene at 8.30 a.m. tomorrow. I've a meeting with the ACC at 10 a.m. to update her, followed by a press conference on Archie Goff's murder, so please do your best, Jack, to get the car park CCTV released well before then. I'm also hoping for a report from our financial investigator by tomorrow morning; I've excused her from this briefing to work on it. And we'll get more from Dr Duncton. Have a good evening, everyone.'

78

Monday, 4 November

It was 7 p.m. when Daniel Hegarty, meticulously applying fake saleroom markings to the rear of the Lowry painting, was distracted by Rocky and Rambo going crazy with excitement and running upstairs. Moments later he heard his wife's voice.

'Good boys, good boys! Has your daddy fed you or has he forgotten again?'

With a twinge of guilt, Hegarty realized he'd been so absorbed in his work he'd clean forgotten the dogs liked to eat at 6 p.m.

'He's a right bastard, isn't he?'

'I heard that!' Hegarty retorted as she came down into the living room.

'Have you fed them?' she asked, walking over and kissing him. She looked drawn and pale, which was not surprising. She had gone to work to help her deal with what had happened and try to get things back to some sort of normal.

'I was just about to!' he fibbed.

'Of course you were,' she retorted, with only the faintest hint of sarcasm.

'How did it go?' he asked.

She shook her head as she pulled off her gloves and bobble hat then shrugged out of her coat. 'It was a good thing that I went in. Two hours on the phone, but I think I saved someone's life. He was seventy-three and had lived with his mother all his life. She did everything for him, cooking, making his bed, and probably wiped his bottom, too. She died two months ago, and he decided he didn't want to go on living without her. But before he topped himself, he wanted my advice on who he should leave her estate to, which was signed over to him. A jerk of a distant cousin, their only living relative, or charity. I think I convinced him to go and enjoy himself, maybe take a world cruise, and think about leaving the money to charity when he died.'

'Good thinking.'

'So did you call the police?' she asked.

He hesitated before replying. 'No.'

Natalie rounded on him. 'What? A bunch of thugs invade our home, threaten us both, we're only saved by the presence of the window cleaners, and you haven't called the police?'

'Let me finish,' he said. 'I was about to, when two police officers turned up.'

'And you told them what happened? What did they say – what did they do? Are they going to arrest those bastards?'

'I need to explain something to you, darling,' Hegarty said.

'I'm listening,' she replied. 'It had better be good.'

'It's good. You're going to like it.'

When he had finished telling her, Natalie shook her head. She didn't like it. She did not like it one bit.

79

Harry Kipling had sat in the pub, deep in thought, nursing his single pint for much longer than he realized. It was 7.15 p.m. when he left, and the pub had filled up a lot in the past hour. He texted Freya that he was on his way.

Twenty minutes later he pulled the Volvo up on the forecourt of their house, in the gap Freya always left for him between her Fiat and his Hilux pick-up, and hurried to the front door. As he let himself in, she greeted him with a kiss, but looked concerned. 'You're late, darling, I was worried. How was your day?'

'Sorry, had to have a drink with the quantity surveyor, Adrian, to discuss Vine Cottage.'

'How did it go?'

He smiled and nodded. 'Good. I have some interesting news! How was your day?'

'Not great.'

He followed her through into the kitchen, and opened the fridge door. 'Glass of wine?'

'A large one, I need it.'

He unscrewed the cap of the South African Chenin blanc and poured a generous amount into a glass, then took a can of beer, popped it open, and carried both drinks over to the island unit. As they perched on the bar stools he asked, 'What's happened?'

338

Freya held up her phone and tapped the yellow LibreLink app. 'Tom's high-glucose alert has been pinging constantly all day. I think he's going through one of his binge-eating moods,' she said.

Harry shrugged. 'Darling, we can't blame him. Poor lad, all his mates are scoffing sweets and eating junk food crap and swigging sugary drinks, and he's having to eat like a monk.'

'There's plenty of good choices he could make,' she said.

Harry shook his head. 'Not when all his mates are eating Haribo Tangfastics, Skittles or Fruit Pastilles, and chips smothered in ketchup, there aren't. I remember when I was his age, that's all the kind of stuff I wanted to eat.'

'You weren't a Type-1 diabetic, your pancreas could cope with all that rubbish. Tom's can't. I rang the head, and he really wasn't that helpful. He said he'd tried to keep an eye on him, and insisted there are healthy options in the school canteen. I gave him a low-sugar meal when he came home tonight, grilled cod, broccoli and mash, and he looked at me like I was trying to poison him. He ate the mash, pointedly left the fish and broccoli, then took a Magnum from the freezer and went up to his room.'

'He's just trying to make a point.'

'A point? What point?'

'That he's fed up being diabetic. That he feels it's unfair, that he's been dealt a shitty hand, which he has.'

'And *your* point is?'

'He's pretty good most of the time. Every now and then he thinks, *to hell with it!* He's a bright guy, cut him a little slack. He'll get it, in time.'

She looked at him dubiously. 'Now, Harry. Now's the time, right? Diabetes attacks the extremities. If he doesn't take care of it now, when he's older he risks losing toes, having legs amputated and going blind.'

He shrugged. 'I've been reading up a lot about diabetes. Whatever he does now is OK, not great, but OK. Once he's north of thirty is the time to really start watching it.'

'I hope to hell you're right,' she said. She sipped some wine, looking dubious. 'So, you said you have some interesting news?'

He smiled. 'I had a call from a guy at Bonhams, the auctioneers. Barnaby Jackson – one of the people I took the picture to. He said they're having a major sale of paintings from that period in January, and they'd like to include ours!'

'He did?'

'He qualified it by saying *if it is genuine*. But he suggested that even if they couldn't establish its provenance as a genuine Fragonard before the sale, they could put it in as "Fragonard or School of Fragonard", and was confident it would go as that for somewhere between £200,000 and £750,000.'

'Seriously?'

'Oh yes.'

'So you are happy to forget trying to find the other three Fragonard Four Seasons paintings?' she asked.

'If you are, I am.'

'You know I am, we've already discussed it endlessly. I'm not interested in millions, however nice that might be. Let's get what we can for it now, and enjoy the money, right?'

'Right!' Harry agreed. 'I'll take it up to Bonhams tomorrow and they'll have it for safe keeping.' He opened his phone and called up the diary.

'Good,' she said. 'I know it should be OK in that place in Worthing, but you do hear of these places being raided or burned down.'

'And auctioneers never burn down or get raided?' he said, smiling.

'I guess – I-I'm just jumpy about everything at the moment.'

'Oh shit,' he said.

'What?'

'I'd forgotten I'm playing golf tomorrow – a charity tournament for the Martlets Hospice. I'll take it on Wednesday or maybe Thursday, there's no rush.'

'The sooner we don't have to worry about it, the better.'

'We don't need to worry about it now, darling, right?'

She shrugged.

80

There was a palpable sense of excitement at the start of the 8.30 a.m. briefing of Operation Porcupine. The feeling that they were closing in on the suspects. And it seemed to Roy Grace that almost everyone in his team assembled in the conference room had something urgent to say. He started with Potting, who was signalling with his arm like a batman at an airport.

'Norman?'

'Chief, I met with Ricky Sharp last night and offered him the five hundred quid bung you got sanctioned. He confirmed he had collected Goff from prison but insisted he was just doing a favour to an old mate. I told him I needed more information if he wanted the money. After a little hesitation he took it. He informed me the garage in which the Audi A6 was parked for some days had been rented by a gentleman called Ross Briggs.'

'Did he give you a description of him?'

'He did, chief, a bit reluctantly. Said he was muscle, spoke with a London accent and, here's the bit that I like, he was wearing an emerald ring that was, in Sharp's view, the size of a knuckle-duster.'

'Twin brother of one with a red ring?' Grace asked.

'I asked him, and he said Ross Briggs was the only person he dealt with, and he told me he had no idea if he had a brother or not and wasn't interested in finding out.'

'Did he say anything else?'

'Other than telling me to fuck off, not really, chief, no.'

There was a roar of laughter from Jon Exton.

'But I think he knows more than he's letting on, chief.'

'He's given us more than enough to be getting on with for now. Excellent, Norman,' Grace replied, then looked down at his notes. As he did so he was interrupted by the financial investigator, Emily Denyer. 'Sir,' she said. 'I have some information on a Maurice Briggs which I think is significant.'

'Tell us, Emily,' he said.

She held up a sheaf of printouts. 'What I have here are copies of the most recent tax returns from Stuart Piper and from his company, of which he is the sole shareholder, Art Recovery UK Ltd. Among the employees of the company are listed a Maurice Briggs and a Ross Briggs.'

'The twins?' Potting queried. 'Port and starboard?'

'Could be,' Grace said and turned back to Denyer. 'Good work, Emily,' he said, then nodded at DS Alexander, who had his hand raised and was looking bleary-eyed. 'Yes, Jack?'

'Sir, I finally got the car park videos released to me late yesterday, and I've been viewing them since, through the night. I've been looking at all the vehicles that arrived and left the car park one hour either side of the time Archie Goff drove his Astra in there. There's one vehicle which strikes me as possibly significant, a Mercedes G Wagon, index GU57 APN. It arrived four minutes after Archie Goff's Astra, and departed twenty-five minutes after the last CCTV sighting of Goff in the Lanes.'

'Coincidence, Jack?' Potting interjected.

Alexander threw the DS an irritated glance at the interruption. 'Not when its index checks out, Norman,' he said with clear satisfaction. 'The vehicle is registered to Stuart Piper's company.'

'Well done, Jack,' Grace said. 'So, not all roads lead to Rome. Some, it seems, lead to this Stuart Piper.'

'We should go and nick him, don't you think, boss?' Branson said.

'On what charge?' Grace asked.

'Conspiracy to murder?' Branson ventured.

The Detective Superintendent shook his head. 'What we have is mounting up, but I don't think we have enough evidence yet to convince the Crown Prosecution Service to bring a prosecution. The evidence against both Piper and the two Briggs brothers is looking strong, but – excuse the pun – there's a bigger picture here. I have the sense these twins might be little more than Piper's pawns. All the evidence against all three of them, at present, is circumstantial.'

He turned to Branson. 'Glenn, how's your knowledge of French artists of the fête galante period?'

'About as comprehensive as my knowledge of hydrogen cell technology, boss.'

Grace smiled. 'You have one hour to bone up on that period, then we're going to pay Stuart Piper a visit and have a friendly chat with him.'

'Did I tell you I failed Art GCSE?' Branson said.

'Now's your chance to redeem yourself.'

81

Roy Grace sat in the passenger seat of the Ford Focus, tight-lipped as Glenn drove, wondering, as he always did, why he'd again let his friend loose behind the wheel. 'How did your swotting up on the fête galante go?'

'Pretty good. Antoine Watteau; Jean-Baptiste Pater; Jean François de Troy; Jean-Honoré Fragonard; Nicolas Lancret; Pierre-Antoine Quillard.'

Glenn's reciting the names had the effect Grace had hoped of slowing down his driving. A few minutes later they arrived, to his relief, and with little thanks to the talent of his chauffeur, at very swanky wrought-iron gates. A discreet plaque fixed to the wall, with gold letters on a black background, said BEWLAY PARK.

Glenn put down his window, pressed a button on the control panel, and gave as good as he got back to the disembodied voice who challenged them. The gates opened and they drove through and up a long avenue of plane trees, with lawns that were almost impossibly green on either side.

'Reckon the grass is dyed, boss?' Branson said, driving now at a civil pace.

'Hand-painted,' Grace replied. 'Every blade.' Then he saw in the mirror of his sun visor that they had an escort behind them. A matt black Mercedes. Branson had seen it, too.

'Stop!' Grace instructed.

Branson obliged, stamping on the brake a little too keenly,

bringing the Ford to an abrupt halt. The Mercedes stopped behind them in a squeal of tyres.

Roy Grace unclipped his seat belt, climbed out and walked up to the off-roader. As he approached, the driver's window slid down, and he saw a piece of shaven-headed muscle with stupid sunglasses, all in black, with a smaller, fatter thug beside him. 'Can I help you guys?' Grace asked facetiously. 'Are you lost, is that why you're following us?'

'Keep driving,' the muscle behind the wheel said in a surly voice.

Grace pulled out his warrant card and held it up a few inches from the man's eyes. 'Can you read English?'

'I can read English.'

'Good. Now here's the deal. Stop following me or I'll start following you, twenty-four-seven. You won't even be able to go to the toilet without a pair of eyes on you. Do you understand?'

He got a sullen nod.

Smiling, Grace said, 'I don't like being followed, understand? So turn around and sod off. And I'm giving you just sixty seconds to do that before I nick you for threatening a police officer. Are we good?'

Without replying, the driver began reversing the vehicle, searching for a space between the trees to turn. Grace climbed back into the Ford.

'Respect!' Branson said.

Grace grinned. 'Drive on, Macduff.'

A short while later, Piper's vast mansion came into view on the far side of a circular driveway around an ornamental lake, across which a pair of black swans glided with supreme elegance. A powder-blue convertible Rolls-Royce was parked outside the front door.

'Reckon anyone could acquire a place like this from honest money?' Branson asked, eyes wide open, pulling up behind the

Rolls. Its number plate had a combination of letters and numbers arranged, illegally close together, spelling out ARTMAN.

'A few rock stars and tech gazillionaires,' Grace replied. 'Or inheriting it from an ancestor.'

'None of these, from what we know about Stuart Piper,' Branson said. 'Must be a lot of dough in art.'

They walked up the steps to the imposing white front door. It was opened, as they reached it, by a hunk of beefcake, all in black, with a coiled earpiece, a large emerald ring on his right hand, and an expression that was about as hostile as a face could look before imploding into a thousand fragments. 'Mr Piper don't see no one without an appointment,' he said, repeating what they'd heard through the speakerphone at the entrance gates.

'Well,' Grace said, smiling pleasantly and holding up his warrant card, 'I think he'd be smart to make an exception for us.' Then he made a play of looking closely at the man's hand. 'Nice ring.'

As he spoke, a figure appeared down the hall, who looked every inch this man's identical twin. And wearing a ruby-red ring.

'My colleague will take you to Mr Piper,' he said.

'Colleague?' Grace said. 'Or brother?'

There was no answer.

The two detectives followed the twin with the red ring along an oak-panelled corridor lined on both sides with framed paintings that were clearly old and probably important, Grace thought.

'Jesus, this reminds me of National Trust houses Ari liked to visit,' Branson said, referring to his ex-wife, ogling both the pictures and marble busts in recesses.

Grace nodded. 'See yourself living in a place like this?'

Branson shook his head. 'I reckon the heating bill's more than my annual salary. You?'

Grace shook his head. 'Nope, wouldn't fancy spending all my weekends mowing the lawns.'

A pair of double doors ahead of them were opened and ruby

ring ushered them into a cavernous room with a domed ceiling. A lean man of about sixty, with an expressionless face, immaculately dressed, sat behind a beautiful desk, flanked on each side by a stationary Dalmatian dog. Neither animal reacted as Grace and Branson entered.

Piper stood up, his eyes cold, his face steely. Confident in his grand setting, Grace thought, he addressed them. 'Yes, gentlemen, what can I do for you?'

'Stuart Piper?'

'Yes.'

Grace held up his warrant card. 'I'm Detective Superintendent Grace and my colleague is Detective Inspector Branson from the Surrey and Sussex Major Crime Team.'

Piper waved an arm at the two chairs in front of his desk. 'Have a seat, officers – or should I say, *detectives*?' His expression revealed nothing. 'So, I've got an upgrade, eh?'

'Upgrade?' Grace was finding his complete lack of expression unnerving. He rarely found people's eyes hard to read, but this man's were.

'Sure.' There was a trace of humour in Piper's voice now, but it was not reflected in his face. 'A couple of weeks ago, I was visited by a humble Detective Sergeant and a Detective Constable. Now I get a Detective Superintendent and a Detective Inspector. I'd call that an upgrade. Enough to have me turning left on an aeroplane, instead of slumming it in economy, wouldn't you say?'

Piper didn't look like a man who ever *slummed it in economy*, Grace thought, but didn't rise to it. 'Our colleagues came to ask you if you'd ever had any dealings with the late art dealer Charlie Porteous,' he said. 'You said you had not. You also said you had no idea why one of the persons we believe may be connected with the murder of art dealer Charlie Porteous in October 2015 had your number on his phone.'

Piper fixed his cold eyes on each of them in turn. 'Well, it's good to know you detectives have such a joined-up team. Is there anything else you'd like to tell me that I already know, or have you just taken a jolly ride out into this beautiful part of the countryside for fun, and to piss away taxpayers' money instead of doing the job we pay you for, of catching criminals?'

Grace glanced at Branson and could see he was riled as he was too by Piper's arrogance. He cut to the chase. 'Mr Piper, you employ two identical twins, Ross and Maurice Briggs. Is that correct?'

'What does that have to do with anything, officer – sorry, *Detective Superintendent*?'

'Quite a bit actually, Mr Piper. An Audi A6 vehicle linked to the murder of Mr Porteous has been also linked to your employees.'

'So?'

'You informed our colleagues, DS Potting and DC Wilde, that you had no knowledge of Charlie Porteous, owner of the Porteous Fine Arts Gallery in Duke Street, and had never had any dealings with him.'

'Correct.'

'Would you say you have a good memory? I'm aware you had an unfortunate incident in your life back in 1979 when you suffered a very severe assault, leaving you with multiple head injuries. You never suffered from an impaired memory subsequently?'

'My memory is excellent,' he replied flatly. 'Pretty much photographic if you really want to know.'

'Well, if that's the case, I'm surprised you've forgotten this.' Grace pulled a folded sheet of paper from his inside pocket, laid it on Piper's desk, opened it, smoothed it out and passed it across to him.

Piper took it and stared at it impassively.

'I imagine you have the original somewhere, for safe keeping, for insurance purposes?' Grace questioned.

'It's a receipt from the Porteous Fine Arts Gallery, dated 15 May 2014, for two sketches by Pierre-Antoine Quillard,' Glenn Branson said.

'Not that long ago to remember,' Grace added. 'Especially not for someone with photographic recall.'

To Piper's credit, Grace thought, the man handled the potential bombshell with aplomb. 'Oh, those – to be honest those are utterly insignificant, mere ephemera.'

'You paid £150,000 each for two pieces of ephemera?' Branson quizzed.

Piper stared back at him so coldly, both his eyes could have been glass, Branson thought. Even though they had the man on the back foot, his gaze chilled him. 'Detective Inspector,' he said, 'most of the art I buy is in multiples of million pounds. You'll have seen some of my collection on the walls as you walked along the corridor.' He waved his arms expansively around the room. 'You can see more of it here. I rarely pay less than five million for a work, and much of what I acquire is well north of twenty million. You'll have to excuse my small memory slip for the purchase of a couple of insignificant sketches, made by my associate.'

'Would that be Mr Robert Kilgore?' Grace asked.

'You two clearly have been doing your homework, haven't you? Let me explain something. Robert Kilgore, who looks out for works of art of the fête galante period for me – the period I collect above all others – has a budget I give him, along with a figure below which he doesn't need to obtain my sanction.' He glanced down at the receipt. 'These two sketches fall well below that threshold. If your enquiry is about these two sketches, you'd best go and talk to him.'

'Can you give us his contact details?' Branson asked.

'Really?' Piper retorted. 'You mean I have something you don't know? Top detectives – two of Sussex's finest – and you've spent all this time, come all this way for a phone number? You could have just called me.' His lips parted, just a fraction, to reveal his veneered teeth. It could have been a smile or a snarl, Grace thought.

'Thank you, Mr Piper.' He stood up, followed by Branson. 'You've been very helpful.'

'Any time, detectives. I'm a big supporter of the police, you know. If you ever need a donation to the Sussex Police Charitable Trust, just ask.'

'We'll bear that in mind,' Grace said.

'Very big-hearted of you,' Branson added.

'I'm all heart,' Piper replied.

82

On the top-right corner of the CCTV on his computer monitor, Piper tracked the movement of the silver Ford Focus heading down his drive. The gates opened. The car pulled out into the road and turned right. Immediately the gates began to close.

The two detectives had gone, but he had a worrying feeling they were not going away for long. It was 11.35 a.m. He picked up the internal phone and pressed a button.

'Bobby, I want you to phone Harry Kipling's mobile, find out where he is. Make out you're a potential customer and you need an urgent quote on a job, a big one, make some shit up that will excite him. Find out his movements – what time he'll be home this evening, say he's been highly recommended but you have to make an urgent decision and could you pop into his house this evening – it's the only time you can do, yadda, yadda, yadda. Get him to agree an appointment at his house tonight, under-stand what I'm saying?'

'Yes, sir.'

'Then get your arse in here along with the boys.'

Piper put the phone down and stared at the monitor again. At the closed gates. Then he tapped his trim fingernails on the surface of his desk, tap-tap-tapping out the same monotone beat he always did when he was anxious. Hoping to hell he wasn't already too late.

83

On the occasions when Harry played a blinder of a first half at golf, the wheels invariably fell off on the back nine. But not this time, no sir! In today's charity four-ball, he'd held it together, scoring two birdies as well as being in the running for closest to the pin on the seventeenth.

Now seated in the dining area of the Dyke Golf Club, surrounded by his pals, he was feeling stuffed after a decent and heavy late lunch of roast pork followed by blackberry and apple crumble. He was still on a high of excitement about the potential of the Bonhams sale, and had confided about the painting's possible value to his teammates, who seemed genuinely pleased for him. Happy days!

He was sipping a cup of strong coffee as Bob Sansom and Roger Moore, the organizers of the event, stood up and made their way to the table laden with trophies to begin the prize-giving. Then he felt his phone, on silent, vibrate in his pocket.

Tugging it out, he saw it was Freya.

He answered it and stepped away from the table. 'How's your day been?' she asked.

In the background he heard Bob Sansom announce they'd raised over £25,000 for the Martlets Hospice.

'Brilliant!' he replied. 'We scored forty-two – which puts us with a really good chance of a prize – we might even have won!'

'Great!' she said, sounding genuinely pleased.

'And I might have got nearest the pin on the seventeenth – that's a two-hundred-quid prize!'

'Fantastic!' There was a brief pause and she asked, 'What time do you think you'll be home?'

He looked at his watch. It was just gone 5 p.m. 'Not late. Why, darling?'

'I've had a call about a job that sounds quite substantial and lucrative, a new-build in Henfield. The gentleman I spoke to said he's been let down by the builders he was planning to use and that you'd been highly recommended to him. But he needs to see you very urgently today, if you're interested.'

'Can't it wait until tomorrow?'

'I thought you were going to London to take the painting to Bonhams first thing? I told him you weren't available tomorrow and he said he couldn't wait until Thursday.'

'What's his name?'

'Mike Elkington – he sounds American.'

'Doesn't ring a bell.'

'He was very charming – I think you should see him this evening, we haven't had a decent new-build in quite a while, and he said if you can give him a price he's happy with he won't go out to tender. What time can you be home?'

In the background, Harry heard Bob Sansom announce the winners of nearest the pin on the thirteenth hole, and he was anxious not to miss the next announcement. Giving himself some margin, he said, 'I could be home by seven.'

'I'll call Mr Elkington and tell him.'

'Love you,' he said.

'Love my champion!'

Ending the call, he sat back down, only to stand up moments later and be awarded his £200 nearest the pin prize. And then again, after just a few minutes, he and his three teammates stood up to be presented with envelopes containing vouchers of £250 each for the pro shop, as well as fancy golfing umbrellas.

What a result! And when he got home, with luck there would be an even bigger result. He just had to hope this Mr Elkington wasn't planning on nailing too hard a bargain, and would be willing to pay for a reliable builder of quality.

84

When he finally left the clubhouse, a little later than he'd intended, Harry was feeling elated. And tomorrow he would collect the painting from the storage depot in Worthing and hand it for safe keeping to Bonhams. Then sit back and wait for the January auction. Maybe, just maybe, if they got really lucky, and it went in as an original Fragonard, they could make so much money from the sale he could forget the building trade altogether. Properly set Tom up, then buy a pad down on the Costa del Sol, escape the rat race and live the good life with Freya. And right now, with all the problems of Vine Cottage, he'd give up this business in a heartbeat.

Shivering against the cold air, with fireworks shooting into the darkness all across the city skyline below him and the volleys of distant explosions, he hurried over the road to the car park, put his golf bag and his sports bag with his golfing clothes into the rear of the Volvo, then climbed into the car, shut the door and immediately switched on the engine, to get the heater going.

Then, before moving off, he googled Mike Elkington and then Michael Elkington on his phone. There were a handful of name matches, but nothing that gave him a clue about the man he would shortly be meeting. No matter, he drove off, very much looking forward to meeting Mr Elkington. And determined to charm him. Oh yes!

Although he was already late, he drove home keeping carefully within the speed limits. And it was good news: although this was Bonfire Night, the roads were quiet. Tom had already been to a big fireworks party at a schoolfriend's house on Saturday, sensibly arranged to not interrupt his studies during the school week.

As Harry drove up Mackie Crescent, he popped a piece of mint gum in his mouth, to freshen his breath for his potential new client. Approaching home, he saw a swanky Tesla on the street outside. Mr Elkington's, he presumed, as he drove onto the driveway and parked as usual between the Fiat and his work van.

He glanced at his watch: 7.25 p.m. – a little later than he'd told Freya, but he was confident she would be charming the client. Deciding to leave his kit in the car for now, he strode up to the front door in a sunny mood. The champion coming home to a hero's welcome!

Not that Jinx gave him any kind of a welcome at all. The cat stood, just inside the front door, its back arched. As he leaned down to stroke it, it sprinted away as if fired from a torpedo tube. The lounge door, to his left, was open and he presumed Freya was in there with Mr Elkington.

He checked his appearance in the coat-stand mirror, straightening his Dyke Golf Club tie and brushing back a few stray strands of hair, then at the last minute, remembering his gum, hurried over to the kitchen and dropped it in the pedal bin. The television was on in there as normal, a sitcom playing. Freya kept it on all the time she was home, whether in the kitchen or not.

He went back into the hallway. Checked his tie again in the mirror and his posture, then with a warm smile for his potential new client, he strode into the lounge.

And felt as though he'd stepped onto a frozen lake and the ice was cracking beneath him.

85

Before his brain could process the surreal sight that greeted him, both of Harry Kipling's arms were seized and yanked sharply behind him. He stared, scared and bewildered, at three hooded strangers in the living room. Each wore a black balaclava, a black oversuit of the style worn by CSIs at crime scenes, and blue latex gloves.

Two of them, man-mountains, stood either side of him. He felt his hands being bound behind him by something sharp that cut into his wrists, and instantly he was forced down onto a chair.

Freya was on one sofa, grey gaffer tape over her mouth and securing her arms also behind her. He could see the terror in her eyes as she desperately tried to signal something to him, but he couldn't figure out what. Tom was on the opposite sofa, his arms similarly taped behind him. His right sweatshirt sleeve was rolled up to his shoulder, revealing his diabetes monitoring disc. On the coffee table, beside a large tray of caramel, chocolate and sugar-coated jam doughnuts, lay a dark blue pen. Tom's insulin pen. Beside it was Freya's phone in its distinctive red cover.

Through the vortex of fear and confusion in his mind, Harry blurted, 'Who the hell are you? What do you want?'

A tall, lean man, eyes, nostrils and mouth visible through the slits in the balaclava, stood beside Tom. He spoke with a Southern American accent in a voice devoid of humour. 'Welcome to our little party, Mr Kipling. I'm real sorry if you're hungry after your golf game, but these are all for your boy, I'm

358

afraid. He's a growing lad. We might need him to eat one or two to keep his sugar levels up.'

'Those things are toxic for Tom!' Harry said in fury. 'What the hell do you think you're doing?'

'Oh, I know exactly what I am doing, Mr Kipling,' he said. 'You see, like your boy, I'm a diabetic too,' he lied, and patted his own left arm. 'I have the same Libre patch as him. Great technology, eh? Before the discovery of insulin in 1921, the life expectancy for a Type-1 diabetic was three to five years.' He picked the pen up off the table. 'Of course, I'm sure you and Mrs Kipling know that, right?' He made a show of removing the cap of the pen, exposing the needle, then twisted the dial, with a series of clicks. Holding the pen up, he pressed the plunger and sent a small spray of the clear, sour-smelling liquid into the air. 'Too much insulin can be just as fatal for a diabetic as too little.' He smiled. 'Guess you know that too, don't you?'

'We don't need a fucking chemistry lesson,' Harry said with impotent rage as he struggled to try to free his arms. He wanted desperately to protect his family and he could do nothing at this moment.

The American nodded his head slowly. 'Oh, I think you do, Mr Kipling. You see, I've already given your lad a very large dose of insulin, way more than he needs. To counterbalance it, he will need to eat and keep eating something with very high sugar content. Doughnuts are perfect for that. But here's the deal, Mr Kipling, before I give Tom one of these lifesavers, I need something from you.'

Harry saw the look of despair Tom gave him. An instant later, the American laid down the pen and picked up the phone. He entered a code, Freya's, Harry presumed, tapped a yellow app that Harry instantly recognized, and held the top of the phone close to the circular Libre patch on Tom's arm. The phone emitted a brief warble sound. Then the American walked over to Freya and held it up in front of her eyes. 'See the reading?'

He then showed it to Harry.

It read 5, in black letters on a green band. Above the number were the words, *GLUCOSE NORMAL*. Beside them was a black arrow, pointing downwards. That was ominous, Harry knew. When Tom had first been diagnosed as a Type-1 diabetic, he had made it his business to learn everything he could about the disease. And one key thing he knew was that the safe range of blood-sugar level was, on the UK calibration system, between 4 and 9. A reading of 5 was fine, but at the low end. And the arrow pointing down indicated Tom's sugar level was dropping.

'I see the reading. What's your point, whoever the hell you are?'

'My point, Mr Kipling, is that twenty minutes before you arrived home, your son's reading was ten. It's come down pretty damn fast, wouldn't you say? Do the math.'

Harry didn't need to. How much insulin had this bastard given Tom? He felt a chill spiral deep through him. He stared at the American belligerently. 'Why are you doing this? You need some-thing? What the hell do you need? What do you want?' He tried to stand up and was immediately pushed back down.

Kilgore jabbed the insulin pen at the Fragonard copy on the wall. 'I think you know exactly what I want, Mr Kipling.'

'That?' Harry said. 'You want that? Be my guest, fucking take it! It's yours! Just leave me and my family alone, please.' He was close to crying in desperation, fearful for his son. He looked at Freya, feeling utterly useless. His heart felt it was trying to twist out of his chest.

'Here's the problem, Mr Kipling,' Kilgore said, quietly and calmly. 'You need to understand it's not that painting there that we want, but thank you kindly for the offer and we may well take that too, to avoid confusion. What we've come for is the original. My boss made you a very generous offer for it some while back and you snubbed him. I'm afraid my boss doesn't like being snubbed.'

'Fifty thousand pounds, right?' Harry said, now realizing what this was about. He glanced desperately again at Freya and then Tom. Freya was trying to say something but all she could do with her masked mouth was make a murmuring sound. 'Fine, I'll take it,' Harry said. 'Do we have a deal?'

'My boss doesn't negotiate, and he doesn't like rejection. I'm afraid we've gone way beyond that, Mr Kipling.'

Kilgore walked back over to Tom and again checked his blood-sugar level on Freya's phone. He showed it to Harry.

It was now reading *4*, the background had changed to yellow, the wording read, GLUCOSE LEVEL GOING LOW. The arrow was still pointing downwards.

Harry realized what he was saying. He'd been here less than five minutes. If the American was telling the truth, in just twenty-five minutes Tom's level had dropped from 10 to 5. At that rate—

Before Harry could reply, the American showed the reading to Freya, who gurgled a sound of desperation.

Then Kilgore laid the phone down on the coffee table and opened his arms expansively. 'There is of course a very simple solution to this problem. All you need to do is hand me the original Fragonard *Summer* and we'll be done and out of here. Could I be any clearer?'

Harry glanced at Freya again, who was nodding vigorously. *Yes, yes, yes, do it!* her eyes were saying.

He then looked at Tom. His beautiful son who was already clearly not himself. Distant. Beads of perspiration on his forehead. He seemed to be shimmying with tiny tremors every few moments. He had to do something, fast. To hell with the painting, it had cost him just twenty quid. Its value in a sale could change their lives but that did not matter any longer and it wasn't going to happen – nothing mattered but his family. They'd been fine before they'd ever bought the damned painting, happy enough. To hell with it. 'You can have the damned painting,' he said.

Ignoring him, the American picked up a caramel doughnut and held it out to Tom, but not quite close enough for him to take a bite from it. As if taunting him. Tom was looking increasingly pallid. 'Wouldn't you like to eat this right now, boy?' he asked, his voice all warm and friendly.

Harry hated this man; if his hands were free he would tear his face off. Instead all he could do was watch, a helpless onlooker.

Tom, turning pale and shaking profusely now, nodded pleadingly.

'Let's check those sugars again, shall we?' Kilgore asked, all patronizing now and putting the doughnut back down. He picked up the phone again, worked the app, held it to Tom's arm, then showed the display to Freya and Harry.

3. The wording on the yellow band continued to read, GLUCOSE LEVEL GOING LOW. The arrow was still pointing down.

He squatted, then leaned across the coffee table until his masked face was just inches from Tom's. Tom, clammy with perspiration now and starting to look disoriented, barely reacted. Then Kilgore picked up the same doughnut and held it out to him once more. 'I think you'd better have a bite, you said earlier you like caramel, would you like a bite?'

Tom was looking at him, bewildered, as if struggling to focus. His neck muscles seemed to be barely supporting his head. After a moment he gave a lolling nod.

Kilgore pushed the doughnut closer to Tom's mouth and he craned forward, chomping off a big piece which he chewed fiercely and desperately. As he did so, Kilgore put the rest of it back in the tray, once more out of the teenager's reach, and turned to Harry. 'That bite will buy him a few extra minutes, Mr Kipling. But you saw how fast his sugar level's dropping.'

'How much insulin have you bloody given him?'

'Sufficient,' he replied.

'Sufficient? What the hell does that mean?'

'Sufficient to get what I need from you, if you want to save his life.'

Harry heard a gurgle from Freya.

'And sufficient to kill him if I don't.'

'I've told you, you can have the damned painting – what kind of sick game are you playing with our son's life?' Harry yelled.

'I'm not playing any game, Mr Kipling. I'm telling it to you plain and simple. Your wife has told me you keep an emergency glucagon injector kit in your fridge. That will restore your son's sugar levels, so long as you don't leave it too late.'

There was another terrified gurgle from Freya. Harry gave her a desperate look. She was pleading to him with her eyes.

The American took a further reading of the patch on Tom's arm with Freya's phone. Another warble. He held it up to Freya and then to Harry.

2.5.

Tom, still chewing, had perspiration gouting down his face and his eyes seemed to be losing focus.

Harry knew that a prolonged glucose level below 2 would damage the central nervous system irreparably if allowed to continue for too long, and any sustained level below 1 would likely be fatal in a short time.

'I'll give you the bloody painting!' Harry blurted. 'I've said I'll give it to you, if you'll just promise to leave my family alone and not hurt us. And give Tom the injection he needs. Do we have a deal?'

'Fine,' the American said. 'We have a deal. You give me the original picture and we're out of here.'

Harry hesitated. 'OK, there's a small issue.'

'Uh huh?' Kilgore said.

'It's not here, it's in a storage depot for safe keeping, half an hour from here.'

The American made a play of studying his watch. 'So, Mr

Kipling, forty minutes to get there, a generous fifteen minutes to retrieve the picture, then forty minutes back. That's a little under two hours before, I'm hoping I'm estimating correctly, your boy lapses into a coma that he may not come out from. Maybe you should get going?'

'Right away,' Harry said, his eyes darting to the doorway.

'I think it might be a good idea if I and one of my colleagues came with you, no disrespect, but just to keep you honest, if you know what I'm saying?'

'I'll take you with me to get the painting if you give my son some more sugar right now. Get the glucagon kit from the fridge, it's on a shelf in the right-hand door.'

'Oh, I know where it is, thank you. And it stays there until I have the original painting.'

'At least give him some more of the doughnut.'

The American shook his head, then said, coldly, 'Mr Kipling, you are not in any position to negotiate. Listen up very carefully. Are you listening?'

Harry hesitated, then nodded.

'Good, here's the deal. I'll give the boy a mouthful of doughnut now. We go get the painting and we bring it back here. Soon as you bring it into the house and I've verified it, he gets his jab of glucagon. Do we understand each other?'

Harry glared at him. 'We understand each other.'

Kilgore walked out of the room. Moments later he returned holding a sealed opaque pack and held it up for Harry to see. It was the glucagon injection kit. 'I'll take this with us, let's call it insurance, hey? Just to make sure we all get back safely.'

One of the heavies stepped behind Harry, freed his hands, then patted him down and removed his mobile phone from his pocket, laying it beside Freya's on the coffee table.

86

As he turned out of Mackie Crescent, steering the Volvo with shaking hands, and glancing in the mirror at the sinister masked faces of the two men on the rear seat, Harry subtly edged the speed up over the 30 mph limit, to 40 mph then 45 mph, hoping against hope he might get stopped by a police car.

The heavy in the back's name was Ross or Russ, he had over-heard in an unguarded moment from his captor-in-chief. Harry felt like he was in a nightmare, and to add to the feeling, the sky through the windscreen ahead of him was constantly lit up with flaring and exploding fireworks.

Fireworks of anger were exploding inside Harry. And frustration at his helplessness.

'You'd better mind your speed,' the American rebuked sharply.

'Yes – sorry – I-I'm a little nervous.'

'Yeah? Well your driving's making me nervous. Stay within the goddamn limit. You don't mind if I smoke?' he said, lighting a cigarette.

'I like the smell, I only quit recently myself,' Harry said, slowing down, trying to appease the man. His brain was in turmoil, he kept thinking about anything he could do, but fear for Tom's life and fear for Freya kept him driving obediently to the limit, as he turned onto the A27, then stuck to a regulation 70 mph all the way towards his destination.

Twenty minutes later, as he turned off the dual carriageway

and threaded through the urban streets of Worthing, the seaside town to the west of Brighton, he suddenly saw a blaze of flashing blue lights ahead – and felt a flip of hope. Maybe it was a roadblock and they'd be stopped? A drink-driver check? Please God.

But his hope faded as he saw ahead a police car either side of a small, beat-up saloon; on the pavement, two officers, with another two standing by, were searching a scruffy youth held face-on to a brick wall.

Even so, this could be his chance, he thought – his last chance. Jam on the brakes and shout for help? The police would see these two in their balaclavas behind him and then what could his captors do?

'Don't even think about it, Harry,' the American said calmly, as if reading his mind. 'I'm not exaggerating about the amount of insulin I injected into your son, it's more than enough to kill him if he doesn't get enough sugar. I have a message on my WhatsApp that's ready to go. If I press that send button on my phone, my associate there will simply stop giving your son a regular bite of a doughnut, sufficient to keep his sugar readings at the minimum of two. If you want to keep your son alive, just keep driving.'

Harry kept on driving. Anger and fear roiling inside him. Thinking all the time if there was anything, anything at all he could do to lash back at this bastard. To get his family out of this nightmare. But he felt all out of options.

He negotiated two roundabouts, drove a short distance along another dual carriageway, then braked sharply, turning left past two modern-looking orange and yellow pillars signed WEST TARRING INDUSTRIAL ESTATE. He drove through into a dark labyrinth of single- and two-storey industrial units, each shining grey and yellow in the Volvo's headlights.

They passed a tyre company, a furniture restorer, a vegan milk depot and several further premises, before Harry made a right and brought the car to a halt in front of a tall steel gate, with equally tall mesh, topped with barbed wire on either side, and a warning sign that it was electrified and monitored by CCTV. Protruding slightly was a numeric keypad. A sign read SOUTHERN CONTROL SAFETY STORAGE.

Lowering his window, Harry reached out his arm and tapped in his code. Moments later the gate slid open, and he drove through into a courtyard, where massive, corrugated-steel hangar-type buildings stood to their right and left. 'This is it,' he announced, switching off the engine, unclipping his seat belt and opening the door. The dome light illuminated his two un-welcome passengers.

Turning to look at them, he asked, 'Either of you coming with me? You'd probably better take your balaclavas off if you do – there are security guards monitoring the CCTV and they might think it a bit odd.'

'We're staying in the car, Mr Kipling,' Kilgore said tersely. 'You have exactly five minutes.' He held up his phone and pointed at the blue arrow button on WhatsApp, then held the phone up closer, so Harry could read the chilling message.

Stop feeding the boy.

Kilgore pressed a button on his watch. 'The countdown has started, Mr Kipling. And don't believe for one moment that if you try to call for help that I won't send this message.'

Harry hesitated for a fleeting second. He hadn't done this before and had never timed it. 'I-I don't know if I can do it in five minutes.'

'Well, that's just cost you several valuable seconds,' the American said in a calm voice of steel.

Harry gave him a quick look, then sprinted towards the

right-hand gates. He entered the code with trembling fingers, *428106*, hoping to hell he'd memorized it correctly.

An error message displayed on the screen: *Two attempts left.*

Shit, shit, shit. He pulled out his wallet and checked the code he kept in there. He realized in his panic that he'd reversed two numbers. He entered it again, with his fingers trembling wildly, this time, *428016*.

The error message again. *One attempt left.*

What the fuck?

He checked the code again. Then entered it again, checking each digit in turn. *Please God . . .*

To his immense relief it clicked open. He pushed it, walked through and it swung closed behind him with a loud clang. Then he ran again, along the row of lock-up units, with roll-up door after roll-up door, until he reached number 257, a small unit, measuring just eight foot by six foot.

There was a combination padlock on the door and, glancing at his watch, he saw he now had under four minutes. His brain seized up and he could not think clearly. What the hell was the combination? For several precious seconds it eluded him. Somewhere close by a flash of light followed by a series of explosions in the air ripped the silence.

He was panic-stricken. He'd deliberately set up this code with a memorable number but his mind was blank. What had he used? Then he remembered, Freya's birthday. Seconds later, to his immense relief it unlocked.

Leaning down, he tugged the handle of the door and hauled it up. Then he tapped the torch app on his phone and shone it at the interior. There were just a few items in here, large objects they had bought on a whim at car boot sales in recent years but had no room for in their current house – their dream was one day to buy a larger place in the countryside. Among the items was a red and green Victorian clothes mangle, a tailor's headless mannequin, an oak wine barrel and a vintage grocer's bicycle with a basket. In the far corner stood a small rectangular package, the Fragonard painting, bound first in protective bubble wrap, with an outer layer of carboard taped around it.

God, so much of their future lay with this painting. Was there anything he could do? Anything at all? He tried to think clearly. The American's threat re. Tom. Really? Was it a bluff?

It wasn't a bluff.

No amount of money was worth risking his life, and God knows what these monsters would do if he tried anything. Nothing was worth the risk.

He picked the painting up, and it felt almost lighter than air. Hurrying out of the unit, he pulled the door down, securing it with the code, then ran back. After negotiating the outer gate, he raced to his car. As he opened the boot, the American said, 'Nice work, Mr Kipling, you still have forty-five seconds to spare.'

'Good,' he panted. 'Phone your mate back at my house and tell him to give Tom the meds.'

'I'm real sorry, Mr Kipling. That's not going to happen until we get back to your house and I have the original Fragonard in my hands. I need to check that package properly. So my advice is we should get going. The clock's ticking.'

Harry laid the picture flat and slammed the boot shut. He flashed back, momentarily, to that late September day when they'd taken this picture to the *Antiques Roadshow,* and security guards had escorted them back to this vehicle. When he and Freya had been so full of excitement, of hope and of almost disbelief. The kind of feeling, he thought, a lottery winner must experience when checking the numbers and realizing they were a match.

And now these bastards were taking all that from him. And he couldn't do a damned thing about it.

Or could he?

As he drove back towards Brighton, in silence, he was still trying to think of something he could do. The occasional wild thought snaked into his mind. And every street light they passed lit up the menace of the two masked faces behind him in his mirror.

He glanced at the car clock: 8.42. They'd be home in ten minutes. Still he kept thinking.

And still he came up with nothing. Nothing but anger at himself for being so helpless.

87

It was approaching 9 p.m. when Harry drove the Volvo onto the driveway of his house. The American took possession of the painting and the three of them walked up to the front door.

'You have what you want,' Harry said. 'Will you now leave us alone and let me give our son his meds?' He held out his hand for the injector kit.

Kilgore replied, 'First we open the package. I don't want to be taken for a fool, Mr Kipling.'

As they entered the house, Harry heard the sound of a football game. He rushed through to the lounge and to his relief he saw that Tom was still conscious, but still looking woozy. There was only a faint expression of recognition in his face. Freya seemed OK, but he could see the terror in her eyes. Their guard was holding the TV remote and watching the game.

'Can you get me a knife?' Kilgore, still holding the package, asked Harry. Then, irked, he turned to the heavy with the remote. 'Turn that goddamn thing off.'

'Boss, it's a big game—'

'Goddamn turn it off!'

He turned it off.

Harry gave Freya a nervous, reassuring smile, hurried to the kitchen and returned with a small serrated knife which he handed to the American. Then he watched as the man cut away the tape securing the cardboard, followed by the bubble wrap. There was no excitement in his actions, no sense of a child tearing open Christmas wrapping; just something coldly forensic about him.

Lifting the framed painting clear, Kilgore held it up to the light and examined it carefully, then turned it over and studied the canvas back. Finally, he turned to Harry. 'This is the painting you bought at a car boot sale, is that right?'

'It is,' he replied. 'Well, just to be clear, it wasn't this painting that I actually thought I was buying. I bought a painting with a hideous old lady's face on it, because I liked the frame, not the painting itself. We later discovered this one was underneath. As you can see, it's the same original frame as you must have seen on the *Antiques Roadshow.*'

Kilgore handed the painting to the heavy who'd accompanied them on the journey, picked up Freya's phone from the coffee table, tapped in the code, then tapped the app and held it to the disc on Tom's arm. Then he showed the readout to Freya and Harry.

2. The arrow was still pointing down.

Harry saw only one doughnut had been eaten.

Kilgore dug his hand in his pocket, pulled out the injector kit and put it down on the coffee table, alongside the phones and doughnuts.

'Guess you folk had better give this lad a pretty big dose after we've gone. I wouldn't leave it for too long, if you know what I'm saying.'

Before Harry could react, he felt his arms seized and pulled behind him. An instant later, grey gaffer tape was being wound around him, pinning his arms back. Then he was forced down onto the same chair as before and taped to it.

'At least give our son a bite of another doughnut.'

He watched the American lift Daniel Hegarty's copy of the Fragonard off the wall. Kilgore turned to him. 'You won't mind if I take this too?'

'Like I have a choice?'

Harry saw the serpent smile through the slit in the balaclava. 'We all have choices in life all the time, Mr Kipling. But choices come with consequences. My employer, as I said, made you a very generous offer of fifty thousand pounds, and your choice was to reject it. Now you have the consequence.' He paused. 'It shouldn't take you too long to free yourself from your bindings. Fifteen or twenty minutes. Tom should still be alive then, and we'll be long gone. Enjoy the rest of your evening.'

An instant later, before he could respond, a strip of gaffer tape was pulled tight across Harry's mouth.

The three men left the room. As he stared at Freya, he heard the click of the front door closing. Then he looked at Tom. He tried to stand but the heavy chair he was taped to dragged him back down. He frantically signalled to Tom, who was barely focusing.

Tom nodded, managed somehow, with his arms still bound behind him, to get to his feet. He sagged, looking around bewildered, then passed out, falling to the floor and striking the side of his head on the coffee table. A stream of blood poured from it onto the carpet.

Harry watched in horror. He had to do something. Powered by desperation, somehow, with the heavy chair attached to him, he got to his feet. Thinking wildly, he staggered a few inches then fell sideways. The impact with the floor was enough to rip the tape holding him to the chair free. He rolled over, got to his knees then pushed himself up, his arms still tightly bound behind him.

Shit, how long did Tom have?

Where was a sharp edge?

The doorway. Of course!

He went over to the door, turned to have his back against it, then began rubbing the tape binding his hands against the edge of the door, trying to find the sharp edge of the brass latch.

He found it.

A minute later his arms came free.

Jesus.

Waving to Freya to hold on, he rushed to the table, broke the glucagon injector free of its container, dialled the one milligram dose he and Freya had learned was what they should give in the event of a hypo, and jabbed it into his unconscious, bleeding son's arm. Then he raced into the kitchen, grabbed a knife and cut Freya free, and she ripped the tape away from her mouth.

'Oh God, oh God,' was all she could say for a moment, as she staggered towards her son and kneeled down, hugging him.

Harry picked up his phone and dialled 999. When the operator answered, he asked for an ambulance, urgently, and the police.

88

Stuart Piper looked at his watch: 10.06 p.m. He was sitting on his sofa in the Hidden Salon, feeling distinctly on edge. And when he was edgy he got angry. And when he got angry he got drunk, which made him even more angry. As he was now.

Where the hell was that fool Kilgore? He should have been here a good hour ago by his reckoning. Had it all gone to rat-shit? Everything at the moment seemed to have gone to rat-shit. Like the police sniffing around a bit too much. Like this damned cigar which wasn't drawing properly. And like the fire in the grate that wasn't burning properly tonight, either. Had his fool of a house-keeper laid it badly?

Even the candles in the two candelabras did not seem to be as bright or steady as normal. They were flickering and it was annoying him.

Even his blasted cognac tasted rank tonight.

He clicked the Dupont lighter and held the flame to the end of his Cohiba Esplendidos, sucking hard. But it was like trying to suck air through a vacuum. Reaching for his silver cutter, he clipped off a further piece of the tip and tried again. Still no joy.

In a fit of temper, he stood up and tossed the £60 cigar into the open fire, went over to the humidor and selected another one. He clipped it, lit it, and drew hard. Better but still not great. *No cigar*, he thought, humourlessly, too angry to even smile at his private joke.

Clamping the fresh Cohiba in his mouth, he picked up the tall bellows beside the grate and pumped some life into the fire, watching his discarded cigar burn for some moments. Then he sat back down and looked at his phone, tempted to call Kilgore to find out what the hell was happening. But they'd agreed radio silence, and he figured if things had gone tits up, it wouldn't be smart to have a traceable call.

He sat back down on the edge of the sofa and drank some more cognac, draining the glass. Restless, he stood up again, went over to the drinks cabinet, feeling a little woozy, and refilled it to a much higher level than usual. And took a large gulp of it as he sat back down, momentarily closing his eyes and wincing against the sharp burn in his throat.

Then he took several hard puffs on the cigar until a reassuring red glow and halo of grey ash appeared. As he did so he felt a draught of cold air; the candles all guttered in unison, and he heard a sound behind him.

The door was open, and Robert Kilgore came through, a broad beam on his face, holding a package encased in bubble wrap.

'What's kept you?' Piper demanded.

Kilgore held up the package. 'Doing what you asked me to do, sir. Mission accomplished!' He propped the package gently against the wall where the other three Fragonards were hung, above, then looked back at Piper proudly. 'I think you're going to be a very happy man, sir.'

'That's for me to decide, I don't need you telling me, Bobby.' He puffed again on his cigar and took another gulp of his brandy. 'So, let me see.'

Kilgore gave him a smile that irritated him, then, seemingly in no hurry, fished a pack of Camels from his pocket and shook a cigarette from the pack. He jammed it between his lips, produced a plastic lighter from another pocket and lit it. 'I could sure use a drink,' he said, nodding at Piper's glass, then taking a long drag of his Camel.

'Would you mind putting that out, please, Bobby?' Piper said sharply.

Kilgore held the cigarette up with a puzzled expression. 'I'm sorry, boss, you're smoking, I figured—'

Piper stood up, abruptly, then swayed on his feet and nearly fell backwards down onto the sofa. Shit, he was very definitely a little bit drunk, he realized. Actually, more than a little bit. Stabilizing himself, he strode unsteadily over to Kilgore, snatched the cigarette from his fingers, carried it over to the coffee table and crushed it out in the ashtray. 'I don't want that cheap thing polluting my Havana. Understand?'

Kilgore looked at him warily. 'I'm sorry, boss.'

'The picture?'

Kilgore pulled away the bubble wrap, lifting the small, framed painting clear, and handed it proudly to Piper. 'It's sure going to look just fine in that gap,' he said.

Piper did not reply. He was holding the painting under the light of the chandelier, examining it carefully. Then, setting it down on one of the sofas, propping it against a cushion, he switched on the torch app of his phone and spent several minutes examining every detail of it, without commenting.

'Looks pretty original to me, I'd say, and the original frame,' Kilgore said quietly. He'd seen the boss's drunken tantrums before. Truth was he was getting pretty fed up with the way the boss treated him.

Piper turned to the reverse and began an equally scrupulous inspection under the torch beam.

Kilgore watched.

'This came from the Kiplings' home?' Piper asked.

'Well, not exactly, sir. I do also have the one that was in their home, which is an obvious fake.' He then explained where Harry Kipling had been storing this one.

Piper continued to study the reverse in silence. Suddenly, to Kilgore's utter surprise, his boss hurled the painting to the floor. 'You moron,' Piper shouted. 'You total and utter moron!'

Kilgore frowned. 'I'm sorry, sir, what do you mean?'

Piper glared at him. 'What do I mean? I thought you were an art expert! This is not an original, it's a fake. It's a fake, for God's sake, man!'

89

Tuesday, 5 November

Kilgore frowned at Piper, then shook his head firmly. 'Sir, you are mistaken.'

'The only mistake I've made was to trust you.' Piper staggered towards him menacingly. 'Are you pulling a fast one on me, Bobby? After all these years of trusting you and making you rich, you're now trying to screw me, right? Think you can take me for a fool or what?'

'Sir, I'm sorry, I'm not with you. I'm honestly not with you.'

'Really? Who are you with? The fairies at the bottom of the garden? I'm telling you this is a fake. A good fake, I'll grant you that one small concession. But it's a fake.' He grabbed Kilgore's jacket lapels, shaking them furiously. 'Where's the original, Bobby? What have you done with it? Where's the bloody original?'

Kilgore was totally flabbergasted. 'This is the original, sir.'

'You liar. You double-crossing liar.' Piper released him and pushed him back so hard Kilgore stumbled, bashing into the sofa. Then, jabbing his cigar at him, Piper sneered, 'You cheating bloody thief.'

Glaring at him, his eyes looking like they were struggling to focus, Piper demanded, 'So where did you park your tiny brain when you visited Daniel Hegarty? When he told you he could fake pretty much any painting if he had enough time? And the only way to tell a fake from the original would be a single groove carved by his fingernail in the back of the frame?' He held the reverse of the painting up to Kilgore's face. 'See that? See that groove?'

To his dismay, Kilgore saw it.

Piper was pointing at a very faint, barely noticeable mark in the back of the frame. He looked up, with cognac-fuelled belligerence, at his employee. 'So?'

'I did what you asked me, sir,' Kilgore said.

'You double-crossing loser!' Piper slurred. 'You Mississippi snake oil salesman. You see that? That groove? You're bloody double-crossing me.'

Piper lashed out with his right fist. But so slowly, Kilgore saw it coming, ducked and parried it. 'Sir,' he said. 'Please, I brought you what Harry Kipling gave me.'

'You fucking liar.' Piper lashed out again, and this time his fist struck Kilgore's face, sending him crashing, momentarily stunned, to the floor.

Piper stood over him, feeling triumphant. 'Anything more you'd like to add, Bobby babe?'

Kilgore looked up at him in astonishment. At his partner-in-crime for the past fifteen years. Together, they'd plundered the art world, lining their own pockets handsomely. Now the man he'd always respectfully called the boss had seemingly turned against him.

And Kilgore wasn't having that.

He lashed out with a foot, striking Piper's right leg, surprising him. Crying out in pain, the cigar falling to the carpet, Piper staggered back, crashed into one of the silver candelabras, sending it toppling over onto the sofa on the far side of the coffee table, and fell over backwards himself.

Kilgore climbed to his feet. Piper lay on the floor, looking up, confused and in pain.

Kilgore saw two of the candles burning holes in the sofa. He hesitated, his anger fogging the deep loyalty he'd once had to this man.

Piper, still on the floor, slurred, 'You total wanker! You've bust my leg. You're a thief. You're fired, get out of my house and don't come back.'

A sudden *whoomph* startled Kilgore. A large part of the centre of the sofa was now well alight, crackling like dry timber. Thick, black, acrid smoke rose from it. Kilgore hesitated, thinking, wondering what the hell to do. Even in the few seconds he stood there, the flames took further hold. It didn't seem to have registered with Piper.

He hurried to the door and ran out into the Long Gallery. There was a fire extinguisher out here, somewhere, he'd walked past it a thousand times – where the hell was it? Strangely, he wasn't panicking, he felt calm. So calm he surprised himself. Calm but very angry.

Fake?

You cheating bloody thief.

The words ringing in his ears smarted, stoking a long-buried furnace of anger inside him. He hurried along, past painting after painting, and finally saw the silver fire extinguisher a short way ahead, beneath a coiled fire hose.

And stopped in his tracks. Thinking.

He looked both ways. There was no one around. The twins had gone off-duty. None of Piper's domestic staff were around after 6 p.m. It was just the two of them at this hour.

Turning, he strode quickly back to the doorway of the Hidden Salon. A blast of heat greeted him as he reached it, and he saw that the ceiling above the burning sofa was now smouldering, looking like it was about to burst into flames at any moment.

'Fuck you!' slurred Piper. 'What the fuck's happening? Jesus, help me up, call the fire brigade!' He held up an arm towards Kilgore.

Without replying, Kilgore backed away, slammed the door shut, turned the large brass key in the lock then removed and pocketed it.

A second later he heard frantic hammering on the other side. Piper's voice screaming his name increasingly desperately, *Bobby, Bobby, BOBBY!*

'Nice knowing you, sir. I never believed I would have the pleasure of this moment where I can actually picture you dead,' he murmured, then strode quickly away, out of the house and into his Tesla.

As he drove off, he felt calmer than he had felt in far too many years. Heading through the pitch darkness down the drive towards the gates, he dug the cigarette pack from his pocket, shook out a Camel and sparked his lighter.

The smoke smelled so sweet, so much better than the aroma of those interminable cigars – and the stench of burning sofa.

He took a long drag, inhaling the sweet taste.

It tasted of freedom.

The gates that opened ahead bade him freedom, too.

Had Harry Kipling pulled a double flanker? he wondered, or more likely was it Daniel Hegarty? It had to be Hegarty, he reckoned. He had talked in the past about dealers in Russia and China and some Middle Eastern countries who would pay big money for stolen works of art. If that was Hegarty's game then he would rumble him, and Hegarty would be forced to cut a deal with him.

Kilgore smiled. A smile that was cold and warm at the same time. The Germans had a word for this, for getting pleasure from someone else's misfortune, and he tried to recall it as the gates opened and he headed out onto the road and away from the Piper mansion for the last time. Then it came to him. Yes. *Schadenfreude.*

In the darkness of the country road, a couple of miles south of Piper's house, he travelled past dense woods on either side.

He checked the mirror for any sign of a red glow in the distance behind him. There was just darkness. But not for much longer, he guessed.

Coming up to his left was a lay-by. He slowed, glided the silent car to a halt and climbed out, leaving the headlights on. There was dense undergrowth, perfect, he thought. Then, removing the large, ancient brass key from his pocket, and wiping it clean of fingerprints, just as a precaution, but a pretty unnecessary one, he figured, he tossed the key deep into the centre of a massive, sprawling gorse bush. Then he got back into the car and drove on, treating himself to another cigarette, and another smile. He'd always liked that word and now he knew why. *Schadenfreude.* Oh yes.

90

Tuesday, 5 November

'Just in here and the hallway – they didn't enter any other rooms, Mr and Mrs Kipling?' PC Alldridge asked.

'Well, I suppose the kitchen, too – Tom was in there having his supper when they – they—' She stumbled on her words.

Harry recognized the burly uniformed police officer in his fifties, PC Alldridge, who had been here before. He was sat on the sofa opposite him and Freya, with his same colleague, a feisty-looking man, who had given his name as PC Simmons, beside him. He was giving Freya a sympathetic smile.

An ambulance was parked on the street outside, the two paramedics still attending Tom, who seemed a lot better now, up in his room.

There were two more uniform police officers outside the house, and a detective in her forties, in civilian clothes, with short greying hair and a businesslike manner, checking around the inside. She had identified herself as Val Remington-Hobbs, the duty DI for Brighton and Hove.

'Please take your time,' Alldridge coaxed gently. 'You've been through quite an ordeal.'

Freya nodded tearfully. 'Just the hallway, the kitchen and here.' She looked at her husband for confirmation.

'I think you said the American had checked out all the other rooms, darling,' Harry replied.

She nodded and said, shakily, 'Yes, yes I'd forgotten. He had a look around.'

'Can you tell us what happened and how come these people got into your house?' Alldridge asked.

'I-I let them in.' She gave a weak smile. 'You see, I was expecting a man called Mike Elkington – that was the name he gave me over the phone – he said he needed a builder, urgently, and Harry had been recommended to him.'

'Did he say by who?' Alldridge asked, making notes on a small tablet.

She shook her head wearily, the sedative the paramedic had given her making her increasingly drowsy.

'Can you try to go through the descriptions of your attackers once more, Mrs Kipling?' PC Simmons asked. 'So we can circulate it to all our patrols, just in case these people are still out and about.'

Harry, holding Freya's hand, responded. 'The main man was tall and thin with a very distinct Southern American accent – you know – *drawl*. His accomplices were big guys, beefcakes, like nightclub bouncers.' Then he remembered. 'Oh yes, one – the one that came with me to the depot in Worthing – was called Ross or Russ or something like that.'

'Ross?' PC Simmons echoed as his colleague appeared to write this into his tablet. 'What kind of an accent did this person – Ross – have?' he asked.

Harry shook his head. 'I never heard him actually speak.' At that moment he noticed DI Remington-Hobbs standing in the doorway, looking around for a moment before coming into the room.

'Mr and Mrs Kipling,' she said, 'you and your son have been through quite a trauma, and we are thankful you are safe now. For your reassurance, I'm going to post an officer outside your house for the rest of the night, so you'll be able to get, hopefully, as much of a good night's sleep as you can. Because of the gravity of this incident, I've requested the involvement of the Surrey and Sussex Major Crime Team, but asked them not to contact you until tomorrow morning.' She smiled, looking at her watch. 'It's past 10.30 p.m. and I don't think it would be productive for them to attend tonight, it looks to me like you all need some rest. They will probably require you and your son to come to the CID HQ for interviews, to see what else you can remember about these criminals, when you are feeling fresher, and your son is better.'

Harry and Freya looked at each other before Harry spoke. 'We've already spoken with two detectives after our break-in.' Then Freya asked her, 'Can Tom go to school tomorrow if he's feeling up to it?'

The Detective Inspector hesitated. 'Well, I think it would be better if he took the day off – or at least the morning, anyway. Just like you and your husband, Tom may have valuable information for us, and it would be good for him to be interviewed while all this is fresh in his mind.'

'Yes, of course,' Freya said.

'We'll do whatever you need,' Harry added.

'I'm so sorry for what you've been through,' the DI said. 'What a nightmare. And obviously we need to consider a link between this and the break-in you had here previously. Hopefully, we'll catch the offenders and get your painting back. Is it insured?'

Harry shook his head ruefully. 'We never insured it because we didn't know what its real value is – we were about to hand it to an auction house who were going to have their experts study it in depth, with a view to putting it into a sale in January – if they could establish to their satisfaction it was genuine.'

'What would it be worth if so?' the DI asked.

Harry shrugged. 'Five million, perhaps more.'

The DI looked astounded. 'Five million *pounds*?'

He nodded and glanced at Freya who said, 'Maybe, but so far it's not brought us much happiness or luck.'

'Let's see if we can change that,' Val Remington-Hobbs said breezily.

'You really think you have a hope of getting that painting back?' Harry asked.

'We will do all we can,' the DI replied.

'Yeah,' he replied. 'I'm already reading your quote in tomorrow's *Argus*. "*We will do all we can to catch these offenders, said Detective Inspector Remington-Hobbs.*"'

Ignoring Freya, who had raised a placating hand, he shook his head at the detective. 'Good luck with that one.'

91

Wednesday, 6 November

Rocky and Rambo raced each other up the vast Downland field, in yet another of their eternally futile attempts at catching a seagull, or indeed any kind of bird. Daniel Hegarty watched the creature wait until almost the very last second, as if taunting them, before taking majestically off and soaring high above them.

It was just gone 6.35 a.m. and the charcoal canvas of the pre-dawn sky was veined with thin streaks of yellow and red.

He should be feeling great. Yesterday he'd agreed a commission for a copy of a Norman Rockwell for a well-known actor, for £15,000. It was his third lucrative commission in as many weeks – and he was rapidly approaching the point where he was going to have to either turn down work or offer far longer lead times. But he was feeling far from great this morning, after his second sleepless night in a row. He was deeply troubled. Vexed.

Afraid.

A wintry chill blew through him as he stared, deep in thought, down at the houses of Saltdean and the grey water of the English Channel beyond. He'd tried to be too clever, he realized, and had crossed a line. Put himself into a place where he neither wanted to be nor needed to be, not at this stage of his life and his career.

When Harry Kipling had first brought the Fragonard painting to him, asking him to make a copy, he'd sensed a real opportunity. Kipling was a decent sort, and he'd done a good job on their building extension here, and at a fair price, but he was totally

388

naïve about art. The builder had explained excitedly how he'd bought the picture in a car boot sale, then, after dissolving the ugly painting over it, the stunning work of art beneath had been revealed. He'd taken it to the *Antiques Roadshow*, where the expert had told him that, if genuine, it could be worth millions. But as Harry had told him, the expert on the show had been unable to ascertain then and there whether it was a genuine Fragonard or not.

That was when Hegarty spotted his opportunity.

Although commissioned to create one copy of the painting, for the Kiplings to display on their lounge wall as insurance while they stored the original safely, until they could get it authenticated or not, Hegarty craftily made two copies. The first, for the lounge wall, was a faithful reproduction, nice quality, but easily detectable as a fake to anyone who knew anything about art. But the second copy was a work he was immensely proud of, one of his finest ever. A true masterpiece!

He used his years of experience in art forgery, even down to his pièce de résistance – mixing pigments with a few clothing fibres from a smock from the mid-1700s, obtained from a mate who worked in the Brighton Museum.

He'd added a few touches to the reverse of the canvas, then, keeping the original himself, had handed both forgeries back to a delighted Harry.

His plan had been simple. Eventually Harry Kipling would attempt to sell the painting, probably through a major London auction house where it would be subject to intense scrutiny – carbon dating, spectrogram analysis and an assessment by a Fragonard expert. That expert, and Hegarty had a pretty good idea who would be called in, would pronounce that painting a fake because of the brushstroke technique – something Hegarty had done deliberately and very subtly, just here and there.

Hegarty's plan had been at some point in the future to produce the original he'd secretly retained, which he was pretty sure was a genuine Fragonard. He would concoct a convincing story about its provenance and quietly sell it to one of his billionaire Russian or Chinese clients for handsome money. Enough money to never have to work again.

Millions!

But he hadn't reckoned on someone already owning the other three works in the series, *Spring, Autumn* and *Winter*. A serious piece of work. Someone who, he had no doubt at all, would not stop at killing to get that fourth painting.

And it would not be long before Piper went after the Kiplings, just as he'd come after him, he thought with a twinge of guilt. And when Piper got his hands on the painting he'd know it was a fake.

Albeit a damned fine one.

And he would put two and two together.

Hegarty loved Natalie and he loved his life. He'd never met Stuart Piper but knew him by reputation. Billy the Brush had told him about two art dealers who had met with fatal accidents that Piper was reputedly behind. And there were possibly more. Hegarty knew from his own criminal background that some villains you could do business with, and some you couldn't. The latter would kill anyone who didn't give them what they wanted. Stuart Piper was one of those.

In the clouds high above he heard a plane. Probably out of Gatwick and heading south. Maybe that's what he should do, jet off to somewhere in the sun with Natalie and lie low for a while? But he had a stack of commissions to fulfil, and he knew that running from a man like Piper would never set you free of him, it would just delay him catching up with you.

A warbling sound distracted him. His ringtone.

Puzzled about who might be calling at this hour, he dug his phone out of his pocket and looked at the display. It was Harry Kipling.

He hesitated. Shit. Shit, shit, shit. He tried to think of the reasons Kipling might have to call him, and could only come up with one. The one he did not want to face. Ignore the call?

No, he was too curious. Taking a deep breath, he answered, trying to sound more cheerful and guileless than he felt. 'Harry! How are you? Must be synchronicity, I was just thinking about you. To what do I owe this honour?'

The builder, sounding deeply distressed, apologized for calling him so early, then told him what had happened. When he finished, Hegarty said, 'Shit. What a bummer.'

'You could say that.'

'You gave him the original, which you had in the secure unit?'

'I didn't have any choice, Daniel. These guys were proper scary, you know? I think they would have killed Tom, our son, if I hadn't done what they demanded.'

'God, I don't know what to say, Harry,' he replied, and at this moment he didn't. He saw his dogs chasing a rabbit, which to his mild relief vanished down a hole. 'Do you have any idea who these people were, Harry?'

'No, I just thought I'd call you in case you have any idea.'

'Can you describe them?'

'One, the bastard in charge, was American. Tall, creepy, he had a kind of Southern accent, but I never saw his face. They were all wearing balaclavas. The other two were like henchmen – bouncer types. One of them was called Ross or something like that.'

The cold wind blowing through Hegarty just got colder. 'Doesn't ring any bell with me,' he lied. 'I'm sorry, Harry, but it doesn't sound like anyone I've ever had dealings with. What did the police say?'

'Nothing really. They'll do their best, and all that. It's been handed over to their Major Crime Team, whatever that means, and we're all going to be interviewed in depth later today.'

'How's your wife and your boy?' Hegarty asked, doing his best to sound sincerely concerned, and that wasn't hard – he *was* seriously concerned, not only for the Kiplings, but for himself and Natalie.

'Pretty bloody traumatized.'

'I can only imagine, what an ordeal. That's terrible, Harry. And you've lost the painting?'

'Both of them. God knows how much the original is worth.'

'And you didn't insure it?'

'No, as I told the police, we didn't know what value to put on it. And if it was worth millions, I probably couldn't have afforded the insurance anyway. That's why I had you make a copy, so I could put the original in a safe place.'

'Is there anything I can do?' Hegarty asked, his mind in turmoil too now, his worst fear confirmed.

'No, I-I just called you on the off-chance you might know something.'

'I so wish, Harry. This is terrible. I wish I did know these people, I really wish I bloody did. I wish I could do something for you.'

'Maybe you could speak to your contacts in the art world in case any of them get offered the painting – they might try to offload it quickly.'

'Of course, Harry, I'll make some discreet calls – I'll bell you if I have any luck.'

'Thanks, I'd really appreciate that.'

Hegarty ended the call with a storm of panic raging through him. This was happening sooner than he'd feared. When Piper realized what he had was a fake, and for sure he would, he would almost certainly come after him. And next time his window cleaners might not be around. Nor anyone else.

He called the dogs. Whistled. Called them again, urgently. He wanted to get home – he had an idea. It wasn't ideal but it might work. He'd always subscribed to the view where possible that if you wanted to conceal something, hiding it in plain sight was often the best idea.

He glanced at his watch. The robbery had taken place around 9 p.m. last night, from what Harry had told him. With luck Piper wouldn't see the painting until this morning. Then it would take him time to get the American and the henchmen for a return visit to his own house. He could just give them the painting and hope that would be the end of it, but screw that. Not after their threats to his darling Natalie and himself. He wasn't going to give those bastards anything.

The more he thought about his plan, the more he liked it. As he headed back down the hill, the dogs lured by a biscuit each, he smiled. It was the first time he'd smiled in two days.

92

Shortly before 8 a.m. the doorbell rang. Harry Kipling peered through the spyhole and saw two men in suits. Keeping the chain on, he opened the door a fraction. 'Can I help you?'

'Mr Kipling?' A calm, direct voice.

'Yes – who are you?'

Through the crack he saw a hand hold up a police warrant card.

'Detective Superintendent Grace and Detective Inspector Branson of the Surrey and Sussex Major Crime Team, sir. May we come in? This is just a quick visit to check you are all OK.'

'Yes, of course, thank you.' Harry closed the door, slipped the chain from the lock and opened it again. Two smartly dressed men stood there, one white, with neat, close-cropped fair hair, the other taller, black and bald, wearing a flamboyant tie.

A few minutes later Harry and Freya were seated in the kitchen, just as last night, with the two senior detectives opposite them. Both of them had politely rejected Freya's offer of tea or coffee.

'I'm very sorry for your ordeal, Mr and Mrs Kipling, and for what your son was put through,' Roy Grace said. 'I'm sure it's no consolation if I tell you violent domestic robberies of this type are extremely rare, and we are taking this very seriously indeed.'

'What chance do you think you have of catching these people – and getting our painting back?' Harry Kipling asked.

'We're drafting in officers to do a house-to-house in this area,

394

looking for any home that has street-facing CCTV,' Branson responded. 'To see if we can get the vehicle's registration.'

'You think it was a Tesla?' Grace butted in. 'You told the officers who attended last night that an unfamiliar car, a Tesla, was parked outside your house and you gave them a description of the model, I believe?'

'I did, yes,' Harry confirmed. 'I-I should have had the presence of mind to note the registration but I . . .' He gestured helplessly.

'Of course,' Glenn Branson said with a warm, sympathetic smile.

'We've already put in a request to the Control Room to check all CCTV and ANPR cameras for the registration plates of any Tesla driving in the area around the time of this attack on you all,' Grace said. 'Do you have a photograph of this painting?'

The Kiplings turned to each other, frowning. 'Did we ever—?' Harry asked. Then he remembered, of course he had. 'Yes, I took several for an art dealer – they're on my phone, I can ping them to you.'

'Good,' Grace said. 'I understand there's an organization called the Art Loss Register which has a worldwide reach. If we can send them an image of the painting, that would block off a number of avenues open to these thieves. We will get it circulated also to all dealers that we can find.'

'Thank you,' Harry said.

Grace glanced at his watch. 'We're going to have to leave, but we will be arranging to bring you both and your son into Sussex CID HQ later today, with your consent of course, to put each of you through a cognitive witness interview.' He smiled. 'That may sound a little alarming, but I assure you it isn't. We'd like to have you all interviewed by trained officers. They might just be able to jog your memories for some tiny nuggets of detail that could make the difference between catching these offenders and not. Will you all be OK with this?'

Freya, nodding, asked, 'How long will this take? I'm worried because Tom has diabetes and stress can play havoc with his sugar levels.'

'We'll make sure the interviewers are aware of that,' Glenn Branson said. 'We could arrange for a doctor to be in attendance if that would help?'

Freya nodded and looked at the Libre app on her phone. 'I think that would be good, his sugar levels are going up and down crazily at the moment.'

Roy Grace stood up and Glenn Branson followed suit. 'We'll arrange for a car to collect you all later,' the Detective Superintendent said.

'We'll be ready,' Harry said, looking at him. He saw honesty there, genuine concern and something else he'd never imagined seeing in a police officer's face. Genuine decency.

He saw it in the Detective Inspector's face, too.

They cared, he realized. They really did bloody care.

93

Natalie was at the kitchen table eating her breakfast and reading the morning's *Argus* when Hegarty came back in with the dogs and removed his fleece. As he gave her a kiss he saw the front-page headline, for the second day running, was about the murder victim on their doorstep, named as Archie Goff, a career burglar.

There was a photograph of him, along with a smaller, inset photograph of Detective Superintendent Roy Grace, who had held a press conference yesterday, in which he was requesting any members of the public who had seen any unfamiliar people or vehicles in the area on Saturday evening to phone either the Incident Room or Crimestoppers, with both numbers beneath.

'Anything new in that piece?' he asked.

She shook her head. 'You OK? You're looking pale.'

'I'm OK, thanks, just didn't sleep well again last night.'

'Me neither. Have something to eat, you'll feel better. Want me to cook you some eggs?'

'I'll just grab some cereal and coffee, something I need to do urgently.'

'Oh?'

He picked the dog bowls off the floor and, as they looked at him expectantly, scooped a generous amount of their dry food into each, took a packet of grated Cheddar from the fridge and sprinkled some over each portion. Rambo barked excitedly. Then he squeezed a couple of drops of hemp oil onto the biscuits in

397

both bowls, something they'd read was good for their dogs' health, made the dogs sit, set down the bowls on the floor and made them wait for a few moments before, with a sweep of his right arm, he said, 'OK, Rambo, OK, Rocky!'

The dogs fell on their bowls as it they'd been starved for weeks. Hegarty switched on the coffee machine, then grabbed one of the chairs from the table, carried it over to the work surface and climbed onto it, balancing precariously.

'What are you doing, darling?' Natalie asked, alarmed.

'Just getting this down.' He reached up and gripped either side of the Banksy copy he'd made, of two policemen kissing, unhooked it and lifted it down. Then he climbed off the chair.

'I liked it there,' she said.

'I'll explain everything later, my love,' he said and carried it through into his studio, removed his current work, the Lowry copy, from the easel and sat the Banksy there.

He hurried back into the kitchen, ignoring his wife's quizzical gaze, made himself a double espresso while gobbling down a banana, then took his coffee back into the studio. Setting it down, he picked up a jar of acetone, selected a fresh paintbrush, dipped it in, and then began, gently coating a small area at the top of the Banksy with the chemical.

Within seconds, that part of the Banksy started to dissolve, revealing a section of the painting beneath. He coated a wider section with the acetone, and as more of the Banksy disappeared, more of the painting beneath, in all its brilliant colours and dense texture, was revealed intact.

In less than fifteen minutes, all traces of the Banksy were gone completely.

Despite the rush he was in, Hegarty could not help taking a couple of minutes to admire what lay beneath. It was sensational. He could actually understand anyone being desperate to own this. It was just glorious. Magical.

Then he set to work replacing the wooden frame with a gilded one, identical to the one which had been on the painting when Harry Kipling had brought it to him. He recalled Harry telling him, ironically, that he'd only bought the picture in the first place for the frame.

He stood back and allowed himself a few more precious moments to admire his handiwork. Or rather, the handiwork of one of the long-dead greats.

And despite the fear roiling through him, he couldn't help himself, he was staring at it wistfully. Respectfully.

Secure on his easel in front of him was the original Fragonard painting of *Summer* that Harry Kipling had brought him to copy, five weeks ago.

94

Wednesday, 6 November

Outside the Kiplings' house, Grace and Branson climbed back into their car. Branson, behind the wheel, said, 'What do you think about their story?'

'In what sense?'

'Like, are they telling the truth?'

'About the robbery?'

'Uh huh. Exactly.'

'Are you saying you think we've just been spun a load of bull?' Grace quizzed.

Branson shrugged. '*ABC*, it's what you've always taught me, boss, right?'

Shaking his head, Grace said, 'Congratulations, it's taken less than five years of being a detective to turn you into a cynic?'

'Better than starting off as one from the get-go like you, right?'

Grace smiled. 'I don't think the Kiplings are lying. They've nothing to gain by giving us a made-up story. I think they're real. It would be a different ballgame if the painting had been insured for big money.'

'If you say so,' Branson replied dubiously.

'What's making you so suspicious of them?' Grace asked him.

He shrugged. 'I don't know, something doesn't feel right about this. They buy a picture in a car boot sale that *might* be a fake, *might* be worth a fortune. Invent a tie-up robbery, hit the press and bingo, the picture must be genuine. Yeah? A clever marketing ploy.'

'Maybe if they still had the painting, but they don't.'

'They *say* they don't.'

Grace shook his head. 'I don't think the Kiplings are wide-boys. They're just decent people, in my view, and they've been to hell and back.' He glanced at his watch. 'Let's get back to base, we've got our next briefing and I'll need to update the ACC.'

For the next ten minutes as Branson drove, Grace made a series of calls. His first was to Jack Alexander, asking him to put back the time of their morning briefing to 9.30 a.m. and asking him to organize a substantial outside enquiry team to do a door-to-door around the vicinity of the Kiplings' home.

Next, just as he was dialling Norman Potting's number, the DS rang him.

'Chief, I've just had a call from Forensic Services in Guildford. They've been experimenting with some new technology on that DNA on the restaurant bill that was in Charlie Porteous's wallet, and they've got a match!'

'Tell me?' Grace asked.

'I think you are going to like this, chief! It's Ross Briggs.'

Grace thought for an instant. 'The man who rented the garage for the Audi A6 from Ricky Sharp?'

''It would appear to be the very same,' Potting confirmed.

'Ross Briggs,' Grace said with clear recall and shooting a glance at Branson. 'He's an employee of Art Recovery UK Ltd of which the head honcho is Stuart Piper?'

'Correct, chief. I have some more intel on him – and his brother – if you'd like to hear it?'

'Go ahead.'

'His brother, Maurice, is a total charmer, like Ross, as you know from when we met them. The twins used to have a security business, doing nightclub doors until they got done for GBH fifteen years ago. A nicer pair of identical twins we couldn't ever hope to meet. Members of the National Front, they also used to advertise themselves on social media as the UK's prime representatives of the Ku Klux Klan. They beat up a black kiddie pretty badly for no greater sin than he tried to enter a Brighton nightclub. The Briggs brothers got two years each, during which their creditors bankrupted their business. Since their release from prison, they have been employed by Art Recovery UK Ltd.'

Grace banged his right fist into his left palm, repeatedly, with excitement, thinking fast. 'Good work, Norman. We know there's another employee of this company, the American, Robert Kilgore. Kilgore and the two Briggs brothers fit the description of the offenders in a nasty tie-up robbery in Brighton last night that I'm about to brief everyone on. One of the witnesses heard the name Ross being used. It all fits. Straight away I felt they were connected. Luke was trying to establish Kilgore's whereabouts, but it sounds like he's in Brighton, or certainly was last night. I want you and Velvet to nick both Briggses on suspicion of the murder of Charlie Porteous. You'd better take a Public Order team with you in case they kick off. I'll also have Kilgore arrested and brought in for questioning in connection with last night's robbery. And I'll ask Jon Exton to get a search warrant for Stuart Piper's house.'

'I think we might be a little late for that, chief,' Potting said.

'What do you mean?' Grace quizzed.

'Just had a call from Luke. Piper's mansion, Bewlay Park, caught fire during the night.'

95

Wednesday, 6 November

At midday, as Daniel Hegarty, following the directions on his Touareg's satnav, turned into Mackie Crescent, he was tormented by doubt. Was this really the right thing? During his time in prison, all those years back, at the same time as honing his painting skills in copying the greats of the past, he'd also tried to catch up on the education he'd missed out on at school, by reading avidly.

He'd discovered to his surprise that he loved Shakespeare, in particular for the colour of his language. And the plays of the grand old bard he had loved the best were the tragedies, in particular *Othello*, which for some reason struck a deep chord in him and inspired some of the work he'd done while inside.

As he shot a wistful glance at the rectangular parcel on the passenger seat beside him, and the envelope beside it, some of the words of *Othello* came back to him.

Like the base Indian, threw a pearl away. Richer than all his tribe.

He was about to do just that now.

But did he have a choice?

If Piper sent his henchmen back to his house and found the painting, God knows what reprisals he might exact. He could cope with a beating, but no way could he risk any harm to Natalie, the woman he loved, the most precious thing in his life. They were happy, they were in a good place, she was all the riches he needed. She was richer than any pearl. Richer than any damned painting was worth.

You are doing the right thing.

There was some quote about *doing the right thing* that he was trying to remember, but in his ragbag-of-nerves state he could not think what the hell it was, at this moment.

The satnav informed him his destination was a quarter of a mile ahead.

Then, as he drove up the street he saw, diagonally opposite tennis courts to his right, a marked police four-by-four parked on the left.

He hit the brakes and pulled into the kerb. A few hundred yards ahead he now saw a uniform copper walk out of a drive-way, followed by Harry Kipling, a fair-haired woman – presumably Harry's wife – and a teenage boy. The copper opened the rear door and the woman and boy climbed in, Harry going round to the front passenger door. Moments later the vehicle made a U-turn and headed back down the road in his direction.

Hegarty shrank down low, making himself as invisible as he could, until he saw the vehicle receding into the distance.

He stayed still for some moments, just in case for any reason they came back. *Close one*, he thought, feeling beads of perspiration popping on his brow. He'd reckoned on the Kiplings being at work and the boy at school. Although it wouldn't really have mattered if one of them had been at home, he had his story ready for them. But this made it easier, less explaining to do. As he was about to drive on, his phone rang, the number withheld.

He answered furtively, even though there was no one in earshot. 'Daniel Hegarty speaking.'

It was Weasel. 'You on a secure phone?'

'No, I don't have a secure phone, I'm legit these days.'

'Haha, that's funny. Listen, you ever heard of the Fates?'

Immediately Hegarty stiffened. 'Why are you asking?'

'Contact of mine has got a billionaire client in China who likes them French artists from the seventeenth century.'

'They're called fête galante,' Hegarty corrected him.

'Yeah, right, that's it. Well I've got a shopping list of artists' names – what's old Billy the Brush got on the back of his business card?'

'I don't know,' Hegarty said impatiently, wanting to get on.

'Filling spaces on rich men's walls,' Weasel said. 'Good, eh?'

'Can we talk later, Jimmy, I'm in the middle of something.'

'I've got to get back with a quick answer. This Hong Kong geezer pays proper money – and he's not bothered about provenance. What he's after, top of the list, is work by Fragonard.'

Suddenly, Weasel had his full attention. 'Fragonard? Jean-Honoré Fragonard?'

'Yeah, that's the one. I think we have an opportunity here, mate, a real one, know what I mean. You could knock one up, but we've only got a few days – this man's buyer is over in London now, goes back next week. He's bent as a nine-bob note – probably be a four-way split of the money – there's another middleman involved. It would have to be a pukka job, the full Hegarty works. Are you in?'

'Let me think about it and I'll bell you back.'

After he hung up, he sat for some minutes, thinking. Tempting, so tempting. But he thought not, not this time. There would always be other opportunities, but right at this moment he only had one chance to do the right thing. He started the car and drove on.

Reaching the Kiplings' house, he saw the open gates, but the driveway was full with three vehicles, a pick-up truck, a Volvo estate and a little Fiat. He pulled up against the kerb, hurried around to the passenger door and took out the painting and the envelope, then walked through onto the driveway of the pleasant if slightly dilapidated-looking house.

There were two wheelie bins to the right of the house, and a narrow path beside them leading through into the lush back garden.

It was a corner property and the garden was completely private, not overlooked by anyone, to his relief. He walked over the wet grass of the lawn to the shed and opened the door. It smelled of creosote and oil. A lawnmower sat in there, along with a row of tools. Garden loungers and chairs and their cushions, stowed away for winter, filled much of the rest of the interior that had not been claimed by cobwebs.

Brushing one out of his hair, Hegarty sidled past a stack of cushions, placed the parcelled painting against the far wall, then left, closing the door firmly behind him. He walked back around the side of the house, onto the driveway, jammed the envelope into the letterbox, then hurried back out to his car and drove off.

As he did so, feeling a massive weight lifted from his shoulders, that expression he'd been trying to remember earlier was actually something Kilgore had said to him.

Integrity is doing the right thing, even when no one is watching.
Yeah.

He'd done the right thing. For himself, for Natalie, and for the Kiplings. He hoped they would appreciate it.

96

Glenn Branson drove on blue lights towards Piper's house, while Roy Grace concentrated on his phone. He had deputized Norman Potting to take the delayed morning briefing, and updated the ACC by email, apologizing for having to cancel their meeting, but trusted she would understand his reasons.

In any event, he would be seeing her Friday. He and Cleo, together with Norman Potting and his late fiancée's mother, Joyce Moy, were going to Buckingham Palace. Bella Moy had been posthumously awarded the Queen's Gallantry Medal after saving the life of a young girl in a blaze and then tragically losing her own. Roy was also receiving the Queen's Gallantry Medal for saving the life of a young boy in a water-filled tunnel at Shoreham Fort.

Twenty minutes later, hurtling past dense woods to their right, the satnav indicated it was two miles to their destination. Then, with less than half a mile to go, they saw a police car angled across the imposing front gates. It reversed to allow them through.

As they drove up the long avenue of trees the air rapidly began to smell foul. The stench of burnt paint, wet, charred wood and other burnt materials. Flecks of ash fluttered in the blustery wind like flights of grey butterflies. Then, rounding a curve, an horrific sight came into view.

The magnificent house he and Glenn had visited, only yesterday, looked in a sorry state. Part of the central portion of the roof had collapsed, leaving it open to the elements, with curls of smoke rising from it, and there were dark scorch marks down part of the facade's upper floors with a row of windows gone.

Several fire engines, one with a turntable ladder, were parked haphazardly in front of the mansion, as well as a Fire Investigation Unit truck, and an assortment of cars and vans, two of which belonged to Crime Scene Investigators, surrounded by pools of water and pieces of blackened debris. Grace also noted a dark green coroner's van, indicating there had been at least one fatality.

Fire hoses lay all over the ground, running into the house, and there was a small army of Fire and Rescue officers in full protective gear, some wearing breathing apparatus.

As they pulled up, a man Grace recognized, also in protective Fire and Rescue uniform, approached. Tony Kent, the Chief Fire Officer for West Sussex. He had the good looks of a movie actor, with short, dark hair, alert blue eyes and, at this moment, a very grim expression. In his free time he played bass guitar with a local band, and Grace remembered years ago attending a gig in a pub with his then wife, Sandy, and Kent's wife, Jan.

'Good to see you again, Tony.'

'You too, sir.'

Grace knew that until a fire was completely under control, the Fire and Rescue officers had primacy over the scene.

'What can you tell us?'

'Well, from what we've been able to establish so far, the fire broke out in a room on the first floor, which has been gutted. But the house's elaborate sprinkler system kicked in, fortunately, preventing the blaze from spreading much further. So far we've found one body. There's a housekeeper who lived in a cottage on the estate who said the owner lived on his own in the big house.'

'Stuart Piper?'

'Yes, she said that was his name. He's missing.'

As Kent was speaking, Grace saw a man wearing breathing apparatus emerge from the front door.

Kent turned and saw him, too. 'Terrence – Terry – Stephens, the Fire Investigator, may be able to tell you more – he's just been inside.' He turned and waved at the man, who removed his head-gear and walked towards them.

Grace and Branson climbed out of the car and Kent introduced them.

Pulling off his thick gloves, the Fire Investigator shook their hands, looking solemn. 'The only good news is we've not found any other bodies,' he said. 'So far at least.'

'What can you tell us about the body?' Grace asked.

'Well, it's early days. But it already looks suspicious to me.'

'In what way?' Grace pressed.

'Well, it looks like the location of the body is pretty much in the seat of the fire, although we can't be sure of that until we've done a lot more investigating. But there's something very odd about it.'

'Odd?' Grace asked. 'Suspicious?'

'Possibly,' Stephens said.

'Can we go in and have a look?'

'Not at the moment, the building isn't safe.'

As if to confirm his words, they were all startled by a loud crashing sound somewhere inside the house, followed by a plume of smoke or dust – it was impossible to tell which – rising through the gaping hole in the roof.

'I might be able to get you inside in a couple of hours,' Stephens said. 'I guess you'll be wanting your Crime Scene Manager and CSIs to go in?'

'When it's safe,' Grace said.

Terry Stephens tapped a camera on a mounting on his chest. 'I can show you the footage, if that would be helpful?'

A few minutes later, seated on a bench in the Fire Investigation

Unit truck, Grace and Branson watched a video replay on a large monitor. And privately, Grace was glad to be watching it here, rather than in situ in the burned room, with all the smells that would accompany it – especially the smell of the body. Like many police officers who'd attended crime scenes or postmortems involving burnt victims, he could no longer stomach barbecued pork.

What was on the video in front of them was the charred shape of a human being, on its stomach, one arm reaching out towards something. As the camera panned round, the two detectives could see that the person had been trying to reach a door but hadn't made it. The door was hanging at an angle on its hinges.

The camera then did a 360-degree pan of the windowless room. It had clearly been hung with paintings, from the hooks and few skeletal charred frames still remaining on the walls, others lying on the floor. Some charred springs indicated sofas, now destroyed. What looked like a fallen candelabra lay on the remains of one.

The camera returned to the body, closing in, then moving slowly, steadily, along it.

'Most likely Stuart Piper,' Grace said. 'His body shape, but it's too burnt to tell.'

'I remember his watch,' Glenn Branson said. 'He had a fancy vintage Patek Philippe, can you wind back a few frames?'

Stephens reversed the playback and zoomed in on the blackened timepiece.

Branson studied it with a frown. 'That could be his watch but it's too badly damaged to be sure.'

'Did the housekeeper say if anyone else might have been in the house last night, Terry?' Grace asked.

'She said he hadn't told her he was expecting visitors, although apparently he had the occasional nocturnal *young gentlemen* visitors, as she politely put it.'

'So, tell me your reasons for thinking this is suspicious?'

'The door,' Stephens responded. 'It's made of steel, which doesn't make sense in a house of this period – all the doors would ordinarily have been made of a hardwood, probably oak. But even more significantly, it appears to have been locked – we had to force entry to the room. It looks to me as if the body was trying to get out. Reaching for the door?' He looked at the two detectives.

They both nodded. 'Died trying?' Branson said and shuddered. 'What a horrible death. I can't imagine what it would feel like to be burned to death.'

'If it's any consolation, most victims die from smoke inhalation before the flames get to them.'

Branson looked at Grace with a faint smile. 'What was it Norman was saying the other day about smoking not being bad for your health?'

'I'm just glad it's us here and not Norman,' Grace said quietly, thinking of Bella.

'Yes,' Branson replied, his smile gone.

'My officers have had a look round for the key to that door, but haven't found it so far.'

Grace frowned. 'So you are telling me the door was definitely locked.'

'It was definitely locked, we thought initially from the inside – we had to sledgehammer it open. We need to take a longer look, but our initial findings – and I stress this is early doors, pardon the expression – is that the victim was locked in this room. I've spoken to the housekeeper, Mrs Coombes, and a couple of other members of the domestic staff who turned up this morning. The housekeeper says that Stuart Piper liked to leave his dalmatians down in the kitchen in their baskets – where they were this morning – before spending the rest of his evening sitting in this room, with the fire and candles lit, smoking a cigar

411

and drinking cognac. She said it's called the Hidden Salon, for some historic reason.'

'Are you implying the victim locked himself in this room or that someone locked him in?' Branson asked.

'I'm not implying anything at this stage,' Stephens replied, a little defensively.

Grace stared again at the image of the charred corpse, with an outstretched hand. As if indeed reaching, desperately, for the door.

97

Harry, Freya and Tom climbed out of the police car that had driven them home, shortly before 6 p.m. They were all exhausted, from a combination of their lack of sleep the previous night, then hours of questioning by detectives at Sussex Police HQ this afternoon.

As they walked across the drive to the front door, they saw a white envelope jammed in the letterbox. Harry removed it, barely giving it a glance, and unlocked the door. As they went inside they were greeted by Jinx, giving a mournful miaow.

Freya kneeled and stroked him. 'Hey, Jinx, are you hungry?'

Jinx miaowed again then shot towards the kitchen, his sure-fire sign that he wanted food.

'I need a drink,' Harry said.

'I'm going up to my room,' Tom mumbled.

'We'll have an early supper, Tom, darling,' his mother said.

'Yeah, OK.'

Harry carried the envelope through into the kitchen, put it on the island unit, then went to the fridge. 'Glass of white?' he asked Freya.

'Sounds a good plan,' she replied and removed a packet of cat food from the cupboard. As she tore it open and tipped the contents into the bowl, nudging Jinx away until she had finished, Harry unscrewed the cap from the bottle of wine in the fridge, poured out a large glass for Freya, then took out a cold beer for

413

himself, opened it and drank a gulp straight from the can, before perching on a bar stool. 'Jesus, what a grilling. I felt at times like we were suspects, not victims of crime.'

'They were just trying to jog our minds. As that detective said, they were trying to see what details we could remember that might be helpful.'

'Jog our minds? It felt like they were trying to prise mine open with a crowbar!'

She sat down next to him and took a sip of her wine, then glanced down at the envelope. 'Who's that from?'

'Probably a bill,' he said. It was addressed in blue handwriting to Mr & Mrs Kipling and underlined with a flourish. He picked it up, ripped it open with his finger and pulled out a plain sheet of white paper. On it was a brief note in the same, rather artistic handwriting.

> Harry, sorry for all the trouble that's been caused for you and your wife and your lad. And for your loss. If you look in your garden shed, you'll find a little memento for you to keep. I always make a copy for myself of any works I particularly love. Hope this compensates you just a little. Daniel Hegarty.

He handed it to Freya and she read it quickly. 'In the shed?' she queried, frowning. '*Hope this compensates you just a little.* What does that mean? I'll go and look.'

'I'll get something out of the freezer for dinner. Veggie lasagne?'

'I'm fine with anything. I can do supper if you want?'

'No, go foraging in the shed!'

Freya returned a few minutes later holding a rectangular parcel, meticulously wrapped in brown paper and bound with Sellotape. Removing a sharp knife from the caddy, she sliced through the tape and removed the paper, to reveal a layer of bubble-wrap packaging beneath. She removed that too, letting it drop to the floor, and held up the framed painting that was revealed.

It was a painting that had become all too familiar. An ornately framed landscape in oil, ten inches wide by twelve, depicting a summer scene. Two beautiful young lovers picnicking together in elegant eighteenth-century dress, the woman holding a pink parasol. It was a woodland setting, with a lake behind.

They looked at each other for some moments. Then Harry shrugged. 'We have an empty space on the lounge wall, might as well hang it there, don't you think?'

Freya shook her head. 'No, Harry, I don't think so.'

He studied it for some moments approvingly. 'Daniel Hegarty's work does have some value. You can see why, can't you, when you look at this?' He turned it so she could see it full on.

'He's good,' she said grudgingly. 'But I don't want it hanging in the lounge. I don't want it in the house.'

Surprised by her vehemence, Harry said, 'Darling, Daniel Hegarty's a really decent guy. He's clearly genuinely sorry for what we've been through – I could tell from his voice when I spoke to him this morning. At least we have this as a memento.'

She looked angry. 'A memento of what, exactly? A memento of being tied up and our son's life threatened?'

He shrugged and stared at his beer can. 'Our dreams?'

'*Our* dreams or *yours*?' She softened a little, seeing how upset he looked. 'I'm sorry, I didn't mean that. Look, even if the police catch those vile people and get the painting back, we still won't know whether it was genuine or just a good forgery, right?'

'We'd soon find out.'

'Fine. And if it turned out to be a forgery and worth no more than the twenty quid you paid for it, would we be any worse off?'

He thought for a moment, then smiled. 'No. But we can all dream, can't we?'

She smiled back, wistfully. 'Harry, my love, do you remember the words you once wrote to me in an anniversary card? Not long after Tom was born?'

He frowned. 'I'm trying to remember.'

'Well, I've never forgotten. You wrote, *To my darling Freya and our baby Tom. We're living the dream. Let's never forget it.*' She smiled again. 'Remember now?'

He did. He nodded. 'Yep.'

'For me that's never changed. Our life, being with you, having this amazing, wonderful son, and sweet Jinx, that's the dream. I don't need to be a multimillionaire to make my life complete. Being with the people I love does that.' She jabbed a finger at the painting. 'Has that damned thing enhanced our lives in any way? Has it brought us any luck? I don't think so, it's just brought a load of grief. The damned thing could have burned our house down. Tom might have died last night. We were happy before that painting came into our lives, screwed with our heads, gave us the fantasy that we'd won the lottery. I don't want to hang it in the lounge, I want to throw it in the bin.'

98

One of the things Roy Grace loved about his job was the constant variety. And there had been plenty of that during the past forty-eight hours for sure.

He had spent part of Wednesday in full PPE treading carefully – and sometimes crawling – around the most damaged part of the interior of Bewlay Park with his Crime Scene Manager. They had discovered that all the CCTV recordings had gone.

Later that afternoon at Worthing Mortuary, he and Glenn had donned surgical gowns and masks for the grim and lengthy Home Office postmortem of Stuart Piper. His body was too charred for visual identity to be formally confirmed, but on the basis of location and build of body, they were confident it was him. DNA and dental records would hopefully confirm it shortly.

Grace was glad the postmortem was taking place in Worthing rather than the Brighton and Hove Mortuary, so Cleo would not have to be present, although Darren had offered to take over from her during these final weeks of her pregnancy any time she didn't feel up to it.

Charred bodies were always a horrific sight, and although he'd seen more than enough during his career, they always disturbed him, as if playing tricks with his mind. Visually, charred bodies looked like props in a horror movie, but the inescapable horror was that each, like the one in front of him now, had been a living human being. And the sweet smell of cooked meat churned his

417

stomach. The postmortems of dead children were the only ones that disturbed him more. And he could see, from the expression in Glenn's eyes above his mask, that he was equally uncomfortable, as was the Coroner's Officer. The only ones in the room who had seemed unperturbed were the CSI photographer, James Gartrell, and the Home Office pathologist, Dr Frazer Theobald.

Yesterday, Grace and his team had spent interviewing suspects, and now twenty-four hours later, on this Friday afternoon, everything was completely different again. He was wearing his full-dress police uniform, crisply pressed, his black shoes spit and polished to a military shine. Just a few hours ago, at 11 a.m., with Cleo elegantly dressed and carrying her pregnancy with real style, Norman Potting spick and span in his uniform, and elderly, frail Joyce Moy, they had been in the grandeur of Buckingham Palace for the investiture ceremony. And, no getting over it, it had felt special. Really special. And he had felt nervous as hell.

The Queen's Gallantry Medal had been presented to him by a resplendent Prince Charles, accompanied by his wife, the Duchess of Cornwall, looking striking. What had surprised him most of all was the warmth of the royal couple, and in particular, just how well briefed the Duchess had been, how charming she was – and just how retentive her memory, especially considering the huge number of people they were seeing that morning.

Her first comment had been to tell him he must be very good at holding his breath. To which he had replied, 'In the presence of royalty, always, ma'am!'

Grinning, she had retorted, 'I understand you swam through a doorway into a flooded room to search for a trapped boy, with no idea whether you had enough in your lungs to reach him, let alone to bring him out to safety – if he was even still alive.'

From somewhere deep inside him, he'd found the wit to reply,

'One of the things this job teaches you, ma'am, is to hold your tongue. I guess holding your breath comes later.'

She had laughed.

And he was recounting this now to the Chief Constable, Lesley Manning, and ACC Hannah Robinson, in an area of the canteen of Sussex Police HQ that had been cordoned off for the reception, hosted by the Chief Constable, in their honour. A lavish spread of sandwiches and cakes had been laid on, as well as a celebratory glass of bubbly for everyone. Those who had been invited included the Mayor of Brighton and Hove, who was due to make a short speech, Emma-Jane Boutwood, Jack Alexander, Luke Stanstead, Velvet Wilde, Glenn Branson and Siobhan Sheldrake, in an off-duty capacity as Glenn's fiancée and not as a reporter, and Beth Durham, Head of Corporate Communications.

Roy Grace's medal hung from a red, white and blue ribbon pinned to his chest. It was a small, silver coin, with an effigy of the Queen's head on one side and the wording of the medal, beneath a crown, on the reverse. It was placed next to his Queen's Jubilee medal. Joyce Moy, standing near him and engaged in conversation with the Police and Crime Commissioner, proudly held her daughter's in its small blue display box.

Behind him, he heard Cleo. 'Prince Charles really was lovely, he asked me when I was due to give birth and did we know if it was a boy or a girl? He was a regular bloke – except I was shaking, almost pinching myself, you know, that this wasn't a Prince Charles lookalike, but the real person, our future King!'

Grace smiled, then said to Lesley Manning and Hannah Robinson, 'I have to say, I've never known Norman Potting so quiet. I watched him talking to the Duchess with total respect – he was genuinely in awe – not many people are capable of having that effect on him!'

The Chief replied quietly, after checking Potting wasn't in earshot. 'His humour can rub people up the wrong way.'

'He's had years of practice, ma'am,' Grace said with a smile. 'But I will be very sorry the day he retires, he's one of the best.'

She nodded, looking solemn suddenly. 'I understand his late fiancée, Bella, was one of the best, too.'

'She was. Something the Duchess asked me this morning was how I felt about all the criticism the police come under. I told her that in an organization with so many people there were always going to be a few bad pennies and they needed to be ruthlessly dealt with. But should we be judged on those or on the good and brave things the vast majority of officers do? That, when everyone else is running from danger, we and the other emergency services are the ones running towards it. I told her that was why the medal means so much to me and to all other officers who receive it. And unlike myself, some, like Joyce Moy's daughter, never get to receive it in person.' He looked at them both. 'I think the Duchess really took that on board.'

99

In the soggy winter months, car boot sales were generally held on firm ground, and one of the largest in the area, which Harry and Freya Kipling regularly attended, was on Sunday mornings in the vast car park of Brighton Racecourse.

Harry drove the Volvo up the long, steep hill of Elm Grove. It was a wide, mostly residential street in the centre of the city that, near the top, climbed past the grimy facade of the city's second hospital, the Brighton General, and on up to the racecourse at the top. He drove slowly, as if reluctant to reach their destination, with deep misgivings about what they were about to do. Thinking about the painting lying in the rear behind them, and all that might have been.

Freya was adamant she did not want the painting Hegarty had left for them in the shed, and which Harry had leaned against the lounge wall hoping she would change her mind. But she didn't. The painting just gave her a bad feeling every time she looked at it – no way could she live with it, after the nightmare they had been through.

He began to see her point. The painting sat there like it was waving two fingers at them. Taunting them. Shouting at them, *Hey, dumbos, if I was the real deal, think just how rich you might become!*

Freya was right, he realized, as she so often was. Keeping this memento of all they had lost would be a constant reminder. A

421

constant wagging finger. There had been no word from the police in the past few days. He'd rung the detective, DI Branson, on Friday and left a message. The DI had returned the call yesterday, informing him that there were a number of developments and he hoped to have further news for him really soon.

There had been a lot of coverage on Radio Sussex and in the *Argus* about a fire in a country house in which a major art collector had died, and a large number of immensely valuable works of art had been destroyed. But the robbery at their house, which had occupied a large amount of column inches a couple of days ago, had now dropped off the newspaper's radar.

Harry paid the entry fee, drove onto the concourse of Brighton Racecourse, followed the directions indicated by a young man in a yellow fluorescent tabard and parked the car. Then he and Freya climbed out into the misty damp morning air. He opened the boot, removed the painting, which they'd wrapped in clear polythene, and together they headed towards the stalls, looking for one that either specialized in paintings, or had some on display.

After a couple of rows, they found a stall stacked with fairly uninspiring paintings – a couple of fox-hunting scenes, a few land-scapes, a terrible portrait of a dog just recognizable as a Labrador. A bored-looking woman with a plump face, and a massive tangle of blonde hair beneath a headscarf, was seated behind the trestle table, sheltered partly by the tailgate of her Toyota off-roader right behind her and partly by a golfing umbrella. She was smoking a roll-up, with a steaming mug of tea beside her.

Harry unwrapped the painting and held it up. 'Might this be of any interest?'

She peered at it. 'Looks like one of those – what d'ya call 'em, French artist fête things – fête galante, that's it – I did actually study art although you wouldn't believe it with the crap I flog here.' She took a swig of her drink then a drag of her cigarette and looked closer. 'Too bad it's not an original, eh? Be worth a few bob.' She took another drag of her cigarette, then suddenly eyed Harry and Freya suspiciously. 'Where did you get this from?'

'It's a Daniel Hegarty copy,' Harry said. 'He gave it to us – a gift – I did a little building work for him. But we don't have anywhere for it to hang. Do you know him?'

'I've had a few of his come through here over the years.' She looked at the painting again, carefully, turned it over and studied the reverse. 'That Hegarty, he always does a thorough job. Clever man he is, big talent. The problem is it's not signed, so is pretty much worthless. If you had Hegarty's signature on the back, it would be worth a few bob – people collect him, you know?' She studied it some more. 'I do quite like this, might keep it for myself, got a perfect place for it in my new home in France. I'll give you a tenner for it.'

Harry, ignoring the *yes* glance from Freya, said, 'We're looking for a bit more. Thirty?'

She shook her head, took another drag of her cigarette and coughed. 'Fifteen.'

'Twenty-five,' Harry said.

'I'll give you twenty, best offer, take it or leave it, love.'

'We'll take it,' Freya butted in.

The woman nodded and handed over a £20 note. 'Yeah, I can see this in my lounge. Got just the place for it.'

As Freya palmed the banknote, the woman took the painting and put it straight into the back of her vehicle.

'Good riddance,' Freya said quietly, as they walked away.

'I guess at least we're even,' Harry replied. 'I paid twenty for it and we've got twenty back.'

Freya gave him a sideways smile. 'Pretty much how you run your business. Maybe with a little coaching you'll learn how to get a better return on your business.'

Harry shrugged. 'We do OK, don't we?'

She squeezed his hand. 'We do OK.'

100

'You know, it seems to me, darling,' Cleo said, looking up from *The Times Magazine*, 'that some criminals are born with a self-destruct gene.'

Grace gave her a wry smile. 'Yep, very fortunately for us.'

'Like your Robert Kilgore. He might have got clean away if it hadn't been for – what – his temper?'

He leaned forward on the sofa and stroked Humphrey, who had snuggled up to his feet, still a bit damp from their long morning run over the fields. 'Sometimes it's almost as if they get to a point where they think they're invincible, and then something happens and they lose the plot. If he hadn't, he could well have got away. Fugitives can still disappear in South America – certainly if they have money, and it looks like he had plenty.'

'What an idiot,' she said.

He smiled, but it was tinged with sadness as he stared at the mobile phone on the coffee table in front of him.

Outside it was pelting with rain, but inside their cottage, with a fire roaring in the wood-burning stove, it was toasty warm. Noah was sitting on the floor, a fireguard and the closed doors of the stove keeping him safe, as he studiously put pieces of Playmobil together.

Showered and changed after his run, Grace was feeling healthier. And the events of the past week had left him feeling much better, having produced a real result for his new ACC on their first case together.

Stuart Piper's burnt body was formally identified both by DNA and by his dental records. The Briggs twin brothers had been arrested in London and were now remanded in custody on a raft of charges including kidnap, aggravated burglary and, most seriously, which would ensure they would not be released on bail before their trial, the murder of Porteous. They had both rolled over during interview and gave their account that they were following orders given by Kilgore and Piper.

Piper's death might possibly have remained a classic locked-room mystery had it not been for Kilgore's subsequent erratic behaviour – the self-destruct gene, as Cleo had said. The Fire Investigators had not been able to find the key to the steel door, though they had established the seat of the fire had been literally a seat – one of the sofas in the Hidden Salon, set alight by a candle. But the key to the door, probably brass, could not be found. Tony Kent's Fire Investigation Team said that brass could melt in a fire but it did not look like the intensity of the heat in the room would have been sufficient.

Then their attention had been brought to Robert Kilgore by the actions of an alert Border Force officer at the airport. A passenger on a flight bound for Buenos Aires had pinged the alarm going through Security. No big deal, that happened all the time. But this one, Donald Saville, had kicked off when asked to go through the X-ray machine, shouting that he was a decorated hero from Vietnam and it was shrapnel in his body from that war that had set the alarm off.

Border Force officers had been summoned to handle the irate Donald Saville. An anomaly in his passport had been detected by one, and Saville was detained. It hadn't taken long for his real identity, Robert Kilgore, to be established. Nor had it taken long for it to be ascertained that this man was wanted by Sussex Police.

It wasn't a big leap for Grace's team from there. The index of a Tesla, registered in Robert Kilgore's name, was fed into the ANPR and two hits came up for the night of Piper's death. The first was travelling in the general direction of Bewlay Park at around 10 p.m. and the second was heading towards Brighton at around 11.30 p.m. the same night. Further checks put the Tesla, possibly, in the vicinity of the Kiplings' home earlier that same evening.

The car was seized and its electronic monitoring systems, as well as its satnav, analysed. It revealed the entire journey of the car that evening, from Kilgore's apartment in Brighton, first to Bewlay Park, then to the Kiplings' house, then back to Bewlay Park. From there it had headed back to Brighton, but two miles from Bewlay Park it had stopped for several minutes. The exact location where it had stopped was identified as a lay-by on the edge of a forest.

Why, Grace had wondered, had Kilgore stopped there – and for several minutes? To have a pee? But surely he would have done that at Bewlay Park before driving off. Unless in a hurry, of course.

Or unless he had another reason. Such as disposing of something? Such as a key?

Unlike the battle for resources he would have faced with Cassian Pewe, Hannah Robinson sanctioned his request for a full search team in seconds.

On the second day they'd found a large brass key, which fitted the lock to the Hidden Salon, in a waterlogged ditch. And despite its immersion in water, Robert Kilgore's DNA was found on it. He was now on remand in custody, charged with all the same offences as the Briggs twins, with the additional charge of the murder of Stuart Piper.

'Bump's busy,' Cleo said.

Grace laid a hand on her belly and could feel the movement.

He grinned. 'Probably wants to get out and help Noah with his construction project!'

'Yep, well, the sooner the better now.' Then she focused back on the magazine.

'What are you reading?' he asked.

'Trying to get ideas for your Christmas presents,' she said, giving him a mischievous smile.

'Really?'

'No, this is really interesting: a large article on criminality in the dog breeding world – illegal puppy farming and puppy smuggling.'

'It's becoming big business,' he said. 'I was talking to some of the Rural Crime team – some gangs are making more money out of it than drugs.' He hesitated. 'Actually, in terms of Christmas presents, I did wonder about getting a companion for Humphrey.'

She looked dubious. 'Another dog? They're not just for Christmas.'

'I know, of course. I thought maybe a rescue one?'

'You're planning a busy Christmas – a new baby, both our families coming, and now a dog?'

'Maybe we should wait?'

'I think so. Plus, we still have our dear little Reggie here until there's a decision about where he will go.'

'OK, good point. Not while Reggie's here. It wouldn't be fair.'

As she resumed reading, Grace leaned forward and picked up the iPhone from the table. It was Bruno's phone, the one he had been looking at while crossing the road and fatally hit by a car. After the accident it had been seized by the Roads Policing Unit, and just returned to him yesterday via Aiden Gilbert. He'd spent much of last night looking through it, trying to understand what had so distracted his son that he'd walked out into the road in front of a car.

It seemed, from what Gilbert had told him, that at the moment of the collision, Bruno had been looking at a genealogy site. What was that about?

There was also a mystery text on the phone. It said:

Good to talk. Speak again soon?

It was from an unknown number. Probably nothing significant, he thought – hoped. Perhaps he should find out.

Cleo closed the magazine and put it down on the table, alongside their copy of *The Week*. 'Interesting piece,' she said. 'I just looked at the forecast for tomorrow – it's looking lovely. Shall we do something? Have an outing? I don't think I can walk too far, but would be good to have a break while I still can.'

'Sure, what are you thinking?'

'A pub lunch, perhaps? How about the Ram at Firle or Rose Cottage at Alciston?'

'Either would be great. Maybe take in a car boot sale first? We've not been to one in ages – we might find a few Christmas presents and some decorations for the tree; and Humphrey's destroyed all his toys – we might pick up a few new ones for him to rip to bits!'

She beamed. 'Sure, great idea. But let's not buy a painting, eh?'

GLOSSARY

ANPR – Automatic Number Plate Recognition. Roadside or mobile cameras that automatically capture the registration number of all cars that pass. It can be used to historically track which cars went past a certain camera, and can also create a signal for cars which are stolen, have no insurance or have an alert attached to them.

CID – Criminal Investigation Department. Usually refers to the divisional detectives rather than the specialist squads.

CSI – Crime Scene Investigators. Formerly SOCO (Scenes of Crime Officers). They are the people who attend crime scenes to search for fingerprints, DNA samples etc.

DIGITAL FORENSICS – The unit which examines and investigates computers and other digital devices.

HOLMES – Home Office Large Major Enquiry System. The national computer database used on all murders. It provides a repository of all messages, actions, decisions and statements, allowing the analysis of intelligence and the tracking and auditing of the whole enquiry. Can enable enquiries to be linked across force areas where necessary.

IOPC – Independent Office for Police Conduct.

MO – Modus Operandi (method of operation). The manner by which the offender has committed the offence. Often this can reveal unique features which allow crimes to be linked or suspects to be identified.

POLSA – Police Search Adviser.

SIO – Senior Investigating Officer. Usually a Detective Chief Inspector who is in overall charge of the investigation of a major crime such as murder, kidnap or rape.

CHART OF POLICE RANKS

Police ranks are consistent across all disciplines and the addition of prefixes such as 'detective' (e.g. detective constable) does not affect seniority relative to others of the same rank (e.g. police constable).

Police Constable

Police Sergeant

Inspector

Chief Inspector

Superintendent

Chief Superintendent

Assistant Chief Constable

Deputy Chief Constable

Chief Constable

ACKNOWLEDGEMENTS

With every new book I write, I so often end up, through a stroke of good fortune, meeting someone who helps with my research way beyond anything I could possibly have hoped for. Here that stroke was a brush stroke – a paintbrush wielded by Brighton-born and raised David Henty, proud bearer of the title of the World's No. 1 Art Forger.

David let me into his world, the secrets and the dark side and all, and I just do not think I could have written this story so authentically or colourfully had it not been for all David's and his wife Natania's kindness and enthusiasm.

As always, too, Sussex Police have helped me so much. I'm immensely grateful to Police and Crime Commissioner Katy Bourne, OBE, to Chief Constable Jo Shiner, and to so many officers and support staff actively serving under them, as well as retirees, from Sussex and other forces. I've listed them in alphabetical order and beg forgiveness for any omissions.

Retd Chief Superintendent Graham Bartlett; PC Jon Bennion-Jones; Inspector James Biggs; Chief Superintendent Justin Burtenshaw; Financial Investigator Emily Denyer; PC Phillip Edwards; Chief Inspector Mark Evans; CSI James Gartrell; CSI Chris Gee; Aiden Gilbert, Digital Forensics; DCI Rich Haycock; Inspector Dan Hiles; Chief Superintendent Nick May; Sergeant Russell Phillips; Chief Constable of Kent, Alan Pughsley QPM; Retd Detective Superintendent Nick Sloan; Chief of Police, States of Jersey, Robin Smith; James Stather, Forensic Services; Retd DC Pauline Sweeney; Detective Sergeant Mark Taylor; Retd Chief Superintendent Jason Tingley; PC Richard Trundle; and Beth Durham, Sue Heard, Jill Pedersen and Katie Perkin of Sussex Police Corporate Communications.

A big thank you also to Theresa Adams, Julian Blazeby, Kate Blazeby, Alan Bowles, Andrew Brown, Marcus Budgen of Spinks, Matthew Collins, Dr Peter Dean, Hamish Dewar, Sean Didcott, Ross Duncton, Anthony Farnham, Dominic Fortnam, Dr Kathleen Ghillies, Anna-Lisa Hancock, Haydn Kelly, Rob Kempson, Andrew Lyons, Dr Francoise Lyons, Dr James Mair, David Mason OBE, James Mayor, Jan McCord, Tony McCord, Simon Muggleton, Producer of *Antiques Roadshow* Robert Murphy, Professor Nick Oliver, Julian Radcliffe of the Art Loss Register, Dr Graham Ramsden, Angela Rippon, Kit Robinson, Alan Setterington, Helen Shenston, Rev Ish Smale, Jonathan Santlofer, Andy Slark, Juliet Smith, Emily Stather, Hans Jurgen Stockerl, Phil Taylor of Gorringes, Neil Wakeling, Tim Wonnacott.

A massive thank you as always to Wayne Brookes, my editor, and the team at Pan Macmillan – to name just a few: Jonathan Atkins, Kinza Azira, Lara Borlenghi, Emily Bromfield, Sian Chilvers, Tom Clancy, Alex Coward, Stuart Dwyer, Claire Evans, Samantha Fletcher, Anthony Forbes-Watson, Jamie Forrest, Elle Gibbons, Hollie Iglesias, Daniel Jenkins, Rebecca Kellaway, Neil Lang, Rebecca Lloyd, Sara Lloyd, James Long, Holly Martin, Rory O'Brien, Joanna Prior, Guy Raphael, Alex Saunders, Holly Sheldrake, Jade Tolley, Jeremy Trevathan, Charlotte Williams, Leanne Williams. And my brilliant structural editor, Susan Opie.

A huge thank you to my amazing literary agent, Isobel Dixon, and to everyone at my UK literary agency, Blake Friedmann: Lizzy Attree, Sian Ellis-Martin, Julian Friedmann, Hana Murrell, James Pusey, Daisy Way, Conrad Williams. And a big shout-out to my fabulously gifted UK PR team at Riot Communications: Preena Gadher, Caitlin Allen, Emily Souders and Angel Pearce.

Whilst writing is a lonely job, I have an amazing support team around me. I'm blessed with two incredibly talented and hard-working people, my wife Lara and former Detective Chief Superintendent David Gaylor, who head up Team James. David

Gaylor contributes so much to every aspect of my novels, creatively, editorially and, very crucially, in terms of the authenticity of the police characters and scenes. He does the same with the stage plays and is now police adviser to the *Grace* TV series also.

The other invaluable members of the team are Sue Ansell, Dani Brown, Erin Brown, Chris Diplock, Martin Diplock, Jane Diplock, Sarah Middle, Lyn Gaylor, Mark Tuckwell, Chris Webb and our fabulous new PA, Emma Gallichan.

My most special thanks of all are reserved for my beloved wife. I've always believed that whilst novels are, above all, stories, they are also so much about how they make you feel. Lara is incredibly in tune with that, and gives me vital help with the emotions of my characters, as well as the storylines and with every aspect of our lives. She has also been of immense help with the stage plays and the television series.

As ever another round of thanks is due to all our wonderful animals in our ever-growing menagerie: Spooky, our labradoodle, Wally, our goldendoodle, our two Burmese cats, our Indian Runner and crested ducks, our forty hens, rescue rabbits, quail, guinea fowl and our very naughty pygmy goats. You do so much to keep us grounded in reality and to put smiles on our faces.

Something else that puts a huge smile on my face is to hear from you, my readers – I owe you so much for your support. Do keep your messages coming through any of the channels below.

Above all, stay safe and well.

Peter James

www.peterjames.com

@ peterjamesuk

@peterjames.roygrace

@peterjamesuk

@peterjamesukpets

@mickeymagicandfriends

YouTube Peter James TV

NOW A MAJOR ITV DRAMA
STARRING JOHN SIMM AS ROY GRACE

DISCOVER
THE ROY GRACE BOOKS

• NOW A MAJOR TV SERIES •

'One of the best British crime writers'
LEE CHILD

Known for gripping stories that put regular people in extraordinary situations, Peter James is the No.1 bestselling author of the award-winning detective series featuring Roy Grace. Discover the darkness that lurks around every corner in Grace's latest case . . .

Discover the Roy Grace series at
www.peterjames.com

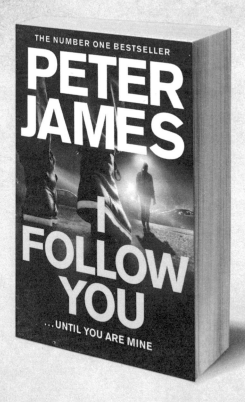

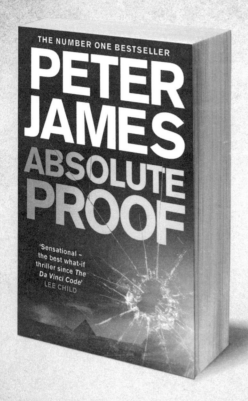

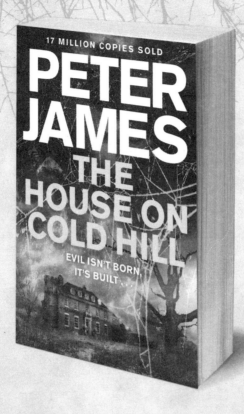

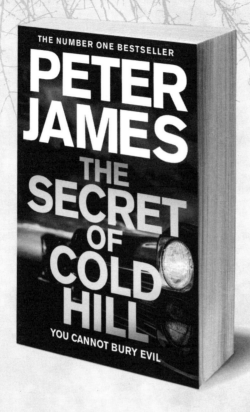

UK STAGE TOUR 2023

GRACE IS BACK!
IN
PETER JAMES
WISH YOU WERE
DEAD

COMING TO A THEATRE NEAR YOU

Myticket.co.uk   PeterJames.com